Double Bucked

USA TODAY BESTSELLING AUTHOR

ADORA CROOKS

Copyright © 2024 by Adora Crooks

All rights reserved.

No part of this book may be reproduced in any form or by any electronic or mechanical means, including information storage and retrieval systems, without written permission from the author, except for the use of brief quotations in a book review.

Book Cover by Wolfsparrow Covers

Editing by Sandra at One Love Editing

Join my newsletter to get a free romance! https://adoracrooksbooks.com/gift/

AUTHOR'S NOTE

The town of Belleflower, Kentucky, does not exist. The mysterious and cultish Belleflower Festival does not exist. The top-secret Wolfpack Special Ops Team (as far as I know) does not exist, nor do any secret societies or government entities mentioned here. This book is not meant to be a reflection of the US Navy in any way.

Trigger warnings and sensitive material include violence, spicy group scenes, bondage, love triangle that turns into polyamorous relationship, drug use, murder, secret small town cults, trafficking, and brainwashing of small town.

Read safely and enjoy responsibly.

XOXO, Adora

1

RANSOM

I'm tongue-deep in Jade. Her fingers curl into my hair, locking me in place.

"Goddamn." She pants. "You work that mouth like you get paid for it."

I smack her thigh. "You giving me a raise?"

"Don't do that."

"Hm?"

"*Don't talk.* You're ruining it."

I flatten my tongue up the seam of her, the way I've learned she likes, and lick upwards, suctioning my mouth around her swollen nub. My efforts earn a shaky moan.

Jade and I are *something* with benefits. Not quite friends. Not quite coworkers. Her husband is my boss. What does that make me?

An asshole, I suppose.

But we recognize skills in each other. I make her come. She makes me forget.

Win-win.

She's got strong thighs—the thighs of a woman who grew up riding, just like ninety-percent of all the other ladies in Belleflower—and they lock around my shoulders as she arches into my mouth.

But just as I feel her start to give, we both hear it—

The downstairs door unlocks.

"Jade!" her husband calls out. "You here?"

Jade jolts up, her head whipping back and forth like a dog that just scented coyote.

"Upstairs!" she shouts. "Be right down!" Her foot finds my chest, and she kicks me backward, off her bed. She swallows her dark skin under a velvet robe, and I snatch my shirt off the floor, tugging it over my head.

"Back door?" I whisper.

She shakes her head as she knots her robe. "He'll catch you."

We can both hear him. Those heavy footsteps climbing the staircase. Jade looks towards the window, then raises her eyebrows at me.

I groan. "C'mon now…"

She goes to the window, flinging open the double panes. "There's a terrace. You'll be fine."

"The hell I will—"

But she's pushing me toward the window, using all her might to get me out of there as fast as she can. "He'll kill you. And me. You get that, don't you? So. What's it going to be? Terrace or a bullet?"

"Well, when you put it like that."

"*Ransom*. Move."

My boots crush her nice satin pillows covering the nook as I shimmy out the window. The panes are tight on my shoulders. I climb out backward and hook the tip of my boot against the wall, finding some kind of purchase on the thin, ivy-covered terrace.

In the twilight, I can make out the shape of the earth two

stories down. My horse—Chaucer—lingers near the side of the house, looking bored with my escapades.

Jade starts to close the window, but I tell her, "Hold up."

She narrows her eyes. I tilt my head towards the hat hanging off her bed post.

She scoops my beige Stetson hat off the post. She leans out the window to fit it on my head.

I risk the uneven grip to tip my hat to her. "Ma'am."

I've earned a small smile, at least. "Get lost, cowboy."

Then she closes the window in my face.

Now, I've got nothing but the night sky and the chirping crickets to witness my sins. I start my descent, and I feel the thin terrace yawning under my weight.

Ah, hell no.

The yellow light from the bedroom flickers, and I can't help but look back through the bedroom window.

He's here.

Arris Dagney isn't a bad man. He isn't even a bad-looking man—he's got a salt-and-pepper wash of hair that curls from his head to his chin.

I watch as he greets his wife. He cups her face, and those lips that were moaning for me only seconds ago are now on his.

Suddenly, it ain't my unspent balls that ache.

It's my heart.

Sure, being a rake has its perks. Hot women. Hot sex. No strings attached.

But, damn, what I wouldn't give to have someone to come home to at the end of the day.

No. Not *someone*.

One gal in particular.

One gal that broke me into a million pieces five years ago.

But I should know better than to linger.

Because I'm a lot of stupid, and the little wicker terrace ain't used to holding that much idiot.

The wooden ladder snaps under my boot. I struggle to hold my grip, but the wood splinters and cracks under my big hands. Before I know it, I'm free-falling down the side of the building, pulling strings of ivy down with me.

My boots hit the ground, sending a shot of hot pain up my leg. I tumble, and my back meets dirt, knocking all the wind out of my lungs.

For a minute, I lie there, catching my breath. I wait for the sound of Arris to come charging at me, but I don't hear anything but the nightlife—crickets and toads.

Hooves pad the ground. Chaucer's hot breath hits my face as he sniffs me, then snorts. He chomps my hat, and I have to swat him away.

"Off. C'mon, then. Let's get home."

I lift up to my feet. Everything hurts when I hoist myself up Chaucer's back.

"I'm getting too old for this," I inform Chaucer. He huffs in agreement.

Even in the dark, Chaucer knows his way home. We leave the Dagney estate behind us, its Greek-revival-style columns reaching to high heaven, golden light streaming out through the windows. Chaucer follows the beaten trail out the back of the Dagney property, through the short stretch of woods, weaving through thick elms and pine trees.

It's early September in Kentucky, and fall is already nipping.

It takes about twenty minutes to ride the overgrown trail through the woods and back home. The trees part, and the darkness lifts. The moon is nearly full, and on a cloudless night like this, it shines bright over the Preacher Ranch.

I've worked and lived on this ranch for nearly going on a decade now. It looks particularly nice in the dark, though. The stables are all put to sleep, illuminated only with soft lanterns that flicker outside each building. Tall, overgrown hedges surround the Preacher house, blocking anyone out.

The Preacher Ranch is an elite horse breeding farm, one of the best in the state. The grounds are well-kept, from the stables to the horses to the freshly cut grass.

It's all in pristine condition except for my digs. The only eyesore in the place.

I've got a trailer parked up on the very edge of the property, tucked away in the woods. Out of sight, out of mind. Mr. Preacher wouldn't have allowed it, except he knows what he pays me, which is a penny short of nothing.

I lift the latch on the wooden gate that separates the Preachers' land from Dagneys'. I'm about to tuck Chaucer in for the night when a shot rings out through the silence.

Then another.

The sounds echo through the empty land. It's coming from the Preacher estate.

Shit.

I kick my heels into Chaucer's sides and click my tongue. He starts forward, picking up the pace and galloping toward the estate. The grass gives way to gravel and red cobblestones as I halt Chaucer, dismount, and step around the hedges to enter Mr. Preacher's private property.

I slowly round the large water fountain with the bronze sculpture of a horse reared up in the center.

Mr. Preacher stands on his porch. He's got a fuzzy, moth-bitten robe hanging over his hairy chest and round belly. He's wearing his boxers this time, at least.

In his hand, he's wielding a double-barrel shotgun.

"Whoa, there." I put up my palms. "Let's take it easy now…"

He rounds on me, swinging the shotgun my way. I freeze.

Those gray eyes are empty and wild.

"It's just me, Mr. Preacher," I continue. "Riley Ransom. You remember me?"

When a horse gets spooked, it's important to keep your voice low and calm. Don't make any sudden movements. If you can, try to meet them with your eyes first.

That's how I approach Mr. Preacher—hands up, body half-bowed, eyes on his.

There's a flicker of knowing in those lost, gray eyes.

Slowly, he starts to settle down. He lowers the shotgun, and I can breathe again.

"That's good," I tell him. "That's pretty heavy, huh?"

He huffs. His mustache quivers.

"How about you let me carry that for you, sir?"

He holds out the shotgun. I take it.

It's loaded. *How in the hell?* Seems like every time I confiscate a firearm from him, he just digs a new one up. I unload it and pop out the shells, shoving them away in my pocket.

Without his shotgun, he's just an old, sad, tired man. His shoulders sag, and he mumbles, "They're coming to kill me."

"Who is?"

"*Them.*"

He narrows his eyes at the darkness.

The darkness hoots back at him with the voice of a barn owl.

I pat his back. "Alright, Mr. Preacher. Let's go on back inside."

The Preacher Estate was once a grand mansion with a full wait and kitchen staff filing in and out of the halls.

Now, there ain't no one here to haunt the halls except Mr. Preacher himself.

The once-dubbed "Tyrant of Belleflower" took a steep decline over the past couple of years. He got paranoid, forgetful, started claiming that everyone under the sun was out to get him. Fired his kitchen staff when he said they were poisoning him. The help went next. Soon, there was no one left but me.

As the on-call farm manager, I've been a firsthand witness to his state of mind going from *weird, eccentric old man* to *downright batshit, liable to shoot someone if they step around his side of the hedges.*

Even entering the estate is a feat of life and death. He's rigged doors and windows with hair-trigger traps, convinced that someone's trying to break in. As I help him inside, we've got to step over the thin, near-invisible fishing line that runs across the hallway. It's attached to a hammer, which is attached to the hanging chandelier, and it'll swing down and knock the daylights out of anyone who triggers the fishing line.

I walk him down the maroon runner and up the winding staircase that empties out on the second floor. From here, I get him down the hallway, past his old office, and into his bedroom.

He's gone from lion-with-a-thorn-in-his-paw to docile lamb. He tucks his robe tighter around himself and ambles on into bed, tucking himself in.

The man's only in his sixties, but you wouldn't know it. When he closes his eyes, his expression tight and worried, he looks in need of a sarcophagus.

I survey the room. It's got that thick, dusty smell. He's got glasses cramped up on his bedside table. Some with whiskey. Some with days-old water. A bottle of pills that looks suspiciously full. "Y'need anything?"

He opens his eyes and peers over at me. Mr. Preacher's most striking feature is his eyebrows. Always has been. He's got these mean, wicked whiskers that curl upward at the tips like wisps of smoke.

"You're the only man I trust," he tells me. "You wanna know why?"

My heart does a surprised little leap. He's never said a kind word to me his entire life, so I indulge. "What's that, Mr. Preacher?"

He squints. "You're too fucking stupid to kill me. You'd muck it up and blow your own brains out."

My smile drops. He starts laughing at that—this rattling, wheezy thing.

Ah. Now, *there's* the Mr. Preacher I know.

I snap my fingers between three of the empty glasses to carry them off. "Ain't you a ray of sunshine. Get some rest, sir."

He's still hacking out his laugh when I exit his room, shutting the door behind me. I carry the whiskey glasses and the shotgun downstairs with me. I set the shotgun down on the dining room table as I pass through toward the kitchen.

This room is a tough one for me. There's a fireplace in here, and above the mantle sits a large oil painting of Mr. Preacher and his daughter, Claire.

She's young in the painting. A teenager. About how old she was when I first met her. Wispy blonde hair. A small button nose. Pink lips she kept closed for all photos as soon as her schoolmates started teasing her about the small gap in her front teeth, but I always thought it was cute as hell. Just a kid but so serious already. It'll break your heart.

I head into the kitchen. I set the crystal glasses in the sink and take a look through his fridge.

Without the kitchen staff, it's just me and Arris Dagney who take care of him.

Yeah—*that* Arris. Arris Dagney is my boss. The co-caretaker of Mr. Preacher. And the guy whose wife I'm licking on the side.

Am I a bastard for it? Probably.

But a man's got needs. Needs that make devils of us all.

I ain't talking about the need under my belt either.

It's the need to *forget* that I've been chasing for half a decade.

The need to forget the fact that I let the only woman I ever loved walk out of my world, and I'll spend the rest of my life paying the price for that.

Arris and I take turns stocking up Mr. Preacher's fridge. It's looking pretty meager now. There's a container of red beans and rice in the freezer, so I set it in the fridge to thaw. I hand-wash dust and smudges from the crystal whiskey glasses and set those out to dry. Finally, I go back into the dining room, get his shotgun, and go back into the hallway. Around the staircase, there's a door. I keep it locked, but the lock's been smashed. *Dammit, Preacher.* I make a mental note to get a sturdier, heavier lock and pull a chain. A bulb flickers on, illuminating the stairs that lead to the cellar.

The temperature drops once I get downstairs. That's mostly because it's a wine cellar, host to bottles of wine that are more money than I'll ever see in my lifetime. Take a turn through the shelves of wine, and there's a gun safe, which— again—should be locked but is wide open.

Mr. Preacher wasn't much of a hunter, even when he had

all his marbles, but that didn't stop him from pretending. He's got a pretty assortment of hunting rifles and shotguns here. I replace the shotgun on the empty hooks and tuck the ammo away in a thin drawer underneath.

I punch in the code to lock the safe. 0-6-1-4-9-5. The mechanism locks into place and beeps, accepting the code.

Just then, I hear footsteps move swiftly across the floorboards over my head.

Sounds like someone's run out the door.

The hell?

I race upstairs to catch Mr. Preacher, but—

When I get upstairs, the front door is wide open.

Worse: the string-trap has been triggered.

The hammer swings back and forth on its rope, making the chandelier cast a swaying shadow on the walls. I touch the bottom of the hammer to stop the momentum. There's a spot of blood on the end.

I step out onto the porch, but there's no one in sight. Nothing but nighttime and night birds.

A bad feeling climbs up the back of my neck.

Something ain't right.

Those footsteps...they sounded too light and too fast to be Mr. Preacher's.

Quick as I can, I run upstairs.

"Mr. Preacher?"

His door's ajar.

Now, my heart is really banging in my chest.

I knock my knuckles against the door. "Mr. Preacher?"

Dead silence.

I press my fingers against the door and push it open.

The sight is so unnerving it takes my eyes a minute to register what I'm seeing.

The bedroom is dark, lit only by the moonlight creeping

in through the blinds. Mr. Preacher is unmoving in his bed, the sheets tucked up to his chest, his purple robe cozy around his throat.

The only problem is that what's above his throat looks like a damn sunrise.

His head has been splattered apart. Red and pink bits of Mr. Preacher cover the pillows. The wall. They seep through the mattress and drip onto his nice white rug.

That's gonna leave a stain.

Mr. Preacher hates stains.

The ground underneath me tilts, lurches, and spins like a carnival ride with a loose screw.

I stumble down the hall. Down the stairs. Through the foyer. Out the door. I barely make it over the porch before I'm on my hands and knees, puking in the manicured grass.

Chaucer nuzzles the top of my head. He lets out a soft huff, as though to comfort me, and then the idiot gently starts to graze on my hair.

2

CLAIRE

I'm on the beautiful Scottish hills, at the beautiful Aivenmoore Club, with my beautiful fiancé and our beautiful friends, and I'm so bored I could scream.

The Aivenmoore Club is a private country club for the rich and pampered. The red wine I'm sipping comes from the very grapes that grow along the highlands, but even that isn't enough to stave off sure death if I have to stand still a moment longer.

My fiancé and I stand under the canopy near the main house, and I'm forced to watch as our friends play croquet below. *Friends* is, perhaps, a generous term, but they are acquaintances in our wealth bracket, which is good enough.

James stands beside me. He's enclosed his body in a tight navy blue suit with white trousers. White AirPods are fitted into the shell of his ears. Sometimes, he's taking calls with clients (as a financial advisor with clients all around the world, the calls come day and night). But most of the time, he's listening to podcasts about ancient history, or post-modern art, or whatever his hyperfixation is at the time.

"Why can't I play?" I ask.

James's eyes are fixed on his phone. Without lifting his gaze from the screen, he answers, "Because, darling, you're the Queen of Hearts."

"What does that mean?"

"When you play, heads roll."

I cross my arms and scowl.

"James!" Addy waves her hand, smile across her mouth. "You're up!"

James takes out his earbuds, tucks them into his blazer pocket, and then steps through the grass to join the game.

If you went to Google and typed in, "Upper-class British Snob Who is Socially Awkward But It Somehow Makes Him More Attractive," this is what would pop up:

James Calloway. Lanky. Black hair knotted into tight, tiny curls. Sky-blue eyes that rest behind slim glasses. He's tall and slender as a pole. His body is quietly toned, with muscles that shy away under button-up shirts. The first time I saw him naked, I was, honestly, open-mouth shocked by the six-pack that lived underneath his unassuming costume. Among his attributes include a wonderfully masculine dusting of arm hair and dark commas of eyebrows that rest above his perpetually downcast eyes.

I watch as he settles his body into perfect form, and he gives a single, sure swing of the mallet.

He has, objectively, a perfect ass in light trousers.

None of this softens the sting of being sidelined while everyone else has fun.

My clutch buzzes. I welcome the distraction and take my phone out.

The area code makes my heart sink.

Kentucky.

The ghost of my childhood creeps like mist around me, and I shiver.

I almost let it ring. I almost don't answer. But then...

Curiosity kills the cunt.

I hold my phone to my ear. "Yes?"

"Miss Claire Preacher?" The voice has familiar Southern grit, but I don't recognize it at all.

"Who am I speaking to?"

"This is Deputy Holden Calhoun of the Belleflower Police Department."

Ice water slides down my spine. I'm trying to sound calm, but my voice pitches. "How did you get this number—?"

He ignores my question. "I'm afraid I'm calling with bad news." He lets his words hang. My heart is in my throat. "Your father has passed away."

The words stretch and bend in front of me, but I can't make sense of them at all at all. "How?"

"He was killed. Shot in his sleep. We're still putting the pieces together. I'm so sorry."

I can hear my own breath, the shake in it. James hits a perfect streak, much to the chagrin of our friends, who grumble after him as he throws the croquet mallet over his shoulder and strides on his long legs back toward me.

"Miss Preacher?" the deputy asks when I've been silent too long.

When James's eyes meet mine, he furrows his eyebrows questioningly. He can tell something is off.

I hang up the phone. I stuff it in my clutch, then push the clutch into James's hands. "Hold this."

He does.

I stomp through the thistle toward our friends. "I need this." I tear the mallet out of Addy's hands. Addy, shocked, releases her grip and stumbles backward. I step in front of James's ball. I coil my muscles, swing the mallet back, and with a fierce shout, I hit the ball with as much force as I can muster.

It goes out of orbit. I watch the satisfying arc it makes through the air before rolling down the hill.

Accomplished, I drop the mallet. I trudge through the thistle and back to James.

"Pack your things," I tell him. "We're going home."

"Paris?"

"*Kentucky.*"

3

JAMES

Nina Simone plays in my ears as Claire and I step off the plane. We've taken a small, connecting jet from New York to Kentucky, and the door opens like a wing on the runway. The cold, recycled air is blown away with a balmy gust of autumn. My first observation: Kentucky smells like sunflowers.

A man waits for us with the name PREACHER printed out on a laminated poster. Claire walks past him, her heels clicking like machine gun fire across the freshly polished airport floors. She dons her dark sunglasses and instructs him to take us straight to the morgue. The driver piles our suitcases in the trunk, and I hold on to my messenger bag.

I watch through the tinted car windows as the tarmac gives way to rolling, green hills, decrepit farmhouses, and worn-down men sitting on worn-down porches, with worn-down dogs on worn-down chains that bark at us as we pass.

A white, painted sign with curly letters says WELCOME TO BELLEFLOWER, KENTUCKY.

The driver—a stout man with a black cap—keeps

adjusting his eyes from the road to the rearview mirror. His name tag says HARDING.

The car lurches over a pothole. I grip the handle above the window.

"Have you ever been to Kentucky, sir?" Harding asks.

"No," I tell him. This is the sixth lie I've told in the last twenty-four hours.

"You should come in the summer seasons. Wildflowers open up. Real pretty."

"I'll keep that in mind."

Claire says nothing. She has a dark camisole pulled over a black dress. She wears large, gradient sunglasses. Her eyes are the color of an oncoming storm, and today, they are as impenetrable as rain clouds.

The wheels click as we roll over the train tracks, and the landscape does a sudden shift. We enter a small, charming town with freshly paved roads and storefronts washed with pastels: soft pinks and welcoming blues. Mothers pushing strollers packed with designer bags. Storeowners stuff their window displays with flower decor. My eyes catch on a stalled parade float with large, brightly colored sculpted flowers attached to it. Decorative horses are frozen mid-leap on the front of the float.

Harding catches my gaze in the rearview mirror.

"You hear about the Belleflower Festival?" Harding asks.

"No."

"Aw, it's our biggest festival of the year! Big draw for out-of-towners," he explains. "Coming up this Saturday. They reveal this year's Belleflower Queen and throw a parade."

I say nothing. Harding takes my lack of input as permission to continue.

"Sorta like a Miss America, you know?" he says. "You get to be the shining star of Belleflower. Big deal here—those ladies get treated like true royalty, I'll tell you what. No one knows who the Belleflower Queen is until the day of the parade, though. They throw a big party about it. Lovely parade. Really pretty. Y'all should go."

"I'm afraid we leave Thursday," I inform him. "We're just here for the funeral."

"Ah." He shakes his head. "Damn shame."

"Quite."

Claire is still staring out the window. Quiet. Taciturn.

I put my hand over Claire's. I thread my large fingers through her small ones, the blocky ring on my ring finger nuzzling hers. She lets me.

The car pulls into the hospital deck. It sinks below to the basement level. The second the wheels stop rolling, Claire opens her door and gets out. I pick up her purse, thank the driver, and follow her inside.

We go in and are met with a woman encased in glass. She informs us that Detective Holden hasn't arrived yet, but we're welcome to take a seat. She gestures to hard, plastic chairs lined against the slim hallway.

Ten minutes pass. Fifteen. Twenty. Claire's heel *tap-tap-taps* against the hard floors. I put a hand on her knee. She stills.

Finally, the doors open. A man in a brown and forest-green uniform steps inside. He has a round belly, a bristle mustache, and a red pocket on his jaw that looks like he cut himself shaving this morning. His utility belt jangles as he walks, and he tugs on his belt as he enters.

"Sorry for the wait, Ms. Preacher," he says. His voice is hoarse with that deep Kentucky drawl, all lazy vowels and slow tenor.

"Any later and we'd be lying in the coffin ourselves," Claire says sharply. "Shall we get this over with?"

The sheriff recognizes that I'm the one he wants to talk to, so he extends a hand to me. "Deputy Holden."

I stand and shake it. "James Calloway. The fiancé."

He nods. "Listen, as I said on the phone, I don't think you'll be wanting to see this...I understand he's your father, but the way it went down...well, to put it frank, it ain't pretty. Remember him how he was. Not like this."

"How he was, was a mean, old bastard," Claire says. "I'm certain whatever he looks like is an improvement. Lead the way."

Claire's tone is tight, businesslike, and leaves no room for anyone to second-guess her. Deputy Holden sways on his boots, as though her words literally knocked him off-balance. But then he fixes his expression, tilts his hat, and says, "Follow me."

He leads us down the thin hallway. He pushes past double doors marked for Staff Only, and we enter a tiled, sterile room. The air is cold and smells sharply of disinfectant.

A woman in a white coat looks up at us with large, surprised eyes.

Deputy Holden tells her, "Bring out Mr. Preacher, if you don't mind. His daughter would like to see him."

The attendant's eyes flicker over Claire, assessing. Then, she unlocks a silver drawer. It rattles as she pulls it out. Mr. Preacher's body is a soft lump underneath the white sheet.

She gives Deputy Holden another unsure look, but he nods in the affirmative. She pulls back the sheet.

Even with a dead body in the room, I'm not looking at the sack of skin and bones formally known as Mr. Preacher.

I'm watching Claire.

Her eyes widen when she sees him. Her lips part ever so

slightly. Her throat concaves as she takes in a rapid, silent inhale, as though she's swallowing a scream.

She turns her face quickly. Quietly, she recovers.

"Yes," she says. "It's him."

"If you'd like a moment with him..." Deputy Holden begins, but Claire doesn't linger. She puts on her sunglasses, swivels on her heels, and pushes back out the door.

I follow in her wake. She exits the building and halts in the parking lot. Her hair looks gold in the Kentucky sun. Claire is standing very still. She stares ahead. I put my hand on her shoulder, but she flinches and shrugs it off.

Deputy Holden steps outside to join us. He's holding his hat by the brim in a sign of mournful respect. "When you're feeling up to it, Ms. Preacher, I'd like to come by the house and get a statement. Go through some of Mr. Preacher's files. See if we can't make some headway into the investigation."

"Do you have any leads?" Claire asks.

"We're compiling a list of people who may've run into trouble with your father in the past."

"You'll need the whole town registry for that." Claire tilts her head. "Come over now."

The deputy hesitates. "Are you sure you don't want to settle in?"

"The quicker we get through this, the quicker I can get back to France."

Our driver pulls up. I open the door for Claire, and she steps a long leg inside.

"I'll follow in my car," the deputy says.

I get in beside Claire and close the door. It's dark in the car, the tinted windows sealing us off from the midday sunlight.

"To the Preacher estate, miss?" the driver asks.

"Yes," I answer for her.

The car rolls forward. Claire looks away from me. As she stares out the window, I notice the rapid rise and fall of her chest.

Claire hasn't eaten in forty-eight hours and wouldn't even touch the tiny bag of airplane pretzels I pushed on her. She's consumed some water, but not enough. She hasn't slept.

She's wound tight, running purely on the fuel of grief and rage.

"Claire." I say her name softly. "You should slow down. Take a breath."

"I'll slow down when I'm dead." She hears the words repeated back in her ears, and her mouth twists.

I crack open the window and let the fresh, earthy air in.

We pass more hills, spotted now with large, looming mansions. Each house has wide swaths of empty land separating one from the other. There are no true neighbors on this side of Belleflower, it seems, only acquaintances who live very, very far down the road from each other.

Our car stops in front of a black iron gate flanked with red brick. Harding gets out, punches in the key code, and the electronic motors on the gate ease open. We roll through the teeth of the gate and turn down a private road blocked in with tall, thick hedges. Through the gaps in the hedges, I can see the sprawling Preacher property, dotted with farm hands, grazing horses, and white wooden ranches.

We drive the bricked road up to the Preacher mansion. It's a looming, Greek-style mansion. Tall, curved windows open out like a many-eyed spider, watching the grounds. The roof is ash-colored, the body limestone white, crawling with green fingers of ivy. We pass a large bronze structure of a horse rearing back on powerful, strong haunches. On either side of the stature sit two stone fountains with cherubs pouring water from large vases.

Now that she's home, I watch some of the fight leave Claire's eyes. This time, she remains seated and allows Harding to open the door for her and help her out.

When I step around to join Claire, I find her pulling through her purse frantically.

"Looking for something?"

"A key. I don't have a key." Her voice is tight and shaky.

I'm about to ask Harding for assistance when we both hear, "Bear."

A man sits on the front steps. He's wearing a rugged canvas jacket, dirty jeans, and a red bandana around his throat. He removes his hat as he rises to his feet, revealing a head full of wild, thick hair and a gentle face full of remorse. "Bear, I'm sorry..."

Something switches in Claire.

I watch as she storms toward the man and smacks him hard across the face.

"I had to hear it from the sheriff!" she hisses. "The sheriff! Where the hell were you?"

"Christ—settle down, woman."

Woman. I've never heard anyone speak to Claire like that and keep their head.

"He's dead!" she snarls. "He's dead, Ransom!"

The man—*Ransom*—takes her anger. "I know. I know. I'm sorry."

"Fuck your *sorrys,*" she chokes out. "Fuck you."

"I know."

"Ransom..."

"*I know,* Claire."

"...Ran...som..."

As she says his name, her eyelashes flutter. My muscles

coil, but it's unnecessary. Ransom tightens his grip on her arms, keeping her upright just as she crumples forward, going limp.

Claire has fainted. Right into this stranger's arms.

I climb the steps and extend my arms. "I'll take it from here."

Ransom cradles her dead weight and furrows his eyebrows at me. "Who in the clam chowder fuck are you?"

"Her fiancé." It's something to see all the light leave a man's face. Gently, I scoop Claire into my arms, and Ransom releases her, transferring her weight to me. She's light, but the weight of her exhaustion is palpable as her head turns against my chest.

"Would you kindly open the door?" I ask.

Ransom eyes me suspiciously, but he reaches for a ring of keys at his belt.

4

CLAIRE

When I open my eyes, I expect to see the rosy walls of my Paris flat, the tiny spaces made bigger by the arched windows that send my gaze over a skyline rolling with rounded rooftops. I expect to smell percolating coffee and warm, fresh loaves from the café downstairs.

Instead, I see the beige curtains of a canopy bed. Dust catches on shards of light and glitters.

"Good morning."

The mattress compresses as James sits down beside me. I groan, touching my temples. My vision feels purple and bruised. There's a migraine on my horizon. "What happened?"

"You fainted. Take this."

In one hand, he offers a glass of water. In the other, an Advil. I take the water from him, pop the Advil, and take a slow, small sip. The pill feels like a rock going down, and my stomach clenches up in protest.

"Now, eat," he demands next. He holds out a plate, upon which sits a plain piece of buttered toast. The plate is ornamented with swirling patterns and Daddy's initials—RCP. A not-so-gentle reminder of whose house I'm in.

A reminder that fills me with a nauseous heat. I ignore the food as memories filter back through my skull. "Where's Ransom?"

James stares at me through his glasses. "Riley Ransom and Deputy Holden are waiting downstairs." He goes quiet for a minute, and then he asks the question that's bugging him. "Riley is—?"

I pinch the bridge of my nose. "Yes."

"The man who—?"

"*Yes.*"

His mouth thins. He's familiar with the entire sad story about my first love…and my first heartbreak. All rolled up into one bumbling, irritating cowboy.

I peel the comforter back. It's so puffy it's like lying underneath a sea of marshmallows. "I should go downstairs."

"You should rest."

"The deputy needs his statement, and I need to finish this."

For one long moment, James and I lock in a stare-off.

He pushes the toast in my face.

"Eat first."

I take the bread and carry it in my mouth like a dog as I get out of bed. The toast is cold at this point, but the butter is good, and I munch as I exit the room and walk downstairs.

The staircase spits me out in a hall beside the sitting room. Ransom and Deputy Holden have parked themselves there, but they both rise to their feet when I enter.

"Miss Preacher," Deputy Holden says with a cautious grin. "You're looking brighter."

"That's a word for it." I finish the toast, brushing crumbs from my shirt.

"You okay?" Ransom asks. He's dropped his voice low, his words meant for only me.

It's too hard to look at him. Staring at him is like staring at the sun. His rust-colored hair shines in the open morning light. The concern in the soft, soulful brown eyes makes me ache. Just the sight of him sends a swirl of tight, complicated emotions through my chest that I don't have the capacity to untangle right now.

"Can I get you anything?" he asks.

"A lobotomy," I answer. I take the leather chair, and the two men sit as well, flanking me. James steps through the sitting room, spreads open the doors that lead into the dining room, and walks to the kitchen. I hear items clattering and water hissing as he gets to work on a pot of tea.

Deputy Holden runs a hand over his slacks. His large brown hat sits on the polished coffee table in front of him. "Well, I won't overstay. Just wanted to make sure y'all were alright. When you're back on your feet, come down to the station. Like I said before, there's no rush…"

I shake my head. "I'm fine. We can do it now."

The deputy purses his lips. "I don't think—"

"Not that drawer!" Ransom shouts suddenly, jumping to his feet, arm outstretched toward the kitchen.

I whip my head around just in time to see James jump to the side. The drawer, already in motion, spits out the sound of a gunshot. A bullet sails through the air where James's head once was and buries itself into the opposite wall.

For a second, all four of us hold our breath in shocked silence.

Ransom rubs the back of his neck. "Mr. Preacher…he got a little paranoid in the past years. Kinda…kept saying people were out to kill him. And I guess he was right. Anyway. There may be a booby trap or ten hiding around here."

Booby traps? My father was a cold man, but that seems extreme, even for him. "Daddy was nothing if not a hostile host," I say.

"What did he have against tea?" James muses. Unfazed, he goes back into the now-tamed drawer, plucking out tea bags.

"James, make some coffee as well," I call through the house. "We're doing this interview now."

Ransom goes toward the kitchen, but I clasp his wrist and urge him back down. "Not you. Unless you're going to unpin more of Daddy's murder traps, you stay here."

Ransom sits down on the couch, looking like a man attending his own hanging. I tilt my head toward Deputy Holden and inform him, "You'll want to talk to him, too, Deputy. We're all part of the same, fucked-up story."

5

CLAIRE

T*hen.*

EVERY TIME RILEY RANSOM fucks me, it's like it's the last time.

When the rest of the staff goes home for the night, we rut like animals in the stables.

My nose fills with the sweet scent of horse and hay and Riley's sweat—that hard, masculine scent—and I tuck into his chest to inhale more of it and stifle my moans.

He has me pinned up against the wooden stable wall. The straps of my dress have fallen down my shoulders, my breasts bouncing in clipped stutters against his chest.

I grip his shoulders and lick the shine from the wiry muscles on his neck. He tastes like salt and grit.

Sex with Riley Ransom is filthy, and I'm obsessed with it.

The only thing that's clean about me is the bottom of my

feet. They haven't touched the ground. Ransom won't let them.

Not his princess.

His arms are tucked around my rear, cradling me tight against him. My pleasure builds, fast and hot, until it bursts like a moonflower on a full moon. I cry out as my orgasm hits me, but he doesn't stop.

I whimper. "Fuck, Ransom…"

"Nuh-uh, princess. I ain't done with you."

He pounds me so hard it hurts.

I feel each thrust in my bones. In the roots of my teeth. And I love every second of it.

Because Riley Ransom is the only person in Belleflower who doesn't treat me like a precious glass figurine.

Ransom treats me like *I belong to him.*

Over the past six months of sneaking around for quickies in the stables, I've become addicted to being his.

His moan is hot against my ear, his breath puffing at my hair. I match his roughness and nuzzle the cloth handkerchief around his neck until I find the heat of bare skin. I sink my teeth in, sucking and pulling the skin there. I squeeze my legs tightly around his hips as he pushes inside of me, as deeply as he can, and finally goes still, emptying himself. I close my eyes, savoring the fullness of his heat.

We catch our breath, panting together, gentle with each other now that our rough passion has burst. I nuzzle my nose to his.

"I like this," I tell him. I use my fingertips to readjust the blue handkerchief around his neck. "You look like a real cowboy."

He grunts on a laugh. "Try it on."

I take his invitation. I unhook the knot and move the

bandana to my throat, tying it in the back. "What do you think?"

"You look like a real cowgirl."

"I *am* a real cowgirl."

He tilts his head. The bite I left from earlier is already purpling. "I had to wear something to hide your vampire marks."

"Aw." I protrude my bottom lip dramatically. "Poor baby. Where does it hurt?"

"Why, you gonna kiss it better? Or just gonna bite harder?"

I grin widely, showing off my teeth.

Riling up Ransom is my favorite activity. He gives as good as he gets, and nothing turns me on more than the push-and-push of our competitive natures.

But every now and then, I give. Just a little.

I tilt in so our noses touch. "I'm going to miss fucking you in the stables," I murmur.

I feel his grin on my lips. "Imagine how good it's going to feel in a bed."

"In a *Parisian* bed. Silk sheets." I kiss his lips. "Warm, fluffy croissants for breakfast." I nibble the scruff on his jaw. "Champagne with freshly picked berries at the bottom." I trace the bulge of his Adam's apple with the tip of my tongue.

He moans and starts to swell again inside of me.

"Quit it."

I nip his lip. "Quit what?"

"You know what you're doing, woman."

Princess when he adores me. *Woman* when I'm being a pain in his ass. Pain in his balls. Pain in his throat.

I still haven't decided which term of endearment I like more.

I grin. He growls and kisses me—hard, playful kisses all over my face—until I'm squeaking with laughter.

We're interrupted when the house bell strikes. Three times. A loud, vibrating *gong* that you can hear miles out.

My good mood deflates, the knowledge of what comes next sharpening. Anxiety rustles around in my chest like a squirrel in a pile of autumn leaves.

"Daddy's calling," Ransom says.

"I have to go. Put me down."

"One more for the road."

He grips my hips and gives me a sudden, rough thrust that makes me gasp. I'm still floating on the unexpected bolt of pleasure when he finally pulls out of me. He lowers me down gently back into my flats, one foot at a time, so my toes don't touch the dirt below us.

As I readjust my underwear over my hips and Ransom fixes his belt, I start to drill him. Because Ransom—God love him—can be thick as a bolder sometimes.

"Are you packed?" I ask.

"Since Wednesday."

"With your passport?"

"Yep."

"And you know to be ready—"

Ransom cups the back of my head and pulls me in close.

"Eleven fifteen," he recites. "Round the back of the main house. You and I will jump in a car to take us to the airport. Get checked in with time to kill, and then we'll be wheels up and Paris-bound and leave Belleflower in our rearview. No looking back."

He strokes a stray strand of blonde hair back with his thumb, those chestnut eyes looking down at me. "How'd I do?"

The anxiety squirrel morphs into butterflies. "Perfect."

I remove the handkerchief from my throat and put it back around his. I adjust it to hide my bite marks and tuck it into his shirt.

I like putting my man back together as much as I like making him fall apart.

He crushes my mouth in a kiss, and it becomes harder and harder to leave him.

Soon, we won't have to sneak around, stealing kisses like criminals.

Once I'm out from my father's tight grip, we'll be free to be *ourselves*. New country. New city. New us.

I lower back onto my heels and force myself to step back. "See you tonight."

"See you."

As I pull away, his hands slide down my arms, over my wrists, until only our fingertips are touching.

"Love you, Bear," he says.

I will never get tired of hearing that.

"Love you more."

Before it becomes officially impossible to extract myself from him, I break our link. I bunch up the bottom of my dress, and the tall grass tickles my calves as I quickly climb the distance between the stables and the main house. With each step closer, the tightness in my chest starts to return.

I'm not sure when my home began to feel like a prison. I'm sure I had good memories here. Didn't Daddy teach me to ride a horse? Or ride a bike? There's no tire swing in our front yard. No hints of a carefree childhood to hold on to. If I have happy memories, they're buried somewhere deep in the recesses of my brain, or they're frames stolen from sappy movies and lines from romantic books with happy endings.

Now, every time I pass the tall Grecian columns in the entranceway, my heart gallops with anxiety.

I'm twenty-four years old. I'm a grown, capable woman.

I shouldn't be sneaking around like a besotted teenager.

But that's the type of fear my father instills.

The doorman stands at the doorway in his suit, hands folded in front of him. I greet him, but he dutifully ignores me. The bottoms of my shoes have gathered mud, so I leave them in the foyer. There's a small oval mirror hanging above a carved oak table. I rake my fingers through my hair and shake out straw. Daddy doesn't like my hair tied back, but he likes it even less when it's messy, so I remove the thin band from around my wrist and pull it back.

I see a woman in the mirror I barely recognize anymore. Small, upturned nose. A forehead slightly too large for my face. Eyes that shift from gray to blue depending on the light. But the most unique feature about me is the two front teeth that sit forward in my mouth, separated by a thin gap. After being not-to-affectionally dubbed "bunny" one too many times, I've learned to conceal my teeth with rosy lips that protrude into a permanent pout.

Lips that, moments ago, were laughing and kissing now look like they haven't smiled in a decade. The house casts a shadow of gloom over every one of my features.

"Claire. Is that you?"

His deep, booming voice sends a stab of dread in my chest.

"Yes, Daddy."

I cross the foyer and step into the adjoining dining room. The table has already been set, and my father's plate sits in front of him. The first thing anyone notices about my father is his eyebrows. He has thick, long hair and a gray beard, but his eyebrows are the star of the show. These thick, bushy cloud wisps above his eyes that seem constantly twisted in disappointment.

"You're late," he says.

The maid pulls out the chair beside him. I take the seat and remain still as she unfolds my napkin and drapes it over my lap. "I was brushing Calypso," I lie.

"We have people for that."

"It's a bonding technique. The more in sync we are in the stables, the more in sync we'll be on the showgrounds."

Daddy's mouth twists in a frown. His plate holds a serving of roasted duck with candied carrots, onions, and sweet potatoes, along with a dinner roll and as assortment of leafy greens plucked from the garden. His knife clicks against the plate as he rips into his duck.

"We need to talk," he says.

He knows. It hits me like an arrow, and suddenly, I can't breathe. *He knows, he saw the charge on his credit card, he's canceled my flight, he—*

"Your performance at the Cantier was less than perfect."

I blink. "Calypso and I received the highest score."

"Do you judge your worth on the failures of others?"

My jaw tightens. "No, but—"

He cuts in, his voice sharp. "You and I both know you could do better. Your form was sloppy. You slouched. What are you doing for core work?"

Getting fucked religiously by Riley Ransom.

"I'm seeing Nina."

"The Pilates instructor?"

"Yes."

"How often?"

"Three times a week."

"Make it five." The twin doors open from the kitchen. The server steps in with my plate. My anxiety turned my stomach to knots before, but now—maybe from my previous nightly *Pilates*—I'm feeling famished, and the crisp skin on the duck makes my stomach pinch.

Just as he's about to set the plate in front of me, however, my father gestures with his knife.

"No need. Take her plate away. Thank you."

Fury rises into my cheeks. The server hovers, unsure, but knows better than to disobey and so, slowly, starts to back away.

I stand abruptly. "If I'm not eating, I won't sit here."

Daddy looks up at me, his gaze flat. There's a shiny piece of duck in his mustache. "Then ask."

My molars grind. "May I be dismissed?"

"You may."

As I start to back away from the table, I suddenly feel as though a string is attached to my palms, pulling me back.

This could very well be the last time I see my father.

If I don't tell him now...I never will.

That knowledge summons up a new courage into my chest. I turn and look square at my father. "Daddy?"

"Hm?" He's already turned his gaze away from me, digging back into his food.

I find my gaze examining him studiously, the way he examines me. I size up the bald patch on the back of his head. The wisps of white hair growing from his ears. The deep valleys of creases along his forehead.

This man loved me once, didn't he?

Did something change in me to make him love me less?

Or did something change in him?

I press my lips together. "You aren't perfect either," I state. "But that never stopped me from loving you. I just wish you'd do the same for me."

He pauses the motion of his fork and knife. His gaze hits

me. There's a ghost of something in his gray eyes. A whisper of regret, maybe?

Or perhaps he's just stunned that his precious puppet spoke out of turn.

It's none of my business anymore. I'm done waiting for him to grow a heart.

The poor server is still hovering, so I take advantage and pluck the dinner roll from my plate. I stick it in my mouth, swivel out of the dining room, and quickly scale the steps. When I make it to my room, my blood is prickling with a new kind of heat. The second I'm inside, I text Ransom.

[TEXT:] One hour, cowboy

HE SENDS BACK A THUMBS-UP.

I pull my suitcase out from under my bed. As I check to make sure I have my passport and the boarding passes, I munch on the dinner roll—even plain, it tastes like sweet victory.

Twenty minutes till, I call the car service and confirm that they have a car scheduled. I perch at my window, the blinds peeled back just enough, and stare down the long, dark road.

Fireflies twinkle by the fence. For the first time, my heart lurches.

I'm going to miss this place.

As much as I hate it, Belleflower is home.

But I need to get out of here. If I don't, I'll never know what it is to stand on my own two feet.

I have it all planned out—the hotel where Ransom and I will stay for the first few weeks. And then orientation, and

I'll be in school, earning my MBA. My acceptance letter is tucked into my purse. Tuition won't be easy without Daddy's money, but it will work out. It has to work out.

I stress eat the rest of the roll until it's nothing but crumbs. Finally, there's light at the end of the tunnel. The cab curls around the side-winding roads and approaches the house.

I shoot Ransom a text: *Cab is here. Come now.*

I grab my bag and pull my purse over my shoulder. I touch the crystal doorknob.

My gaze gets caught on my promise ring.

That glint of diamond on my ring finger. The ring I've worn every day of my life since I was thirteen.

When I put this ring on, I promised to be perfect. A good, obedient, intelligent little girl. Pure of heart and body. Dedicated to my own excellence. The perfect future Belleflower Queen.

But over a decade has passed, and the dream of wearing the Belleflower Queen crown gets further and further every day. It's a stupid dream. Like holding on to the fantasy that every Christmas, a man on a magical sleigh will leave me presents. But...

It still hurts. Even all this time, it still hurts that I was never good enough. A bruise on my heart that won't heal.

Hell with it.

I twist the ring off my finger and set it down on my dresser. Then, I open my bedroom door and quietly slip out.

Sometimes, Daddy spends his evenings drinking whiskey and listening to music in the sitting room. Tonight, it's quiet downstairs. I exhale a tight breath. Small graces.

I take my luggage and hobble downstairs with it as quietly as I can. I wanted to bring more, but I couldn't shove too much away without arousing suspicion. Besides, I've calculated that once I'm there and making some money of my own, I'll be able to buy clothes of my own—

The night air is brisk. I've made it this far. The car is already parked outside, the driver standing near it. He greets me and takes my luggage. I look around, but...there's no sign of Ransom.

[TEXT:] where are you???

I STARE AT MY PHONE. A couple of minutes later, it pings.

[TEXT:] I'll meet you at the airport.

MY HEART HICCUPS. This was *not* the plan.

I'd scheduled everything so meticulously. I'd reminded him. Countless times. There is *no room for deviation.*

I send him a scourge of texts. He doesn't reply.

"Ma'am?" The driver holds the door open for me.

I get inside, but I feel as though I've swallowed a horseshoe whole, the metal bend stuck in my throat, making it hard to breathe. He shuts the door behind me, and all the crickets and owls and nighttime Kentucky sounds get sucked away into a vacuum of silence.

The ride to the airport is a blur. I pay the driver, check my bag, go through security, and find my gate. But I can't focus on anything. I spend the whole time clutching my cell phone and staring at the blank screen, praying for it to ring.

And then, finally, it does.

I answer quickly. "Ransom. Where are you?"

My voice is tight. Even I can hear the tremble.

Then he says my three least favorite words in the English language. "I'm not coming."

All the blood leaves my face.

"What do you *mean* you're not coming?"

His tone is sad but decided. "I can't leave. This is my home."

"I thought...I thought *I* was your home."

"I'm sorry."

I'm sorry.

Two words that could never mean so little.

I unpin my tongue from the roof of my mouth. "If you're staying, I'm staying."

His voice is firm suddenly. "No. Bear. You said it yourself. You stay here, you'll never be anything but your daddy's prize. You gotta go."

"I can't do this without you."

My voice hitches. People are starting to stare. I bow myself over and let my long hair fall like a curtain in front of my face.

Ransom's voice comes through the phone so clearly that if I close my eyes, I can imagine he's holding me and whispering in my ear. "You can. And you will. If leaving me means finding yourself, you're going to get off your tight little ass and march your way up to that plane. You hear me?"

I swallow. Everything is too tight to speak.

Ransom continues, his voice soft now. "You're the strongest, most capable woman I know. You can do this."

Over the loudspeakers, the attendants are calling. It's time to board.

I close my eyes.

"I hate you," I whisper.

Meaning it. But meaning something else, too.

There's a long pause. "Go catch your plane, Claire."

The very sound of my name in his voice hurts me.

How many times has he moaned my name in my ear?

How many times have I heard it grunted in frustration when I piss him off?

How many times has he said that word through rumbling bouts of laughter?

Anger lashes my heart like a whip. "Fuck you."

I end the call, white-knuckle my purse, and line up with all the other travelers. I hand over my one-way ticket to Paris and board the plane.

I don't let myself cry until I'm thousands of feet in the air, where no one down below in Belleflower can hear me break.

RANSOM

ow.

CLAIRE FINISHES TELLING OUR SAD, messed-up tale.

I stare at the ashtray on the table. If I stared at it any harder, the whole thing might combust. I can't look at her as she recounts one of the worst goddamn days of my whole sorry life.

My jaw is so tight I might just crack a molar if I'm not careful.

"So," she continues, speaking to Deputy Holden, "to answer your questions before you bother asking them—no, I don't know who killed my father. I don't know his enemies, though I imagine half the town wants his head on a stick. I don't know his friends, but I can tell you they were always few and far between. The truth is I don't know anything about him. I haven't heard from him in over five years. Not a single phone call, email, or Christmas card. I left. I never looked back. And he resented me for it. We've been perfect strangers ever since."

With that, she's finished.

The place goes silent. I force my eyes to meet Claire's face.

She's empty of emotion. The perfectly poised picture of perfection she's always been.

The way Mr. Preacher trained her.

But I can hear it. The echo of sadness underlining her words. She pretends her father's absence doesn't affect her, but it does.

She hated him, but I know well enough—she was the only daughter of a single-father narcissist, and that man was her entire world, once upon a time.

Deputy Holden flips his little notebook shut. He jams his pen in the spiral top.

"This was useful," he says. "Thank you for your time. I'll be in touch if we need anything else."

He gets up, and immediately, I'm on my feet. "I'll walk you out."

I need to breathe fresh air.

A pot of tea and fresh coffee sit on the table in front of us. James has settled into the couch next to Claire, but he reaches over and takes her hand. I already noticed the big rock on her hand—a princess-cut diamond the size of the Eiffel Tower. Now, I notice his own sigil-style diamond ring as they thread their fingers together. And—dammit—I hate the guy, and I hate his stupid rings, but maybe that's right.

She sure as hell doesn't need a bad memory like me hanging around her.

Deputy Holden jangles with every step. The house spits us out, and when the chilled afternoon cold catches on my skin, I feel a little better.

"Hey." I stop the deputy before he reaches his car. "Any leads on who got Mr. Preacher?"

His mouth folds in a frown. "If I did, I couldn't very well tell you."

"Mr. Preacher was right, wasn't he? Someone was trying to get him? It's the mafia, isn't it?"

"*Huh?*"

"You know—Don Corleone? You know how they get—horse heads and all. Threatening people with them. If you need help, you know, getting those mafia sons of bitches—"

"Where the hell're you getting *mafia*?" Holden growls.

I hold my ground. "Mr. Preacher and I, we didn't always see eye to eye, but I owe it to him."

He sizes me up. "You mean you owe it to *her*."

I shove my hands in my pockets. "I just want to help. However I can."

Deputy Holden comes face-to-face with me. He's a good deal shorter than me, but that doesn't stop him from frowning like a bulldog. "You want to do me a favor? Quit stepping into trouble. Right now, you're the only one who was here at the time of the crime, and the way I see it, you've got a motive, sneaking around with Preacher's daughter all those years ago."

I blink. "You don't think I—?"

"No! Goddammit, I've known you since you were a sprout. You wouldn't hurt a horsefly. But you're not making it an easy case for me to prove. Keep your nose clean, you hear?"

"Yes, sir."

Deputy Holden shakes his head. He waddles back to his car, and I follow behind him. I close his door car, pat the roof, and step out of his way. His wheels crunch over gravel before rolling out the gate.

I turn and climb the steps back to the house. When I try the door, however, it's locked. I knock loudly, and thirty seconds later, the door opens up.

"Can I help you?" James asks. He's annoyingly tall. Like a human gargoyle frowning down at me.

If Claire's eyes are a storm cloud, James's eyes are the opposite. They're this bright, piercing blue, but I hold his gaze.

"Yeah. I got locked out."

"Claire is resting. I think you should go home as well."

"Alright, well, can I just make sure she's alright?"

"I'm afraid she's already in the shower."

Lying son of a bitch. I can see it on his face. That British accent makes everything that comes out of his mouth sound so damn polite, even when he's telling me to screw off.

He nods. "Goodbye, Riley Ransom."

With that, he closes the door in my face.

Son of a bitch! Ain't been here twenty-four hours, and already, he thinks he owns the place.

Should've let Mr. Preacher's booby trap take him out.

I step backward, my boots clicking on the stone walkway. I tilt my hat back so I can look upstairs. Second floor. Where they keep the bedrooms.

I swear, for a moment, I see Claire in the master suite window.

But just as quickly, she vanishes, the curtain fluttering in her wake.

7

CLAIRE

The bedroom door clicks as James opens it. My eyes don't leave the window, though.

Through the thin curtain, I can still see the shadow of Riley Ransom lingering outside the house.

"They've left," James announces.

"We'll stay here," I tell him. "Get unpacked."

I can feel James lingering. His silences are the loudest. "This was your father's room," he states.

"Yes."

"This is where they found him."

His words are like nettles under my fingernails. I turn, arms crossed. "I'm told it's been cleaned. Mattress replaced. Demons exorcised. Are you afraid of ghosts?"

Those blue eyes meet mine. "I saw your old room down the hall. Wouldn't you prefer to sleep there?"

I push my lips together. "You know how when a little girl dies, their parents keep the room as a memorial to their daughter?"

"Yes."

"That girl is dead. We don't open her room. Understand?"

James nods. "Understood."

What I can't say to him is *there is too much in that room.* I'm afraid if I open the door of my childhood bedroom, memories will come flying out like so many black-winged moths, and I won't be able to compartmentalize them.

I've worked very, very hard to suppress the rotten memories of growing up in Belleflower.

And yet...

Part of me is still drawn to them.

I look out the window again. I nudge the curtain back, but I'm too late.

Ransom has vanished like a ghost.

James comes up behind me. He slides my hair to the side. His mouth presses a small note of affection to my throat. I close my eyes, leaning into it. "I need sleep," I admit. "Lots of it."

His hand slips up the column of my throat. He covers my mouth with his palm and pinches my nose between his thumb and forefinger, closing off my air. The heat of his breath hits my ear.

"Should I suffocate you?" he asks. "It'll be the deepest sleep you've ever had."

James is an enigma. A tall, socially awkward, prim and proper geek.

And then.

He says things like *that* in a deep, dark voice that makes my pulse skip because I can't tell if he's kidding or not.

He holds me in this breathless embrace only for a moment. Just long enough to make my lungs ache. A whisper of the things he's capable of. A gentle reminder not to stare at old boyfriends out the window, maybe.

He drops his hand, and I suck in air. I'm light-headed.

I twist to face him and slip my arms around his shoulders. "Put me to bed," I tell him, and he lifts me off my feet.

8

CLAIRE

Running clears my head.

Normally, James and I wake up when the sky is still kissed pink with dawn light. We're late today, jet-lagged, and we don't make it out of the house until nearly nine. It's a cool morning. My emerald-green, velvet tracksuit keeps me warm. James is dressed in matching green (I got us a set for Christmas) with a smart watch to calculate his movements and his AirPods. His bare neck and cheeks pinken in the chill.

In Paris, we run loops around the city parks. Here, we have actual woods.

He slows his pace to keep alongside me, and I pick up mine to match his.

"It doesn't make any sense," I say.

"Tell me," he encourages, opening the door for me to vent.

As we cut deeper into the woods, the sky dims, hooded with thick oak trees.

"I couldn't sleep last night," I tell him. "So I started going through Daddy's finances."

"Alright."

"Most of it is pretty standard—breeding expenses. Horse care. Equipment for the stables. Salaries."

"Mmhm."

"But he's been sending money to something called the Semper Fi Fund."

Twigs snap under my feet. My thighs burn, and I push through the pain.

"What's that?"

"I don't know. Some sort of...nonprofit for veterans. Military fundraiser bullshit."

"I didn't know he served."

I scoff. "He didn't. Ever. I don't think he's ever even *voted*. Daddy hated politics."

"Maybe he became patriotic in his old age."

I take a couple of seconds to inhale. Exhale. Jog. "It's just...it's just *off*."

We're coming up to a river. "Left or right?" James asks.

"Right. We can circle back to the house."

We swoop to the right like geese on a migration path. James's feet fall quickly and quietly in line with mine, and for a minute, we pick up the pace. I let the beating of my heart do the talking.

But then I say, "What if it's a front?"

James's breath is light. I can hear his soft inhales and exhales.

"A front for what?"

"I don't know. Maybe Daddy was...cheating on his taxes. Something. He always thought he was invincible. Better than everyone else. What if he was doing something illegal...and it caught up with him?"

"You think the tax man killed your father?"

A strand of hair springs free from my ponytail. I blow it

out of my face. "No…I don't know. It's just a theory. But it's strange, isn't it?"

James is quiet for a minute. "You said it yourself," he says. "You really didn't know the man in the past five years."

"So?"

"I think you're reaching."

I stop. I put my hands on my thighs.

James stalls. He keeps moving, though, jogging in place. "Are you okay?"

My chest is tight. I grip my knees and lift so I can look him in the eyes.

"Daddy is dead," I tell him. "He had his head blown off in his own bed. What part of that sounds *normal* to you?"

The edge of his mouth tucks downward. He says nothing to his own defense.

I bow my head. Air hurts. Breathing hurts.

Being alive hurts.

When I stand up again, my gaze moves beyond James. We're almost back to the house. And then I see it—three familiar figures perched like flamingos in front of the gate.

"Oh, *fuck*," I swear.

He follows my gaze to the women at the house. "You know them?"

"They're my…Promise Sisters."

A pink, puff-pastry-shaped form steps toward us. She holds her hand over her brow to see us through the morning sun and then waves her hand.

"Claire!" Mary-Kate shouts. "Is that you? Running in the morning—aren't you fit!"

Like a skittish deer, James starts to take off for his second loop. Cobra-quick, I grab his arm and yank him back.

"If you leave me alone with these vipers," I hiss at him, "I swear to God, I will eviscerate you."

He slips his arm around my back instead. Cordially, he waves at the women.

The second we're close enough to the Promise Sisters, they descend on us. The flock of pastel dresses swarms around me, and one by one, they pull me into a hug.

"Claire! I can't believe you're home!"

"You and me both," I wheeze between tight squeezes.

"I'm so sorry about your daddy, bunny," Violet says, and her eyes are instantly wet, a cry-on-command trick she picked up from drama school. Terrified she's about to burst into tears just for the applause, I quickly change the subject.

"This is my fiancé, James."

I put my hand on James's back. Their eyes snap to him, and immediately, they begin assessing. Elsbeth even squeezes his bicep.

"Oh," she says pleasantly. "Well done, Claire."

"Thank you. What are you doing here?"

"We're picking you up." Mary-Kate smiles. "We're going to brunch at the Equestrian Club, and you're coming with us."

"It's a Friday *must*," Violet emphasizes, her dark curls bouncing as she nods.

"Oh...I don't know. We have a lot to do before the funeral—"

"But you *must*," Elsbeth repeats, her fingers flying frantically together, twisting.

I glance at the car they drove up in—a white Pontiac. "Is that Hudson?"

"Oh, yes," Mary-Kate says. "And Jake, my youngest. Wave hi."

We wave. Hudson looks tired, but he spots us and lifts the infant on the steering wheel. He manipulates the baby's hand so it waves back, and the child starts chewing on the wheel.

"Do they want to come inside?"

Mary-Kate waves them off. "No need. I cracked a window. Do you have bubbles?"

It quickly becomes clear this isn't an invite I can talk my way out of, so I open the gate. Once we're all inside, they invite themselves to Daddy's bar while James and I excuse ourselves to rinse off from our run.

We share the shower. It's quicker this way.

"What do I need to know?" James asks. The hot water steams as it hits his strong chest.

I cover myself in suds. "Mary-Kate is the daughter of my father's bloodstock agent, so we were forced into friendship. We grew up together. Then Elsbeth, Violet, and Bonnie joined our crew. We called ourselves the *Promise Sisters*. I didn't see Bonnie downstairs—maybe she actually left this godforsaken town."

"Promise Sisters?"

God, this town is so bizarre. Trying to explain it to an out-of-towner feels like unraveling a mummy's tomb and reading some ancient inscription.

"You know...purity rings? How little girls get a ring when they promise to stay *clean* for their future husbands? And it's all...bizarre and culty?"

"Sure."

"Well, we had a tradition like that in Belleflower. Sort of. Except instead of purity rings, if you were *very, very* good, you would get a ring from the Benefactors' Society. It was called a Promise Ring. It's a term for *promising* young girls who are on the path to be future Belleflower Queens. Sort of like...junior queens, I guess. Only a handful of girls ever got them."

"And you all had your Promise Rings."

"Yes. It was like...an elite group."

"You take this Belleflower Queen thing very seriously, don't you?" James says.

"It's a religion," I say without a hint of humor.

He stares at me. Droplets of water hang over his long eyelashes.

"Switch," I say.

We do a small dance to swivel around in the shower so I can rinse off while James takes the soap. He suds up under his arms. Over his strong chest.

The most shocking thing about naked James, probably, is his tattoo.

Everything about him is so prim and proper...*and then.* The lower half of his left arm is engulfed with the image of a dark wolf head swallowing a dagger. The first time I saw it, I asked him what it meant. He showed me the purpled skin underneath.

"The tattoo is to cover the burn," he told me.

"What's the burn?" I'd asked.

He gave me a strange smile. "To cover up the boy."

I tilt my head back into the stream of hot water. I close my eyes under the downpour. "Anyway. We were spoiled, entitled teenagers. We rode our horses everywhere and terrorized the town."

"You? A terror? I can't imagine it."

"On weekends, we took our horses to the river, where we went for a swim and sunned in our bathing suits and teased the old men who fished there. Then—still bathing suit clad —we'd hop back on our horses and ride bareback into town, where we'd hitch them up and go to Margie's Cafe, and we'd get free coffee—no sugar because we weren't allowed to intake sweets."

"So not much has changed." I open my eyes to see James wearing a sly, sideways smile.

I elbow him for it, and he grunts as I exit the shower. I grab my towel and shake my hair dry.

There's a double knock on the door before Elsbeth bursts in. I barely have time to cover myself with my towel.

"Knock, knock! We brought you a dress!" Elsbeth says. To my dismay, she holds up a matching, fluffy, pink dress.

Dear God.

"You're too kind." My smile could kill kittens.

"I know," Elsbeth says.

The shower cuts. James opens the shower door and blinks when he sees our company.

Elsbeth, unashamedly, gawks.

I guess I can't blame her. My fiancé is wonderfully endowed. To be honest, I get a small surge of pride when she loses her tongue and simply *stares* at his handsome, naked figure.

James clears his throat. He nods to the towel rack. "Would you be so kind?"

Elsbeth fumbles. She goes in the direction of his nod but hands over his glasses instead of a towel.

I have to bite back a laugh as James, crestfallen, adorns his glasses. Naked, wet, but at least he can *see* now.

"Thank you."

"Don't mention it. See you dears downstairs!" Before Elsbeth leaves, she mouths to me, *Oh my God.*

I quirk a grin. I shrug. I've won the fiancé lottery.

James crosses the bathroom and finally grabs his towel.

"Blink twice if you're in danger," I tell him.

"I'm in danger."

I wind my arms around his shoulders. His body is shower-warm and pink against mine.

"If I can survive a pink dress, you can survive being my arm candy."

"So stay quiet and look pretty?"

"Yes."

"And if they eat me alive?"

"The Promise Sisters might be the Belleflower matriarchs...but lucky you, you're engaged to me. And no one touches what's mine."

I touch my nose against his and rest my hand on his hip. He stirs underneath his towel, the hard swell of him nuzzling my belly.

I'd love nothing more than to let him take me right now. To remind myself that he's mine, and I'm his, and we can get through this shitshow as long as we're together. But—

"They're waiting. Come on." I lift my arms. "The quicker we're in, the quicker we're out. Help me into this monstrosity."

9

CLAIRE

The Equestrian Club looks just as I left it.

The building is a rounded, glass-encased structure shaped like a horseshoe. The curve allows onlookers a perfect view of the racetrack, where horses and riders parade back and forth for the diners sipping mimosas underneath fascinators.

The Promise Sisters have a standing reservation, apparently. You need an invite to get into the country club. The host—who I've never seen before in my life—recognizes me. He bends in his stiff dinner jacket and says, "Mr. and Miss Preacher. Welcome. Right this way."

Greeters stand straight-backed and welcome us with polite smiles. As we walk toward the table, I let my body bump against James's. "How does it feel to take my last name?"

"Dangerously good," he murmurs in my ear.

We sit at a prize table catty-cornered to the glass windows, lending us a perfect view of the race track. There's a bountiful bouquet of dripping lilies as a centerpiece, which is delicately removed and replaced with a carafe of orange juice and prosecco.

Hudson straps the child to a harness at his chest, its bare, chubby feet kicking and bouncing. Just when I think James might have some male company, Hudson kisses the side of Mary-Kate's face. "Do you need anything?" he murmurs.

She shakes her head and waves him off. He gives us a polite nod and then vanishes into the other room, bouncing little Jake against his chest and squeezing his small foot.

"Where's he going?" I ask.

"There's a playground outside," Mary-Kate responds with a flick of her hand.

"They've made some updates." Violet smiles. "Isn't Jake precious?"

I can't tell one baby from the other, but I say the thing you're supposed to say when confronted with a squealing freshly born.

"He looks just like Hudson," I say.

The girls exchange a fugitive look and then burst out laughing.

"What am I missing?"

Mary-Kate takes my hand and squeezes it too hard. "We have so much to catch up on."

THEY DELIVER finger sandwiches with mayo and cucumbers. Small bowls of creamy, white mushroom soup. Pimento cheese on crackers lined up perfectly on a slim plate.

Nibbles that aren't meant to fill you up but to pad the stomach for the bottomless mimosas that pass back and forth across the table.

My Promise Sisters have grown up. Everyone has had kids. Jake is Mary-Kate's second. Elsbeth has one. Violet has three.

"That's amazing," I say, meaning it.

"It's a pain, is what it is," Mary-Kate says as she plucks through the finger sandwiches, pushing them around the plate until she finds the one with salmon and cream cheese. "You really have to be careful about what you put *inside* of your body. You do all this work for them and—for what?"

"And they're ungrateful." Violet sighs. "All my children said *Daddy* first. Can you believe it? I carried them for nine months, and they have the nerve to learn his name before mine."

"It's infant identity transference," James says.

He's been quiet the whole brunch, so when he speaks up, the girls stop what they're doing and blink at him, as though just remembering he's there.

"Go on," I encourage.

"I take it you're the primary caretaker," James says.

"Yes," Violet agrees.

"In the beginning stages of life, psychologists theorize that infants fuse their own identities with that of their primary caretaker. In short, they don't think to give you a name—*mama*—because you are the same as them. *Daddy* comes easier because they can differentiate between themselves and him."

Violet tilts her head as she considers the information. "That's...strangely comforting."

"He's like that," I muse. "Strangely comforting."

James's eyes catch mine from behind his glasses. I smile at him.

Our attention is derailed when a tremor rushes through the room, like a flutter of birds taking off all at once. People lift up in their seats and crane their necks to look out the large, open windows.

On the racetrack outside, I see men leading their horses, one by one, across the field. Onlookers strain to watch the parade.

"What are they doing?" I ask.

"Showing off the studs," Elsbeth says dreamily. Her eyes are fixed on the men, not the horses.

"I'm going to have a look," James says. He stands and touches my shoulder on his way over.

What he means is *I am overstimulated. I need space.*

I grant it. I watch him leave. He perches like a cat on the benches by the big windows to peer down below. He fits his earbuds back in his ears. He's settling himself.

His ass looks *amazing* in those pants. Tight. Asking to be gripped.

I may have also had too many mimosas.

My bones are looser. I want to sink into my puffy dress the way one sags into a beanbag.

"What about you, Claire?" Mary-Kate asks.

"What about me?"

"Are you and James thinking about children?"

I turn to James and call out, "James, what do we think about children?"

James takes out his earbud. "They're wonderful. Especially when you can hand them back to their owners."

Violet touches the back of my hand to comfort me. "He'll change his mind when you're married."

I can't help the grin that tickles my lips. "I certainly hope not."

My gaze fixes on the nape of James's neck. I want to draw my fingers through that fine, dark hair.

I don't want kids, but...I *do* want this man to bury himself inside me, fist his fingers through my hair, and...

I shift in my seat. I'm leaving a puddle in my underwear at the thought.

"Excuse me," I say and drop my napkin on the table. I make my way to the restroom. My feet know the way, even if I haven't been here in years—around the corner, through the narrow hall, to the door marked "Mares."

As I'm entering, someone is exiting. She wears a large, floppy-rimmed hat and chunky, square sunglasses rimmed with neon green.

"Bonnie?" I ask.

She slides her glasses off her nose to look at me. "Claire?"

I'm flooded with a sudden rush of joy for seeing this woman. Bonnie and I weren't closer than any of the other women—but right now, she's not sitting at that Kafka-ian nightmare of a table where I feel like I'm on trial for some imaginary crime, and that fact alone is enough to make me pull her into a hug.

Her pregnant belly nudges between us. I soften my hold.

"I'm sorry about your father," she says breathlessly.

"Don't be. He was an ass." *Oh. Okay. That champagne tongue is really kicking in.* I back up and rest my hands on her shoulders. "How are you?"

Her face pinches. "I'm a Belleflower Queen. As of last year."

I squeeze her shoulders. "That's huge. Congratulations."

Somewhere inside of me, a little blonde girl is screaming with envy.

Stop, Claire. Just stop it.

"It's quite the honor." Her voice is strangely hollow when she says it, though.

I point to the table. "We're all sitting over there if you want to join us."

Bonnie tucks her chin. Her straight, dark hair falls around her face. Immediately, she shoves her glasses back on, as though she's in witness protection. "I can't. I'm only here to sign Hank up for the polo match this weekend. We're married." She flicks the back of her hand dismissively to show a blocky diamond ring. "He loves polo. He's quite good."

The hand holding up her ring trembles lightly. "Are you okay?" I ask her.

"Please don't tell them you saw me."

"Sure, why—?"

"Got to go." She gives me a quick kiss on the side of my face and then hurries off, her flats shuffling as she goes.

How bizarre.

When I get back to the table, the girls are refilling everyone's glasses.

"Was that Bonnie?" Violet asks immediately.

Before I can confirm or deny, Mary-Kate lets out an exhausted sigh. "Ugh. She thinks she's so much better than us since she became last year's Belleflower Queen. But she's been nothing but a disappointment, in my opinion." She drops her voice, low and secretive. "Some women crack under the weight of the crown, you know."

"She's our friend," I hear myself saying.

"Oh, Claire. You've been in Paris for so long."

"Not that long." My refilled mimosa tastes pulpy and stringy. I've lost the taste for it. I scan across the room, and my eyes find James. He's still sitting on the bench, tall body hunched over his phone, scrolling through it.

"I'll be right back," I say, excusing myself. I get up and

walk over to James. It's not until my shadow touches him that he finally looks up from his phone.

I climb into his lap. He immediately uncrosses his legs to make room for me. I wind my arms around his shoulders, look him in all four of his eyes, and say, "Save me."

"You're drunk," he observes.

His tall form makes me feel small. Like a little girl in Daddy's lap.

Especially when he chastises me.

Except there's nothing familial about the bulge between us.

I shift ever so slightly in my spot. "You're hard."

"You're in my lap," he says by way of explanation.

"Is that all it takes?"

"Every inch of your body turns me on, Claire."

Those blue eyes. I could lose myself in those sky-blue eyes.

"Prove it," I tell him. He tilts his head against mine. I whisper in his ear, "Come back to the table. Let me sit in your lap. Put it inside of me."

"You're being a brat." His voice is a low rumble, like far-away thunder. It makes me shudder.

"Then tame me."

I've never been submissive. To any man, ever, in my life.

Except James Calloway.

His dominance is a heady, erotic fog that makes it hard for me to catch my breath.

Dizzy, I unwind from his lap. He takes my hand, and together, we walk back to the table with the Promise Sisters.

"James! You've returned!"

"Just in time," Mary-Kate says. "They just brought out dessert."

Tiny egg cups with barely half a scoop of perfectly orange sorbet sit in front of us.

James takes his chair and casually pulls me onto his lap. I adjust my dress, and for the first time, I'm grateful for the huge, gaudy skirt. It covers both of our laps completely. No one notices when James slides a hand underneath my ass and tugs down his zipper.

"Sorbet?" Violet asks, motioning to the cups in the center.

"No, thank you."

"She'll have one," James says. "Pass them over."

I rise just enough to collect a cup. When I sit back down, I find James's hand and his bare cock. He pushes my panties to the side and guides his erection inside of me.

My heart is hammering in my chest. I sit back slowly, easing him inside of me. It's hard to swallow back my whimper, but I succeed.

He's so thick. He feels wonderful.

"Claire," he says.

"Hmm?"

"A spoon, please."

I give him a dessert spoon. James hooks an arm around me, holds the cup, and leans over my shoulder to scoop a bite of sorbet into his mouth.

The women have dissolved into speculation about the polo match this weekend. I shift, trying to adjust to the feeling of him so full inside of me without anyone knowing.

God. We're terrible people. But there's such a rush to it.

I love knowing that this man owns my body completely. He can take it whenever he wants it...and no one has the slightest idea.

"How is it?" I ask. Because I need something to distract

from the heat pooling between my legs. I want to badly to grind down on him, but I can't. I can't bring attention to us.

"Sweet," he replies. "Try it."

While everyone's attention is on their conversation, his hand drops to my thigh and slips underneath my dress.

My spine stiffens. His fingers are freezing from holding on to the small glass cup. He draws his cold touch up the sensitive skin of my inner thigh and then finds my hot sex.

I suck in a quick breath. He doesn't flinch. His cold fingers nestle between my lips and nudges my swollen clit. It takes everything within me not to move as he teases me. My sex is burning, and the chilly sensations are a sharp contrast. He pets me with slow, teasing motions, drumming his fingers languidly, playing me.

I'm vibrating on the edge of pleasure.

"Claire," he says.

"Mmm?"

"The sorbet."

Right. I grab the spoon. My hand shakes when I lift it to my mouth. It's a burst of mango sweet, but I can barely taste it. His touch has warmed with the heat of my arousal. His fingers are hot and slick in the same way I'm hot and slick, and with every pass, I edge closer to the height of my pleasure. My body contacts around his stiff muscle.

James is made of metal. My tin man. Impossible to tell that he's cock-deep inside of me. He doesn't move. Doesn't flinch. If I put my hand to his chest, I'm not even sure his heartbeat will have changed.

No one knows he's driving me crazy underneath my dress.

His tempo changes. He stops teasing and starts to flick me. Lightly. Over and over. Rapid, tight little taps directly on my aching nub.

The taps themselves? Not bad. But when they're delivered in *rapid succession*...

Everything in me clenches. All of my attention zeroes in on each small...teasing...flick of his fingers until...I come undone. I grip the tablecloth as I grind my orgasm out, twisting in his lap.

I can't help it. A small moan escapes me. I catch the attention of the girls at the table.

"This...sorbet..." I gasp. "So good..."

As calm as ice, James removes his hand from between my legs. He wipes my wet on my thigh. I feel filthy, slutty, and exhilarated.

"That," he states, "is the best dessert I've ever had."

I shift in his lap. His hard cock rubs against my throbbing sex in such a delicious way a quiet, tiny whine escapes the back of my throat.

James doesn't budge, but he swells suddenly between my legs. From rock-hard to diamond-hard.

What did it? The orgasm? The exhibition of it all? The whimper?

For science, I test him. I part my lips at the shell of his ear and exhale another quiet, desperate whimper. Just for him.

His hand clamps around my arm. He lifts me suddenly off his lap. I make a small noise of discomfort as he leaves my body, and in a single subtle move, he tucks himself back into his pants and stands.

He uses my body to shield his dignity, though. His pants don't leave a lot for the imagination right now.

"I'd like a tour of the club," he says. There's a dark note in his tone only I can detect.

"Now?" My voice is breathless.

"Now."

I walk like a newly fawned calf, wobbling my way

through the sea of people, ignoring the Promise Sisters' inquisitive stares. James remains right behind me, his grip tight on my arm, cutting off circulation.

"What do you want to see first?"

"This will do."

He pulls me to the bathroom. It's a multi-stall room with tiled floors, sea-shell-pale doors, and a long, marbled sink.

James checks the stalls, and once he's satisfied we're alone, he flips the lock on the door.

Those dark eyes burn from behind his glasses.

"Are you angry?" I ask.

"Fuming."

I cock my head. I have to tilt so far back to look up at him. "What did I do?"

He cups my face in the shell of his palm. He smears my bottom lip with his thumb. "Don't play dumb. You're far too smart to play dumb."

A grin teases my mouth. "I suppose I am."

"Hands on the sink."

I hold his gaze only a second longer before turning toward the mirrors. I drop my palms to the sink and bend over, presenting myself to him.

I lift my eyes to the mirror. I watch James take his place behind me. His large hands grasp my thighs and slip upward, bunching the ruffles of my ridiculous dress. He pushes it to my hips, and I watch him drop to a crouch. He rolls the thin, soaked fabric of my underwear down my legs. The point of his nose touches my rear. The heat of his breath warms my sex. Is he...inhaling me?

He stands, leaving me tingling with want. I remain still as he pulls on the sleeves of my dress, yanking them down my arms. He handles the fabric roughly, and I hear it rip as he yanks it down my chest so my breasts fall free.

He's staging me. Exactly how he wants me.

He wants to see my tits when he fucks me.

My throat is dry. I wet my lips. "Are you punishing me?"

Those dark eyes meet my gaze in the mirror.

"Get on the tips of your toes. Don't come down until I tell you to."

I lift my heels from the floor, rising to the balls of my feet.

I watch him unbuckle. I swallow when his zipper hisses. My back arches, and I push up even taller on my toes. Beseeching.

I want him so badly my core aches.

He pushes his cock inside of me. His hands bunch at my hair. I can feel him so deep. My toes want to curl, but they can't. They're too busy trying to hold me up.

He thrusts into me once. Twice. Three times.

That's all it takes. I'm so worked up I explode.

The woman in the mirror loses it. She disassembles, slumping forward—a boneless heap as he clutches her hips and gives a final thrust before pouring himself inside of her.

I cry out. I close my eyes. Sweet, sweet heat.

My body craves it. Tightens for it. Milks his hardworking cock, pleading for more.

He gives more. More thrusts. More spilling. *More.* All of it. Everything that is his is mine now, living inside of me. When he pulls out, I'm not empty long. He pushes those long fingers deep inside, and I choke on a gasp when I realize he's pushing *it* inside me.

"Don't clean up," he tells me. "Keep it inside. I might not want children, but I can still make you my breeding pet."

Holy fuck. My cunt, which thought it was done coming, suddenly gives a tight throb that makes me whine.

He uses his grip on my hair to lift me and pull me

against his strong body. He opens my mouth with his tongue. His kiss is strong. Possessive. It sucks the air out of my lungs. I curl my fingers on his shoulders, pulling him closer, needing more. Needing everything.

He makes me so fucking needy.

My thighs part. If he asked, I'd let him fill me again.

If he asked, I'd let him do whatever he wanted to me.

But he reaches between us, pulls the teeth of his zipper together, and buttons his pants. Our kiss sent his glasses askew, so he fixes those as well. He lost control for a minute there. He's pulling himself back together. One button at a time.

"We should go back out," he says. "Your friends are waiting."

"You tore my dress."

He attempts to fix it until he sees that I'm right, and the damaged sleeve falls limply down my arm. He takes off his blazer and hangs it over my shoulders.

"That should hold until we get you home."

"Where you can rip it off me properly."

A smile threatens the edge of his mouth. "You're insatiable."

"I'm drippy." I'm in that giddy, postorgasm euphoria. I pluck one of his earbuds from his ear and hold it close so I can hear the music. "What did we fuck to?"

"The Eurythmics."

I press the front of my body to his, like a cat. I tilt my forehead at his chest and reach upward to tuck the earbud back into the shell of his ear. "Will you think about breeding me every time you hear them now?"

I drop my hand down his middle and cup his groin. What was dormant starts to swell for me again.

His fingers grip my wrist, chastising. "Don't ruin the Eurythmics for me."

"You have a funny way of using the word *ruin*."

He weaves his fingers through mine, extracting me from his dick and taking my hand in his own. Holding my hand, he unlocks the bathroom and escorts me out.

There's a rush of AC-chilled air when we re-enter the Equestrian Club, and for a second, I'm dizzy. I find my eyes bouncing around the room, zeroing in on the women. A lot of maternity dresses. A lot of virgin mocktails.

Is it just me, or does there seem to be an abnormal religion around pregnancy here?

Is this what I would've been if I'd stayed?

Mimosas and mothers' brunches.

Then that terrible whisper of a thought—

If I'd had a litter with Ransom, maybe I wouldn't have minded.

Acid rises in my chest. The bitter taste of *could've-beens*.

I clutch James's hand tighter. "I'm ready to leave."

He doesn't argue. He doesn't ask questions. He lifts our hands, presses his lips to my knuckles, and then guides me out.

10

CLAIRE

But there will be no *dress ripping* at home because the champagne made me forget...

I scheduled a meeting with Daddy's lawyer today.

The poor, short man is waiting outside the gate when we get back. He's clutching a briefcase, the hot sun beating down on him and reddening the back of his neck.

I invite him in, and the three of us settle into Daddy's office.

I wasn't allowed in here much as a child. It was an off-limits room, unless Daddy was chastising me or training me. The wallpaper is a deep red that makes the whole room look splashed with blood. It's lined with wooden book-shelves and Daddy's impressive desk.

Fletcher Waters is calm and professional, but his face betrays him. He tinges pink every time he's forced to give bad news. And right now, he's beet red.

"What happened to your arm?" James asks.

Mr. Waters's arm is tucked into a sling. It makes his work

challenging as he attempts to shuffle papers against the glass coffee table with one hand.

"Golfing accident," he replies. He goes back to badly aligning the papers. "I usually do this after the funeral, but—"

"We have a plane to catch."

"Right."

The grandfather clock behind him ticks.

I always hated that clock.

It's this hulking, golden monolith that stands in the corner of his office. The pendulum swings back and forth. Each time it swings, it clicks. Each click feels like a finger tapping against my skull.

Yet I can't stop staring at it.

"Your father was a man of considerable wealth," Mr. Waters says. "He made quite the legacy with the Preacher Ranch. His finances are...well..."

He's fumbling through his words. *I don't have time for this.*

"I don't want his money," I tell him flatly.

"Oh, well, that's good news." Waters removes a tissue from his bag to wipe the puddle of sweat on the back of his neck. "He didn't leave you any."

I blink. I feel James go stiff beside me. "What?"

More paper shuffling. *Stop fucking with the papers.* "In his will, he made a clear divide of his finances. Firstly, the farm debts should be paid off in full. Whatever remains will be split in half. Half of it is to be donated to the Belleflower Benefactors Society. The other half is to be donated to the Semper Fi Foundation."

"That fucking foundation again," I mutter.

Waters blinks at me. "I'm sorry?"

My ears are ringing. Waters is speaking, explaining the next steps, but I can't hear him.

All I can hear is that fucking grandfather clock.

Tick. Tick.

I didn't want his money. I *don't* want it.

But to be cut out of the will entirely?

Money was Daddy's love language. This message is clear.

You bitch. You selfish, ungrateful bitch. Choke on this.

"The Preacher Ranch, he's left in the care of Arris Dagney. Your father *did* leave you something," Waters continues, and through the fever in my skull, I manage to tune back in. He says, "And...please be aware, I'm quoting directly. These are his words. Not mine."

"Just spit it out," I say.

He clears his throat. "*To Claire*, my—ah, again, this is a direct quote—*to Claire, my thankless bitch of a daughter, I bequeath this paperweight as a reminder of what she was to me. A weight.*"

And then he slides a round rock paperweight across the table. It's a smooth rock with the image of a closed eyeball etched into it.

I could laugh.

There are papers that need my signature. The pen scratches against the page as I scrawl my name over and over. The words blur in my vision. I can't read it. I just want to get this part over with.

At some point, James realizes I haven't said a word. His hand falls to my thigh. He squeezes. "We have a long night ahead of us."

"Yes." Mr. Waters awkwardly shovels the loose papers back into his briefcase. "The funeral tomorrow."

James stands. Ever the gentleman. Politely, he gestures to the door. "I'll walk you out."

James leads Waters out of the room. I should rise to say goodbye to him, but I can't.

I can't move. I can't blink. I can't do anything but stare at that grandfather clock.

Tick-tick.

There's a knock on the door. I glance up.

James stands in the open doorway. He leans against the frame, his elbow propped up. "Waters is gone. How are you feeling?"

I shrug. "Fine."

He presses his lips together. He steps through the room and then crouches to put his hands on my knees. Here, he bends down until he's eye to eye with me—or eye-to-glasses-to-eye, anyway.

"Hi," he says.

"Hi."

Even crouched, he's still taller than me.

"I sent Harding out with a grocery list," he says. "We'll have everything we need to make an all-American burger."

"Oh?"

"When we were in London, I asked you what you missed most about America. You said hamburgers. With American cheese."

A small smile touches my lips. "I did say that. But I don't think I can eat."

"Not even a burger?"

I shake my head. The edge of his mouth pinches downward, but he nods.

"Come downstairs if you change your mind."

He rises to his full height. His large fingers sift through my hair as he cups the back of my head, and his lips touch my forehead. Then he pulls away, steps out, and closes the door behind him.

I'm alone, but I don't feel alone.

My father's office space was always the scariest room in the house. The only time I was invited in was to have a "frank conversation" about my grades or my posture or my competition rank. The velvety red walls are lined with bookshelves—all rare books, many first editions. He has a standing bar in the corner of the room. A coffee table for casual conversations.

And then there's the desk. Flanked by the gruesome grandfather clock, his desk is pure mahogany and exquisitely hand carved. An onyx, horse-shaped paperweight marches on top of a stack of in-progress papers. The desktop is impeccable—my father was nothing if not orderly—with his ledger in the center and a fountain pen lying neatly beside it.

The chair is practically a throne, with carved animal feet and a soft padding that matches the wall color. Even empty, there's a heaviness there.

I swear, I can see him sitting in it now.

A creeping feeling crawls up the back of my neck. I get up and go to the bar. I fix Daddy's drink—two fingers of scotch, neat—and take the drink to his desk. Maybe to clear the dust or shake out the negative energy, I sit in his chair.

It's harder than I imagined. I lean into it, trying to make myself comfortable. I sip the scotch. It burns, and I wait for the unpleasantness to subside before I take another swallow.

If you'd told me a couple of days ago that someone had planned to burn the Preacher Ranch down, I would've provided the gasoline.

But now, faced with the very real prospect of losing the ranch, I surprise myself with a strange pinch of nostalgia.

The booby traps, the strange donations to strange foundations, the way he let the house go to rot...

Is it all my fault? Did I push him to it? Depression, drinking, paranoia?

Did he lose it all when he lost me?

I twist in the chair and tilt the glass to my lips, finishing it off.

Through the arched windows, I see a sky streaked with reds, oranges, and pinks. From this chair, Daddy had a perfect view of his kingdom. The various houses on the property, as well as the large, open training rings and the well-groomed, expansive garden.

A light catches my eye when it flickers in the stables.

Everyone should be home by now. The horses should be resting.

So who's pulling the all-nighter?

I have my suspicions, but curiosity gets the better of me. I put my glass down, pick up the rest of the bottle, and leave the office.

I walk down the hall, passing my bedroom. The door is cracked open. I can hear James's voice inside.

"Yes," he says. "I know what *indefinitely* means. I just don't know what it means in this context."

He goes quiet. I glance in the crack of the door. His tall body paces the length of the bedroom. He has his earbuds in, and he's talking to someone on the other end. He stops pacing to run his fingers over a stuffed horse that sits in the window shelf.

"Yes, sir. I understand."

His voice is low, and there's an intense edge to it I'm not familiar with. I get the strange feeling I'm witnessing something I shouldn't.

I take a step backward. The floorboard creaks under my weight.

I sidestep quickly and round the corner, toward the stairway.

"One moment," James says. I hear him walk to the bedroom door. There's a silence, and I can only imagine he's checking the hallway. Then the door clicks shut, and whatever he says next is too muffled to make out.

I keep moving. I sneak out the front door and, quietly, shut it behind me.

The sky is still in ribbons, but the colors are turning pale as the sun sets lower in the sky. The night has turned sharp with the mid-autumn chill, and I regret not taking a jacket with me.

Too late to turn back. Besides. I still have my whiskey.

I shouldn't be sneaking around. But here I am, tiptoeing like a criminal in Daddy's shadow.

I step over the stone walkway until my feet hit dirt. The grass tickles my bare ankles as I walk up the sloped hill toward the stables.

I won't lie. It feels good to have grass between my toes.

As I get closer to the stable, I hear sounds of some sports program blaring on the television. It's so loud he doesn't even notice me step inside.

"Boom!" Ransom shouts. He throws up his fist high. "In your face, Cagney!"

He's built his own personal tailgate. He's pulled out a couple of box cartons to make a bench. He's also pulled out the arm of the television from Chaucer's stall so he can see it clearly. Chaucer, meanwhile, is roaming around free. There's a coin-operated horse—an old, rusty thing that's been around since I used to live here—and Chaucer stands beside it, chewing lazily on its rope hair.

Ransom has a cooler beside him, and he yanks out a beer, cracking it open in his palm.

"Nice setup you've got here," I say.

Ransom jumps in his seat. His beer sprays him. "Jesus—all that is holy, woman, don't sneak up on a guy like that."

I roll my eyes. "You're not exactly being stealthy."

He looks me over. "You want a beer?"

"Sure."

I pull my dress tight around my legs so it doesn't hike up and sit down on the carton beside him.

I can feel his eyes on me. "Nice dress."

"The Promise Sisters got me."

He lets out a *huh* of a laugh. "Yep. Sounds about right."

The ripped sleeve makes my dress drop just slightly, exposing the top of my breast. I can feel Ransom's eyes on the bare skin.

A terrible, awful part of me doesn't bother adjusting the sleeve.

"Watch this," he says, then turns to the horse. "Chaucer. Beer me."

Chaucer ambles over toward the cooler...and picks up a brush between his teeth. He drops it at Ransom's feet.

"No—goddammit. Chaucer. *Beer* me."

Chaucer brings over a shovel and drops that in front of us too.

I snort a laugh. "Impressive."

He lifts a finger. "One day, he's actually going to get a beer."

Ransom does it the hard way. He leans over and plucks out a beer himself, opens it up, and then hands it over to me.

We click necks and both take a swallow. It's cheap beer, but it's cold and somehow comforting.

We both stare at the TV without watching.

A shiver comes over me before I can stop it.

"Cold?" he asks.

"I'm fine."

"You're stubborn. Here."

He takes off his jacket and throws it over my shoulders. It's a canvas jacket with soft lining on the inside. I slip my arms through it, tug the collar close to me, and inhale.

There's that scent. Smoke, ash, and dirt.

When I open my eyes, Ransom is watching me sniff his jacket.

Oh, God. I look insane.

I quickly pretend to scratch my nose instead. I motion toward Chaucer and the coin-operated horse, drawing attention away from me. "I can't believe Daddy kept that old thing."

"What? Miss Penny? Sure did. He'd have to pry it out of my cold, dead hands. Chaucer loves that girl."

"It's *old.*"

"What's wrong with that? Some of us never forget our first love."

His eyes follow me. I shrug his gaze off. "Someone should throw that thing out."

"Claire Preacher. You touch a hair on that penny-horse, and I swear to God, I'll never forgive you."

I can't help the smile that crawls over my mouth. "I forgot that."

"What?"

"What a hopeless romantic you are. You wear your heart on your sleeve."

He shrugs. "I love hard. I don't know how to do it any other way."

I pull a slow, cold drink from my beer.

I can feel Ransom watching me. He asks, "Does James?"

"Does James *what*?"

"Does he...love you? Hard enough?"

I rub my thumb over the neck of the beer. The low ache in my cunt says *yes*. James loves me very hard. On the other hand...he's been pulling away. Ever since we arrived in Belleflower. There's a coldness to him that I love, but this coldness...

It's new. Unnerving. Troublesome.

I want to choose my words carefully, but it's hard to hold myself back with Ransom. When I'm with him, everything comes flooding out. "Sometimes...I'm afraid James doesn't want me the same way that I want him. He's so stoic. A tin man. I think that's what attracted me to him in the first place. He was a challenge. I wanted so badly to crack him open. But what if there's nothing inside?"

"He might've been a tin man when he met you, but no man can stay heartless around you for long. That's your... Claire power."

"My *Claire power*?"

"It's like being a superhero, but more of a pain in the ass."

I bite back on a grin. I rub my thumb over the smooth neck of the glass bottle.

I can't help but watch Ransom's hands out of the periphery of my vision. Big hands. Calloused hands. He's picking at the label of his beer, distractedly peeling it from the glass.

He can't seem to keep his hands still either.

"What are you doing here?" I ask.

"Watching TV. My trailer doesn't have one."

"Your...trailer?"

A sideways grin cuts across his face. "What, you didn't see my castle on the way in? I don't blame you. It's pretty well hidden. Mr. Preacher let me park it on the property, so long as I keep it behind the trees and out of sight."

"Oh."

Ransom stops picking at his bottle. He stares at me. "Don't do that."

"What?"

"That pity sneer. It might not be a yacht in the Hamptons, but dammit, I like my life."

I lift my eyebrows. "And you have no regrets?"

He shakes his head. "You know better than to ask me that."

The air between us is thick. Heavy.

Chaucer lets out a small, sweet huff and nuzzles his love.

"What about you, Miss High Horse?" Ransom says.

"Excuse me?"

He shrugs. "I might not have a fancy TV, but at least I'm not Rodeo Barbie."

My jaw goes tight. "Fuck you."

Those brown eyes meet mine. "Go on. Tell me I'm wrong."

I strangle my beer. "I came out here because I was suffocating inside, and now, somehow, you and your idiot mouth made me feel ten times worse. So. Congratulations."

I start to rise, but I'm halted when he grabs my wrist. "I'm sorry," he gets out. "Stay. I'll keep my idiot mouth shut."

I waver. But those chestnut browns are soft now.

He means it. Ransom apologizes with his whole chest.

I sit back down, but this time, I let my ass hit the floor at Ransom's feet. I settle down between his legs, and he knows what to do. He sets his beer down beside me. His hands collect the blonde hair at the nape of my neck. I feel the gentle tugs as he starts to braid my hair back in a thick rope.

When Ransom and I couldn't talk with words, we spoke with touches. This feels right.

"Tell me about you," he says after a long stretch of easy

silence.

"What about me?"

"About your life since you left. I wanna hear about...tea and crumpets."

I tilt my head back to look at him. "I got in a plane, not a time machine, you know that, right?"

He chuckles.

I settle back in. "Yes. There was tea. And crumpets. I went to school. Learned a lot. Worked hard. Got a degree in business. Then another in psychology. Modeled to make ends meet—you'd be surprised by how similar it is to show riding. Chin up! Back straight!"

"Sounds like a perfect fit," Ransom says.

"Doesn't it? But in reality, it was just...one stroke of bad luck after the other. Money was hard. I bounced around places for a long time. I had no friends. My French was rusty. Oh, and to top it all off, my apartment burned down."

"What?"

I wave it off. "It's fine. I wasn't in it." My tongue goes heavy. I go quiet, debating, and then finally admit, "The worst part of it all was...I kept thinking that all of it would've been bearable if you were there."

His hands still in my hair.

"Why didn't you get on that plane?"

"Bear..."

"Don't *Claire-Bear* me. I deserve an explanation. Now."

He lets out a deep sigh. "You got a hair tie?"

"No."

"Check my pockets."

I dig into his jacket. In the big pockets, I find a lighter, a bottle cap, a utility tool, his wallet, and...a hair tie. A woman's hair tie.

I'm shocked by the hot jealousy that roars through my

veins.

Does Ransom have a girlfriend?

Is he having sex with other people?

Is he braiding another woman's hair?

Of course. He's no priest.

It's been five years. He's allowed to move on.

I've moved on. I have a fiancé.

So why is my only thought *Fuck you, he's mine?*

"No," I lie.

"Ah, well. Nice while it lasted," he says. He gives my braid a little tug before releasing it. He drains his beer and tosses the empty in a pile of hay.

"Chaucer," he says, "Beer me."

The horse picks up a mitten and drops it at his feet. Ransom begins his story.

11

RANSOM

T *hen.*

"*Ça va?*"

"Sar-var."

"*Ça va.*"

"Sah...what?"

Claire lets out a low wail of frustration. "It means *how are you* in French. We're one week away, and you can't even get that right!"

I can see Claire's boots pacing back and forth on the other side of Chaucer as I brush the dust off the big horse. Chaucer, who is used to Claire's temper tantrums, doesn't even bat an ear at her complaining.

I grip the brush, band around the back of my hand. "How about you do the talking, and I'll just grunt and point?"

Wrong thing to say. Even with Chaucer between us, I can

feel her energy shift. Claire walks around Chaucer to look me square in the face. She looks particularly intimidating in her dressage outfit, all navy blue suit, crisp pants, and round helmet. As I brush him, I can feel her quizzical stare.

"Why aren't you taking this seriously?" she asks.

"Who says I ain't?"

"Things are going to change when we get to Paris."

"How's that?"

She clutches her little translation book to her chest. She looks off, and even though she's staring at nothing but the stable walls, I can tell she's seeing the Eiffel Tower in her eyes.

"Can't you picture it? Croissants and coffee in bed. Sharing a bottle of wine as we watch the sun set on the Seine. Eating macarons by the handful."

"What's a macaron?"

She swats me with her little book. "It's a cookie."

She can't escape me. I hook my finger under the chin strap of her helmet and tug her in. "You're a cookie."

She gives my chest a push. I lose my balance, sitting back on a block, and pull her down with me. She fits in my lap perfectly, straddling me.

Whenever I've got Claire to myself, it's hard to keep my hands off her.

"Screw the horse," I say. "Ride me."

She nuzzles that button nose against mine. Her helmet bumps my forehead. "Say it," she says.

"*Ça va.*"

"Good boy." That's pleased her, at least. Her breath patters on my cheek and makes my heart race.

"We get to reinvent ourselves," she says. "I'll go to school, and you can be...I don't know. A cop."

"A *cop*?"

"A firefighter. A doctor. The first cowboy to put his spurs on the moon."

"I like that the last one."

"What do you want to be?" She looks down at me, genuinely curious now. "You can be whatever you put your mind to."

And it feels like someone tossed a lasso around my neck. Most of my life, no one's ever asked me what I wanted to do. They all just figured I'd pick up whatever low-hanging fruit my dumb, greedy hands could grasp.

When this woman looks at me, she sees the potential for something good. No—something *great*.

Ain't no one ever looked at me like that before.

I slip my hands into the back pockets of her pants. Her body fits so snugly in my hands. "I wanna be yours, princess. Only yours."

She blinks at that, surprised. A small smile touches her mouth, and it sets my heart on fire. "We can reinvent ourselves, Ransom." She pushes my hair back, and her lips brush mine. "It'll all work out."

BUT THAT'S the thing about girls who grew up with silver spoons in their mouths.

When Claire Preacher says *it'll all work out*, she believes it.

Her whole life, she's had a little trust fund fairy godmother on her shoulder. Anytime she's needed a soft place to fall, there's her daddy's dollar bills giving her that nice, green cushion.

What she doesn't get is once he cuts her off—and he will —that's it.

Life ain't so easy when you're scraping pennies to get by.

I should know. All my life, I've lived paycheck to paycheck. I've learned to beg, borrow, and, yeah, sometimes, even steal. I know firsthand that it doesn't always work out. In fact, sometimes, it's really fucking shitty.

The closer and closer we get to our departure date, the more it weighs on me. Claire's a tough girl. If the going got tough, I know she'd survive it.

But I don't know if I can. Can I survive the disappointed downward turn of her lips the first time her card gets declined? Can I survive watching her rake her fingers through her hair as she pores over the unpaid bills?

Can I survive knowing she won't be able to eat all the macarons her sweet tooth deserves?

It makes my stomach twist up in knots. We're less than a week out from departure, and I can't barely focus on work.

"Ransom! Come get your crazy-ass horse!"

The shout of my name shakes me out of my haze. I drop the rope I've been wrapping up and get to my feet, quickly making my way through the stables.

I see one of the hands, Rafe, giving me a mean glare. Rafe and I have been friends since we were too small to fit in our boots. He's a joker off the clock, but he's serious on the farm, and he's got a guilty-looking Chaucer by the halter.

"What'd he do now?" I ask.

"Your stallion keeps breaking out. I caught him riding Miss Penny again."

I take Chaucer's halter and pat his dusty neck. Affectionately, I say, "You dumb, horny bastard. C'mere."

I lead Chaucer back into the stable, hooking him up. He jerks his head disapprovingly.

But Rafe still looks irritated. He shakes his head. "You

gotta get rid of that penny-horse. This horse pumps out gold bars, man. You can't have him wasting that."

I shift back on my heels. Wheels are turning. "How much gold are we talking?"

Rafe takes off his gloves and leans against the gate. "Fifty thousand."

"Huh."

Rafe clicks his tongue like a disapproving mom. "*Huh*, he says. If my stuff went for fifty thousand a pop, you better believe I'd buy some gold briefs. Put these eggs in a nest. Strict, pineapple-only diet."

I side-eye him. He shrugs. "Keep him away from Miss Penny. I mean it."

BUT NOW MY brain is working overtime.

Technically, it's against the rules to collect semen manually from thoroughbreds. That's why what we do at the breeding farm is so important. The only way these thoroughbreds are allowed to breed is the old-fashioned way— stallion meets mare, they do what animals do, and then eleven months later, boom. A beautiful, purebred foal.

Of course, *if* someone, say, collected the semen of a prize-winning thoroughbred...well. That'd be incredibly valuable on the market.

Sell it to the right person with the right mare. She starts pushing out race-winning foals, and her value goes up... everyone wins.

It's a victimless crime, if you think about it.

And I think about it.

Long. Hard. I even start talking to Rafe about it.

He's in. In fact, he tells me if I can get the *goods*, he'll sell it. He's already got a buyer with a ready mare. But—

"It's all about the timing," Rafe says. His Corona hangs between his knees. We sit on the steps outside Maeby's Bar, watching the dipping sun bruise the sky.

I thumb my beer cap, making little rigid indentations in my palm. "Go on."

"*Hypothetically*," Rafe continues—which has become his new favorite word, *hypothetically*, "we'd have to collect and get it to the mare within twenty-four hours. *Plus*, it's gotta be in the window when she's ovulating. If she doesn't produce a foal, we don't get paid, and then this is all for nothing."

I squint at him. "*We?*"

"Yeah. Fifty-fifty."

"Fifty-fifty! I'm doing all the damn dirty work!"

Rafe clasps my shoulder. "Yeah, but you look so pretty doing it. C'mon, I've got something to show you."

He pushes up to his feet, choking his beer by the neck. We walk through the parking lot, and he pops the trunk of his car. It's stuffed with bags of feed, tattered clothes, and other bits. He pulls a utility bag forward and unzips it, motioning me closer.

"I've got everything you need," he says, "*hypothetically*." He lifts out the items as he goes through them. "This vial here is where you'll put the collection. You mix it up with this extender to preserve it. Then you've got to store it in this ice pack immediately to keep it from spoiling. Keep it out of sunlight. We've got six hours from storing to insemination, so there isn't a hell of a lot of wiggle room. I spoke to the mare's handler—he said they can get her prepped and ready to go on Friday."

"Claire and I are flying out Friday."

"Well, you can consider this my bon voyage present."

"The hell is that?" I say, pointing to the bag.

Rafe winks, wearing this dumb, wide grin. "Your stallion's new girlfriend. Artificial lady-horse bits. Wanna try it out first? See how it compares to Claire?"

"I'm *this* close to knocking your teeth out, pal."

I swallow the rest of my beer. It tastes warm and clots in the back of my throat. I stare at the bag and its dubious contents. Rafe stares at me.

"What are you thinking?" he asks after a beat.

"You ever wonder if your parents are looking down at you and wondering, *why the hell didn't I throw him out with the bathwater when I had the chance?*"

"Don't be ridiculous," Rafe says. He slaps me on the shoulder. "They're Ransoms. They're definitely looking *up.*"

Claire isn't happy.

When I tell her I'm going to meet her at the airport, she blows up my phone about it. It's a hurt I'll smooth over later.

Twenty-five grand makes for a pretty nice Band-Aid, the way I figure it.

And she can't know anything about this. I can't implicate her like that.

Better or worse, this is all on me.

The night of our departure, I check my watch. Just near eleven. My suitcase is in the back of my truck. I'm all ready to roll out. Just one more thing I have to do.

My truck growls like a guard dog as I keep it loitering in neutral. Rafe's utility bag sits in the passenger seat beside me, feeling a bit like an unpinned grenade.

From my spot, I watch as the car rolls up around the back of the main house. Claire leaves, bag in hand. I can barely make her out in the dark, but I see her looking around for me.

My heart lurches. *I'm coming, princess.*

Just a little later.

She finally gives in and gets in the car. I hold my breath until it leaves.

Alright. Go time.

Now or never.

I drive my truck up as far as the dirt roads will let me and then park it. I climb by foot the rest of the way to the stable.

Luck would have it, the stable is empty. The horses are quiet, except for the occasional nighttime whinny.

I pull off a lantern from the shelf and turn it on. It splashes light over my boots and across the floor. I take the coin-operated horse out, set her up, and strap the device on Rafe's bag onto it.

What'd you do this week?

Ah, you know. Just set up a sex toy for my horse.

Normal people stuff.

Once Miss Penny is situated, I quickly walk down the hall to Chaucer.

Lazy bastard is lying down, nose tucked into the ground, sound asleep. I click to get his attention, and he blinks an eye open.

"Hey, buddy. Wake up."

He flicks his ear and turns his head away from the light.

"Wanna go on a date with Miss Penny?"

His ears perk up at that. He lifts his head.

My heart is pounding so hard, but that gets relief fizzling through my blood. "That's what I thought. C'mon, Romeo."

Quietly, I hook the lead on Ransom and guide him out

of his stall. I take him into the pen in back, where I've already got Miss Penny waiting for him.

Now, Chaucer is wide-awake. The second I release him, he trots over to the coin-operated horse. He knocks his head against hers, nuzzling her stiff frame.

It's almost romantic, if I weren't here to steal his guy stuff.

"Make me proud, you kinky stud," I mutter under my breath.

Chaucer is quick on the charm. After a little flirting and necking, he and Miss Penny get into it. With a satisfied snort, he hops off his girl and yawns. Back to bed for him.

I crouch and unfasten the device. I'll be damned, the damn thing worked. Carefully, I transfer the collection into the vial. I tilt it up so I can make sure I've got enough. I swear, the stuff nearly sparkles in the lantern light.

But just like that, I feel like I've been kicked in the throat by a pair of hooves.

What the hell am I doing?

A common thief, stealing horse jizz in the middle of the night.

Claire deserves better.

But ain't that why I'm doing this in the first place?

Claire deserves *everything*.

After the hell her father put her through, hasn't she earned a little...cream off the top?

But his ears must be itching because out of the dark, I hear—

"Riley Ransom."

I startle. I lose my grip and drop the vial.

And just like that, fifty thousand dollars spills out over my boot.

But even that doesn't compare to the dread I feel when my gaze meets Mr. Preacher's cold, gray eyes.

He stares at me, unmoved. The lantern light flickers like flames around his face.

"My office," he says, his voice low and firm. "Now."

THE GRANDFATHER CLOCK CLICKS. Its pendulum swings back and forth like a bad omen.

Mr. Preacher and I sit in silence otherwise. My heart is pounding like a jackhammer in my ear, and my leg won't stop shaking. I latch my fingers together to keep them from trembling.

"Listen," I start. "What you saw, it wasn't—"

"I have a panic button," he interrupts. "Underneath my desk. If I press it, Deputy Holden will be here before you can get out of that chair."

I swallow a lump the size of an ostrich egg.

All I can think about is Claire. Claire in the airport. Claire clutching the handle of her bag. Claire all alone. *Waiting* for me.

I cast my eyes to the floor. They land on the dark, shameful stain on my boot.

This much anxiety can make a man sick.

His dark voice carries through my cloud of fear. "Or we can strike a deal."

I lift my head. Those gray eyes don't move an inch.

"What kinda deal?"

I'm trying not to sound too hopeful, but Jesus H. Christ, I need a Hail Mary right now if I'm ever going to see Claire again.

If she'll ever *want* to see me again after all this.

"I know all about Paris," he says evenly. "She purchased the tickets on my card, after all. I learned long ago that I can't control Claire. If she wants to leave, she'll leave. There's nothing I can do to stop her. But I'll be damned if she runs away with a useless degenerate like you."

Rage loosens the knot in my throat. "That ain't fair."

"There are two people in this world, Ransom. Winners and losers. My Claire is a winner. Can you guess which you are?"

"I love her, sir." I can hear the shake in my voice, but I can't stop it. My heart is bleeding all over his perfect oriental carpet. "I'll do whatever it takes to spend the rest of my life taking care of her. You can be damned sure of that."

"You couldn't successfully steal sperm off a fake horse. What makes you think you could take care of my Claire?"

My Claire.

And just like that, it's like a cold splash of water in the face.

What the hell am I doing?

I don't need this. I don't need to sit here and take this from him. Claire is waiting for me—*my Claire, not his*—and Paris might not be perfect, but hell, she's right.

We'll figure it out.

We can do anything, long as we're together.

The grandfather clock ticks. I've still got thirty minutes before takeoff.

I can still make this right.

"All respect, sir, she ain't your problem anymore. She's mine."

I grab my jacket off the back of the chair, and I stand to leave. Before I can get a foot toward the door, however, his voice cuts through the air like a knife.

"If you go that way, you'll leave in handcuffs."

I stop in my tracks.

"How did you think this was going to go?" Mr. Preacher continues. "That I would let you leave and destroy everything I've worked so hard to create?"

"Claire is who she is in spite of you. Not because of you."

His eyes darken, and I know I've hit a nerve.

"Sit down, Ransom," he says.

This time, I have no choice. I retrace my steps and sink down into the hard leather of the chair.

He watches me. Exhales. And then starts cutting me apart, piece by piece.

"She will make something of herself in Paris, but you… you will lie. And steal. And cheat your way through life. Because when faced with a hard thing, you will always take the easy way out. It's your nature. It was your parents' nature. The Ransoms are a family of weak hearts. Claire has a strong heart and an unbreakable spirit. But if you insist on following her, you will slow her down. You will drag her down with you. And she will let you because despite everything I've done to train it out of her, my Claire still believes in the best of people."

My blood is roaring in my ears. My chest is so tight it's hard to breathe.

For a second, I close my eyes.

I'm so sorry, Claire.

"You'll break her fucking heart, you know that?"

"Don't flatter yourself. It will take more than a deadbeat ranch hand to destroy her. She'll cry for a night, and then you'll be nothing but a mistake she's learned better from." He takes a stack of papers from the table, meticulously lines them up, and then slides them across to me. "Sign this."

I don't budge. "What is it?"

"Your work contract. I won't press charges. Your event

with Chaucer will stay between us. In return, you stay here. Continue to work on the farm. You were expecting, I imagine, somewhere in the range of fifty thousand for your efforts? Let's call it fifty-five with interest. I'll dock the difference from your earnings until you've paid in full. In return, this can stay between us. No law enforcement. You can keep your freedom and your job."

"And what about Claire?"

There's a lengthy pause. "Claire will thrive without the burden of either of us holding her back."

My heart is shaking apart in my chest.

He opens his hand, motioning to the chair. "You can make the call here."

I dial Claire's number and put the cell phone to my ear.

"Ransom." Even angry, her voice makes my heart skip. "Where are you?"

I swallow hard. I lift my gaze.

Mr. Preacher nods. *Go ahead.*

I take in a breath and break her heart.

12

CLAIRE

ow.

RANSOM FINISHES HIS STORY, and we both sit in the silence that follows.

The game plays on the screen, but the noises are soft and muted.

Crickets cry out, singing softly outside the stables.

I clutch the smooth glass of the bottle. "Daddy black-mailed you into staying."

"I dug myself in that hole. He just filled it." Ransom takes a slow pull from his beer.

"I suppose that doesn't surprise me. He was a heartless bastard. I was his trophy, and he'd do anything to control me."

Ransom gives a hum of agreement.

My braid brushes against my back as I twist to look up at

him. "But you surprise me. The Riley Ransom I knew wouldn't let anyone tell him what to do."

Those chestnut-brown eyes meet mine. "The Riley Ransom you knew was an idiot."

"Don't sell yourself short. You're still a dumbass."

He lets out a humorless *huh* at that.

"I wish you'd told me," I say.

"You would've tried to stay."

"Maybe," I say sharply. "But it would've been my choice. You don't get to make that decision for me. I'm so goddamn tired of men controlling my life."

The beer turns bitter in my mouth. I plant it in the dirt and push against Ransom's leg to rise to my feet. As I brush the straw and dirt from my dress, Ransom says my name.

"Claire."

The sound of my name on his tongue is like a bell ringing on my heart.

Bear. Woman. Princess.

These are all words I'm used to Ransom using for me.

When he says *Claire*, he means it.

His eyes are sad when they find mine. "I wasn't trying to control you. I was trying to love you. The only way I knew how. I loved you then, and I love you now."

My breath catches in my throat. My heart splatters against my rib cage.

He continues. "I don't expect anything to come of it. If I thought James was your true love, I'd keep my mouth shut, but—"

"Don't," I snap. "You don't know anything about James."

"What do *you* know about James?" he asked pointedly.

"I know he'd never leave me alone at an airport."

That knocks his words back into his mouth. But then he

stands and closes the distance between us. My heart trips in my chest when those chestnut eyes stare into my own.

"I haven't stopped thinking about you," he says, his voice low, intense. "Not once. Not for one night. You're the only woman in my brain. The only woman I want in my bed."

"Stop it," I say. A quiet whisper.

His gaze doesn't budge. "Do you think about me?"

"*Stop.*"

His hand catches the side of my face. His thumb touches my bottom lip. I fight back the urge to suck the digit into my mouth. There's fire in his eyes, a dark rim around those soft browns. "Do you think about me when you're with him?"

And...

I'm tired, suddenly.

So, so tired.

I'm tired of hating him. I'm tired of loving him. I'm tired of fighting both feelings battling around in my chest like pissed-off farm cats.

I feel like my muscles have been tensed and ready to fight ever since I got that call that my father was dead. And now...

I don't have the energy to fight this. Not tonight.

I take his hand from my face. I know this hand. I remember these strong fingers between my legs. I touch my lips to his rough palm. With my eyes on his, I guide his hand to cradle my face.

We're close. So close. His thumb strokes my cheek. I can see the rapid rise and fall of his chest, as though just being *near me* is enough to get his heart racing.

"Daddy's funeral is tomorrow," I say pointedly.

He nods. "I know."

"I need you there. So whatever you're feeling right now... I need you to button it up and sleep it off."

I use every reserve of energy left to put my hands on his chest and shove him. Hard.

His solid frame moves a step back.

"Claire."

"What?"

He gives a small, nearly imperceptible tilt of his head. "Sweet dreams."

The look in his eyes says, *I'll see you in them.*

I leave the stables and don't look back, even as I can feel Ransom's eyes following me. I run my fingers through the tight braid in the back of my head and shake it out as I walk, letting the strands unravel until it's just a wild, tangled mess.

I slip through the break in the hedges and walk back inside the house. I kick my shoes off in the foyer. The house is dark but not quiet. There is a presence. The creaking of old wood. The ticking hands of the clocks. Even the walls seem to have their own beating pulse.

There's a ghost in this house, but I don't know if it's my father's or my own.

James is upstairs. I can hear the floorboards creak as he walks from one end of the bedroom to the other. He's talking to someone, the sound of his voice soft and muted. I climb the staircase and move toward him, but I find myself pausing in front of my old room.

Little ghost girl.

I touch the crystal door handle. The rough pattern bites gently into my skin as I twist and push it open.

I'm met with a gush of stale air. As though the ghosts are saying, *Finally. Finally, we're free.*

There are the powder-blue walls I was forced to stare at when Daddy locked me in here as punishment. There are the books that kept me company. A line of stuffed animals sitting on a shelf above my bed—to look at, only, not to touch. There's my trophy case, each blue ribbon set out on proud display.

And then there's the wall of Belleflower Queens.

I walk toward the wall, remembering how I used to study each poster meticulously. They're mini posters, each framed and hung along the wall. Not every Belleflower Queen, but my favorites. 1974, Lynn Beckett, with a stern but handsome expression. 1994, Maeve Belladonna "Maeby" Katherine, with her effortless, pixie-like beauty. Cassie Sinclaire, 1999, with a cat-that-ate-the-canary smile. Some of the newer posters have signatures scrawled at the bottom. My own personal collection. These were the women I looked up to—their beauty, their grace, their *strength*.

The Maeby poster is special. She signed it with a pistol shot. The exit wound is ripped through the poster paper, making it pucker outward like a white clover. My fingertips touch the picture frame, and I scrape a line of dust across the glass.

This used to be my entire world.

The dream to be a Belleflower Queen was my *entire existence.*

Even now that I'm a different person, a grown adult, with her own apartment, her own fiancé, her own life in Paris...

There's a longing here. Like a phantom limb.

But all dreams turn to dust. Eventually.

I sneeze. This room is going to make me sick with allergies.

There's one more artifact I want to uncover first.

I crouch down and run my fingers along the lowest rung of my bookshelf. All the way to the right, I press my fingers against a panel in the shelf. It wobbles, loose, and I push the panel so it slides back.

My secret place. The small, hidden spot where I kept my journal with all my young, angsty teenage thoughts.

But when I slide the panel back, there's nothing but an empty gap in the wood.

My diary. It's gone.

Unbidden, rage swells up inside of me.

Daddy found all my secrets, then. Found them and burned them, probably.

Maybe it's for the best.

Maybe it's better to leave the past in the past.

I replace the panel, get to my feet, and exit the bedroom, closing the door behind me.

When I go to the master bedroom, James is off his call. He's in bed, iPad in his lap, finger on the screen. The lamplight halos his dark curls, softening his features. The screen reflects in his glasses.

My heart wiggles and twists like a fish on a hook.

Yes. The past in the past.

I'm worn to the bone, and I'm too exhausted to shower off. James has unpacked us, and my bottle of Ambien sits on the oak bedside table, along with a glass of water. I take a pill and swallow it down. Then I shed my hellish dress, leaving it in a puddle on the floor. I climb under the sheets and into bed with James. He opens his body to me, extending his arm out around me, and I rest my head on his chest. His body is hard and sturdy, and his heart has a nice, predictable thump against my ear.

"Everything alright, love?" he murmurs.

"Who were you on the phone with?"

"Work."

He strokes a hand through my hair. I peer at his iPad screen.

He's watching a captioned documentary about the Jurassic period.

Thump-thump. Thump-thump.

My steady, predictable James.

I close my eyes. "I just want to sleep."

His breath is warm on my forehead as he lands a kiss there. He takes an earbud from his ear and slips it into my own. A droll, British voice informs me of flora and fauna that will never see this earth again, and I'm out before the meteor hits.

13

CLAIRE

She's here. The Belleflower Queen.

The Kentucky sun beats down on the crowd as we part like a wave to accept her. The float rolls down Main Street, painted in striking colors with large reliefs of flowers on the sides. Statues of horses rise like figureheads around the bow of the float, their hooves lifted in a strong gallop.

As the float gets closer, the crowd pushes in from either side. Everyone wants to get a rose. My heart catches in my throat. I'm small and too short. When I get nudged forward, I can't see a thing.

I lift my arms. "Daddy!"

The sun has turned him into a silhouette. He turns away.

"Please!"

He ignores me. His jaw goes tight.

"C'mere, little one."

Strong hands fit under my arms. My father's friend, Dagney, lifts me, settling me onto his shoulders.

Tall now, I can finally see.

The men in horse heads around the rim of the float unsettle me. I rear back was one tries to shove a plastic flower at me.

But then she appears.

The Belleflower Queen. Her dress shimmers like silver in the sunlight. A crown of flowers wraps around her hair, pulled back in beautiful, tight braids.

She's the most beautiful woman I've ever seen.

She smiles at me. She leans over the edge of the float and procures one, beautiful rose. A real rose.

She holds it out to me. I take it in my tiny hands.

"I want to be you!" I shout to her.

She smiles, but she's silent. She opens her mouth to speak, but no sound comes out. There's something wrong with her mouth. Red in her teeth.

Blood falls from her gums, through the cracks in her mouth, and drips down her lips. It stains her throat. Her white dress.

All the while, she keeps smiling.

I push myself backwards, and fall off of Dagney's shoulders.

I JERK IN MY SLEEP. It's the sensation of falling without falling.

I catch my breath. The room is swathed in deep blue.

A nightmare. It was just a nightmare.

But my heart keeps pattering all the same.

There's a sawing sound. Like chains rattling. Or tree branches scratching the window. I find the culprit: James, asleep beside me.

I smack James in the chest.

"*James*. You're grinding your teeth again."

He lets out a *mmph* noise. "Sorry," he mumbles, still half asleep. "Sorry."

He rolls onto his stomach, smothering his sounds in the pillow. I stare at the ceiling and wait for the fingers of fear to release their grip on my heart.

14

CLAIRE

The morning of Daddy's funeral, I wake up with an emotional hangover the size of Texas.

Sun is pouring in through the windows, and the room feels too brightly white.

I groan and roll over.

"Good morning," James says.

He's sitting up in bed. The sheets pool around his hips. He has a silver platter on the bedside table beside him. On it rests two cups, a pot, and a couple of plates of pastries. The herbal scent of tea and the warm, fresh bread remind me that I went to sleep without dinner last night.

My father can't punish me anymore, so apparently, I've taken it upon myself to do it for him.

Silly girl.

My stomach complains.

I rest my head on his strong thigh. I admire his lean torso. His messy bed head. The peppering of morning scruff that he'll shave off later.

"Hungry?" James asks.

I nod.

He pinches off a corner of scone and hand-feeds me. The bread is soft, the blueberries are sweet, and there's a crunchy layer of sugar crystals on top.

I may not be happy about being back, but the decadent pastries are helping.

"Do you think we could just not go?"

"To your father's funeral?"

I nod.

His thumb pets my chin. "Say the word and I'll take you to the airport."

If I just look at him, I can pretend I'm not here.

I can pretend we're in our Paris flat, and Daddy isn't dead, and Ransom doesn't love me.

I take his hand. His hands are so large they make me feel small. I pull his hand to my face, and his fingers curl instinctively at my cheek. I kiss the space between the rounded mounds at the bottom of his palm.

There's a swelling, aching in my chest. I'm so *grateful* for this man.

James makes me feel safe. He is, perhaps, the only person on earth to accomplish that task.

"Can you make all the decisions today?" I ask him.

Without missing a beat, he says, "I command you to stay in bed for another fifteen minutes."

"Okay."

"Open your mouth."

I obey. He feeds me the rest of the scone. We're getting crumbs in bed, but I don't care.

This is the kind of domesticity I could get used to.

But there's a nagging in me. A ripple that disturbs our placid peace, and it's getting larger and larger the longer the silence between us stretches out.

"James?"

"Yes?"

I can't contain the words anymore. "I spoke with Ransom last night. Alone. In the barn."

"Okay."

His voice is calm the way a violin note is calm.

It's the peaceful sound of a string pulled very, very taut.

I trudge forward anyway. *Honesty is the only way forward.* "It's strange talking to him. When I'm with him, it's like...I'm that sweet, starry-eyed girl again."

"Claire." My name is a protest on his tongue.

"What?"

"You were never *sweet* or starry-eyed."

I frown. "He brings up feelings, is what I'm saying. Complicated feelings." I pause. I force myself to say the quiet thing out loud. "I used to love him. Hard. And when I see him now, it's difficult to pretend like those feelings never existed."

James, to his credit, doesn't bat an eye. Instead, like a weathered professor, he simply chastises with, "You're mistaken."

I blink. "Sorry?"

"Marriage is a period."

"A...what?"

"A period. The punctuation mark. A period is an end to things. It's the end to you looking at other men. Thinking about other men. And it's certainly an end to you having feelings with old flames in the stables, darling."

A hot flush of anger rises in my cheeks. I sit up and remind him, "We're engaged. *Darling.* We're not a period yet." I steal a scone from his plate. "If anything, we're a *semicolon.*"

15

JAMES

A semicolon.
A semicolon.
A fucking semicolon.

INHALE. Exhale.

THE SEMICOLON first made its unwanted appearance on parchment in 1494 when Aldus Manutius included it in his publication of a Latin text. It's a combination of two separate, perfectly reasonable grammatical devices—the colon and a comma. The semicolon is a mad scientist, messily stitching together two independent clauses with ruddy tools like a drunken Frankenstein.

Writer Donald Barthelme once said the semicolon was as "ugly as a tick on a dog's belly."

Disgusting. Bloodsucking. Leech.

I will never, ever use a semicolon. As long as I live.

I'm cursing the written language, Aldus Manutius, and Herman Melville as I check my watch. Again.

"Harding is late." Even I can hear the terse anger between my teeth.

Claire side-eyes me. She folds her arms over her chest. "What's Daddy going to do? Get up and walk out of the coffin? I think he'll wait for us."

She's wearing a conservative black dress with a keyhole neckline and quarter-length sleeves. A slender, dark purse hangs over her shoulder. Kitten heels adorn her feet.

I've put on a black turtleneck underneath a blazer and crisp slacks. It seemed like a good idea at the time, but now the fabric around my neck feels like a noose, and it takes everything in me not to pull at it.

I dip my hand into my pocket and press a button on my phone, activating the white noise. The hushing sound in my ears acts like a blanket, smothering the punch of my heart.

The gates open, and for a second, I'm relieved. But just as quickly, my hope is dashed.

It's not Harding.

Ransom's ugly, weathered red pickup truck bounces down the gravel toward us.

I watch Claire. She runs her fingers over her hair, touching the two tiny braids pinned to the crown of her head.

The truck comes to a stop in front of us. Ransom hops out. He hangs off the open door. He's wearing a black button-up, dark pants, and a black bandana around his neck. His "funeral bandana," I assume.

He cleans up well. How annoying.

"Morning," he says.

"Good morning," Claire replies.

Tension echoes in the space between them, but they're both being very polite about it.

A fucking semicolon.

"Just wanted to check in. See if y'all needed anything."

"We're fine," I answer.

His gaze moves between us. "Y'all need a ride?"

"No," I say at the same time Claire says, "Yes."

But just then, the rusted hinges of the front gate squeak.

I'm not a praying man, but I'm tempted to thank God.

Our black limo slowly meanders toward us.

"That's us," I say. I close my hand around Claire's bicep. *Mine.*

Ransom tilts his hat. Everything he does is like staples underneath my fingernails. "See y'all there, then."

"See you," Claire says. Wistfully.

Hmm.

Ransom gets back in his shitty vehicle and gets out of the way. The limo winds around the fountain and creeps up to the front of the house.

The back door opens. A silver-haired man steps out of the limo. He drops his black hat to his chest.

"I'm sorry we're late," he says. "I had to get you these."

He procures a bouquet of flowers, extending them toward Claire.

Claire does something unexpected. Her expression goes soft. Gentle as a duckling, she bypasses the flowers and folds herself into his arms, cuddling against his chest.

"*Arris,*" she says, her voice like a prayer.

ARRIS DAGNEY SITS across from us in the limo. It's a small, square space, and it's hard to keep our knees from knocking together. We cross the train tracks to get to the church grounds, and the roads make a swift shift from smooth, paved asphalt to bumpy, uneven ground. Arris clutches the handhold above the window and presses his mouth into a tight, *we're not in Kansas anymore* smile.

Here is what I've surmised from Arris Dagney:

He looks to be in his forties, but my guess would be late fifties. The oil-black of his hair suggests he's been dying it ever since the grays started coming in, and the lack of wrinkles around his eyes makes me think he's had some work done. Appearance is important to him, and the cut and fabric of his black suit suggests he's paid a pretty penny to keep appearances up.

The collar of his shirt is fitted with little silver triangles, and he wears horseshoe-shaped silver cufflinks.

He owns and runs the Equestrian Club, and he's a founding member of the Benefactors' Society. He befriended Mr. Preacher over thirty years ago and has been working with him ever since as his bloodstock agent, organizing and coordinating the sales made from breeding the Preacher horses. His close relation with Mr. Preacher made him something of a second father to Claire, hence her soft affection for him.

I also recognize his face, but I don't know from where, and being unable to place it is driving me crazy.

Not-knowing is my least favorite state of being.

Arris tightens his hold on the grip handle and leans forward. His leg touches mine, and I force myself to allow it. His eyes are deep blue, and they fix on me.

"What's the score?" he asks.

"I'm sorry?"

He taps his ear, motioning to the earbud in my ear. "Are you listening to the game?"

"No. Mozart."

He smiles. His teeth are perfect. "I don't know how they do it in the UK, but here, it's a touch rude to be all wired in when you're with people."

His tone is collected, but there's an undercurrent of threat running through it.

The worst thing you can be in Belleflower, I've come to learn, is rude.

Claire's hand slides over my thigh, settling at my knee. She gives a small squeeze. "James gets sensory overload," she explains. "He focuses better when there's white noise. This *is* him being polite."

Arris cocks his head. A mea culpa. "Ah. That makes more sense. Here, I thought maybe you were a spy. Relaying your every move to your team."

I laugh. It's a tight sound in my throat. He laughs in turn.

I don't like this man very much.

The limo pulls up to a narrow, white church with a thin, pointed spire that looks as though God himself pinched the building between his thumb and forefinger and gave it a sturdy tug.

A ramp zigzags the front of the church, and people dressed in black somberly walk in. A gravel lot flanks the church, and I see Ransom's red truck in there. He's in the bed of his truck, unfolding a wheelchair. He pulls it out, climbs down, and assists an older man into the chair.

Of course he helps the infirm.

Annoying, bleeding heart.

The three of us climb out of the limo, and I help Claire to her feet. Immediately, I notice the heads turning toward Claire. She ignores the attention, avoiding eye contact with the expertise of a Hollywood star, looking up at the church instead.

"Are you ready?" I ask.

She lays her arm lightly in the crook of mine. Claire and I fall behind Arris Dagney, and together, we walk through the twin church doors.

A willow tree spreads an umbrella of shade, leaves rustling like wind chimes. The sound climbs my shoulder like a horde of spiders. I crank up the volume of my earbuds.

We're greeted at the door by a somber pastor who looks half Grim Reaper himself, cheeks long and sallow. The church inside is surprisingly humble, with simple wooden pews, stained glass windows, and open beams that spread across the ceiling like the rib cage of a giant beast. There's an overwhelming smell of cedar and sawdust.

An ornate mahogany coffin sits in the pulpit. Closed. A framed picture of Mr. Preacher stands beside it, the man serious and unsmiling in his portrait. White calla lilies bow their heads as though in reverent respect.

It's a slow descent down the aisle as Arris Dagney stops to share small talk with everyone. I've gathered that the Dagneys and Preachers are Belleflower royalty. When people talk to them, they clasp their hands and speak in reverent voices. I half expect them to get to their knees and kiss the gold signet ring that adorns Arris's pinky finger.

Claire, to her credit, shakes hands and politely thanks people for coming. The Promise Sisters briefly flutter around Claire, each wearing thick black dresses and small black fascinators and the same crocodile tears. Second to the front, we pass a very pregnant woman, who takes Claire's hand.

"Thank you for coming, Bonnie," Claire says. This one, she looks genuinely pleased to see, and I watch the women exchange a squeeze of hands.

Arris slides his hand over the bump of Bonnie's stomach. "How's our girl?" he asks.

The man beside Bonnie—her husband, I presume—nearly trips over himself as he gets to his feet. He clutches his hat, worrying the brim in his tight grip. "She's great, sir. Thank you very much. Doctor says she's in great health."

"Wonderful."

Arris's hand cups the back of Bonnie's head far too affectionately for my liking. Bonnie's expression goes blank.

Hm.

Finally, the four of us take our seats in the front pew.

"No, Grandmimi, you can't see him—it's closed. I ain't telling them to open it up."

Ransom's voice is a big, booming thing, and it carries, even when he's trying to be quiet. I glance over the back of the pew. He's seated far in the back, between the old man in the wheelchair and a matching old woman beside him.

The woman fusses at him. He folds his arms across his chest.

Our eyes connect across the church. I slide my arm around Claire's shoulders.

"Are you okay?" I ask Claire.

Her jaw is a thin, tight line. She stares ahead at the coffin containing the remains of her father.

"If you ask me that again," she says, "there will be two bodies in that coffin."

I shut my mouth. Her shoulders are tense and tight under my embrace.

The Grim-Pastor takes the stand. He nods toward the pallbearers at the end of the hall, and they begin to close the door.

"Hold on! One damned minute."

The doors shutter back open to allow the latecomer to

enter. She's in a classic, elegant funeral dress. Her heels click loudly across the marble floors. She walks with purpose around the pews, all the way to the front, and takes her seat beside Arris.

This, I take it, is *Mrs.* Dagney.

She fits the bill. The epitome of trophy wife—beautiful, poised, and elegant. Her dark skin is without blemish. Her hair is strung into perfect ringlets. Her makeup is sharp. She walks with the confident air of someone who owns the entire town.

Arris's mouth is a bitter, thin line. "You're late."

She drops her purse beside her. "You left me at home."

"I assumed you were getting a ride." There's a pointed edge to his tone.

"Mm. You'd be so lucky."

The pastor clears his throat. Loudly.

Even the Dagneys go quiet under the narrowed eyes of the man of God.

"Let's begin," he says.

16

RANSOM

This is hell.

I can't sit still, knowing Claire is in pain and there's not a goddamn thing I can do about it.

Pastor Jones mumbles through his ceremony, but his voice just sounds like a bunch of rocks rolling together. I can't focus on the words.

I can't focus on nothing but Claire.

Funny how the town I've spent my entire life in changed color the second Claire stepped back in it.

Through the sea of feathered hats and fascinators, I can see the quarter turn of Claire's face. She keeps her chin up, her eyes straight ahead on her father's casket. Her bottom lip juts forward, just a bit, but her expression remains hard stone.

She's the toughest gal I know.

My Claire-Bear.

To others, she might look emotionless. Me? I know what she looks like when she's grieving. She's got herself stitched together with pins and prayer, and as soon as she's somewhere safe, she's going to shake to pieces.

I want to be beside her. I want to scoop her up in my arms. I want to tell her it's all going to be okay, but I can't. I can't because I'm stuck in the back, and she's got a James, and I gave up the privilege of taking care of Claire, and now it's my penance to watch another man do the job for me...and do it badly.

Every time James tries to put his arm on her, Claire pulls away from him.

Guess things aren't all gravy in paradise.

To top it all off, Jade keeps peeking over her shoulder at me. She's in one of her moods.

Meaning: she's angry at her husband and horny for me.

The last thing I needed was my forbidden flame sitting next to my past flame, but ain't nothing to be done about it now except wait and see if they can keep far enough apart so they don't combust each other.

I should leave it well alone, but...

I can't take my eyes off Claire.

I want to hold her hand. I want to rub my thumb over the back of it. I want to tell her it's all going to be okay.

I want so much, and this longing thumps inside of me like some sick, swollen organ, black and corrupted. If I let it get any bigger, I swear it's gonna burst and kill me.

Pastor Jones says a few formal words. Then, a few coworkers and partners go up to talk about what a good sort of man Mr. Preacher was.

Finally, the pastor asks if Claire would say a few words.

I can see her stiffen in her chair. Then, slowly, she rises. She drops her purse in James's lap and steps up to the pulpit.

Everyone is quiet as they wait for Claire to speak.

I can see her choosing her words. When she addresses the crowd, it's with a clear, sharp voice.

"My father was a cold man," she says. "Hardheaded. Stubborn. But he believed in me, and he pushed me every day to do better. Be better. Be more. For better or worse, he made me the woman I am today. So. Thank you for the thorns, Daddy."

She turns and stares at the casket. There's a hush as she touches her fingers across the top of it. For a second, my heart pounds, and I'm afraid she's going to open it. But then she quietly walks away and returns to her seat beside James. He offers her a handkerchief, and she uses it to clean her hands.

An old biddy, Mrs. Bridges, sits with her husband in front of me. She whispers too loudly as she leans toward her husband, "Not a tear shed. She knows who did it, I'll tell you that."

I nearly launch out of the pew, but Grandmimi fixes me in my spot with a glare that could tame a wild cat. I thread my fingers together and stay put.

There isn't much more to the ceremony after that. The pastor says his peace, and then the organ kicks up, and everyone stands as they move to carry Mr. Preacher out. I watch as Arris Dagney goes to stand by the coffin, and then so do a few other members from the Benefactors' Society. I know these men. Have worked around the ranch while these men were milling about. Have heard the things they said about their "friend," Mr. Preacher—how they gossiped like hens about him losing his marbles in the end. How they picked at the carcass of his reputation like vultures before it'd even gone cold.

It doesn't seem right that, at the end, there ain't a single person up there carrying his coffin that had a lick of sympathy for the man—devil though he might've been.

I can't help it. I get to my feet and approach. Their eyes turn to me warily when they see me getting closer.

I clasp my hands together. "Mind if I lend a hand?"

I'm about ten years younger and fifty pounds stronger than any of the men there. They should welcome the help. Instead, they look at me like I've lost my damned mind.

Abernathy, a thick-necked man with boots that never have and never will see a lick of dirt on them, looks at me with skeptical eyes. "We've got this, boy."

Boy. As in: South of the Railroad kid. As in: you're not one of us. As in: you're lucky we even let you through those church doors, you ho-dunk piece of—

"Let him," Claire says suddenly, her voice breaking free.

Her face is placid and expressionless, but she has a command in her voice that no one can ignore. Arris can't argue with Preacher's daughter, not today. He doesn't look happy about it, but he nods at me. "Grab a handle."

We bury the old man behind the church.

Claire doesn't shed a tear. Not once. But her bottom lip blows up as though she's been stung by a bee.

When it's all said and done, she gets swallowed in the sea of people offering their condolences. Maybe hoping for a Preacher handout. I head back to check in on my grandparents. Turns out, they don't need a ride back; they're going to catch an early dinner with their friends. Good for them.

Me? I'm exhausted.

I get into my truck and take off my hat, setting it on the dashboard. I rake my fingers through my hair. I let out a sigh. Deep sigh. It feels good. I've got my peace.

...For about three seconds.

Then my passenger-side door opens and shuts. Claire hops in beside me, fixing her dark sunglasses over her face.

"Drive," she says, like some starlet in a heist movie.

I don't budge. "What're you doing here?"

Claire snaps her seatbelt into place. "I can't go back to the ranch. Not yet. Besides. James is driving me fucking crazy."

Speak of the bitch, and he'll appear.

As if summoned, the back door opens. James—the giant he is—has to crouch down in order to climb in the back of my truck.

"Claire." He snaps on his seat belt. "There you are."

Claire scowls at me, as though this is all somehow my fault. "Here I am."

"Here you both are," I counter. "Now, get out."

My truck doors open a fourth time. This time, it's Jade. She blinks when she closes the door behind her and sees the other seats already taken. "Oh!" Jade says. "It's a party in here, isn't it? No one saw me, did they? I had to leave before Arris notices. That man truly knows how to spoil a good time."

"A good time," James says simply. "You mean the funeral?"

She tilts her head toward James. "I don't think we've been introduced."

He sticks out his hand. "I'm Claire's fiancé."

She shakes it. "Claire's fiancé. Does it have a name?"

"James."

Her eyes flicker over him. Scanning him from head to toe. Giving him *that look*. "And the giant peach, *indeed*."

Alright. That's the last straw. I blow a gasket and smack my hand against the steering wheel.

"Goddammit! The hell is this, a clown car? Everyone out of my truck!"

"Ransom!" the women snap, their voices in horrible, perfect sync. "Drive!"

Cursing, I put the truck into gear and kick dirt.

CLAIRE DOESN'T WANT to go to the Preacher Ranch. Jade doesn't want to go to the Dagney estate.

Everyone, it seems, is on the run, and somehow, I've been designated the getaway driver.

So I take them to the best spot I know.

Maeby's Tavern is a hole-in-the-wall bar on the south side of the tracks. It's not long until we're underneath a loud, neon red sign with the words *Maeby's Tavern* scrolled across in loopy, cursive letters.

This was *our spot*, once upon a time.

The four of us exit the truck. In our funeral suits, we're all far too overdressed.

"Charming," James says. But he says it the same way a cat person tries to compliment a coworker's dog.

I fill him in. "Claire and I used to come here all the time. It was the one place Mr. Preacher wouldn't think to search for her. Sorta her own personal…"

"Escape," James finishes.

"Yeah."

We enter, and I'm hit with the stench of old wood and stale beer. Smells like home. There are booths flanking the windows, a pool table in the back, and a small platform where they sometimes have music. Looks like they're setting up for tonight, but they've got old rock playing on the sound system.

"This place is cute," Jade says. "How did I never know it exists?"

"Welcome to the south of the tracks," I tell her.

Her hand touches my arm, grasping it. Which is weird. We've got rules. No flirting. No PDA. She's picked a hell of a time to break those rules.

I can feel Claire's gray eyes digging holes in the back of my head.

"C'mon." I tilt my head. "Let's grab a seat."

I guide the sheep into a booth. It's a seat-yourself kind of place. You have to order at the bar, so I find myself playing waiter. I grab a few laminated menus and slap them on the table.

"What do y'all want?" I ask. "Drinks? Food?"

"Definitely drinks." Claire takes off her jacket and hands it to James. He folds it beside him.

I wish I was sitting next to her. I wish I was folding her jacket.

I find myself getting green with envy over the strangest things.

There's a pop of a gunshot. I know what the sound is—James doesn't. Like a viper, he suddenly grabs Claire and shoves her under the table. She yelps as he crouches over her, his head jerking back toward the noise.

"Oh God!" Jade says, lifting her palms as though she's being held up.

I can't help it. I chuckle. "*Relax*. Ain't no one in danger. There's a shooting range out back. Just some jackasses popping off cans."

James releases Claire from his hold. She touches her hair as she rises back up to her seat.

"A shooting range in a bar," James says, his voice tight. He snaps the collar on his shirt. "Bloody brilliant idea."

"It's a BB gun," I say. Even I can hear the defensive edge in my voice. "Nothing but blanks. But. Sure. Real killers out there."

Jade laughs. She fans herself with her hand. "Whew!" she says, her eyes sparkling. "Exciting! James, are you in the military?"

"Accountant," he says.

"Claire, he's protective." Jade wiggles her eyebrows. "I like that in a man. I can see why you married him."

"Oh—we're not married. We're engaged."

Jade suddenly reaches forward and touches her fingers over the back of James's hand. I watch him go still, the way a viper does before it strikes. Unbothered, she taps her finger over the silver ring around his ring finger. "This looks like a married man to me."

"Yes, well." Claire flicks her wrist. "He wanted an engagement ring, too."

James lifts his hand and splays out his fingers to show off the ring to us.

I tilt my head. "Guy with an engagement ring. That's a bit unusual, isn't it?"

Claire glares at me. "And?"

I can't stop myself. "So he wears the ring, you wear the pants?"

She touches the back of James's neck fondly. "It's romantic."

Now that we've all settled down, the women turn their attention to the laminated menus in front of them. "I'm famished," Jade says.

But James's gaze remains on mine.

When Claire isn't looking, he lowers four of his fingers, leaving the middle one up at me.

Flicking me off. Right at the table.

What?

Did that—?

Did that just happen?

He's rubbing it in my face, and there isn't jack or shit I can do about it. Then he drops his arm, resting it around Claire's shoulders. Impotent, quiet anger pounds inside of me like a second heartbeat.

"I can't read this," Jade complains. She pushes the menu away. "Just get me a cosmo."

"And a pitcher for the table," Claire says.

"Yep." I need to get out of this booth before I strangle him. I go to the bar and square my forearms on the wood.

My hands are *shaking*.

Someone smacks me on the back. My buddy—Rafe— stands beside me. "Hey, how's it going?"

My voice trembles. "I'm so mad I think I'm having a stroke."

He twists, propping his elbows on the bar. Rafe has golden skin, jet-black hair cut in a clean fade, and a smart tongue. He also wears a single golden stud in his left ear, which started some kind of trend because now a lot of the workhands wear the same single-ear piercing. But that's just Rafe. He's got this magnetic energy about him that makes people warm to him. They wanna be him. Wanna be like him. Wanna be *with* him.

I should know. We grew up together. Got into the sort of innocent trouble boys get into and then never mention again. Now, we work together, drink together, and spend most of our free time complaining about life, money, and women. I watch his dark eyes scan the booth I just came from.

"Is that Claire? And Miss Jade?" He squints. "Who's the guy?"

"James. Claire's fiancé."

Rafe whistles low. "Kinda stiff, isn't he?"

"*Kinda*? He's a tin man."

Rafe clicks his tongue. "Got that lone coyote rizz. You think he'd recognize his mother tongue?"

"Don't—"

Rafe lets out a couple of loud animal yips.

A couple of barflies give us curious looks. James looks our way, eyebrows furrowed.

Rafe laughs. I can't help it. I drop my head and chuckle into my arms.

"You dumbass."

"Takes one to know one, amigo." Rafe lapses into thought and then asks, "You think they fuck, or do they just assemble like IKEA furniture?"

I don't want to think about that. I change the topic.

"You didn't see them. Any of them. Especially Jade, you got that?"

Rafe drags his eyes over me. "I've never met a man who's so incredibly good at getting himself into hot water the way you are."

I sigh. "Yeah, I'm a regular lobster."

Finally, Maeby appears. Her story is nothing but a fall from grace. Once a Belleflower Queen, she now owns her own tavern and spends her nights slinging beers. She's still elegant as all hell if you ask me, but she wears her roughness on her sleeves now. She's got a chipped tooth, leathery skin, and when she wears a strappy shirt like tonight, you can see hints of deep scars that peek out from around her shoulders.

This is a woman who, literally, took life's licks and lived to tell the tale.

No one knows why Maeby left her life of Belleflower

privilege to slum it with the Sooters down here. Sooters—
that's what they call us. South of the Railroad kids. At this
point, I think everyone's too afraid of Maeby to ask.

Even I wouldn't dare ask, and she's practically family to
me. When my folks were alive, they spent so much time at
this bar it was my school, my afterschool, and my higher
education. Maeby, my whip-smart and wiseass professor,
helping me with homework between pitchers.

Which is why I know she's got nothing but love for me,
even when she rolls her eyes at me and Rafe. "What do you
two want, then?"

Rafe nudges his empty glass forward. I give my order. "A
couple baskets of fries, four shots of whiskey, a pitcher of
Yellow Canary Pils, and a cosmo." Even I wince hearing it
back. I'm probably the first man to ever order a cosmo here.
"Please don't spit in it."

Maeby sets four shot glasses on the table. She fills them
up, then looks me dead in the eyes as she gathers a glob of
spit and drops it into the fourth glass.

"That's for you," she says. "For insinuating that I'd do
such a thing."

Without hesitation, Rafe takes the spit-shot and knocks
it back. He holds his hands up in prayer.

"Another, please. Heavy on the spit, Miss Maeby."

She narrows her eyes at him. She fixes our drinks,
setting them on a tray. She tells me, "No animals allowed in
here. Tie your stud to the post out back, Ransom, or I will."

Rafe puts his chin on the bar and looks up at her with
big moon eyes. "I'd let you tie me to anything you'd like,
ma'am."

He's got a thing for MILFs.

I fight a grin and jab him with my elbow, a sign to cut it
out before Maeby kicks us out on our asses.

We might be grown men, but some friendships never grow up, not really.

"Be good," Miss Maeby tells me as she hands over the tray.

"Yes, ma'am."

I take my truck keys out of my pocket and drop them on the bar. Maeby takes them and stashes them by the cashier. That's our deal. When I'm here to have fun, I leave my keys with Maeby and leave the truck in the parking lot. I'll come collect it in the morning. I don't drive with a drop of liquor in me, and Maeby knows that. No exceptions.

I bring the drinks back to the table and hand them out.

"Drinks." Claire brightens. "Yes."

I take my spot beside Jade. James tents his fingers around his shot glass. "To Mr. Preacher," he says.

I tilt my glass. Claire does the same. Her gray eyes meet mine as she puts the rim to her lips.

I don't know if it's the whiskey or her stare, but it burns all the way down.

Jade lifts her glass. "Za vashe zdorovie," she says before knocking her shot back. Her face pinches at the taste, and she shivers as she puts the glass down. "It means *to your health* in Russian."

"Are we in Russia now?" I ask.

"I've visited," she says flippantly. "A few times. Very cold."

Like it's nothing. I ain't ever even left Belleflower.

"There's a Russian superstition," Jade says suddenly. "It is said that the soul travels."

"Oh, yeah?" I ask, only half listening. Mostly staring across the table.

"Three days after death, the soul ascends to paradise," she continues. "On the ninth day, the soul goes to hell. And then, on the fortieth day, it returns to paradise to be with God."

That gets my attention. "So everyone spends forty days in hell?"

James corrects me with, "Thirty-one."

"No matter how good you are?" I protest.

She smiles at me, a sly grin. "Everyone has something to repent for."

"Think I might need more than forty days," I reply.

"Have a lot to repent for?" Claire asks.

My gaze finds Claire. Her gray eyes find mine right back.

"You know it," I tell her.

"I think She will find ways to forgive you." Jade slips her hand over the back of my neck and squeezes. I can feel Claire's eyes.

"God's a she now?" I ask.

Jade shrugs. "All the powerful creatures are."

Claire is over this heaven and hell talk. Her gaze is roaming. "I want to play," she says suddenly.

"I don't know if that's a good idea," James interjects, but Claire's made up her mind. She stands and takes her pint glass as she heads toward the pool table.

I look at James. Those dark eyebrows are pinched together. "You ever see her play pool?" I ask.

"No."

"You're about to see a side of Claire you ain't maybe experienced yet."

His mouth turns downward, and I get a kick out of it.

Claire ignores James. She ignores everything as she makes a beeline to the pool table. I watch as she carefully picks out her pool cue and starts to grind chalk on the tip of it.

I can feel the shift in the room. One by one, everyone

starts to recognize the Preacher prodigy. Around here, Preachers are something like royalty—something I never much envied Claire for.

I can walk into a room and turn into wallpaper. Claire? She'll always shine bright.

The gossip flies start to buzz. I hear phrases like—

"—Preacher's daughter."

"—Big-city girl now."

"—Such a shame."

Claire turns and examines the green chalkboard behind her. It's a running scoreboard with the names of the winners etched in white. "Who is Kane?" she asks, immediately zeroing in on the name at the top of the board.

From a round table in the center of the room, a burly man lifts his hand.

She points at him with her cue stick. "You first."

17

RANSOM

Claire takes on her first victim. Jade, James, and I move into a closer booth where we can get a clear view of the action.

And it's a show, alright.

Claire is in her zone. Claire plays solids. He plays stripes. Without breaking a sweat, Claire wipes the table with him.

Then, she does the same to the next guy.

And the next.

She invites James up. He doesn't stand a chance.

Jade is next. She, too, gets pulverized.

Claire's drug of choice is *winning*, and right now, she's overdosing.

She unpins her hair, letting it fall down. She's wild, bits of braid sticking out. James stands near her in the corner, holding her whiskey like a cornerman. There's a small dark patch of sweat underneath her arms. She lays her body across the table, scissors her fingers around the length of the pool cue, and fires her shot.

Her ball sinks into the pocket.

The small crowd of admirers breaks out into a round of

cheers. Claire lifts herself from the velvet green and swipes her hand over her hair, tucking it back.

And—ouch.

My dick is bruising itself on the zipper of my jeans.

A fly tickles the back of my neck. I swat it.

"Ow!" Jade pulls her hand back.

"God...dammit," I fumble. "What the hell are you doing?"

"What do you *think* I'm doing?" She pouts and sucks her fingers. "I'm giving you a hand, darling."

"Come again?"

She rolls her eyes. I can tell she's drunk because she's mindlessly picking at the remains of the fry basket on the table. "*Please.* Everyone can see the way you look at Claire."

I buck up. "What about it?"

She waves a fry. "Don't you know the way to a woman's heart is jealousy? She sees you with me, she'll lose her damn mind. *You're welcome.*"

"You're a pal," I say dryly.

"Besides," she nibbles her fry, "if you two pair up, that leaves James free. I'm always on the look-out for my next *ex-husband.*"

"What the hell does everyone see in him? He looks like he cuts the crusts off his PB&Js."

"Look enamored, darling."

I lift a fry. I let her eat it from my fingers.

When I glance back to the pool table, Claire's gray eyes are on me.

She pulls her cue stick and scratches the ball.

There's a light groan from the audience. The look she's giving me could kill.

Her opponent sinks a couple of balls before he misses the shot. The next time Claire goes up, she clears the table.

There are a couple of feeble claps, but mostly people have gotten tired of her winning, and it's stopped being impressive.

But when the Bear is on a rampage, she doesn't know when to stop.

She's beautiful, unkempt, the feral version of Claire that's always gotten into my bloodstream, but...she's in pain. I can see it. As clear as if she tipped a bottle of whiskey to her lips and started inhaling it.

Claire hides her tears behind her pride.

And it's getting hard to watch.

She shoves her cue at James. He takes it. I watch as Claire takes a break, stepping off the platform and heading to the bathroom.

"Excuse me." Jade climbs over my lap.

I get a bad feeling about this. "Jade." My voice is a terse warning.

She gives me that Mona Lisa smile. "*Relax*. I know what I'm doing."

But I can't relax.

I feel downright rotten—but what the hell else is new?

18

CLAIRE

I t's right at the top of my list of things I don't want to witness. Ransom and Jade pawing at each other like cats in heat.

Yet here I am.

I push my way blindly into the bathroom. I let the door slam shut behind me. I go to the sink and clutch the cold material.

Do not let them smell blood.

Do not let any of them know you're wounded.

I breathe.

I only get a second of peace. The door opens. Jade comes in. She takes the sink next to mine, plops her purse down, and begins reapplying her makeup.

I want to stab her with her lipstick. I restrain myself.

My hair looks a wild mess. I start to pull it back, fixing some of the stray frizz underneath.

"Quite the performance out there," Jade says. Her voice is this elegant, velvet purr. "Really showing the boys who's boss, aren't you?

There's an insult in her tone. I ignore her. "Thanks."

One of the faucets is leaking. The water ticks as it taps against the bowl.

She wants girl talk? Fine.

Let's talk.

"You and Ransom," I say bluntly. "What's that about."

An amused smile stretches across her freshly sharpened lips. "You know what they call him, don't you?" Jade says. Her eyes flicker from her image in the mirror to mine. "*Wiley Riley*. The fox in the henhouse. There are so many unhappily married women in this town...and that man... well. He gives them all a reason to smile."

Then she pops her lipstick back in her purse, snaps it shut.

"See you on the battlefield," she says and leaves.

I look in the mirror. My father's gray eyes stare back at me.

"You're Claire Preacher," I tell myself. I make my voice hard as stone. "And you're not going to let one dumbass cowboy ruin your life."

19

RANSOM

I head back to the bar. I rest my elbows on the bar top and try to ignore this sick feeling churning around in my belly.

"Another pitcher, please, Miss Maeby."

James's tall form slides in beside me.

Great. Just what I need.

"And two whiskey gingers," James adds. This close, I notice he even *smells* good. This clean, floral scent, like tea leaves. It's fucking irritating. He pulls his dumb man-purse over his shoulder, and he reaches into it to pull out a wallet. "This round is on me." He pushes a crisp hundred-dollar bill across the bar.

I can't help it. I snort a bitter laugh. "Your generosity knows no bounds, chief."

"It's the least I can do since you've been kind enough to drive us around."

Every word he says feels like fleas nipping at my skin.

Drive us around. Like I'm some goddamn taxi service.

"Yeah, well. Claire and I go way back. It's the least I can do."

"Oh, I know," he says plainly. "I know all about it."

I can't stuff my anger down anymore. I tell him, "You know what people hate more than an outsider? An outsider who pretends he knows it all."

His blue eyes meet mine. He's exceptionally, infuriatingly calm when he says, "But I do know it all. I know everything about you, Riley Ransom."

"Yeah? What do you think you know?"

He tilts in. I can feel my heartbeat pounding in my throat when he drops his voice, low enough just so only I can hear him. "I know you chase married women because you don't feel adequate. You'd rather take the sure thing than risk rejection. I know the last time you felt like you were worth a damn was your teenage years, and life has been an uphill battle for you ever since, so you long for the things you left behind the way a weened child cries for its pacifier."

Everything in me goes cold, and the hair stands up on the back of my neck, but he doesn't stop. He continues. "I know that you're operating on the assumption that if you can get into Claire's bed, she'll remember how good it was with you, and she'll leave me. But that's where you've miscalculated. In fact, the best thing you can do is keep your mystery. Because once you're inside of her, you'll lose that sweet, puppy-love charm. She'll see you for what you are. A memory made rosier by time. And all Claire is going to think about is me. The man who made her a woman. A woman who likes to get fucked and spanked and choked. By me."

I jolt as Maeby sets the drinks on the bar with a clink. James straightens his spine, pulling away from me. He takes the two whiskey gingers. "Keep the change," he tells her and gives Maeby a chillingly polite smile.

The man's got this haunting, cat-who-ate-the-junkyard-dog smile.

With that, he leaves. My heart is pounding, this heavy, thudding beat that won't let up.

"Ransom," Maeby says. Her gaze flickers over me. "You good?"

I watch as James meets Claire back at the pool table. He holds out a drink for her. She takes it, and they sip together.

Thu-thump. Thu-thump.

"Yep," I tell Maeby. "All good."

I take the pitcher back to the booth.

"Ransom!" That's Claire's voice. When I turn, I see Claire twirling her cue between her fingers. "Are you going to hide in the shadows all night, or are you going to put on your big-boy pants and get up here?"

I get a couple of curious stares from the barnacles at the bar. James watches me from the sidelines, gauging my reaction.

I step up to the pool table. "Don't you think you've played long enough?"

"Can't handle the competition? I guess you can only take it when it's easy."

Claire's eyes lock on me. A challenge.

I'm pissed, my heart's all tangled up, and—

Fuck it. She wants a fight, I'll give her a fight.

I shrug. "I was just thinking...it'd be a shame."

"What would?"

"To knock your pretty ass off your very high pedestal."

Her eyes flash. I'm in.

"You're welcome to try," Claire says. She grinds her tip against the chalk, like a swordswoman sharpening her rapier.

I pick out my cue. "You know, you're a real pain in my—"

"Chaps?" James interjects.

I click my tongue. "Wasn't talking to you, Mary Poppins."

James has an uneasy expression on his face—but he can get fucked, honestly.

Claire and I are locked in battle, and she's only got eyes for me right now.

Her pale cheeks have a soft, red glow. The rickety ceiling fan blows a tassel of unrestrained hair against her pouting lips.

What I would do to those lips.

Claire at her worst is, unfortunately, the Claire that makes my heart beat the fastest.

We were good at loving. At fucking. But, damn—

We were always best at fighting.

I rack up the balls. When she looks at me with those intense, gray-sky eyes, I feel her gaze singe the hair up arms like an electric current.

Being this close to her *hurts*. In my chest. In my groin. Cock and heart swelling to the limits of their confines. I know better. I know I ain't doing anything but hurting myself by testing these lines. Yet, like some idiot dog choking itself on its own leash, I can't stop pulling.

"Bitches break," I tell her.

She motions to the rack. "Then be my guest."

I take off the rack, line up my shot, and hit it.

Balls click and go scattering. I've got solids.

Claire might have the mean streak of a perfectionist robot...

But I've got the slow grind of someone who had nothing better to do with his free time than come down to Maeby's and play round after round of pool.

And I'm fucking good.

I sink three balls before I miss. Claire rounds the table

like a lioness on the hunt. Her fingertips graze the green velvet.

"Wiley, Wiley, Wiley," she muses. "What should we play for?"

Wiley. I bite back a cringe at the nickname. *Goddammit, Jade. Stop helping.*

"You tell me."

She finds an angle that suits her and lines up her shot. "Money wouldn't be fair. It means more in your pocket than it does mine."

"Whatever you say, princess."

Fun fact: Claire's got a kink for arms.

At least, she used to.

I test my theory by unbuttoning my wrist cuff and rolling the sleeve up over my elbow. Sure enough, her eyes flicker from the table to the dark hair that climbs my exposed forearm.

She hits. It's a miss. My turn.

As I line up my shot, she asks, "What about Miss Penny?"

The cue jumps in my hand. It knocks the ball out of place, sailing past its target. "You said you wouldn't get rid of her."

Claire bends her lithe body over the table. Her chest nearly touches the green, and she threads the cue between her fingers. "I just don't see the point of keeping the thing around."

Claire is so focused on the game, when she goes to line up her next shot, she nearly walks straight into me. She catches herself at the last second, her hand on my chest.

Her hair tickles my face. Our eyes meet briefly.

She smells sweet. Like honeysuckle.

"The point is," I tell her, "Chaucer loves her."

Her mouth twists. She turns away from me and leans over the pool table. The balls click. Claire sinks her shot. We're neck and neck now. "It's an object, not a *her*."

My jaw tightens. "Not to him."

Claire stops playing. She looks up at me, and this time, there's real fire in her eyes. Cold, black embers. "Studs don't love," she says simply. "Chaucer has fucked every mare in Kentucky. He's not going to even notice she's gone."

"He'll notice."

She lines up her shot again, ignoring me. But I press on.

"He thinks about her every day," I continue.

She glares at the end of her cue. "You don't get to say that to me," she says, her voice quiet and angry. "You don't get to stand there and fucking *lie*."

"It ain't a lie, princess."

Through gritted teeth, she says, "I. Am not. Your. *Princess*."

She hits the ball with too much force. It skips and goes flying off the table.

James, eyes still glued to his phone, headphones in his ears, flicks out his wrist and catches it effortlessly in the palm of his hand.

"Play nicely," he chastises before setting the ball back down on the table.

But Claire doesn't budge. Her eyes are stuck on James, eyebrows scrunched, her pretty little mouth twisted like she's trying to solve a puzzle.

"You caught that. Perfectly." She speaks slowly, like she's sounding out the words as she goes.

"I suppose I did," he says.

"You have perfect reflexes," she repeats.

"They come in handy."

Her next sentence is a fine, lethal point. "*You let me win*."

James's expression flickers the second he realizes he's made a mistake. "Claire—"

"Did you," she seethes, "let me. *Win?*"

He weighs his answer on his tongue before he gives it to her. "You're getting worked up."

Her jaw goes tight. "Get the fuck out of my sight."

Claire storms out, her eyes a gray hurricane, taking the fury of all-mighty Zeus with her.

Not gonna lie, I almost feel sorry for the guy.

Almost.

There's a part of me that wants to enjoy James getting his ass chewed out. But the pain on Claire's face makes me queasy.

James goes still. When his robot brain is done calculating the damage he's done, he says, "I think I'd better go after her."

"Yep." I nod. "I think that's wise."

Fucking dick.

I watch as James follows Claire out. I rest against the abandoned pool table and take a swallow from my beer. Jade sidles up beside me. She's been uncharacteristically quiet. She's wearing the face of a princess whose carriage has turned into a pumpkin. We both know: the fantasy is over.

For good.

"I called a car," she says. There's no anger in her voice. Just a flatness. "He's waiting for me. Escort me out, cowboy."

"Yes, ma'am."

I clean my beer and walk her outside.

Claire and James are in the wind. Jade's black car whisks her away. Back in the bar, I find Rafe playing hook and ring. We kill the rest of the pitcher and close down the bar.

The Kentucky night is cold, dark, and bitter when I stumble outside. If I breath it in deep enough, I can almost get the taste of Claire's perfume out of my lungs.

I hear the jingle of dropped keys. Rafe curses as he drunkenly fumbles around his car.

I step up behind him. I snatch his keys off the gravel and pocket them. "No, sir," I tell him.

The sound of a car horn breaks us up. I look up to see Maeby in the driver's seat of her blue pickup. She jabs her thumb to the back of the truck.

"Degenerates in the bed," she says.

Rafe and I climb into the bed of the truck. My back hits the hard bottom. Rafe grunts as he collapses beside me like a dead fish. We lie on our backs and stare up at the dark sky scattered with stars.

"Women," Rafe sighs.

"Women," I agree.

But I ain't thinking about women.

I'm thinking about one woman in particular.

20

RANSOM

T *hen.*

"I'M *NOT* LOSING my virginity in the back of a truck."

Claire folds her arms as she stares into my truck bed.

I hop up. "No. You're not. *We* are."

I made it all romantic and everything.

A nice, soft quilt lines the back of the truck, stuffed with pillows. I rolled out a sleeping bag on the bottom of the bed to even out the ridges. There's a basket with cheese, crackers, and strawberries and a sparkling cider. A bouquet of flowers is wrapped up beside it, and a lantern spills soft light on the whole spread.

I think it's cozy. But Claire's got the edge of her mouth turned downward.

I like the way she frowns. Makes me wanna kiss the frown right off her face.

I pat the spot next to me. "Room for one more."

She gives in. I extend my hand, and she takes it. I help her up into the bed. Her dress is spotted with daisies, and it bunches up around her legs as she crawls in beside me.

We lie down together, side by side, and stare up at the sky. It's streaked with pink and orange.

"You see that?" I ask.

"See what?"

"You know, anytime I feel trapped or lost or just...*hell, I'm gonna die in Belleflower*...I just look up. We're lucky to live here. It's one of the last places in the world you can feel the wild in your bones."

When I turn to Claire, she's staring at me. Those gray eyes have a hint of curiosity in them.

Her chest rises and falls with small breaths. My heart patters.

"You know," I say, "we don't have to—"

She stops me with a kiss.

I love Claire's kisses.

Claire Preacher is the picture of poise. Pretty, round face. Blonde hair all pulled back. Plump lips and a stern mouth. Not a hair out of place.

But when she kisses, she throws her entire body into it. It's like breaking a dam, and suddenly, she's a desperate, hungry thing.

I cup her head. I roll us over so I'm on top of her. She sighs into my mouth, and that sound is an angel's song.

Her fingers make quick work of the buttons on my shirt. I push her dress up and feel the warm, creamy skin of her thigh. She unclasps my belt buckle and unbuttons me.

"I want to feel it," she says.

I give her permission. "Go on."

She slips her hand underneath my briefs. I groan when her soft, warm fingers envelop me. She pulls my hard length through her fingers, slowly, learning me. It takes everything within me not to rut into her palm.

She grins. I love that smile. "Riley Ransom, you're perfect."

Hell. My heart does a flip.

She's the only person in the world who can say those words and make me believe them.

Her touch leaves me. She raises her hips and pushes her panties off her legs.

"I want it inside of me."

A breeze ripples, and cornstalks hiss. I've parked the truck in the middle of a field, where no one will walk in on us. It's better than having our own room. That's what I tell myself.

Nothing but me, Claire, and the stars here.

I reach between her legs. She's molten here, wet and hot. I slip my fingers around her slit and find her entrance. When I press a finger inside, she moans, her eyes rolling back.

I could do this all night. I don't want her to ever stop moaning.

She grabs the collar of my open shirt and pulls me against her. Her lips crush mine, and then she murmurs against them, "Need you."

Give the lady what she wants.

I remove my hand from her sweetness and guide my cock against her instead. My heart is beating out of my chest.

"Ready?" I ask her.

She grins. "Are you?" She pets her fingers through my hair. "You're shaking."

"Chills," I lie. "It's cold."

"Let me warm you up." She drags the tip of her tongue

from the base of my chest, over my Adam's apple, and up my chin. She sucks my bottom lip into her mouth.

My cock jumps in my hand. I hear myself grunt.

"Yes," she says. "I'm ready."

Slowly, I ease myself inside of her. Her sweet heat is so tight she clutches the head of me. I push in further, and she gasps. I stop.

"You okay?" I ask.

Her mouth twists. "It hurts."

I pant against her lips. "Just a couple more inches, princess. You're doing so good."

Her eyes go wide. "There's *more*?"

I can't help it. I snort on a laugh. "Put that on my gravestone."

That earns me a stinger on my cheek. "Don't be funny right now."

"Okay. Sorry. Here." I take her hand and guide it onto my shoulder. "Dig your nails in when it hurts. Real hard. Don't be shy." I meet her gaze. "If you hurt, I hurt."

Her expression softens at that. Her fingers curl at my shoulder, those nails digging in at the crook of my neck.

I shiver at the prick of pain. "That's good. Keep going," I tell her. "We're in this together."

Claire's breath patters against my lips. I push in the rest of the way. Her nails shred my shoulders, my back. Her mouth connects with my throat, and she bites. I groan, arching into her ferocious affection. I roll my hips against hers, and she mewls—but those are pleasure noises now. Her legs wrap around me tightly, and she pushes her hips against mine, meeting me thrust for thrust. We roll together, riding each other, ripping and licking and clawing and kissing—messy, hungry love.

My brain is in my balls. Words start spilling from me.

"Fuck, princess, you feel so good."

"So do you." Her breath is light and flutters against my sweat-damp skin.

"I'll never be inside another woman," I tell her.

Those gray eyes flash. "You promise?"

"I promise. It's you. Only you."

Her body goes tight around me suddenly. So tight. Her head falls back, and she cries out, her nails making welts in my back. I moan and spill over as she throbs around me, pulling, draining my pleasure from me.

I pant into her shoulder. She laughs. It's this light, airy sound.

"I ruined your back," she says.

"I ruined your hymen. We're even."

Her eyes lock on mine. Those beautiful, wild grays.

I can see my entire future in those eyes.

"I hate you," she says. But I know she means the other thing.

I slip my hand in hers. She laces her fingers in mine.

"I know," I tell her.

We lie there, kissing and touching, until the stars fall out of the sky.

21

RANSOM

ow.

MAEBY DROPS me off at the Preacher estate.

The crickets chirp. It's a clear night. Lots of moonlight for me to walk in as I pass the entrance. I glance down the tunnel of thick hedges, down the gravel walkway that leads to the Preacher house. There are lights on. Strange to know Claire and James are in there, and Mr. Preacher isn't. I walk past it, through the groomed lawn and into the tall grass.

My trailer is a metal junkyard thing that's tucked away in the woods on the fringe of the Preacher property. It's mostly hidden except at strange hours when the sun hits it through the trees just right and makes the whole thing shine.

My trailer ain't much, but it's mine. That counts for something. It feels good to be home.

I need to cry. Or jerk off. Maybe both. At the same time.

You're a damn mess, Ransom.

I hear the rustle of fallen leaves. My bones go stiff, until I see the culprit.

"Dammit, Chaucer, you scared the hell out of me."

He sneezes and flicks his ears.

He escapes. All the time. Can't figure out how the hell he's getting out. Even if I knew, I'm not sure I'd stop it up. He always comes back.

He wanders half a mile up the hills, into the Dagney estate. They've got some weeds growing he can't get enough of, I guess. He eats his fill, and then he ambles back down.

That's how Jade and I first started hooking up. She returned the horse after she found him messing around behind her house.

Better not to think about that now.

"C'mon." I guide Chaucer back to his stable.

He's restless when we get inside, though. I take the brush and run it over his neck.

"Rough night?" I ask him.

He huffs.

"Yeah, me too."

But as I run the brush over him, each swipe calms me. I feel myself start to shed the weirdness of the day. Mr. Preacher in that closed coffin. The unbridled rage James unleashed inside of me. Claire. The agony of Claire. Of being so close and being unable to comfort her. Hold her. Love her.

Barred from loving her. Yeah. That's the worst of it.

I can't tell her, so I pet Chaucer's velvet-soft snout. I drop my forehead to his neck. His hair is soft against my cheek.

"Love you, old boy," I mumble. He nuzzles my shoulder affectionately.

God bless these pain-in-the-ass horses.

My phone buzzes. When I lift it out of my pocket, all my blood freezes up in my veins.

It's Claire.

One single, simple text that makes my heart damn near stop in my chest.

NEED YOU. *Now.*

22

CLAIRE

E *arlier.*

THERE'S a deadly silence between us.

James and I don't speak the entire way from Maeby's Tavern to the Preacher Ranch. Harding seems to sense the tension—he doesn't ask questions, and he doesn't try to make small talk. We leave the bumpy roads, cross the tracks, and sail across smooth pavement until we get to the ranch.

It's not until we're inside, door closed, alone, that James finally tries to break the quiet.

"Claire—"

"I'm going to bed," I announce. I shrug out of my shoes and quickly climb the stairs before he can get in a word edgewise.

It's the day of my father's funeral. I'm allowed to be a bitch.

I'm angry at James. I'm angry at Ransom. But most of all, I'm angry at *him*.

The one person I can never rage at. Ever again.

I cross the hall, enter the bedroom, and slip into the bathroom. I flip on the light and stare at myself in the mirror. I've fallen apart. I take myself down the rest of the way, plucking bobby pins from my head and arranging them on the sink.

The bedroom door creaks. I can hear James shuffling about. Even his *presence* annoys me.

I wash my face. I take my birth control. I remove cotton balls from my kit and start removing my makeup.

Be gone, Claire Preacher.

"You're overreacting," James says. He lingers in the bedroom—in case I turn into a dragon and start spitting fire, I suppose.

I scrub my face so hard it leaves little red marks. "You couldn't have picked two worse words to piss me off."

"Three."

I shoot him a glare through the open door. He doesn't express nearly enough remorse.

"I let you win one game of pool," he continues. "One. On the day of your father's funeral. Most people would consider that a mercy."

I start fishing through my travel bag. "I don't. I consider it a lie."

"Claire—"

"Where's my sleep mask?"

"Did you pack it?"

"Of course I fucking packed it. It was right here."

Our suitcases are half-unpacked, lined up neatly beside the dresser. I tear apart my suitcase, hunting it. Then I grab

James's leather satchel that he used for a carry-on and rip into that.

"Let me," he says. He grabs the strap and yanks it.

But something's caught my attention.

I hold my grip on the bag. I pull out a small, purple, floral journal.

I look at James. His face is a mask.

"What's this?" I ask.

"I found it," he replies.

It's a diary. *My* diary. I recognize the beaten, worn cover. Except the pages are littered with thin strips of multicolored Post-it notes. I flip the book open. My words. My teenager ramblings. Highlighted. Sections circled. With James's compact, neat handwriting in the margins.

My heart launches itself into my throat. I nearly choke.

Even through the rushing surge of adrenaline, I force myself to keep my voice neutral.

"You found it," I repeat slowly. "With your handwriting in it."

I turn the page. I read James's note scribbled in the margins.

"Obsessed with Colin Firth's rendition of Pride & Prejudice. Must watch to understand the hold it has on her." I snap the book shut. "What the *fuck* is this?"

His lips thin. He goes quiet.

"Answer me, James."

When he speaks, his voice is dark and cold. A stone dropped down a well. "I can't."

The way he says it—it chills me to the bone.

This is a fear that wraps its fingers around my throat and squeezes.

"Is this a game to you?" I ask. "Reading my diary? Learning

all the right things to say so—what? So you can get my inheritance? Well, the laugh is on you because he left me jack shit. No—you know what? Take the paperweight. All yours."

I spin around. My head feels light on my shoulders. I can't catch my breath.

You're in a nightmare. A terrible, insane nightmare.

Wake up.

Wake. Up.

As I rush down the stairs, I text Ransom.

Need you. Now.

"Claire."

I ignore James's plea. I grab my jacket.

When my hand touches the doorknob, he grabs my arm. His grip is so tight it reminds me of his strength. What he's capable of.

What *is* he capable of?

Have I ever known him, really? The man in my bed.

"You're in danger," he says. His voice is low, intense.

I meet his gaze. Those blue eyes.

I want to pluck out those blue eyes.

"Yes," I say plainly. "I'm in danger of breaking your nose. Get your hand off of me."

My father couldn't lock me up.

I'll be damned if I let my fiancé try.

There's a beat of silence between us. Then James relaxes his fingers.

I rip away from him and exit the house. The stone steps are cold under my bare feet.

Ransom is there. *Thank God.* Sitting on top of Chaucer like a knight.

He failed to run away with me once. But he's here now.

My heart cracks open and spills warm, honeyed relief

through my body. My body seems to register that I'm safe now, and my knees go weak and nearly buckle.

It takes every last bit of strength to reach him.

"You came," I say.

Ransom looks down at me. "You asked me to. You alright?"

I shake my head. "Get me out of here."

He reaches down. I clasp his strong forearm.

He hoists me up. I climb into the saddle behind him and wrap my arms around his strong middle. He clicks his tongue, and my legs squeeze the leather of the saddle as Chaucer takes off, his hooves clicking on the walkway.

I glance over my shoulder only once. James stands on the porch, his form getting smaller and smaller in the distance.

And then, the strangest thing. When we exit the mouth of the estate, breaking free from the iron gates, I notice a black car waiting on the side of the road. For a second, the headlights flicker on and off again.

23

CLAIRE

We ride in silence.

Chaucer's hooves click along the pavement, then thump down a dirt trail that cuts between the Preacher and Dagney properties. Ransom hooked a lantern to the saddle to help guide us, but even in the dark, Chaucer knows his way.

Ransom's body is strong and solid in my arms. He's like hugging a tree—thick and hard—and I rest my cheek on his back and inhale his scent.

We pass a familiar sight—a length of cornfield—and I say, "Stop."

He pulls on Chaucer's reins. I slide down first, and then Ransom gets off next.

The cornstalks shiver and rustle. They've set up an elaborate maze, decorated with fairy lights for the Belleflower Festival. Like a moth, I find myself drawn to the lights. I follow them, letting the corn maze swallow me whole.

The ground is soft, broken with the occasional scratch of fallen stalk. Crickets sing. Ransom follows behind me, letting me lead the way.

During the Belleflower Festival, there will be kids playing in here. Families. But at midnight, it's just the two of us.

The maze drops us into a clearing. There's a gazebo, tangled in ivy and drenched in the soft glow of string lights.

I'm spinning out underneath the nighttime sky. My lungs are so tight, and I can't catch my breath.

My chest feels so empty I want to kneel on the soft dirt, rip my rib cage open, and shove cornstalks inside the hollow space just to feel something rattling around inside of there.

I enter the gazebo. I squeeze my eyes shut. I slip my fingers into my hair and grip until it hurts. I want to pull it off my skull.

Gently, Ransom's hands slip over my wrists. He guides my hands behind my back. His big hands wrap around my wrists, holding me in place.

"This okay?" Ransom says.

A tickle of comfort in my chest. "Yes."

This was our thing. I'd get overwhelmed and self-destructive. Ransom would tie my hands back until the episode passed.

I'd forgotten how much I needed it until this second.

With my back to him, lost in this private maze, there's an uneasy truce. An openness between us.

"Did he hurt you?" Ransom asks.

I shake my head. "No. Nothing like that."

Ransom holds my wrists. The tightness feels good. It feels healing.

I'm a moth that's climbed back into my cocoon. I'm too tired to be a butterfly anymore.

"What was Daddy like?" I hear myself ask. "In the end."

"Paranoid. Thought everyone was out to get him."

"Maybe it's a curse, you know? Preachers can't trust anyone."

"You can trust me."

I suck in a breath between my teeth. "That's rich, after tonight."

"You mean with Jade?"

I yank my arms. He releases me. I turn so I can face him. In the flickering lights, those brown eyes look haloed in gold. "Ransom. The other night, in the stables, you spun pretty poetry about how you only have eyes for me. And now I hear you're some playboy, *Wiley Riley*, fucking married women—?"

His jaw sets. "It ain't like that."

Angry heat licks my chest. "You made a promise."

"You got engaged."

"Yeah. After you *abandoned me*." Rage makes my throat tight. The backs of my eyes sting. "You promised it would be only us."

He shifts, uncomfortable on his feet. "I made a promise you'd be the only woman I'd make love to. And...*technically*...I ain't broken that promise..."

His words whip through me. "Stop. Immediately. Stop talking before you put pictures in my head you can't take back."

Like a smart boy, Ransom shuts up.

I pace the gazebo. I want to tear at myself. I growl, "I hate it here. I hate Belleflower. And I hate you. The sight of you. The smell of you. Every goddamn thing about you that gets under my skin."

I shove his chest, but he grabs me suddenly. He takes me by the arms and yanks me in so my body is flush against his. I have no choice but to meet his gaze now.

Just having him close makes the tips of my fingers tingle.

"You've got it twisted." His voice is low. Serious. "Stop raging for a second and listen. I'm not a playboy. I don't go after married women for the sport. I do it because they don't ask anything of me. I've got nothing to give. Nothing. I can't belong to them because my heart already belongs to you. So I go with women who have a family. Who have a husband and a life. Because I will never be that for them. I won't ever be anyone's husband or the father of their kids. I found my one. That's it. That's all it is for me."

I'm shivering. My teeth chatter.

Not from the cold but from the pure, undiluted adrenaline whipping through my veins.

I curl my fingers in his shirt. I inhale deeply.

Earth. Embers. Home.

Riley Ransom is my own personal calming scent. One deep breath and my feet are on firmer ground.

I rest my head on his chest. "I feel like I'm losing my mind," I whisper.

His thumb rubs against the base of my skull, the pressure dissolving a headache pinching the edges of my vision. "If you lost it, we'll find it together."

"James will—"

"You don't gotta make any decisions about James right now." Ransom cradles my head in his hands, and he tilts my chin up gently. Those chestnut eyes look down at me. "You don't gotta make *any* decisions at all."

A strand of hair sticks to my lips. He brushes it off. His hands are so big, and I feel protected in them.

Ransom lets out a sigh. "You carry so much, princess."

"Someone has to."

"So let that someone be me." He drops his forehead against mine. I close my eyes. The air is mixed with autumn and Ransom. His hands drop to my arms, and he squeezes me there. "I've got you," he says, and I believe him.

Oh, God. I believe him.

Before I can second-guess myself, I take his face in my hands and pull him in.

His mouth presses against mine. The prickles of his stubble scratch my cheek. Ransom is hard and rough in every inch of his body.

But...

He's gentle with me.

He unlocks. Our mouths meet, and I open to him. He's hot and intoxicating, and when he kisses me, my chest isn't full of thorns anymore.

My heart is a seed. Planted, rooting in the deep, warm earth that is Ransom.

I crave him. Years of longing crack open inside of me and spill out. I need more of him. I need his heat. His raw body against mine.

The way he kisses me, he needs it, too.

This isn't the shaking, sweet boy I used to know.

This man is strong, and confident, and he takes what he wants.

Me.

Our bodies crash against the railing, and it's a miracle the old bones of this gazebo don't crack underneath us. I rip at his shirt, eager for the hard, warm flesh underneath. His body presses against mine, and I nip at his throat as I run my fingers down those hard, strong muscles, made tight with the backbreaking work he does day in, day out.

But when my hands pull at the buckle of his belt, he stops me, cuffing my wrists in his grip. "Hold up," he says. "Slow down."

My throat squeezes. *You idiot, Claire.*

You're five years too late.

"I'm sorry," I blurt out. My voice hitches on the words.

Something has broken inside of my chest, and it burns the backs of my eyes.

"Oh, God. I'm so sorry."

"Hey." Ransom takes my face in his hands. I hate the heat that burns my cheeks. His thumb brushes my tear away. "Dammit, woman, you make me dizzy," he sighs. His forehead drops against mine again.

For a second, we breathe together in the silence. And ache. This longing is like a third heartbeat pounding between us.

Then, beyond the bubble of our little gazebo, we hear, "Bit late to be wandering about, isn't it?"

The presence of strangers makes my bones turn brittle. Two men walk through the maze, entering our little clearing.

What are they doing here?

It's late. And there's no reason for anyone to walk this way...unless you intend to neck in the gazebo.

And they don't look like they've come to neck.

Something about the way they're looking at us makes my blood go cold.

I quickly turn away. Strangers don't get to see me cry. I lock it up, pushing back my tears.

"You're on private property," one of them says.

"Yes, sir," Ransom replies, ever congenial. "Sorry about that. We'll be on our way."

"Is that Claire Preacher with you?"

Fuck me.

I turn and peel on a smile. "Hi. We're just leaving."

"Ma'am." He tips his hat. "Where's that fancy husband of yours?"

Needles tickle my skin.

This feels very, very off.

"We're just having a conversation," Ransom butts in.

"Uh-huh." A leery grin cuts across his face. "How about that?"

My stomach is churning. *Fuck them.* Fuck this whole town and their puritanical mindset.

"Have a good night," I tell them, clipped. Which is Southern for *go away now*.

"Actually, Ms. Preacher, we're all about to have a very bad night." Then he takes a pistol out of his holster and aims it at Ransom. "You're coming with us."

24

CLAIRE

I can't move.

One second, I'm spilling my secrets and kissing the man who I despise as much as I love.

The next...

We're surrounded.

The man in the black hat steps forward, extending his spindly leg across the gazebo steps. He twists his lithe frame to a dramatic bow. He outstretches his hand and wears a smile that looks like it's been carved into a Halloween pumpkin.

"Miss Preacher, let's not make this any harder than it has to be. You're coming with us now."

Immediately, Ransom wedges his body in front of mine. His hand touches my waist, holding me back. "What do you want with her?"

That smile sends a shiver through me. "'Fraid there's a debt that needs settling. Nothing personal."

I rear up. "Leave before I have the authorities called."

He takes off his hat and puts it to his chest like an apology. "Darling, they're not going to get here in time to save you."

That sends a chill through me.

Who are these people?

Ransom acts first. He launches himself at Black Hat, throwing his weight into the other man. As the two scrabble, Black Hat's companion locks eyes with me.

I try to move backward, but I only hit the back of the gazebo. *Shit.*

He rushes forward, grabbing me by the arm. I throw my elbow into his face and get a satisfying yelp. When he loosens his grip, I grab onto the railing, shove my foot in the bottom, and start to leap over it. But I'm not quick enough. He grips my waist and yanks me back. The air wheezes from my lungs when my back hits the ground. He's on me, but I don't make it easy for him. I kick and hit, throwing my limbs at him.

He sits on my hips. His weight crushes me, and he grabs my wrists, using his strength to pin me back.

"Settle down, lil' lady," he sneers. "You're damaging the goods."

The...*what?*

Limbs bound, I do the other thing left.

I spit at him.

The glob of spit hits him right in the eye. He squints, then gives a low, menacing chuckle. He fits both of my wrists into his hand so he can wipe his eye clean.

"You're going to regret that," he says. Then he grabs me by the hair.

The pain is blinding as he uses his grip to yank me to my feet. My scalp is on fire, and I shout, clawing at his wrist.

But I go still when I feel the hard kiss of metal against my cheek.

The hedges rustle. Two more men appear through the maze's entrance. They surround the gazebo. All of them are holding pistols.

Ransom and Black Hat stop scrambling. Ransom got a couple of good licks in, it looks like, by the state of the other man's face. But he freezes in place when he sees that we're suddenly, woefully outnumbered.

Black Hat wrestles out his own gun. He pushes back his hair, smearing his own blood in the process, and points his gun at Ransom.

He pants. "On your knees, cowboy."

My heart is beating out of my chest. Ransom looks at me, and there's nothing but calm in his gaze. "It's okay, Claire," he says.

"Let him go!" I snap. But when I try to move to him, my assailant wraps his arm around me, binding me tightly against his body.

"It's you we want." His breath is hot against my ear. "You should've come alone. Now you get to watch your boyfriend die."

This isn't happening. That's all I can think as I watch with a weird, out-of-body feeling as Ransom slowly lowers himself. His knees hit the dirt, and my stomach lurches.

Black Hat aims his pistol right at Ransom's head. "Any last words?"

Ransom's jaw goes tight. "Look away, Claire."

"No."

"Goddammit, Claire! Quite being stubborn for once in your life!"

"I hate you!" I shout at him.

He chokes out a laugh. When Ransom looks at me, it doesn't matter. It doesn't matter that we're surrounded by gunmen. It doesn't matter that our lives are hanging on by a thread.

When Ransom looks at me, it's like I'm the only person in the world.

"I hate you, too," he says affectionately.

The words fill my chest and make it so tight I can't hardly breathe.

There's a click as Black Hat pulls back the safety on his gun. Suddenly, I'm screaming. I scream and claw and struggle. I scream for Ransom. I scream for help. I scream for him to *get the fuck up* because we sure as hell aren't going down like this.

But he won't move. He won't budge. Black Hat presses the barrel to his forehead, and Ransom just closes his eyes, grits his teeth, and his lips move as he murmurs something quietly under his breath.

And then the gun goes off.

Or, rather, *a* gun goes off. Because Black Hat's head suddenly jerks back unnaturally. His hat tumbles off his head, and a small, black spot grows between his unseeing eyes.

He's dead before he hits the ground. His corpse collapses with a soft thump.

My breath shudders.

Even my assailant gasps. "What the—?"

He doesn't get to finish his sentence, though, before another buzz rips through the air. His head jerks back, and he loosens his grip on me as death takes him, too, pulling him down to the ground.

I scramble out from underneath his limp body and run forward. "Ransom!"

He gets off his knees. He's wonderfully, beautifully still

in one piece, and I find my hands touching his chest, his face, to make sure he's really alive. "Ransom..."

He grabs my shoulders, holding me close. His eyes aren't on me, however. They're scanning around, hunting.

We're still outnumbered. The two other men surround us, but they suddenly seem less interested in us and *more* interested in the mysterious gunman no one can see.

That's when they start firing.

At the corn. At anything that moves.

Ransom wraps me tightly in his arms, shielding me with his body.

It's hard to understand exactly what I'm seeing.

One of the gunmen screams as he's yanked back into the maze. The stalks themselves seem to swallow him whole, and suddenly, the screaming stops.

Now, there's only one man standing.

He looks at us, and I see the same fear in my heart reflected in his eyes.

Now's our chance.

Black Hat's gun lies only a couple of feet away from us.

I push away from Ransom and grab the gun from the ground. I lift it, pointing it at the man.

My hands are shaking, but my voice is hard. "Go," I demand. "Leave. Now."

But he doesn't leave. Instead, he turns his head back and forth like a spooked horse. "Who the hell is out there?" he shouts.

I *feel* him before I see him.

Someone behind me.

No. Not *someone.*

A body I know well.

"Don't move," James says. His breath tickles my ear.

His tall body presses against mine. My breath catches in my throat.

He puts his hand around mine. Like a puppeteer, he lifts both my arm and his. He directs the gun toward the last man standing. Before the other man can ever lift his weapon, James slots his finger against mine and presses in, pulling back the trigger.

The gun bucks in my hand. The shot lands perfectly between the other man's eyes, and he falls to the ground.

It's a strange, uncanny feeling. My soul leaves my body.

The gun feels like hot hell in my hands. I quickly yank my fingers away from it and spin around to look at him.

James. It's James, but it's not-James. He wears James's tall build. James's cropped, dark hair. James's neat clothes.

But that hard look in his eyes. That's not the man I know.

That's not my fiancé.

He carries the gun in his hand.

He looks at me, and his voice is unbearably calm but firm. "There may be more," he says. "We have to get you out of here."

Then he extends his hand to me.

I can't stop staring at it. Around us, the air is tinged with the metallic smell of blood.

The veins in his arm. Those long fingers that cradled my face. Those fingers that, seconds ago, guided me to end a life.

The silver engagement band around his finger.

None of it seems real.

"Claire." He says my name, and his voice rings in my ear. "Come."

But I can't.

I won't.

Instead of moving forward, my feet step backward.

Away from this demon that's swallowed my fiancé whole.

But the second I step back, my knees give out. I take in a breath, but my vision swims.

Someone says my name, but I don't know who.

Ransom. James. The demon.

I can't tell because I'm falling, and the darkness wraps me in its arms and takes me down.

25

CLAIRE

T *hen.*

I HANG my head between my hands and close my eyes. The steam from the cup of tea tickles my nose and warms my face.

I know that when you live someplace long enough, you're supposed to acclimate to the climate.

Three years in and I haven't. Instead, my soft, Southern skin reacts to Europe like an allergy. My face is cracked and rough. My lips are peeling. I've broken out in stress hives. Nothing is the way it was supposed to be.

So much for dreams of bon-bons and French wine.

My Parisian dream has turned into a Parisian nightmare. The worst part of it all is that I can't admit defeat. I'm too deep in it now, and I'll keep kicking this dead horse until it kills me.

And it might kill me.

My aunt has made it clear she won't tolerate indulgences of self-pity under her roof, so I have to lick my own wounds in public.

This little café has become my small escape.

I slip my fingers through my hair and look around. A couple is enjoying a cupcake between the two of them. A family of tourists counts out their coins on the counter. A man in a dark peacoat is flipping through his iPad.

One thing I like about Parisians: they don't care. No one cares that I'm in the middle of a mental collapse. No one bothers to come check on me.

They leave me to suffer in peace, which is how I like it.

At least, that's what I tell myself as I sniffle in public.

The peacoat stands. He collects his suitcase, goes to the counter, thanks the barista in French, and leaves a tip before leaving.

It isn't until the bell chimes that I realize that he's left his book behind.

I get to my feet to run the book to him. If I can do one good deed today, maybe that'll make getting out of bed worth it.

But when I see the cover, my breath catches.

It's a weathered paperback copy of *The Sacred Stallion*. The first book in the *Wild Hooves Chronicles*. The cover has one of those old-school, thrift store–style watercolors of a horse rearing up against a sunset.

I used to devour these books when I was a little girl.

Page after page of animal fantasy. I spent hours escaping into a world of wild, anthropomorphized horses that had their own culture and politics. Herds clashed, heroes fought hard, and good always, *always* prevailed.

It was all a bit silly, maybe, but even now, when I'm far

too old to be holding on to little-girl fantasies, I find myself getting sucked back in.

These books faded out of existence in the States. You could only find the rare copy, bruised and battered in a thrift store, a charming picture of the English teacher turned author in her eighties updo on the back.

What are the chances I'd run into this book here?

Before I know it, I've taken the seat, and I've completely forgotten about my bad mood. Instead, I'm cast away into the epic, fantastical world of wild horses.

I barely hear the bell chime as the café door opens and shuts.

"Engrossing, isn't it?" a deep, British voice asks, and I nearly drop the book.

Peacoat is looking down at me, a small smile lifting the edge of his mouth.

"Sorry, I was just...I love these books. Or I used to. When I was younger." My cheeks get hot. A grown woman caught reading a middle grade novel. I need to be euthanized.

I nudge the book toward him. "This probably belongs to your child."

He touches the cover. He has large hands, with fingers that touch both corners of the book, adjusting it to line up with the table. "It doesn't. It's mine."

I blink at him. He has black, curly hair. A clean shave. A nice, crisp suit. He looks like he stepped off the cover of a *Fortune* magazine...not the type of man to be caught dead reading middle grade animal fantasy.

I tell him, "No one writes about—"

"Heroes anymore," he finishes my thought. "I know."

Those blue eyes meet mine. I'm burning again, but this heat rides lower.

He pushes the book back toward me.

"Hold on to it. It should be in the hands of someone who loves it."

"But you're reading it."

"I've read it already."

"Still. I have a copy at—"

I almost say it.

Home.

But the Preacher Ranch hasn't been my home for three years. And it won't ever be again. My tongue stumbles over my words.

So why do I still find myself reaching for it like an amputee trying to scratch a phantom limb?

My handsome stranger cocks his head. "Can I get you a tea?"

"I have a cup."

"Then what would be an acceptable way to convince you to spend more time with me?"

I can't help the smile that lifts my lips. My skin, no longer used to the sensation, feels tight at the edges of my mouth. "You can sit."

He does. I extend a hand. "Claire Preacher."

"Claire." He says my name like a prayer. He takes my hand. "James Calloway."

26

CLAIRE

Now.

THROUGH THE THROBBING pressure of my headache, the muddled sound of arguing comes into focus.

I'm lying across the hard leather of my father's couch.

There are voices. Two voices, arguing back and forth.

"—can't stay here. It's too dangerous."

"The way I see it, seems like danger follows you around like a goddamn stray cat on a fisherman."

"*Quiet*," I say, and they shut up.

Ransom crouches down in front of me. "You okay? Are you hurt?"

I don't answer him. I'm too busy watching James.

James looks at his phone. He answers a call with a "Yes" and then steps out of the room and into the kitchen to take it.

"Water?" Ransom continues. "Tea?"

I get to my feet and follow James as though there's a thread pulling me with him.

My heart pounds in my ears as I push the door open.

The kitchen is drenched in white. James has his back to me. He's touching his ear.

"—She's compromised," he says. His voice is low, serious. "I need a safe house."

I push myself onto my tiptoes, snatch the earbud from his ear, and fit it in mine instead.

"Hello?" I say quickly. "Who is this?"

I hear nothing on the other end. The other line disconnects immediately.

James turns to me. He holds open his palm. "Claire. Give it back."

I drop the earbud on the ground, fit it under my shoe, and press down until I feel it crack.

James's lips tighten. "I wish you hadn't done that."

"Who are you talking to?"

"Someone who can help us."

"*Who*?" My eyes scan him. "Who are you?"

"You know me, Claire."

"No. My fiancé is a boring stick-in-the-mud whose idea of a wild Friday night is a 500-piece puzzle. I just watched you kill four men without batting an eye."

His gaze is measured, his tone cool. "I trained up in self-defense. I suppose it came in handy tonight—"

"No." My voice is brittle, and it cracks. "No more lies, James. No more games. Try again."

He says nothing. He just stares at me like I'm some animal that's gained the ability to speak.

The kitchen door opens again, and Ransom stands in it. He glances between us, caught in a standoff. "Everything okay in here?"

Beside me is a stovetop and a block of knives. I pull one of the knives out by the handle and point it at James.

Ransom sucks in a breath. "Claire. Goddammit. Put that thing down."

James doesn't even flinch. Those blue eyes just watch me with passive curiosity.

Yelling, I can handle.

Anger. Sadness. Passion.

I can take it.

But James's glacial indifference is more than I can bear.

So I turn on the only thing he's ever cared about.

I turn the blade and hold it to my throat. *That* gets the desired response. A brief, momentary flicker of fear in his eyes. "Tell me who you are," I say, "or watch me bleed out. Your call."

James takes a single, slow step toward me. All my muscles go rigid. Suddenly, his hand whips out, and before I can react, he has my wrist in a tight grip.

"Claire." There's a deep, dark edge to his voice that swoops through my belly. "Never hold a weapon unless you intend to use it."

The knife is cold on my throat. With his hand on my wrist, he guides it closer. The blade presses deeper, stinging my skin, and I gasp.

"Get the hell away from her," Ransom growls.

Ransom starts toward us, but James says, "Be a good boy and stay put."

Ransom stops. I don't blame him.

I would, too.

James's eyes are locked on mine. Those blues are so cold, so compassionless, and I can't wrap my head around it.

"This," he says, "will only slice your trachea. You'll live, but you'll breathe out of a tube for the rest of your life." He guides my wrist, shifting the blade to the side of my throat. I can feel my pulse pounding against the thin line of the knife. "If you want to die, you cut here," he explains as simply as if he were reciting words from a dictionary. "Your carotid artery..." He guides the tip of my knife down my belly until it's resting right underneath my breasts. "Or the heart." And the knife travels lower still. The pointy blade scrapes down the center of my body, down my pelvis, and then nuzzles between my legs. He presses the flat of the blade to my thigh. "Or here. Your femoral artery. A slow way to bleed out, but without quick intervention, effective all the same."

His breath hits my cheek. Then, his voice drops to a low whisper. "Am I still boring you, Claire?"

His accent. It's gone. No trace of the British gentleman I once knew.

There's nothing but this hard, dark, American voice now.

He releases me. I'm shaking. I drop the knife, and it clatters to the floor.

Ransom goes to me. He puts an arm around me protectively. His hand pushes my hair back, inspecting my throat. "You okay, princess?"

If he cut me, I don't feel it.

I don't feel anything but this heavy ice in my chest.

"Meeting you," I say, "that day in the café. It wasn't an accident."

James grips the granite island to steady himself. He stares at me.

"No," he admits. "It wasn't an accident."

"You were waiting for me."

"Yes."

"Why?"

"I'm a special agent. I work for an organization that takes missions no one else will. Your father hired me to keep you safe."

There it is.

The truth that turns my entire body numb.

I can't feel anything except this blood rush, this red heat that flames over my face.

He's been lying to you the entire time, and you were too self-absorbed to see it.

"You. You're Semper Fi. You're the one he's sending this money to."

"Yes."

Knowing I'll get the real answer now, I ask again, "Who are you?"

James—no, the man-formally-known-as-James—straightens up. He leans his tall body against the kitchen counter, turning to face me. He rakes his fingers through his hair and when those blue eyes meet mine again, I don't know who, or what, I'm looking at.

"My name isn't James," he says. "It's—"

27

EVERETT

T *hen.*

"Everett Hollow."

There is a small fleck of lint on my trousers. I pinch it off and let it fall to his very nice rug.

My job as a Wolfpack Special Forces Operative is to be invisible.

But like Hansel, I itch to leave little breadcrumbs of myself everywhere I go, as though I'm daring someone to find me.

I pry my gaze away to turn my attention to the man behind the desk.

Mr. Preacher is an impeccable man tucked in a tailored gray suit. The curve of his white mustache is impressive.

His polite smile twists. I sense he's irritated with me.

"Yes?" I ask.

He mimes plucking something invisible out of his ear—

a gesture encouraging me to remove my earbuds. "Do you think you can remove those so we can talk?"

Currently, my earbuds are filtering in a soft, rhythmic low-fi. If I disconnect it, I'll be forced to withstand the irritating click of the ancient grandfather clock in Mr. Preacher's office.

I inform him, "No."

His expression goes slack. I gather he's unaccustomed to the word.

What would Mr. Schilling say? *You get more bees with honey than vinegar.*

"Mr. Hollow—" he protests again.

Mr. Preacher has a syrupy, old-world, Deep South accent. An accent reserved for Civil War reenactments.

I've trained myself into a neutral accent, but when my vocal cords relax, there is a Kentucky grit that I can't get out. Like sand.

But I have an ear for accents. I pay attention to the way he accentuates the consonants in my name.

Huh-AL-oh.

I try to smooth the ground with, "Call me Everett."

Mr. Preacher fixes his expression and presses on a waxen smile. "Everett, then. Are you listening?"

"Yes, sir."

"Because this is important. This is my daughter, after all. We haven't spoken in...some time...but she is my only child, and if anything were to happen to her, well..."

He runs his hand over his mouth.

He is composed. A powerful figure. But his hands are trembling.

"That's why you hired Wolfpack," I tell him. "We're the best at what we do. As long as Claire is under my protection, she'll be safe. You have my word."

His mustache relaxes.

"They're after me," he says. "They want my fortune and my legacy. When I'm done for, they'll turn to Claire next."

"*They?*"

He pets his mustache again. His irises go unfocused. There is an edge of madness to this man, and I feel I'm losing him to it. "The society," he says. "They've been trying to kill me for years."

"Why?"

He looks out the window. Searching. "I put myself in debt to them," he says. "A long time ago. Now, they want to collect. They don't want my money. They want my flesh. Claire's flesh. And they won't stop until they find her."

Okay. Let's redirect.

"What does she like?" I ask.

"Who?"

"Your daughter."

He thinks. "Horses."

"*Horses?*"

I'm no good at regulating my tone. I can't control the bite. He shifts uncomfortably. "Yes. Horses."

He's proven himself useless, so I move on to a different tactic. "Does she have a room here?"

He nods. "Yes."

"I need to see it."

He stands. I take his cue and get to my feet as well. He glances up at me, and I don't miss the downturn in his mouth. I have an uncanny ability to annoy people simply by getting to my feet. The height difference between us is staggering. The crown of his head reaches my chest.

I've learned to keep pace a couple of feet away so I don't crowd him.

Before we exit his office, my feet stop at the doorway.

I cast one last glare at the grandfather clock. "You need to dismantle that clock."

His eyebrows furrow. "I'll take it under advisement."

He leads me out of the office and down the hall. We come to a locked door. He opens it but then steps back.

Like a vampire, he can't seem to cross the threshold.

I give him an out. "I'll find you if I have any questions."

He nods tightly, but before he leaves, he makes sure to tell me, "Don't move anything."

I step inside. The air is stale, as though the room has been kept like a museum.

The room is bathed in a soft, purple hue. I close the door behind me. I open the blinds. The light catches on dust, and I crack open a window.

It's quiet in here. I take a breath. I pull out my phone, turn off the music, and turn on the mic.

I touch my glasses. "Do you have eyes?"

"Yes. Eyes and ears."

The smooth voice in my ear is Aaron Schilling—my handler.

The frames of my glasses are fitted with two small, invisible cameras in the screws.

Likewise, my headphones are connected to Schilling's device.

What I hear, Schilling hears. What I see, Schilling sees.

It doesn't always connect directly to Schilling. He's made a point to join me for the preliminary exam of this operation in order to make sure it's a legitimate request. Most of the time, I'll get wired through to one of the remote intelligence agents. While I'm in the field, they're behind a desk, researching my findings, geo-tracking faces, and occasionally quickly searching things like *how to land a helicopter*.

My job is a lot of things. Boring isn't one of them.

"Sweep the room," Schilling instructs.

I make a grid around the room, careful to aim the lenses in every corner so I make sure I'm not missing anything.

People are not unlike puzzles. There are pieces of Claire Preacher scattered all around this room, begging for someone to pick them up and put them together.

On her bedside table sits two photographs in hand-painted wooden frames. One is a picture of a chestnut horse. The second is a picture of small child with straw-colored hair cuddled up to her stern, unsmiling father.

She has posters on the wall. Rows of beautiful women in striking poses.

According to Mr. Preacher, he hasn't seen Claire in three years.

Which makes her twenty-four when she left.

This isn't the room of a twenty-four-year-old. This is the room of a sixteen-year-old.

Which begs the question:

Who, or what, was she hiding?

"Do you really think Oculus is involved in this?" I ask.

"It's a thin lead," Schilling admits, "but right now, it's the only lead we've got to work with."

We've been hunting down whispers of Oculus for years now. Oculus is an organization responsible for, primarily, the black-market trade of stolen goods, drugs, and, occasionally, trafficking people. The deeply secretive organization has fingers spread all across the world.

But why would they put roots in small-town Kentucky?

It doesn't add up.

"What's your read on Preacher?" Schilling asks.

"He has too much money, no friends, and his isolation has made him paranoid. But you know what they say about insanity. The only thing worse than being paranoid...is to be paranoid and actually have someone after you."

"We'll keep eyes on him. I'm forwarding you a plane ticket to Paris now. Leaves in the morning. I need you to watch the daughter. If even a sliver of what he's saying is true, she might be the lead to draw out Oculus."

"The bait, you mean."

"You'll be there to protect her. She'll lead us to Oculus. It's a win-win."

I touch her sheets. The soft, pink fabric is squared into pillowed puffs. I lean in close. Her pillow smells like lavender.

I stand. I go to her bookshelf.

Nancy Drew—both the modernized version and the old, yellow-edged hardback covers. Willkie Collins. Mary Shelley. This is a woman who escapes her life by diving into darkness. But how dark will she go?

I draw a single fingertip over the tops of the books but come to a stop at a familiar one.

I tilt the spine.

"*The Sacred Stallion*. Volume one. I used to love these books."

"Focus, Everett."

When I pull the book out, my knuckle hits the side of the shelf, and the board shifts. It's loose. I press the board aside and find a secret compartment inside. There's a small stash of journals in here. I pull one out and open it. *Her diary*. All her secret, private thoughts jotted down for my eyes only.

I pocket the book. "I have all I need."

28

CLAIRE

N *ow.*

The fireplace crackles and pops.

I watch James—

No.

Everett.

Fuck. My head spins. I have to close my eyes. I take in a breath. Count to three. Exhale.

When I open my eyes again, those blue are watching me.

"I was hired to protect you," Everett continues. "The men who killed your father tried to kidnap you tonight. And they'll try again."

"Why?"

"Your father was in debt to a criminal organization. They call themselves Oculus. Does that mean anything to you?"

I shake my head.

"Well, you mean something to them. They have a

bounty out for you. Your father hired me to keep you safe. Now you know as much as I do."

I'm numb. My entire body is numb.

Everett's dark eyes rest on mine. "This group is professional and dangerous. They won't stop until they have you. In Paris, we were safe. I could hide you. But here...they have the upper hand. They know everything about us, and we still know very little about them. They could be anywhere. Anyone."

I stare out the window. The tall grass ripples like water. Fireflies glow brightly, fade, and then blink awake. Everything outside is dark and silent, and there's a lovely, peaceful calm to it.

I close my eyes. I take in a breath, inhaling it all.

Daddy, what have you done?

I do the math.

Your fiancé does not love you. He's a man who was paid to keep you alive.

Your father does not love you. He put you in danger with a criminal organization.

You cannot trust anyone. They're liars and con artists.

I shake my head. "No."

"No?"

"*No.* I'm not leaving."

I step forward. I stand in front of the-man-formerly-known-as-my-fiancé and tilt my head. I scan his eyes and measure his gaze. I try the new name on my tongue. "Everett Hollow."

He looks down at me. "Claire Preacher."

"You're my protector. Right?"

"Yes."

"So. Stand by the door and *protect.*"

I twist and turn away from him. I grab Ransom's arm and

tug him.

"I'm going to bed. And Ransom is coming with me."

29

RANSOM

I can't tell if I'm the luckiest guy around or the biggest idiot to follow Claire up to her room.

Both, maybe.

The second-floor hallway is a long stretch of wood-paneled walls with a red carpet that stretches out like a tongue.

Every floor feels haunted. I expect Mr. Preacher's hollering to kick up any minute now. The quiet, somehow, is even worse.

Claire has showered. Changed. She's standing on the other side of a huge four-poster bed. The moon is high, peeking through the trees in the window behind her. She's got a soft glow on her from the lamplight as she threads a knot into the cream-colored robe that hangs around her form.

The robe clings to the perky lift of her tits. The slim curve of her hips.

A knot of want tightens around my throat.

Settle down, boy.

Just as I'm backing towards the door, without looking up

from her robe, Claire states, "Where do you think you're going?"

I fit myself in the entrance, leaning against the doorway. "I'm just...not sure if I should be here."

Claire looks in the mirror. Her mouth dives into a tight frown. "Four men tried to kill me tonight. My fiancé may or may not be an assassin. As much as I'm loath to admit it, you're the only one I trust right now. You're not going anywhere."

I can't help it. A bitter chuckle climbs my throat. "You sound like your father."

Her eyes sharpen. "What do you mean?"

"He used to say, '*Ransom, you're the only one I trust. You're too damn stupid to kill me.*'"

"You're not stupid," she says plainly. "You're earnest. To a fault. There's a difference."

She reaches to the back of her head, tying her hair back.

The sheer fabric lifts, and I can damn near almost see the outline of her small breasts.

"Can you handle sleeping in the same bed as me?" Her eyes swoop to my groin and then back to mine, and her voice takes on a condescending edge. "Or is that too much for you?"

A heat rises in me. I cross my arms. "I can handle it," I tell her. Maybe too forcefully.

"Good. There's a man's robe in the bathroom. Help yourself."

"Yes, ma'am."

I go into the bathroom, closing the door. Their bathroom is bigger than my trailer. Big soaking tub, a tall shower, a row of mirrors and sinks. I kick up the shower and drop my clothes. My belt hits the tile hard, and mud on my shoes leaves smudge marks on the white floor.

I get in the shower. It's like a damn sauna. The hot water pelts down on me, and for a second, I let myself get submerged in it.

But that's dangerous because the second I get comfortable, all my dumb brain can do is think about Claire.

Claire, in bed. Waiting for me.

Needing me.

Wanting *me*.

She chose me. That thought alone is enough to make my cock swell up.

I've gotta settle down if I'm gonna be any sort of comfort for Claire tonight.

The temptation to stroke one out to relieve this building pressure is strong, and I curse myself for it. So I flick the water to cold, shiver under it until I'm less riled up, and then hop out and towel off. I find the robe—a matching beige, satin thing—and I toss it on, feeling a little silly in something so decadent.

When I get back in the bedroom, Claire is quiet. She's lying on her side in bed, facing the window. I slip into the spot beside her, pulling up the blankets, which puff up like marshmallows.

"Shower's nice," I tell her.

"Mmhm."

Silence creeps in.

"You okay?" I ask her.

She rolls onto her back. She looks up at me. She's taken off her makeup and taken down her hair. Now, she just looks like—Claire. My Claire.

"I want to go to sleep," she says plainly, "and wake up and find out that all of this was a strange, bizarre nightmare. And...why are you smiling?"

"Sorry. It's nothing. Strange nightmares."

"No, you first. Tell me what's funny?"

"It's not funny. It's just...this is the first time we've ever shared a bed together."

Slowly, she blinks at me. A small smile touches her own lips. "I suppose it is."

"Is it exactly how you imagined it?"

She reaches forward. Her fingers tickle down my bare chest, playing with the hair there. "No."

I draw her hair underneath her ear.

"I wanna kiss you," I tell her. I draw my hand down and press my fingers into the soft skin above her breast. "Right here."

Her fingers curl in my hair. She nods. "Then do it."

I tilt down and press my lips to her skin. I inhale her smell—buttery and vanilla. I want to lick every inch of her, but I refrain.

Instead, I touch her cheek. "And here."

Those eyes flit over mine. "Yes."

I nestle against the side of her face. I draw my lips over the softness of her cheek. Her small gasp patters against my ear.

I draw back just enough to bump my nose against hers. Our lips are so close now. The heat of her breath hits my mouth and makes my skin tingle.

"And here, most of all."

Dark eyes meet mine. She leans in and brushes her lips against mine.

That's all the permission I need to lose control.

I scoop the back of her head in my grip and close my mouth over hers. She exhales a muffled moan against my lips, her shaky breath pattering on my cheek. She parts her lips, and I dive in, my tongue sweeping along the heat of hers. Her fingers coil in my hair, tightening.

It's happening. We're here.

I'm kissing the woman I thought I'd never see again.

Her lips on mine feel like a gift from God, and I'm going to savor it.

Claire isn't passive or submissive. Her lips push back. She slides her tongue over mine. She's curious and bold, and I let her.

I want her to invade me.

I want to be hers.

We can't get close enough. I hold the back of her head up from the pillow and kiss her as deep as I can. Her back arches. Her robe has come loose, exposing her breast, and I can feel her hard nipple graze my bare chest.

I wanna enjoy her. But it's hard when her nails dig into the back of my neck. It's hard when she peppers my mouth with tight, frantic kisses. It's hard when she dances the tip of her tongue skillfully against mine. I grunt, and my hips pull forward.

She's gripping me hard, and her kisses are coming too fast. She sucks, heatedly, at the sensitive skin of my throat, right under my jaw.

"You're wild," I tell her. I damn near don't recognize my voice with all that roughness in it.

"So tame me."

She rakes her claws down my chest, opening my robe. She finds my nipple and works the sensitive spot under her thumb as she pulls my earlobe between her teeth.

"Tie me down," she pants in my ear. "Take me. Make the headboard rattle."

"*Claire.*"

My voice is tight. My head is spinning. My need is so swollen, so full, one more kiss might make me burst.

She's breathless. Her lips are so close to mine I can feel each shudder.

"Make me scream your name," she says. "Let him hear it."

Him.

James. Everett.

Her fiancé.

Fiancé.

Downstairs. Listening.

Fuck. *Fuck.*

Reality hits me like a horseshoe to the head.

I peel away from her and get out of bed. I need distance. It's the only way I'm going to be able to think.

"I can't do this," I say.

Claire sits up in bed. Her hair is a wild tangle. Her robe hangs off one shoulder, small breast exposed, pink nipple peaked. My ache tightens, and I pace.

"What are you saying?"

I shake my head. "This ain't right. You don't want me. You just want to punish him."

Her mouth twists into a scowl. "Jesus Christ, of all times not to think with your dick, Ransom."

I pull my fingers through my hair. "Trust me, both my dick and my heart are screaming at me right now."

"What are they saying? Ransom, *you're an idiot*?"

I stop pacing at the foot of the bed. I wrap my hands around both posts and look Claire dead in the eyes. "They're saying...when you love a woman that hard, you can do better by her."

Claire stares at me. Her nostrils flare and then subside.

She whips herself out of bed, yanking her robe around her chest. "Go to hell."

My mouth tastes like metal. "Classic Claire. The second I open up, you shut down."

"You don't get to use those words with me."

"What? *I love you*? Well, I do! I loved you back then, and I love you just as hard now. Trust me, I tried to get you out of my system. I tried it on every goddamn woman in Belle-flower. But no one could hold a lick of a candle to you."

She gets in my face and snaps, "Then why is it that every time you say *I love you*, it sounds like *I win*?"

"Claire?"

"*What*?"

Her eyes are blazing, her cheeks flushed with pink fire.

I tell her, "You win."

This time, when she kisses me, she's all mine.

He may have her heart. Her ring finger. The last few years of her life.

But, goddammit, I've always had her anger.

I yank the tie on her robe. It hisses as it comes free. I pull her in my arms and we both fall to our knees, and then I push her down so her back hits the floor. Her breath catches, splayed out on the rug underneath me, her eyes wide and wanting.

I wrap the tie around my fist. "You want me, princess?"

Her thighs part. "Yes."

I get low, my knees around her hips. I take her hand. With my gaze on hers, I suck her ring finger into my mouth. Her diamond catches around my teeth, and I slide it free from her hand.

I spit it out. The metal hits the carpet.

"Then show me your hands."

She knows what I want. She puts both her wrists together, holding them up for me. I take the tie from her robe and wrap it around, crossing the satin, binding her in a tight, clean knot.

Her tied wrists fall back above her head. I stand up over her. I drop my robe. Claire's eyes drop to my briefs. There's a dark patch where I've leaked, and she wets her lips. "What a mess you've made already," she says, goading.

I kick her legs apart. She gasps. Her bare, pink cunt is swollen, and it glistens for me.

"Pot calling the kettle wet," I tell her.

Her cheeks go red, but her thighs part a little wider.

I snap my briefs off my legs. I relieve the tight ache in my groin by wrapping my hand around my erection and giving it a squeeze.

Claire would never beg for me. But she doesn't have to.

Her body does all the begging.

She bites her lip. Her throat bobs as she swallows hard.

"This is what you want?" I ask. I stroke it. Slowly.

Her mouth parts. "Yes."

I lower myself to meet her body. Her hips arch. I drive my cock into Claire. She chokes on a gasp, and when her eyes meet mine, there's a flash of surprise in them.

I know: she's remembering.

She remembers now what it's like to be claimed by Riley Ransom.

She remembers how much she loved it.

How much she *loves* it.

Engulfed in her tight heat, I'm already up against my edge, but I'm going to hold on to this feeling as long as I can.

She's going to remember how good it feels to be in love with me.

"Look at me," I tell her.

Her bright eyes lock on mine as I hook her knee in the crook of my arm and push in all the way so our hips kiss.

Her gasp is shuddery.

Those pretty little hands turn into fists, splay open, and fist again. Wanting to touch, clenching nothing but air.

Those eyes close. That's when I see it. A wet streak slides down from the edge of her eye to her ear.

"Bear? You with me?"

"Don't stop," she begs. "Fill me. I want to feel it inside."

I slip my hand into her bound fingers. She grips me back, entwining her fingers with mine.

Something switches in me.

Our palms together, I feel the energy of her. We connect, entwining together. Body and soul. "I'm here," I tell her. "I'm right here." I kiss her. I taste the heat of her. The warmth of her. Those soft, small whimpers.

I pull our bodies together. Riding her. Driving deep. Over and over, until she's trembling. She breaks our kiss to throw her head back and gives the smallest, tiniest whine as her body clenches around me...

Pleasure floods through me and into her. I moan and I fill her, torrents of want. Her hips roll upward, encouraging, riding every wave of it until I've got nothing left.

There's nothing of me that's not hers.

We collapse together on the floor. We pant, catching our breath.

"Claire?" I say after a moment.

"Yeah?"

"We were so close to finally fucking in a bed."

She laughs, a small sound.

I tilt her chin toward mine. Her lips are soft now, delicate as glass when I kiss them. I kiss her mouth and each of her eyes, tasting the salt of her tears.

"Don't pull out," she says. "Not yet."

"Okay," I say, thinking, *I'd stay here forever if she just asked.*

30

EVERETT

I can hear them.

Clawing. Thumping.

Like animals in the walls.

I watch the fire roar, and I imagine what it would be like to be inside of it. Flesh and muscle melting away from bone. Stripped clean of all our mortal follies: love, lust.

Hate.

Not for Claire. I could never hold hate for Claire. After all, this is on me.

I couldn't have shepherded her better into his arms than if I were a dutiful collie and she a wayward sheep.

After all my lies and the deceit...how can I blame her for craving familiar comforts?

How can I fault her for clinging to her former flame, with his calloused hands and his messy hair and his stupid, charming, lopsided smile?

I hold the gun I took from the cornfield earlier. I can visualize the bullet inside of it, sleeping soundly in its chamber. I lift the gun and point it to the ceiling, directing it at the sounds. It clicks when I pull back the safety.

"Boom," I hear myself say.

Then I tuck it underneath my chin. I point it at the noise in my brain. I close my eyes.

"Boom," I repeat.

I press my thumb into the nodule and hear the safety click back on again. Only then do I lower it back to my side.

This is what she wants. To punish me.

My Claire would have made a great swordsman. She knows where to hit where it hurts.

And I don't even have my headphones.

The fire pops. Claire moans. Ransom groans. My molars hurt. Like biting directly into the heart of an ice cube.

I begin to hum. Something. Anything. A song from my youth, maybe. I can't quite place it. But the vibrations in my throat and in my ears soothe me.

The pain lessens. I grip my gun.

I dream about all the ways I'm going to end Riley Ransom's life.

31

RANSOM

Claire sleeps like the dead.

That is, if the dead reanimated themselves and had asthma, maybe. That angelic, sweet face snores loud enough to wake the spirits all night.

I'm not sure when I crash out, but I wake up to an empty bed.

The sheets are crumpled beside me. I run my hand over the space. My fingers remember the heat of Claire's skin underneath them.

The pillow smells like her. Sweet as flowers.

Just the scent of Claire makes my blood rush south.

I gotta get out of this bed now, or I never will.

Claire is sitting up already. She's got a dress on, and she's fixing her shoes on her feet.

"Morning," I tell her.

"Morning." Short. Clipped.

Even the way she laces up her boots turns me on.

The hell is wrong with me?

"We should talk about last night."

Her eyes don't leave her boots. "What's there to talk

about?"

Oh. That's like a double-barrel shotgun to the chest.

Last night, she was mine.

This morning, she's got her armor back on.

That's when I see it. The glint of her engagement ring fixed back on her finger.

My stomach gets all knotted up when I think of Claire waking up early in the morning, getting on her hands and knees to find it in the carpet.

And ain't that me and Claire in a nutshell? Her, fully dressed, fixing her boots. Me, butt-ass naked, hanging in the wind for her.

"Nothing, apparently."

I roll out of bed, take my briefs off the floor, and yank them over my hips.

Her eyes flicker over to me. "Go to your trailer and pick up a few clean clothes. Toothbrush. Whatever you need. You can stick them in Daddy's room."

"You sure you want me to stay here?"

"Of course."

"You could've fooled me."

She starts, "Last night was—"

"Amazing."

"—familiar. You and I. We've always taken care of each other. That's what it was. That's all I have the capacity for right now. If you can't handle that—"

"I can handle it."

"Ransom..."

I take her face in my hand. "I'd rather have a piece of you than none of you at all."

Her breath trembles against my mouth. I tilt my chin down and brush my lips against hers. But she startles suddenly, like a spooked horse. Her hands fly to my chest, and she gives me a powerful shove back.

"Off. We've got things to do."

"Sure thing, princess."

She shoots me a look that would turn a better man to stone. I need to learn how to keep my mouth shut. But the pink in her cheeks...hell. That makes riling her up worth it.

Claire shuts the door behind her. Hard. I pull on last night's clothes, grab my hat, and head downstairs. There's noise in the kitchen, and when I peek inside, I find Claire and Everett dancing around each other. From what I can gather, he's trying to make her a cup of coffee, and she's not having it.

I jab my thumb over my shoulder. "I'm heading to the trailer for a minute."

"Fine," they both say in the same clipped, short tone.

Guess mommy and daddy are still fighting.

I get the feeling that if I hang out any longer, I'll get sent to my room, so I don't linger.

It ain't more than ten minutes to walk from the Preacher house to my trailer. But the second I step outside, there's a bad feeling in the air.

I squint against the blinding sun. Overgrown stalks of grass and cattails stick up like swords from the ground. There's the normal morning hustle—people walking in and out of the stables, taking care of the horses. People I know.

Or do I?

Hard to tell who's friend and who's foe after last night. Fear climbs me like a wayward June bug, little legs tickling the hairs on the back of my neck.

I see my trailer sticking out like an oasis in the distance.

A short jog. That's all it is.

But my feet don't wanna leave the house.

My parents died when I was fourteen on account of

them being "bad seeds," as Grandpops put it. Got themselves in a car wreck after getting drunk and driving straight off a bridge. My grandpops and grandmimi raised me. Which meant a lot of superhero comics, replays of *The Lone Ranger*, and old, dusty movies where the good guys are really good and you can always tell who the bad guys are because they've got these twisty handlebar mustaches.

I wanted so badly to be a good guy, a real hero. Except I grew up mostly afraid of my own shadow until one day, Grandpops pulled me aside and said, "Being scared is *smart*. Just means you know there's danger ahead, but you've got the stones to move forward anyway."

So I guess I'm feeling *really damn smart* when I force myself to step down the brick steps and leave the safety net of the Preacher house.

I walk around the circular gravel walkway. Head down, hiding under the brim of my hat, I veer off the path and through the grass toward my trailer.

"Hey, Ransom!"

My nerves smack me in the face when Dodger, our gardener, steps out and blocks my path.

He's got a grim frown, and all my bones go stiff.

"Yep?"

"Sorry to hear about the old man," he says. He pulls off his hat politely. "Look, I don't mean to be insensitive, but I gotta ask—where's the next paycheck coming from? I'm a day late, and...well."

"I'll get it sorted," I promise. "Don't worry about it."

He grins. "Thanks."

As he walks away, I feel my blood come back into my body.

Is he working for us? Or them?

I'm paranoid, I know it, but I can't help the thoughts racing through me.

Maybe I don't trust this Everett fellow as far as I can throw him, but I sure as hell would feel better with his trigger finger by my side right about now.

I quicken my pace to avoid anyone else. By the time I make it into my trailer, my pits are wet with nervous sweat. I wipe my brow and lock the door behind me.

Alright, Ransom. Focus.

My place is the way it always is: a doggone mess. The bed is unmade. There are clothes and mugs on every surface.

I already feel like a different version of Riley Ransom. Like the Riley Ransom that used to live here doesn't belong to me anymore.

I pull out a bag and start blindly yanking out clothes and shoving them in. I take down a couple of belts. I open my bandana drawer.

Don't everyone got a bandana drawer? I guess not. It's a drawer in the kitchen that's supposed to be for utensils, I guess, or something like that. Instead, I've got my bandanas all tightly rolled up and ready to go. I like picking them out at the start of my day. Blue is my happy, "thank God it's the weekend" bandana. Yellow is my good-luck bandana. Red is for when I'm feeling bold and frisky.

The color am I today? Orange, for the panicking way my heart is rabbit kicking in my chest.

When I touch the bandana, however, I see the dark stain on my sleeve. I twist my forearm and touch it, examining.

Dark. Red. Blood. Not mine.

My gag reflex jolts in my throat. I flip on the sink, pop the buttons off my shirt, and toss it in. The shirt gets dark as it soaks. I squeeze soap on it and rub the shirt hard, but the stain doesn't budge.

I'm cleaning up a crime scene, and I ain't even sure what the hell crime was committed. Still, I can't shake the feeling—

I've done something wrong.

The gun pressed to the side of Claire's head.

The surprise in that man's eyes when Everett put a bullet in his brain.

The way Claire's fingers laced with mine as her cunt gripped me.

The way she moaned in my ear as her engagement ring gleamed from its spot on the rug.

I rip the shirt out of the sink and throw it in the trash. Hell with this.

I pull off my belt, drop my pants, my underwear, and my socks, and shove those in as well.

I wrap up the bag, drop it by the door, and jump in the shower. It's a quick rinse, but it feels good to get yesterday off of me. I towel off, yank on a fresh pair of underwear and jeans, and pull on a dark button-up.

Already, I'm feeling better.

My fingers linger over my bandana choice. No. Not orange.

Blue.

Blue like a clear day. Like a bird's back. Strong, reliable blue.

I twist the ends, wrap it around my throat, and tuck it neatly under my shirt.

We ain't giving in to the fear today.

I toss my bag over my shoulder and head out. Before heading back to the house, I make a quick loop around the property.

Arris Dagney's office is a small, narrow building behind the Preacher house. As our bloodstock agent, in charge of buying and selling breeding horses, he's only ever here a couple times a week, tops. Most days, he's busy with the Equestrian Club and Benefactor's Society. So it's 50/50 when I knock on his door, but I hear from inside: "Come in."

I enter and I'm hit with a blast of AC. He's behind his desk, but he glances up at me when I step in. Even in this ice box, he's got a fan going, and his papers flutter in the manufactured wind.

I take off my hat and hold it. "Mr. Dagney. You got a minute?"

His gaze falls back to his papers. "Ransom. What can I do for you?"

"Some of the men had some questions about their paychecks. Said they were running late."

He scratches his jaw. The scruff makes a rough sound. "I'll get it sorted. Thank you. Remind them that we're shut down for the rest of the week."

"How's that?"

He glances up at me. "The Belleflower Festival."

Right. Keep forgetting about that damn festival.

Everything shuts down for the festival.

Between Mr. Preacher's death and Claire coming back to town and the shitstorm that was last night, I haven't exactly had time to think about a parade.

As if he can read my mind, Arris closes his ledger book. He looks me in the eyes when he says, "Losing Preacher was hard on all of us. Get some rest. When we start back up again, we should talk about your place on the ranch."

I shift my weight from one foot to the other. "Am I getting fired?"

A low chuckle. "You're getting promoted. You really...put

your back into your work here. That kind of loyalty should be rewarded, don't you think?"

The way he's looking at me has me wondering...what isn't he saying?

Does he know something? About Jade? About Mr. Preacher?

I can't tell, but there's a jagged edge to his stare that leaves me uncomfortable.

I play it off. "Well. I'll let you be."

Before I can leave, I hear him ask: "How's Claire?"

I stop, hand on the doorknob. "Surviving."

"She's a fighter, that one. Perhaps she should stop."

"Stop what?"

"Fighting so hard."

The papers shudder and flap.

I exit, leaving him to his work. The Kentucky sun hits me in the face. Something doesn't feel right, but everything's off kilter. Too much to wrap my head around. I head back to the main house.

It smells good when I step inside. Like eggs and coffee. I go into the kitchen. Claire's sitting at the table, brow furrowed at her laptop, fingers tapping over the keyboard. Everett has a plate of breakfast in hand and he nudges it across the table to her.

"Claire," he says lowly, "you have to eat."

"I don't *have* to do anything."

Everett glares at me when I enter the room. Like this is somehow my fault.

"Picked up a couple things," I announce, adjusting the bag on my shoulder. "Where do you want me to put them?"

"Ransom." Claire jumps out of her seat. "Thank God you're here."

Her hand grips my wrist.

Even if it is wrong, even if I am going to hell, it's worth it for that look in her eyes. The relief when she sees me. Like I'm her hero come to rescue a kitten out of a tree.

That's worth a trip to hell, I reckon.

She pulls at my arm. "Come." Like a dog, I follow her. But not after snagging a piece of bacon off her plate—can't let it go to waste, right?

Even if Everett frowns at me for it.

Claire pulls me up the stairs and into her father's old study. Everett, the tall shadow, lurks a step behind us.

"I've been thinking," Claire says. "Daddy kept records of everything. *Everything.* He was meticulous. If he owed someone money or he'd gone into debt or...*whatever the case*...it'll be here. Somewhere."

"Somewhere," I echo.

The study is thick with books. Journals. Record logbooks. Stuffed into shelves, cluttering the desk, piled in corners.

I drop my bag. "Let's get to work, then."

32

CLAIRE

Together, the three of us dismantle Daddy's study.

We empty the filing cabinets and skim through his heavy, dusty ledgers.

"What exactly are we looking for?" Ransom asks. He's sitting in one of the high-backed leather chairs, flipping through an old accounting book.

"Something," I mumble. "Anything."

Daddy has accounting books reaching as far back as the eighties. I've got three stacked on the desk beside me and one open in front of me. In dismantling Daddy's desk, I've found a stubbornly locked drawer (annoying), a stack of unopened mail, and his secret liquor stash.

It only feels right to drink while I work.

I feel Everett watching me.

He keeps trying to feed me, but I can't bring myself to swallow any more of his bullshit. Even if my stomach pinches in protest.

So I have a liquid breakfast instead.

Expensive whiskey. Neat.

Everett crosses the room. His long legs make quick

work of the small space. He stands in front of Daddy's framed Belleflower Queen poster. It's original artwork. Each year has its own unique design. They're collector's items. This is a rare one—one of the first Belleflower Queen posters.

"Your people take the Belleflower Festival seriously," Everett says.

It's still so fucking strange to hear him speak without a British accent.

Everything about him tilts my axis.

I put my whiskey glass to my lips. "Ransom," I say. "Give him the song."

Ransom has one leg folded over the other, the ledger sitting in his lap. As he turns the page, he hums, his voice a low, brassy thing:

"When dawn light played a summer's day,
    Twenty miners went with picks in hand
    Into the yawning mountain's clay
    To earn their backbreaking pay.

"But in the belly of the beast,
    The miners screamed and shouted,
    The mountain trembled and began to feast,
    As rocks closed in and all sound ceased.

"For three days they stood still,
    And choked on smoke and coal,
    Just as they were losing hope and will,
    The darkness broke in burst a chill,

. . .

"WHAT GOOD GLORY did they see?
But a goddess with flowers in her hair,
Who with strong horses three,
Pulled down the rocks and broke the men free.

SO SING the song of the Belleflower Queen,
Who saved the miners from death unseen.
Sooty hands and faces washed clean,
Flowers in her hair, she washed our sins clean."

RANSOM'S VOICE IS LOW, calming. I've heard that song a million times. From the kids at the playground. From my father's own lips, late at night, on the rare moment when I could get an inch of attention from him.

We've piqued Everett's curiosity. "It's an old folklore."

"Sorta," Ransom explains. "It was an old story from the twenties. Miners got trapped. This beautiful woman came out of nowhere and rescued them. No one ever saw or heard of her since. So we throw a celebration for her every year. Honor her."

"Blackdamp," Everett says.

Ransom blinks. "What?"

"Blackdamp. It's an asphyxiant found in mines. Common source of death in mine collapses. When the oxygen level drops dangerously low and the carbon monoxide levels rise, you'll start to feel light-headed. Perhaps even hallucinate. Much like those men did."

"Yeah," Ransom says, his voice sharpening as he get defensive, "or they got saved by the Belleflower Queen."

I hiss between my teeth. "Belleflower Queens. Penny horses. Don't fuck with Ransom and his fantasies."

Ransom narrows his eyes at me. Whiskey makes me mean. I take another swallow anyway.

"Should we put on something while we work?" Ransom asks. "Music?"

Everett perks up. "Music would be nice."

I know he's still sore about his AirPods.

Tough titties. I'm still sore about being lied to for the past year.

"Let's play a game," I announce. "Twenty questions. The objective is to get Everett to tell the truth."

Everett turns to me. Dust hangs in the shaft of light between us. "You can ask me anything. Whatever you want to know."

Ransom watches us. I take another nip of the whiskey as I roll my first question over my tongue. The alcohol has stopped burning. A bad sign.

"Do you have a wife?" I ask.

"No."

"A husband?"

A small flicker of surprise in his gaze. Did he think I wouldn't remember? That soft, intimate night in Paris when I, feeling safe, came out to him as bisexual and he replied, *We have so much in common.*

Did he think I wouldn't hang onto his every word?

Doesn't he understand that this is why *lies hurt* when they come from your fiancé?

Former fiancé.

"No, again," he answers.

"What about family? Parents? Siblings?"

His lips thin. "I grew up in an orphanage. I never knew my biological parents."

"And you're…on a special forces team. Like James Bond."

"Wolfpack Special Operations," he says. "Not quite James Bond."

"You got a pen that turns into a poisonous dart?" Ransom asks.

"No, but my glasses have a camera in them that can record images. My watch doubles as an emergency beacon. If I'm in trouble, I hit the crown and I can relay a message to my team. I hide a revolver in the stitching of my satchel."

I press my lips together. "So why did you take *this* job?"

"I was assigned your case. It's as simple as that."

"And that's all this is to you?" I wave my hand. "A job?"

Everett says nothing to that, so I continue.

"You could have watched me from a distance."

"I did. For a time. But in order to properly keep you safe, I had to be closer."

"Did you have to be *that close*?"

He goes quiet. I can almost *hear* the gears in his brain turning over his answer.

"Alright," he says. "Truths. I like podcasts about history. I love puzzles and crosswords. And, yes. I let you win at pool. In fact, I let you win all the time. Because you're a royal bitch when you lose."

My cheeks go hot. I suck in a breath to argue with him, but he continues—

"You have a temper. You're spoiled. You're the most stubborn person I've ever encountered. You are a lot of things. But you're not *just a job*. You, Claire, are the first thing in my life that ever felt like home. So, yes. I had to be that close. Because any distance between us was physically unbearable."

The pain in those blue eyes. The intensity in his voice. The way that vein in his neck lifts and strains. He seems so sincere.

But, worse, I believe him.

Why, after all the lies, do I still believe him?

I can feel Ransom watching us. Quietly. Waiting to see what I do.

Waiting to see if I go running back to him.

And then, I'm saved by the bell.

Or, rather, the clock.

That old grandfather clock chimes on the hour. Its old ring echoes in a slightly distorted, vibrating sound.

Everett cringes as though he's been stuck.

The chime of clocks, I know, is an auditory trigger. He once described the sound of chimes as the feeling of flesh being ripping from bone.

I hate the clock, suddenly.

I hate the clock that hurt the man who hurt me.

The twisted Stockholm syndrome of it all makes me dizzy.

A kaleidoscope of emotions whips through me. *Sadness. Pain. Guilt.*

And then I settle into the only emotion I've ever been comfortable with.

Anger.

I wrap my fingers around the paperweight stone. I growl, "I hate. That fucking. Clock."

I throw the rock as hard as I can. It hits its target—the clock—which gives a groan and a pop as the face collapses and pins spring free. The glass shatters and scatters to the floor.

But at least the chiming has stopped.

Everett exhales a breath of relief.

"You see that?" Ransom asks suddenly. He gets to his feet. "There's something in there."

Everett goes over to the smashed clock. He reaches into the glass and pulls out the stone.

It's split in half. A clean split. Too clean.

When he takes the rock apart, there's a small key inside of it.

A key...

Oh! A key!

"Give it," I say. I lift my hand. "I think I know where it goes to."

Everett closes the distance between us and hands the key over to me.

I drop to a crouch in front of the bottom drawer on Daddy's desk. My fingers are shaking as I snap the key into the lock and—eureka!

"Claire, wait—" Everett says, but it's too late.

I've already twisted the key and started to pull out the drawer.

But, idiot that I am, I forgot Daddy left his little, lethal traps all over the house.

When I pull the drawer out a quarter of the way, I hear a strange *click* from inside the drawer.

Something launches forward at me. I freeze in place and brace for an impact that never comes.

Everett is behind me suddenly. In his hand, he grips an arrow. The tip of the arrow grazes the hollow of my throat. The arrow, attached to a spring catapult inside the drawer, vibrates in his hand, itching to sink into my neck.

I can't breathe. I can't move. A thin, red line of blood pools in his palm.

Everett's breath is hot in my ear. "Move aside," he instructs me. "Slowly."

Every hair on my body tingles as I inch away. The tip of the arrow lightly kisses my throat as I pass it. It's not until

I'm fully out of the line of danger that I let myself tumble away—and straight into Ransom's arms.

"You okay?" he asks me. His hand cups me under my throat.

"Fine," I say. My words shake.

Everett tilts his body out of the way and then releases his grip. The spring unloads, and it launches the arrow past Everett, sinking it with a thud into the spine of one of Daddy's books.

Everett's eyes meet mine. There a kinetic, dangerous calm in those blues.

"Claire," he says, "I do believe you've found something."

33

RANSOM

We've found a piece of the puzzle.

Or a piece of the piece.

Once we're sure the damn desk isn't gonna try to kill us again, Everett pulls out an old, leather-bound book.

He hands the book over to Claire. She sits on the floor and thumbs through the pages. Her cheeks are soft and pink, and her eyebrows furrow intensely.

"It's a breeding record book," she says. "But the prices are...well. Astronomical. Even our best studs don't go this high. And they don't have names. Only initials."

I look over Claire's shoulder, trying to help her make sense of it. "These don't sound like any of the horses we've got in the stables. You think he was selling on the side?"

"Or he wasn't selling *horses*," Everett juts in quietly.

It takes me a second to realize Claire has gone very still and very quiet. She's stopped at a page, and she's staring down at it.

"What? Did you find something?"

"He wasn't selling horses." Claire repeats. Her voice is so

quiet it's like a whisper. She puts her finger on one of the dates. "Purebred mare. 6.5 pounds. Good health. Sold for two million on June 14th, 1995." When her eyes lift from the page and meet mine, they're blank, big as owl eyes. "My birthday. It was me. The day I was born, he sold me."

Everett moves behind Claire, looking over her shoulder. His eyebrows furrow. "And now they've come to collect."

The air goes still.

The silence only breaks when Claire snaps the book shut. She goes skittering out of the room, stumbling over her boots. She's half crawling, half stumbling when I chase after her. I watch as she shoves through the bathroom door and barely makes it to the toilet.

I can't fix this.

I can't make her old man a good person.

I can't help her wrap her head around the fact that she was sold off like an animal.

I can't tell her any of this is going to be okay.

But I can kneel on the floor behind her, pull her soft strands of hair over her shoulders, and weave it back while she pukes.

She's got nothing on her stomach, but her body heaves anyway. I get up only to wet a hand towel and hand it off. She pats her face dry, flushes the toilet, and leans back into me. She's caved over, and her little body is trembling.

"How could he do this?" she asks.

I pet her back. "He made a mistake. He made a...damn awful mistake. One he must've regretted because he hired Everett to look after you. He wouldn't have done that if he wasn't trying to protect you."

She tilts her chin to look up at me. Those eyes are gentle and watery. My Claire—full of teeth and iron—is caught without her armor. I wanna tuck her away inside of me and keep her safe. "Why the hell do you defend him?" she asks.

I shake my head. "He was a rotten, mean old pain in the ass. He made my life a living hell—and he enjoyed it, too. After how he treated you...well. He deserved anything he had coming to him. I ain't defending him. Just trying to make sense of it."

"There's no sense." Her hand touches her mouth. "Nothing makes sense."

Her body trembles. It's those quiet, hiccupping sobs. I hold her, and she curls tighter into me. Her fingers twist in my shirt, clutching.

"I hate him," she cries. I can feel the wet through my shirt, against my chest. "I hate him, I hate him, *I hate him*."

But I know she means the other thing.

Hate doesn't hurt like this.

"I'm here," I tell her. I kiss her forehead, the damp sweat that's collected there. I pet her back and inhale the scent of her hair. "I'm here."

34

EVERETT

It's been a trying day.

Ransom has assumed charge of cleaning up the pieces of Claire that today's revelations smashed apart. For my part, I'm doing my best to let him.

It's not *me* she wants to see right now.

I understand this very clearly.

Claire has friends, and Claire has enemies. Right now, I'm an enemy. Someone who can't be trusted. I don't blame her for putting a length of space between us.

Even if it takes every ounce of willpower within me not to rush upstairs, peel Claire's clothes off, shower her, and tuck her into bed.

The urge to *care* is a throbbing organ inside of me, split and bleeding and poisoning me internally.

I can't take care of Claire. So I focus on the one thing I do have control over.

My palm is slashed in the middle. Mr. Preacher's trap left a red line across it like a new lifeline. It's a thin cut and I run cold water over it, cleaning it.

I hear Ransom approach. His heavy footfalls. He's the

opposite of stealthy. He hangs in the bathroom doorway, shoulder on the frame. "Need a hand with that?"

I don't reply. He steps inside anyway and gets in beside me. His shoulder bumps into mine as he opens up the mirror, finding an antibacterial.

"Give me your paw," he says.

I hold up my hand. He douses it. The cut stings, fizzes. I hold it steady.

"How's Claire?" I ask.

"Down for the count. She's taking a nap. Think she wore herself out."

There's wrapping tape in the cabinet as well. Ransom takes it out and binds it around my hand, snaking the tape through my finger and thumb and around again.

His hands are calloused and rough, but he works with a surprisingly gentle touch.

Against my better instincts, I find myself letting him.

"Just...gonna say this out loud," Ransom says. "Claire's in danger. The way I see it, we're the only two looking out for her right now. So as far as I'm concerned, between you and me, there's no bad blood."

He snaps off the tape. I touch it.

"How's that feel?" he asks.

The cut throbs, but it's contained. "Fine. Thank you."

"So." Those brown eyes lift to meet my gaze. "What're you thinking?"

"Don't worry, Ransom," I tell him. "You're a semicolon."

He blinks at that. "Thanks. I think. A semicolon. That's good, right?"

I leave him guessing and exit the bathroom.

Claire is asleep. Ransom is lingering. I give myself a task. Because Ransom is right about one thing—Claire is in danger, and we need to be prepared.

Operation: How Many Guns Do We Have In This House?

The answer is: many, but not many that are worth a damn.

Much of the late Mr. Preacher's collection is for show. For example, the double-barreled shotguns hanging above the mantlepiece are covered in dust and rusted. Collector's items, but more likely to blow the user's hands off than reach their target.

So I keep searching, until I reach the basement.

And this is where it gets very exciting because I find his hunting locker.

It's locked, but the lock comes apart easily with a little muscled encouragement. He owns hunting rifles. Shotguns. Pistols.

The Smith & Wesson revolver is a comfortable classic. Not too heavy in my hand. I open the chamber. It'll give me seven shots, so I'll need to make them count.

And then—bless Mr. Preacher—I find a SIG Sauer.

Not unlike what we carried in the Navy. 10mm auto cartridge. Accurate in close range. Good for hog hunting—or, in my case, Oculus hunting.

I carry both guns, a shotgun and a long-range rifle, upstairs with me. I set them out on the dining room table and begin taking them apart to clean and grease them. I enjoy taking them apart. Knowing each piece intimately. Understanding it.

I have to run through these details in my head because I don't have my headphones, and the silence in this house gives me the same sensation of having a thousand needles poking through my skin. Every time there's a new sound—a dog barking in the distance or a clock ticking—the needles tremble and shudder.

I am an exposed nerve.

I stop greasing the weapon when I hear a creak coming from the stairs. I glance up from my spot. Claire is in a soft, pale nightgown. It clings to the small roundness of her breasts and flows along her legs. Her bare feet thump lightly on each step before rounding into the dining room. I watch as she pulls out the chair, takes a seat, and folds her hands in front of her.

I'm glad she sat across from me, not next to me. I need the distance. I need to put a leash on the temptation to reach under her nightgown and feel her soft skin prickle to my touch.

I temper my hands by locking them around the wooden knobs of the chair. "Do you need something?"

Her gaze flickers briefly over the guns. Her eyes are glassy. Her nose is red. She sniffles. "What's all this?"

I chose the least frightening descriptor. "A precaution."

She seems too exhausted to argue. She has something in her hand and she sets it on the table.

"I found these in my bag," she says. "A spare."

She pushes a small case across the table. I thumb it open and find a pair of new, working AirPods inside of them.

Thank God.

"Thank you," I say. I put them aside.

"Aren't you going to put them on?"

"Not now. I don't need them now."

Everything feels better when Claire is in the room.

She watches me. There's a deep, curious intensity in her gaze.

It makes me feel like a dragonfly on a pin.

"Your pancakes smelled...really good this morning. I'm sorry I didn't eat them."

The edges of my eyes crinkle. My heart fucking explodes.

But my tone remains, somehow, neutral. "Stay put," I tell her.

She obeys like a child. I clear the weapons from the table and set them aside. Then I go into the kitchen, wash my hands, and start pulling out pans.

I make Claire three blueberry pancakes, two slices of bacon, two sausages, a mushroom-and-onion medley, and a bell pepper, onion, and cheddar cheese omelet. Then I sit at the table across from her and watch as she carefully uses the edge of her fork to slice the fluffy pancake into small, square pieces.

Each bite she takes heals something inside of me.

I could watch her eat all night.

She finishes her meal in silence, minus the clicking of her fork against the plate. She swallows down half the glass of orange juice. She looks more herself now, her skin rosy and warm, the blues of her eyes brighter.

"Thank you for cooking," she says.

"Thank you for eating. Feeling better?"

She sets the glass down on the table with a soft thump. "I think I'm taking this admirably well."

My body prepares itself by quietly turning to steel. "I agree."

Those gray eyes stare at me from across the table. In the soft lamplight of the night, there are no hard walls between us.

For the first time since my confession—Everett, agent, *Wolfpack*—I feel an openness from Claire. Not anger. Not pain. Her gaze is a quiet, genuine invitation for honesty.

One I am willing to accept. Even if it means removing the mask.

Even if it means being more exposed than I've been in a very, very long time.

"You lied to me," she says plainly. "Thousands of times."

"One thousand, five hundred, and thirty-eight times, to be exact."

She blinks. "What?"

"That's how many times I lied to you."

"You kept count?"

"I was raised in a Catholic orphanage. We were trained to keep score of our sins."

Her gaze measures me. My skin tingles as though her stare were a physical touch.

"I'm a bitch," she states. "But I'm not an unreasonable bitch. You were a man doing a job, and you performed it admirably."

Her tone is cool, but there is no hint of sarcasm in her voice.

So I give an inch. "I lied to you. I manipulated you. And I betrayed your trust. And I'd do it again to keep you safe."

The clock on the fireplace mantle ticks in the silence between us.

Why does Mr. Preacher fill his house with the loudest clocks?

"I don't fault you for doing your job," Claire says plainly. "But moving forward, I'll require complete honesty. No more lies. Even if you think it's for my own good. I've had enough men in my life who lie to me, and I won't tolerate one more. Is that clear?"

Claire is setting boundaries. Making rules. Laying down the foundation for a future between us.

There's a future between us.

My blood goes hot at the prospect of it. "Yes. Crystal."

"Good. Because there is one thing I was curious about."

"Alright."

"How far were you planning to go?"

My tongue recoils from the truth, so Claire continues.

"I mean, eventually, the lies were going to catch up with you, weren't they?" Ever so slightly, her head cocks. My pulse beats along the side of my neck. "We were engaged to get married. What happens on the wedding day? When you go to sign the papers...does James Calloway appear out of thin air? Do you forge a marriage license?"

"Possibly. I hadn't worked out the details."

"I find that hard to believe." She taps her finger against the table. "One thousand, five hundred, and thirty-*nine*."

She's not wrong. Fuck.

I've spent the last year and a half lying to her, and yet still, she knows me too well.

"The plan was to change my name. Legally."

Her eyes narrow. "All that...to protect your cover? Eventually, the job was going to end. And then you've got a new name and a very legally binding contract to your target."

"It's just a name."

Those perfect, pouty lips purse together. I want to kiss them. I refrain. She looks away for a moment, debating her words, and then her eyes return to mine. "You're a lot of things. But you've never been stupid. I need you to be honest with me. Complete, ugly honesty. Where did the job end and the fantasy begin?"

Truths slither like pythons in my throat, entwining and tightening until I can hardly breathe. I turn away from her piercing gray eyes.

Outside, night's fallen. The moon is three-quarters full. It's too bright. It blinds the stars.

"*July twenty-fourth,*" I recite, "*Dear diary. I slept in the barn last night. Daddy found out I've been going to the river to see Ransom. He told me he'd teach me a lesson. I was certain he was going to put Calypso down. I stayed in the stable with her all night. I fell asleep on her body, listening to the sound of her breathing. I'll sleep here again tonight if I have to. I'll sleep here every night. There are worse fates than straw in your hair. Maybe that's how scarecrows are made. Scarecrow? ScareClaire."*

When I look back at Claire, she's wearing a soft, confused expression. "You...memorized my diary?"

"Part of it. You wrote a joke at the end of your diary entry. Why would you do that if you were the only one reading it?"

Her lips purse. "Maybe I wanted to remind myself that I was funny, once upon a time."

"You were an attention-starved young girl in a single-parent household where your only company was a man who wanted a prodigy, not a child. Every entry is a cry for someone to read it. To see you."

I'm compelled to lean forward—to put my elbow on the table, to be closer to her. A magnetic, impossible-to-deny yearning.

"You wrote this wanting to be seen," I say. "I see you, Claire."

Her gaze measures me. "You know everything about me. Everything. Every dirty secret I wrote in my diary."

"Yes."

"So tell me something about you. Something no one else knows."

"How will you know if I'm telling the truth?"

She doesn't bat an eye. "I'll know."

I take my time, considering. And then I start.

"I grew up in an orphanage not far from here. That's why I was assigned the job. Familiar territory. Stone Hollow Home for Boys." I brave her gaze. It's unwavering. "Hollow," I repeat. "It's where my name comes from. When small children are dropped off without a name or note, they belong to the home. The surname *Hollow* is intended to be a temporary fit until you're adopted into your new family. Only boys like me—boys who never got adopted out—got stuck with the name. So when I say it's just a name, I mean...*it's just a name.*"

Claire listens. She doesn't flinch. She doesn't interrupt. She is quiet and considerate, so I pull the truth like thorns from my throat and continue.

"Life at the home was...difficult. Being a child with auditory sensitivity living in a communal space with fifteen to twenty teenage boys at any given time...it's a bit like walking around with a full body rash, only no one can see it, and no one believes you when you tell them you're itchy. So I found other ways to ask for what I needed.

"There was this dragonfly that would hover outside my bedroom window. I told myself that the dragonfly was my friend. When the Sisters asked—well, it wasn't me who didn't like noise—the dragonfly didn't like noise. The dragonfly needed calm. The dragonfly didn't like the cafeteria. The dragonfly was my brother. My friend. My companion. My voice, when I felt voiceless.

"You asked me why I took the job. You asked the wrong question. I *took* the job because of the money. I stayed on the job because...for the first time since my dragonfly, I felt like I wasn't alone."

I reach across the table. I thread those soft, lithe fingers in my own. "Everett Hollow is the fake. James Calloway...he was a real man. With real feelings for you."

Claire looks down at our hands. Her fingers detach from mine, and the absence of her touch leaves me cold as well stones.

But then she rises, walks around the table, and puts her

hands on my shoulders. I swivel my legs toward her, and she sinks down into my lap, straddling me.

She looks me directly in the eyes and says, "I'm not your dragonfly."

"Alright."

"I'm your Claire. I'm a real person. Not a fantasy. I'm tough. I can handle you." Her forehead drops against mine. I close my eyes. Her hair whispers against my cheek. Her breath beats against my skin. "No more lies. No more deceit." She whispers, "Let me know you. Let me know *Everett*."

Her palm falls to my chest and rests at my heart.

Can she feel it pounding through the fabric?

Her head tilts against mine. I can't breathe as her fingertips trickle down my chest. They find the bare skin of my arm. The hair there. They dance along my marked skin— the wolf tattoo that curls around my forearm. She clutches my arm. Pushes her thumb against the tattoo. Tracing it. Learning it.

Learning me.

I catch the back of her head and take her mouth in mine. She melts against me, giving herself. Her lips part, and I take the invitation. I taste the inside of her mouth as my hand slips up her thigh. She lifts her hips, and I take off her pants, pulling them down the curve of her rear, then off her legs. She nestles her sweet body against mine, and she whimpers as she pulls at my belt.

We need this.

She takes my cock out and rocks over me, guiding me inside of her. When she lowers herself down, we both take in a short, tight breath.

Her head curls against my shoulder. "Fuck, James—" She catches herself. "Sorry, *Everett*. I'll get used to that."

I grasp the back of her head. Her soft hair bunches in my hand. I murmur against her mouth, "Call me whatever you want. Name me. Claim me. I'm yours."

She gasps. I use the opportunity to hook my fingers in her mouth.

"Open wider," I instruct.

The problem is:

I know everything about Claire.

Every dark fantasy she penned in her diary. Everything.

I know she acts tough and hard, but secretly, she gets off on being knocked down a peg.

Degraded.

Forced to submit.

She trusted me to take her there when I was James.

But does she trust Everett?

Her blue eyes flare, but then she opens her mouth, accepting my fingers.

That's a yes.

I coax two of them inside, pressing against the soft muscle of her tongue.

"Suck," I demand.

She wraps those beautiful lips around the digits and closes her throat, tugging. It's as though there's a direct line from the pull of her soft lips around my fingers to my cock. I swell inside her, and my blood sings.

"Good girl. Now, ride."

I draw my fingers from her mouth and drop my hand between her legs. My darling is very, very wet. I slip against the crease of her. I touch the space where our bodies meet. I trace her entrance, pleased to feel her stuffed full of me. Her breath shudders against my cheek when I draw my fingers back and find her small, swollen nub. I butterfly my fingertips around that sweet, sensitive part of her.

She rocks over me, gliding against my hand. Her thighs squeeze me, and her arms wrap around my shoulders. Her nails dive into my hair and sharply trace my skin, sending a shiver up and down my spine. She moves with slow, deliberate purpose, chasing her own pleasure with every rut of her hips.

The gentle, rhythmic beat of her breath on my neck twists me open, like turning a lock.

I feel my lower muscles tensing. Wanting. Aching for a release I won't permit.

Not yet.

Not until my Claire has had her fill.

I can't, anyway. Not like this. Her movements are too slow. Too subtle. There is a feral hound inside of me. Something with no home and no discipline. Something that bites the hand that feeds it. Something that can only get off with a hard, deep, animal fucking.

But the gentleman prevails.

The gentleman will wait his turn. Will let Claire crumble and shake to pieces in his lap. Will kiss her, and hold her, and lick her through every wave of pleasure.

The gentleman would spend every second of his life devoted to Claire's pleasure, if she permitted it.

"Ever—" she starts my name, but she chokes on it when I pinch the swollen nub of her clit.

"*Ever.*" I breathe against her neck. "I like the sound of that. Do it again."

Her legs tremble. "*Ever.*"

When she comes, it's a tidal wave. She muzzles her cries into my shoulder. Her body shivers and squeezes me, pulling me with tight, needy pulses.

In this moment, Claire is *mine*, and that thought alone is nearly enough to push me over the edge.

Nearly.

Claire settles her hips so I'm buried in her to the hilt. Her hot core pulses weakly in the aftershocks. A wicked twitch sends a lash of ache through me. She nestles, her small nose nuzzling mine. Her blonde hair tickling my cheek. Those light, rapid breaths slowly resetting against my mouth.

I don't mean to let the dog off its leash. But when she surprises me with a single lick—the tip of her tongue running a path up my lips—the animal growls behind my teeth.

Claire smiles.

"How're you holding up, Ever?"

"Perfect."

She touches my collar, her fingertip tracing the bone there. My entire body is an erogenous zone. "Tell me what you want."

I nestle against her ear. "You. Just you."

"You have me. Take me."

I don't need to be told twice.

I lift her. She gasps when her back hits the table. I claim her mouth and her cunt, pushing my tongue and cock deep inside of her. She whimpers, soft and pliant and open, as I ravage her without grace.

A plate clatters to the ground and crashes. We're going to break the table. Its old, antique legs creak with every brutal push of my hips.

She wants Everett? She'll get Everett.

"Just like that," Claire begs. Her hair is splayed out so far it waterfalls down the other end of the table. Her body bounces with each thrust, her mouth open in half pain, half pleasure. "Don't stop, don't stop, oh *God*, Everett, don't stop."

I close my hand around her throat. I push my thumb

into the side, restricting her air, and she comes immediately. Rapid, needy pulses that must be borderline painful because she tries to writhe underneath me, but I only tighten my grip, trapping her in the prison of her own pleasure. I pound deep inside of her, and then—

I lose control, groaning her name. "*Claire...*"

She kisses me, and I pant in her mouth as I empty inside of her. My beast brain growls for *deeper, more, fill her, fucking fill her*—and this time, I let it win. I clutch her thigh, pushing upward, and bury myself as deep as I can, giving, giving her more. She whimpers into my mouth, and I take that, too, swallowing her sounds.

The world is blue and quiet when we come down. I can hear my blood in my ears, but we're stiller.

The passion is cooling. The beast is satisfied. I can pull myself back into comfortable order now.

But when I start to rise, Claire grabs my face suddenly—

"Stay," she pleads. "Just a second longer."

—as if she can feel me pulling away. As if she can feel the locks turning.

Against my instincts, I allow myself to soften for her.

I stay. The heat of her skin kisses mine. Our lips touch. Gentle now. Nurturing.

I linger here. I let the seconds stretch into minutes. Our breaths, slowly, even out.

She cups the side of my face. A strand of her hair is stuck under her thumb, which she pushes against my cheek.

We're irrevocably tangled.

"Everett," she says softly. Learning me. *Relearning* me. She hums on the name. "I think I like him."

"I think he likes you, too."

She smiles, and my heart smacks into my rib cage.

"Now?" I ask.

She nods. "Okay."

I pull away. I ease out of her and tuck myself away. She sits up. I help her back into her pants, and she takes my hand to get off the table.

She drops a couple of inches and has to lift her chin to meet my gaze.

"Well," she says as she buttons her pants.

"Well."

We have now entered the *where do we go from here?* phase.

"I should clean up." I motion to the scattered remains of Claire's meal and the broken glassware.

"I'll help."

I shake my head. "My mess. My job."

Her mouth twists, but she accepts.

"Come to bed when you're done," she says.

My heart hiccups. But I've locked everything away now, so my voice betrays no emotion when I say, "Alright."

She nods, satisfied, then turns and leaves. I watch her wobble a couple of steps (*I did that*) before she grasps the railing and climbs the staircase.

Come to bed. It's not a marriage invitation. It may not even be an open door. But it's a window, cracked open just enough for me to crawl back into Claire's life.

It's mine, and this feeling is so sweet I can taste it like sugar melting on my tongue.

I'm floating an inch above my body when I clean the dishes. I don't mind picking the pieces of ceramic and food off the floor. I don't even mind the skin-ripping, clinking sound the broken shards make as they clatter together in the bottom of the trash bag.

I can endure it. I can endure anything right now.

I can even endure the dumb, irritated look on Ransom's face when I enter the bedroom.

He's tucking away his bandana on the nightstand. Claire is at the edge of her bed in her robe, which parts slightly as she reaches over to moisturize her legs.

Like a child, he looks at me, then at Claire, then back at me again. His face pinches.

"What's he doing here?"

"I invited him," Claire says. Long blonde hair cascades over her shoulder as she rubs moisturizer over the soft curve of her strong calves.

Ransom blinks. "You kicking me out?"

"No," Claire says as though it's obvious. "There's room enough for three. Move over."

Ransom gives me a dubious look. Then he pulls up his legs in bed and leans his broad body against the headboard. "Long as I ain't middle spoon."

Claire slides her body into bed. She folds back the edge of the sheet, inviting. I get in behind her and wind my arm around her soft belly. She curls herself into the crux of my body, her silk robe against my chest, her hair tickling my throat.

Even after our foray in the living room, I start to awaken.

She lifts her swan neck to glance over her shoulder at me.

"Can you keep your hands to yourself?" she asks me.

Her hair shivers in the wake of my exhale.

"Let's find out."

Across the bed, Ransom's eyes catch on mine.

I hold his eye contact as I kiss Claire's shoulder.

"G'night, crazy kids," he says.

He reaches over and turns out the light, swathing all three of us in darkness.

35

CLAIRE

The morning breaks over the bed like warm yolk, spilling bright sunshine over the cream duvet. I should be hungover. Thick-throated, head-pounding, ugly hangover. Instead, I feel better than I should.

Better than I deserve.

Two million. That number keeps pounding through my head.

Not a lot of people have a quantifiable number for their father's love. Two million. That's not bad, right? A decent sum?

He might as well have said *zero.*

Just when I thought he couldn't hurt me anymore, his ghost haunts me. Twisting the knife. Reminding me that I'm nothing but a decorated show pony, bred and trained to perform for everyone else's enjoyment.

I want to stay in bed. I want to drink until my liver gives out. I want to rub all my *fine breeding* in his face.

Look at your prize mare now, Daddy.

I yank the covers up my shoulders to burrow deeper into

the bed, but when I kick my leg out, my foot hits something warm and solid.

"Ow! Watch the tootsies, princess."

Ransom's voice sounds like it's coming from...the foot of the bed?

I prop up on my elbow. "What are you doing?"

Everett, still beside me, wakes up at our commotion and sits up.

Ransom is lying with his head at the foot of the bed, his feet up by my face. His hair sticks out at odd angles. He rubs his face where I, no doubt, kicked him. Somewhere between sleepy and grumpy, he complains, "You snore! He grinds his teeth! It's like sleeping with the damn circus!"

Everett frowns. "I like her snores. It lets me know she hasn't died in her sleep."

Ransom throws up his hands. "Y'all need Jesus."

I can't help it. A laugh bubbles up from inside of me. A real, genuine, *what-the-hell-is-my-life?* laugh that builds in my chest and comes pouring out my mouth until my eyes are stinging and I'm wheezing for breath.

I don't think I've laughed since I've gotten here. It feels good.

Ransom and Everett make me feel *good*. Even when the rest of the world is collapsing around me.

I pull up my legs so I can scoot halfway down the bed. I cup Ransom's jaw and rub his rough stubble underneath the pad of my thumb.

"Poor Ransom," I coo. "I'm sorry. How can I make it up to you?"

He pouts. "You can stick a nasal strip on that pretty nose."

I press my mouth to his, kissing away his pout. "How's that?"

He hums. "It's a start."

The bed creaks as Everett shifts. *Shit.*

Kissing Ransom was instinctive. But I've never kissed him in front of Everett before. A sliver of guilt cuts like a knife down my sternum.

Everett gets out of bed and fixes his glasses onto his face. "I'll make breakfast."

"I'll help," I say, guilt rising.

Be a better daughter.

Be a better wife.

But when I look at Everett, there's no hatred there or resentment. Instead, he says, "No need. Stay cozy."

Then he mimics my motion with Ransom; he cups my chin, tilts my head, and presses a gentle, chaste kiss to my mouth.

And like that, we break.

Like that, it's *normal.*

Kissing Ransom. Kissing Everett. Having them both in my bed.

Why not?

My father sold me like livestock.

I have a bounty out for my head.

Why can't *this* be normal?

"Any requests?" Everett asks.

"I'd murder my grandmimi for more of those pancakes," Ransom says.

Everett nods and looks at me. "Anything else?"

"Whatever you make is perfect. Thank you."

He slips on his sweatpants, dons a shirt, and then leaves the room.

Ransom's hand slips over my knee. "He's in a better mood this morning."

"We worked things out last night."

In the chair. On the dining room table. Messy, hard work. The memory of it lights up like fireflies through my blood.

Ransom's thumb rubs over my knee. "I'm glad for that. I am. But I've gotta ask...what's that mean for us?"

I look him in the eyes. Ransom. My sweet Ransom. Those chocolate-brown, soulful eyes. I could spill any of my secrets to those eyes, and now, when he looks at me like that, I feel compelled to tell him the truth. The honest truth.

"I need you right now," I tell him. "Both of you. I don't know what that means, or what that looks like, I-I don't even know if it's fair to either of you, it's selfish, but..."

He silences me by gripping my legs and yanking me, pulling me nearly into his lap. Ransom's forehead touches mine, and the heat of his breath warms my cheek. His voice is that deep, sincere rumble when he says, "You, Claire Preacher, deserve all the love you've got coming to you." With those strong hands clutching my thighs, he presses a sweet kiss to the bridge of my nose. "I just needed to know I wasn't out of the picture."

I shake my head. I trace my fingers down the bulk of his chest. The soft, curly hairs there. "No. You're very much in."

"Then I've got one request."

"What's that?"

"Nasal strips. Just try 'em."

I smack his chest and laugh. "Ass."

"Princess."

He kisses me fully on the lips this time. A warm, lingering kiss I could get lost in. My legs splay, and my body melts. His skin warms, and he's flushed when we break.

"Everett never complains when I snore," I tell him.

I know that bringing up *Everett* when we're like this could be dangerous.

But I'm testing the waters.

Seeing how truly *good* he is with sharing me.

His breath patters on my throat. He murmurs in my ear, "There are gonna be some new rules now that I'm here."

I tilt my head, giving him better access. "Like what?"

"Rule number one. If Everett gets you at night...I get you in the morning."

I'm on my knees, my legs splayed on either side of his, and I can't close them like this. All I can do is shiver at his touch. My nipples tighten until the soft satin of the robe feels like fire every time it brushes against them.

"You know what I want." Ransom's voice is that syrupy, dark demand that makes my heart flutter. "Fix your hands."

I'm putty. I obey.

I move my arms behind my back. Ransom slides the cord from the robe. His body is warm and strong against mine as he reaches behind me. Even blind, I can feel him wrap the tie around my wrists and knot it expertly. It's tight enough that I can't move but loose enough that it's comfortable on my skin.

"How's that?" he asks. Always checking in.

"Good."

Better than good. My skin is humming.

I'm vulnerable now. Slowly, he parts my robe, baring my breasts. His eyes light up as they drink me in. Ransom paints his thumb down my chest. He flicks over my hard nipple. I gasp, that one single stroke sending a bolt of want straight through me.

I'm ruining a perfectly good pair of panties.

"You're a gem," he tells me. "You know that?"

Ransom worships me with his gaze. With my words. With his touch.

My entire body aches for his particular brand of sweet, dominant affection.

I crane my chin upward, arching my chest forward. Wanting more of his touch.

"Please, touch me," I beg.

"I am touching you, princess."

He keeps me hungry for it. He dusts the tips of his fingers down the center of my body. He circles my navel.

"Or do you want me to touch you here?" He dances over the elasticity of my panties. My abdomen clenches, and my core throbs.

"Yes," I say, breathless.

"Your fiancé is expecting you downstairs," Ransom says. "You think it's nice to keep him waiting?"

Oh.

Here, I thought mentioning Everett would make Ransom jealous.

I didn't consider that, maybe, Ransom likes sharing.

No—Ransom likes *stealing*.

When I was eight, a stray cat wandered onto our property. It was an ugly, feral thing. I called it Horatio and left a bowl of water and food for it every morning, trying to lure it inside.

The cat never took the bait. He stole from the barn instead, helping himself to the horse's troughs and feed bags.

Feeling like I'd done something wrong, I cried about it to my father. He hoisted me in his lap and told me, "It's a wild animal. Wild animals have never been loved properly. They don't trust it. They're thieves. They steal." He touched me under my chin so he could look me in the eyes. "If you want that cat to love you, you have to make it work for it."

Which, in retrospect, is a strange thing to say to an eight-year-old.

But now I have to wonder...

Is Ransom too wild to accept my love from an open palm?

Does the water only taste good when it's forbidden?

If the erection in his briefs is any litmus test, I'd say he likes stealing.

And if the way I'm drenching my panties means anything, I think I like being stolen.

I twist. The binds hold tightly against my wrists. "I need you."

"Naughty girl." He slips his hand underneath the blanket. He invites himself between my legs, dipping underneath my panties, feeling the wetness that's collected at my core.

He slides two fingers on either side of my nether lips and pinches them. It sends a sharp, pleasurable pain through me, and I gasp. "Do you think you can come before he notices you're getting up to no good?"

My throat is dry with want. I don't want to tell him that I'm burning so hot I feel like I might explode from just the right amount of pressure.

"I think I can try."

He growls in my ear. That sound sends a shiver through me. His fingers dip against the crease of my slit, pushing my wetness around. He curls his two fingers, strumming one after the other against my clit. "Go ahead," he grunts in my ear. "Give me my bad girl."

The pleasure is almost blinding. My thighs ache being held apart like this, and I can feel my feet going numb, but I don't want it to stop. My toes curl, and everything in me focuses on the steady, unceasing drumbeat of his fingers. It only takes seconds. I tremble apart, unable to stop the cry that escapes me as I come on his hand. My body clenches, and he moans darkly in my ear, a sound that makes me hot.

"There she is." His breath is hot on my cheek. "You're flooding me, princess."

I whimper. My thighs try to shut, but they can't, pinned apart by his strong legs. I crumple forward instead, my forehead resting on his shoulder, as his tickling strokes draw out each hot pulse.

"Good girl." He kisses the top of my head. "That's my girl. You're my girl, ain't you?"

"Yes," I murmur, drowsy with pleasure. "Yours."

He removes his touch. I whimper in his absence.

I lift my head and watch as Ransom lifts his hand. His fingers are shiny and wet with me. He sticks them in his mouth, and the way he works his tongue around the digits makes me weak.

"Sweet as honey," he says. "Won't even need syrup for my pancakes."

A breath of a laugh escapes me. "If I had my arms, I'd smack you."

Suddenly, my hair is in his hands. A small cry leaves me as he grips me tight, pulling at my scalp.

"If you wanna be a brat, I'll leave you here for your fiancé to find," he growls. "Arms tied back. Legs spread. Pussy dripping. What d'you think he'll do to punish a dirty slut like you?"

My breath is short and tight in my throat.

Ransom is enjoying his role a little too much. And, truthfully...

So am I.

My heart is racing in my chest.

"Please, don't," I beg, playing the part. "I'll do anything."

"Anything?" With my head yanked back, his lips touch the exposed skin of my throat. "I'll hold you to that later."

His hard cock nudges against my thigh. *I wish he'd hold me to it now.*

I want him inside of me so badly it's a deep, painful ache. I came. Hard. But it wasn't enough. It's never enough. I need more. I need *him.*

But his fingers find the satin rope around my wrists. He pulls the quick-release knot, and I feel the threads flutter and slide down my wrists.

It means *we're done here.*

"We better get down there," Ransom says. His voice is lighter now. Playful. The Ransom I know. He gives my ass a small smack. "Before breakfast gets cold."

But my throat is suddenly tight. Knotting. I can't explain it, but I feel like if he pulls away, I might burst into tears.

"Kiss me first?" I ask.

His gaze meets mine. He must hear the tightness in my voice because I see surprise there, and then his eyes go soft. "Yes, ma'am," he says. Gently, he cradles my face in his hand. He brushes his lips to mine and kisses me. Softly. Sweetly. Lovingly.

Not the dominant, dirty man he was moments ago.

Now, he's Ransom again. My Ransom.

"Like that?" he asks.

I nod. "One more, please."

A gentle smile unfurls on his lips. "Princess, I'll kiss you until the stars fall outta the sky if you ask for it."

His mouth is so sweet on mine—asking for nothing, demanding nothing, but pure love, given without strings.

My wrists are tingling where the rope once was. Slowly, I reach forward and touch Ransom's chest. I flatten my palms on his bare skin.

I can feel it. His heart, strong and steady, like the beat of hooves against dirt. Pounding to meet my palm.

The tight knot around my throat slackens. I can breathe again.

"Okay," I say. "I'm ready to eat."

"Let's go," Ransom says. Then, before I can react, he stands and hoists me up, taking me over his shoulder.

36

EVERETT

Claire's screams of laughter carry through the bones of the house.

I increase the volume on my podcast.

Volcanoes, even dormant, can erupt at any time under the right circumstances...

The new headphones will take some wearing in, but it feels good to have my old crutch back.

I'm setting the plates at the table when Ransom and Claire come barreling down the stairs. My bones stiffen. He's got her tossed over his shoulder the way a caveman might carry a woman. She lets out a happy shriek as he hoists her off him, lowers her to her feet, and then pulls out her chair for her.

"M'lady."

"Thank you, Ransom."

She's wearing a too-long flannel, underwear, and nothing else. The red flannel kisses the tops of her thighs.

She's wearing his shirt.

I'm seized with the sudden impulse to rip it off her. I

want to clear the click of each scattered button as I fuck her on this table—our table.

My heart is pounding. I can feel it.

Control yourself, Everett.

"Holy shit," Claire says, eyes wandering over the spread, "this looks amazing."

It better.

Fresh slices of oranges. Fluffy pancakes. Crispy bacon. Over-easy eggs. A blueberry and blackberry mix.

"Coffee?" I ask.

"Please."

I pour her a fresh cup. Ransom sits down beside her, so I fill his cup as well.

Claire slices the side of her fork into a square of pancake and takes a bite. My heart flips.

My Claire has her appetite back.

She has her *everything* back, actually.

Her eyes are bright. Her perfect posture has returned. Even her hair seems more golden this morning.

I sit across from them so I can watch Claire devour her breakfast.

"I've been thinking," Claire says. "I know who I need to talk to. My father's business partner. Arris Dagney. He was the only one Daddy confided in. The closest thing I had to an uncle. If anyone knows anything about Daddy's nefarious friends, it would be him."

"It sounds like a good place to start," I agree.

Ransom shakes his head. "You won't have any luck cornering him today. Arris is having the polo match up at the Equestrian Club. They do it every week."

"Then it sounds like that's where we need to be," Claire says, cocking her head.

My smart, smart girl.

I'm obsessed with her brain.

"Hot damn." Ransom interrupts massacring his plate and points his fork at me. "I don't know what you put in pancakes, but it's amazing."

Cornmeal. But I won't tell him that. "Trade secret."

Ransom shakes his head. A dollop of syrup clings to the scruff around his mouth. "If this secret agent thing doesn't work out, you could make a decent living as a chef."

"Noted."

I hope he enjoys it. I want him to enjoy it.

Every man deserves a decent last meal.

You see, I figured it out.

Claire will never choose between us.

That's okay. I can't fault her.

Her father—the only family she's ever known—broke her. He gave her a heart that craves love the way a sponge craves water. He deprived her of affection, and now she's gone greedy for it.

Well, I'll give her all of it. I'll give her the love she needs.

The love she deserves.

And she'll learn that my love is all she needs. All she'll ever need.

I am all she will ever need.

Which is why...

I am going to kill Riley Ransom. Today. At the polo match.

37

EVERETT

We're back to the lion's den.

The Equestrian Club is bustling by the time we arrive. Event trucks are parked outside. They have workers on ladders looping streams of flowers on the overhang.

Tomorrow is the Belleflower Festival. They're in crunch time now.

My music app plays a playlist called "calming, chill vibes." I need it.

I may be on pins and needles, but even I have time to notice...

Claire looks fucking stunning.

She's wearing a beige pantsuit with a dark brown trim, a loose ribbon at her collar, and thin-strapped, dark heels. Her makeup is subtle but sharp, deftly highlighting her smoky, dark eyes. She's curled her hair, and it falls in buoyant, swoopy waves around her shoulders.

Since we arrived in Belleflower, Claire has been teetering on the edge of a complete and utter breakdown. This is the first time I've seen the Claire I know—confident, with her chin tilted upward, her posture perfect, and a look in her eyes that says, *Go ahead. Try me.*

Even the click of her heels is an aphrodisiac.

When we enter, the hostess gives us a distressed smile. "So sorry," she says. "We're closed for a private event."

I can feel Claire puffing up like a cat with its tail trampled underfoot. Before Claire can argue her way in, a hand slips over the hostess's shoulder. "Don't you recognize Belleflower royalty?" Arris steps around the podium. He's dressed in a maroon suit with dark fringe around the shoulders. He takes Claire's hand and gives it a kiss. "Apologies, dear. Come on in."

He moves his hand to the small of Claire's back, guiding her inside. Ransom and I follow in their wake.

"It's busy," I comment.

"Everyone's excited for the festival tomorrow. Limited service in the meantime."

We enter the dining hall with its round, white-clothed tables, where Claire and I came with her Promise Sisters. Also where Claire sat in my lap and clenched around me over sorbet.

Focus.

A chandelier blooms above the space, but it fills mostly with the natural light of the curved, floor-to-ceiling windows that look out into the arena. The brunch crowd is familiar, everyone dressed in their regal best. Claire's "sisters" are at a table in the corner, and when they see us, Elsbeth breaks into a wild wave.

I adjust my glasses on my face. As I do, I pinch the rim where it folds around my ears, activating the small camera. It'll take a series of pictures and shoot them off to the Wolfpack, where they can analyze the faces for any suspicious characters.

I wager there are more than a few in this bunch.

I'm particularly interested in the arrival of the special security—men in dark suits who hover against the wallpaper like mute statues. *Brunch* seems like a peculiar place to need firearms.

Arris guides us to an empty table by the window, but Claire catches his wrist. "Arris. I was hoping we could sit down and talk. It's important."

He gives her hand a squeeze. "Of course. Make yourself comfortable. Help yourself to the buffet. I'll be right with you."

He parts ways with us.

"Thirsty?" I ask Claire.

"Just a sweet tea," she replies.

"I've got it," Ransom and I say at the same time.

The Promise Sisters are descending. We both break to go to the buffet table, which sits adjacent to the windows. It's piled with mini sandwiches, finger foods, and a host of drinks.

Ransom beats me to the tea (bastard), so I collect three glasses of water.

"You should unbutton your shirt," Ransom tells me. "You're looking a little stiff."

My gaze flickers to him. Specifically, to the handkerchief around his neck. "Blue. Interesting choice."

"How's that?"

"Have you heard of the hanky-code?"

"The what?"

"In the seventies, queer people would safely flirt by wearing handkerchiefs. It was dubbed *flagging*. The different colors signified different intimate acts they were comfortable performing. The position of the handkerchief denoted giving or receiving."

"What's blue mean?"

"Anal sex." I hold his eye contact, unflinching. "Bottoming."

His expression sours. "You're making that up."

"Am I?"

As I lift the glasses to take them back to the table, I hear Ransom mutter, "*Dammit*," before removing his handkerchief and stuffing it in his pocket.

I have to work hard to keep the smirk off my lips.

When I return to the table, the girls are all standing around together. I set the waters down, and Ransom gives Claire her tea.

"Riley Ransom!" Mary-Kate exclaims. "What are you doing here?"

Her eyes dart greedily from Claire to Ransom, back and forth like a pinball, eager for the latest gossip.

I can feel Ransom gearing up for an elaborate lie, so I come out with the truth: "We all sleep in the same bed these days."

The girls break into a flutter of laughter, thinking I'm joking.

Yes. How absurd.

Claire changes the topic. She twists toward the window and asks, "What's going on down there?"

Men in tight-fitting suits and helmets linger around the racetrack. Some walk with horses that wear dark socks around their ankles and braids around their tails.

"They're having a polo match," Mary-Kate says. "Look at them," she whispers, her voice soft and reverent. "Those strong legs...the way he fills out those pants..."

"Are we talking about the horses or the riders?" Claire asks.

"You know what they say," Mary-Kate grins. "Save a

horse." She puts her hand on my chest. The uninvited touch makes my skin crawl.

I retreat into James. "Polo originated in Iran," I say. "But it's a popular sport among modern English gentlemen."

Ransom squints at me. "Oh, yeah? You play often?"

I stand my ground. "When the opportunity presents itself."

"Wicked cool, gov'ner!" Ransom says, with the worst British accent I've ever heard in my life.

The urge to put my hand around his throat is strong.

"You should sign up!" Elsbeth squeaks. "It's an open game."

I press my lips together. "I don't think so—"

"*Yes,*" Claire says enthusiastically. "They absolutely will." She sets down her glass to grip me and Ransom, then pulls us aside. "*Go,*" she says, dropping her voice. "Arris will speak freely with me. He might clam up if you two are breathing down his neck. Besides. It will give you a chance to...mingle with the locals."

"Mm." All I can think is *horses. Dust. Sweat.*

"Knock 'em dead," Claire says, trying to be encouraging.

"May I?" I ask.

Her mouth twists. "Ransom. Hold his hand."

Ransom smacks me on the back. "C'mon, James. Time to cowboy up."

38

RANSOM

I've never seen a grown man look more uncomfortable on top of a horse.

Everett's boots are hooked in the saddle's stirrups, and he's poised as though he's about to leap straight off the horse. He's clutching the horn like it's a lifeline.

I pat the horse's neck. "How're you feeling?"

"Fine," he says stiffly. He's had to put away his moral-support headphones so they don't fall out while he's riding. It's made him cranky.

"You should be riding comfortable. We had to get you a special saddle and everything, you tall princess."

He grimaces.

"You ever been on a horse before?"

Everett stiffens. "How hard can it be?"

Oh boy...

"Alright, quick lesson in two minutes." I move my hand to his middle, but I hover it in the air. "It alright if I put my hands on you?"

He blinks. "Go ahead."

I put my hand flat on his stomach. Even through his

shirt, I feel his hard muscles clench at my touch. "Keep your core tight here. Back straight." I take the reins in my hands and give them to him. "Use this for steering." I give Everett's thigh a pat. "This is your gas. Squeeze your thighs when you want him to move forward." I give the reins a tug. "And that's the brake pedal."

"Copy that," Everett says. I can see those pesky gears turning overtime in his head, processing the new information.

Never been on a horse before, and he's about to enter a polo match.

God, help him.

Our lesson is interrupted by the click of a tongue.

"I'll be. Riley *fuckin'* Ransom. I thought that was you." The intruder is a neat blond with wiry whiskers on his upper lip, which is currently curled into a mean smirk.

My stomach sours. "Loren."

We've had bad blood for a long time now. Of course he's come to make my life hell.

He's already gussied up in his riding uniform. He swaggers over to us. "They let anyone in here these days, don't they? Hey, saddle up my horse, will you?"

"Do I look like I work here?"

His eyes don't leave mine. "No. Actually, you don't look like you belong here at all."

"How about you mind you and yours, and I'll mind me and mine?"

"*Lauren*," Everett says suddenly from atop the saddle. "That's a lady's name, isn't it?"

Loren scowls at him. "Who the fuck is this?"

Everett just smiles. It's a haunting, scary thing. "The man who is about to shove the mallet so far up your arse you'll be picking splinters out of your teeth."

Loren goes pale. He can give, but he can't *get*. He spits on the ground before walking away. "See you idiots on the field," he says.

Once he's out of earshot, Everett asks, "Friend of yours?"

I unlock my clenched jaw. "That's Arris's son. Son of a bitch, if you ask me. Before I worked at the Preacher Ranch, I used to ride with him some at competitions. His horses were always jumpy. Spooked-like. Be a dick to me all you want—fine. I can take it. But be a dick to a horse? You skip home, go straight to hell for that one. I laid him out for it. He's been a pain in my ass ever since."

"Hmm."

I glance up at him. "You didn't have to stand up for me, you know. Those are strong words from someone who can barely hold on to his reins."

Those intense, blue eyes bear down on me. "No one gets to talk to you like that but me. Cowboy up, Riley Ransom."

He clicks his tongue, squeezes his thighs, and moves his horse into action.

Oh. Damn. Maybe I get it.

This strange heat crawls up my neck as I watch them saunter onto the field.

39

RANSOM

I feel fucking stupid.

For all my bluster, I'm actually not much better off than Everett. I might be good in the saddle, but I've never played polo.

I get to mount this beautiful filly named "Fancy." I walk her out to the field and stand side by side with Everett.

"The word on the field," Everett says, "is that Arris is watching. If a player impresses him, he'll invite them to the Coronation Ball."

"Huh. Is that something we want?"

"If we want to get to the bottom of this, *yes*. From what I've gathered, the most important people in town will be there." He glances at me, and his voice hardens. "Mr. Preacher's killer will be there."

Resolve fixes around my veins. "So we'll be there."

Everett measures me with his gaze. "You know how to play, don't you?"

"Hit the ball with the bat. How hard can it be?"

"A mallet. Not a bat." His voice is tight, like a warning.

"There are two teams. Two goals. Try to hit the ball into yours."

"What's my team name?"

"I don't think they don't have names."

"That's lame." I tug at the strap of my helmet. "This uniform sucks. Helmet's too tight."

Everett's mouth crosses in a thin, tight line, and I feel like I've come to the very long tail end of his patience. "Any other complaints?"

"Yeah. How come I've got the pink bat?"

"*Mallet*."

Loren rides up to us, sneer stamped across his face. He yanks his horse's reins too sharply, and the horse's head whips back. My stomach twists. "Hey, dumbass," he says.

"What?" Everett and I snap in unison.

He blinks. Probably surprised two grown men responded to his insult without flinching. He's got the face of a kid who has just walked in on his parents mid-decision to get divorced. Now, he's too thrown for whatever great comeback he was amping himself up for, so he just says, "Uh...good luck."

He kicks his horse's flank, and it lets out a whine before bolting forward.

Everett gives me a look. "Try not to make an ass of yourself."

Dick. Give this man a little kindness and he hangs me on it.

"I'd say *same to you*, but I think it comes naturally for you."

Everett squeezes his thighs (like I taught him), and we guide our horses toward the center of the clearing, where everyone else is already lined up.

A woman in a tight-fitting outfit and cream pants meets us in the center of the field and explains the rules. We've got the red team and the green team, four horses on each. The horses have bands on their ankles to designate the different colors. Everett and Loren are red, I'm green. The field is wide, green, and has two goalposts on either side. The object of the game is to be the team to hit the ball through the opposing team's goal.

Seems easy enough. I look around at my competition. They're all stiff-backed and got silver spoons sticking out of their mouths. They may've been playing polo ever since they've been in diapers, but no one knows how to handle a horse the way I do.

"Ready to knock 'em dead, Fancy?" I ask.

She twitches her ear and huffs, which I translate to *Eat the rich, sir.*

But then the game kicks off, and I'm eating dust.

The players zip around the arena like wasps, swarming around the ball. Mallets whoosh through the air and click as they connect with the ball, hooves beating against the ground.

I follow the ball and even get a couple of whacks at it, but the mallet is harder to swing than it looks, and I keep kicking up dirt, leaving the ball in my wake.

I've got my eyes on Everett. He's fighting his horse, giving the gal mixed signals with his reins, but every time he swings that mallet, it's a perfect hit that sends the ball sailing through the goal.

Their team scores. My team glares at me.

Even with the autumn chill, the game is more exerting than it lets on, and between the strain of riding and the sun beating on my fleece, I feel sweat sticking to my sweater.

Through pure rage alone, I manage to knock my mallet into the ball with a few hard swings. I've finally got some kind of flow on this, and Fancy and I weave down the field as I knock the ball forward. Through the edge of my vision, I can see Loren and Everett flanking me, trying to chase me off the ball. But I'm on it now, like a hound dog, and I kick it closer and closer until I'm within reach of the goal. I swing my mallet back for the killing blow, but—

Everett hooks my mallet with his. I was holding on too damn tight because the force of his tug not only knocks me off-balance, but it yanks me right off my horse.

Fancy darts ahead, and I hit the dirt. I hear myself swear, and I just manage to roll out of the way before Everett's horse come pounding past me, hooves inches away from my face.

Son of a bitch!

The ball lies in the grass, a mere couple of inches away from me.

I'm pissed, I've got grass between my teeth, and I don't like being yanked out of my saddle.

Without thinking, I grab the ball and chuck it at Everett.

It hits him square in the back.

Ha! Take that!

But then he tumbles off his saddle, too, and guilt seeps in my chest.

Well, shit.

The horses move like a thundercloud, getting further way. I walk over to where Everett is lying on the ground. His glasses came off, so I pick those up and hand them down to him.

He props himself on his elbows. He's got a mean grass streak across his shirt and pants. He puts his glasses on his face and then shoots me an icy look.

"That was not very sportsmanlike of you," he chastises.

"Yeah, neither was your move." I offer him a hand. He takes it.

"I was following model rules," he says.

"They're *dick* rules."

I yank Everett to his feet. His tall body sways and, briefly, brushes against mine. The heat of his breath hits my cheek when we nearly collide. This close, I can nearly taste the sweat and dirt on him.

Everett doesn't release my hand—not right away, anyway.

He drops the British act. In a low murmur, he says, "Imagine how insidious we'd be if we worked together instead of against each other."

"Yeah. Also. I'm thinking we'd make a good team."

There's polite eruption of applause from the stands as Loren's team scores. The board is now even—four and four. The next goal settles the game.

Those steely blue eyes flash. "Do you want to destroy Loren?"

"I thought you'd never ask."

As if on cue, Fancy trots up beside us and flicks her tail as if to say, *What're you waiting for?*

Everett and I make eye contact, and somehow, that's all we have to say.

I swing myself up back in the saddle and hold out a hand for Everett. He takes my hand and pulls himself up, mounting the horse behind me.

Gotta say—I'm not used to riding double saddle with a guy, but we fit. Everett's body is flat, all coiled, tight muscles pressed against my back. His arm hooks around my middle. He wraps his hand around the horn of the saddle between my legs and grips.

Head in the game, Ransom.

"Hup!" I kick my heel into Fancy's flank, and she obliges, taking off.

Loren is hungry for the win. He's hot on the ball, and his powerful stallion pounds dirt, keeping the other horses a healthy distance.

Fancy isn't afraid. She's light and quick, and I weave her up behind him. Loren's horse grunts, and Loren glances back. He does a double take when he sees the both of us on the horse, and his mustache nearly jumps off his face. He swings for the ball, but this time, Everett hooks him, knocking Loren's mallet back. In the same swing, Everett hits the ball, and suddenly, it's ours.

Everett deftly knocks the ball to another team member. He guides the ball into the goal, and—like that—we win the round.

But more importantly, Loren loses.

Apparently, someone's shaken the skeletons awake because our audience breaks into the liveliest applause they've had all day. We even get a couple of hoots and hollers.

"How do you like that?" I call back at Loren.

The sneer on Loren's face? That's priceless.

I lift my mallet in the air. "Three cheers to Team Dumbass!"

There's a puff of breath against the back of my neck, and I swear to God, I think I made Everett Stick-in-the-ass Hollow laugh.

Loren—giant man-child that he is—throws a fit. He rips off his helmet. I can see him shouting at the referee.

But his words get drowned out because then I see it.

A notch on the back of his head. Stitches and a shaven patch of skin.

The kind of mark a hammer might leave, for example, if it hit someone in the back of their head when they went running from the murder scene.

40

CLAIRE

I'm sipping my sweet tea, nodding without listening to the mindless banter of my former Promise Sisters, when the room tilts.

At least, that's how it feels.

The commotion from the crowd watching the polo game outside draws the interest of everyone *inside*. It's as though we're on a ship, and suddenly, the ship has tacked, sloshing everyone to the other side of the room, noses pressed to windows, breath fogging glass.

I peer outside the wide, observatory-style windows myself, expecting to see the tail end of an accident—a horse and rider flailing on the ground.

What I find instead makes my blood temperature rise.

Ransom and Everett are riding the same horse. Cuddled tightly together, they play the game as a single unit and are, subsequently, demolishing the competition.

In any other circumstance, I might find this cute! Entertaining! Amusing!

But when they're making a mockery of the Equestrian

Club...right when I'm about to have a meeting with its owner...

It's *infuriating*.

They're like children. I can't take my eyes off them for two seconds.

"Goddammit," I mutter under my breath.

"Quite the game."

I recognize the voice behind me immediately—dark, deep Arris.

I quickly turn to face him. "Christ. I'm sorry...I honestly have no idea what they're doing—"

Arris chuckles. "Don't be. This is the most entertainment the crowd has had in a long time." His eyes sweep past me to the chaos below. "A little fresh blood can be a good thing every now and then." He turns back to me. His hand finds my shoulder. "You wanted to talk with me?"

"Yes..." Now's my chance. Everyone is distracted by the show below; they ignore us completely. Still, I take Arris's arm and pull him aside, sitting down at a table at an empty table at the far end of the room. We have, at least, a little privacy here. Nerves tremble through me, but I fit my hands together, locking my fingers in place. *Breathe, Claire.* At a young age, I learned to pluck every thread of worry or anxiety from my expression. Daddy considered it *unfitting* for a woman of my standing. So when I look at Arris now, I'm confident I'm wearing nothing but a blank, calm expression.

"I've been going through Daddy's things," I explain. "Organizing and cleaning his records."

He nods, understanding. "I'm sure that's quite the endeavor."

"Quite. He was meticulous, as you know. But the truth is I've found some things that are, frankly, disturbing."

His gray eyebrows knit together. "*Disturbing?*"

"Daddy considered you family. And you worked so closely together. I just thought if anyone knew what was going on, it would be you."

Arris's large hands sweep around the table. He encloses my hands in his own.

"Whatever I can do to help," he says. His voice sounds so sincere, so earnest, my heart aches for it. "Tell me what you found."

I want to believe him. I want to trust him.

But...

Perhaps it's my black Preacher heart that knows no one is above suspicion.

There's a nagging here I can't release.

I look him dead in the eyes. "Oculus," I say. "Does that name mean anything to you?"

There. Right there.

A flicker in his gaze.

"Oculus?" He stretches the word out. "No. I'm afraid not."

But he's nodding as he speaks. A tell.

He knows. Fuck. *He's known all along.*

I start to pull away, but his hands tighten, trapping me in place.

"I wish I could be more help," he continues. "But the truth is, as close as we were, your father shut me out in his final years. He shut everyone out. I hope I'm not overstepping here, but...I would hate to see you tread the same path."

"Which path? The path to a sudden, violent death?"

"The path to isolation," he corrects. "He trusted no one. Loved no one. I hope you know you have friends here. People who love you."

Yes. Ransom. Everett. Those people love me.

Not you.

Daddy knew. Now I know it, too.

But I play nice. For now. "I know," I tell him.

A look of relief crosses his expression. His entire face warms. He releases his tight hold on me now and relaxes back into his chair. "I'm glad you pulled me aside, Claire. I wanted to talk with you, too. I hope to see you here tomorrow."

"Tomorrow? That's the Belleflower Festival."

"Yes. And it would be nothing without its Queen." He reaches into his inside jacket pocket and pulls out a thin envelope. He slides it across the table. "I would have put it under your pillow, but I figured you're too old for that sort of thing."

I stare at the envelope. It has a red wax seal.

The Benefactors' Society.

All attempts to keep my composure shatter.

I run my thumb over the smooth, buttery wax seal. Like a blind person hunting for the meaning, I trace the seal. The closed eye. The ridges of the lashes.

The phrase skitters like a skipping stone across my mind: *see no evil.*

I slide my thumb underneath the lip of the envelope and pry open the seal.

The cackling laughter of the Promise Sisters, the clinking of tiny spoons against porcelain teacups, the hushed murmurs of gossip...all of that dissolves into a single, piercing buzz as I remove the letter from its sleeve.

The card stock is thick with fraying on the edges. The golden words curl in stylish, cursive script, the embossed letters giving the impression of it leaping off the paper.

. . .

You've been Chosen as this year's Belleflower Queen.

My pulse pounds, excitement racing through me like a herd of horses, all stampeding in powerful, thumping, synchronized rhythm.

Underneath the announcement, the invitation continues in small, strict font:

This Honor granted to you is a testament to your Perseverance, Purity, and Steadiness of Character. Your Promise has matured into unwavering Ambition, and we have made the decision to grant you the Gifts of the Benefactors' Society to fund and support your Life's Mission.

At the end of your term, you will be Welcomed into the fold of Queens, a Community like none-other, where you will find Support, Love, and Empowerment. This position is an honor For Life.

You have been Matched to a King, who shall be revealed at the Coronation Ball on the Eve of the festival.

The members of the Benefactors' Society humbly anticipate your acceptance at 10:00 AM on the fourteenth of September at The Belleflower Ranch.

Signed,

The Benefactors' Society

THE INCONSISTENT CAPITALIZATION IS STRANGE. The old-world language is unsettling. But as I hold the invitation in my hand, I feel nothing but longing, and gratitude, and a sudden wish to burst into queen-appropriate tears, despite the dryness in my eyes.

In one ear, I hear Everett's warnings. *Benefactors' Society. Oculus. It's too dangerous. Don't trust them.*

But in my other ear, Daddy's ghost murmurs without breath, *That's my girl. I always knew you were number one.*

This is what I wanted. What I've wanted my entire life.

And if something *is* rotten in Denmark...if there *is* someone scheming behind the scenes...

Wouldn't the best place to uncover the mystery be from *inside* the very society itself?

All I have to do is accept it.

I hear my voice echo, as though it's coming from someone else. "I don't know what to say."

The edges of Arris's eyes crinkle. He's pleased with my reaction. "Say nothing. Just be there." His hand grasps me again, but this time, it's a gentle touch on the wrist. A fatherly embrace. "Belleflower hasn't been kind to you in the past. It's here for you now. Your place is here, Claire. With us. It's what your father would have wanted."

He gives me one last pat on the hand and then rises to join the rest of his crowd.

He leaves me staring at those glimmering letters, rubbing the embossed words over and over like a worry stone.

41

EVERETT

The polo game comes to an end.

Our referee approaches us, a stout man sweating through his shirt. He wipes tears from his eyes as he laughs. "Whew! That was the most entertaining match I've seen in a while."

Riding is using muscles I'm unaccustomed to using. I can already tell my thighs will be sore tomorrow. I can feel the horse panting underneath us. Ransom fits peculiarly well in my lap, his body warm and bulky against mine.

"What'd we win?" Ransom asks.

Loren and his team ride up alongside us. Playing unfair was worth it to see his mouth twisted in a sour expression underneath that whiskery mustache. He answers, "You get to go find the ball, idiots."

At the edge of the field, I see one of Loren's teammates smack the polo ball hard. It sails into the woods, vanishing behind the trees.

Petty but effective. Ransom's muscles tense against me.

"Pick your battles," I murmur to him.

As the rest of the men lead their horses back to the tables, we pivot and ride into the woods. Ransom stalls the horse. I dismount first, and then he follows.

Under the canopy of trees, the light dims. The woods are thick here, and they swallow us.

I look toward the Equestrian Club. The people are small dots from here.

I can't see them. They can't see us.

We're alone out here.

Ransom's heavy boots crunch over dry leaves and snap twigs. He has no sense of stealth. His head is down, hunting for the ball. Quietly, I follow behind him.

Completely alone.

"Good riding out there," Ransom says.

"You did all the riding. I did the swinging."

"Guess we make an alright team, huh?"

I crouch down on a knee. I slip my hand into my boot. My fingers wrap around the hard steel of the small hunting pistol.

"I guess so," I reply. I take the bullet out of my pocket, thumb it into the barrel, and click it into place. I'll only need one at this close range.

Ransom gets to his knees and brushes aside a pile of leaves, hunting for the ball.

"Listen," he says. "There's something about Loren. I saw something, and—I don't know. Might be nothing. Might be that I'm seeing things, but..."

Ransom is rambling as he hunts. He's distracted.

Adrenaline pinches, and my heart quickens in my chest.

Now's my chance.

I lift my gun.

Goodbye.

I understand that word now. *Goodbye.*

This is a *good* bye. A wonderful bye. The best *bye* there ever was.

Goodbye, Riley Ransom.

Goodbye to your stupid jokes and your filthy clothes.

Goodbye to your crooked grin and your color-coordinated bandanas.

Goodbye to your need to always get in the last word.

Goodbye to that big, bleeding heart you wear on your sleeve.

Goodbye to the way Claire looks at you with those soft doe eyes.

Goodbye to the way she wrote about you in her diary with such painful longing.

Goodbye to the shadow of you that hangs over us every moment I'm with her.

Good. Bye.

But as I aim the gun directly at the back of Ransom's skull…

A dragonfly flutters in front of my vision.

It hovers in the air. Buzzing. Its blue-green body flickers. Then it settles, landing on the muzzle of my gun. Its tiny legs cling to the silver metal.

Everything within me turns to glass. Thin. Cold. Glass. The kind of glass that might shatter apart at the slightest touch.

My dragonfly.

Ransom turns to face me. The dragonfly lifts and zips away.

Ransom's jaw goes slack when he sees the eye of my gun. "What the hell—?"

"Don't move," I tell him.

He goes still. I fix my aim and fire.

The pistol goes off with a crack. The bullet sinks into the soft dirt an inch from Ransom.

The leaves shudder with movement. A brown copperhead snake whips around and quickly slithers away, its diamond-studded body weaving through the autumn leaves as it goes.

Ransom's body deflates with a sigh. "Y'don't like snakes, huh?"

"I don't like snakes," I agree.

I slip the pistol back into my boot. I step over beside Ransom and point to the white ball beside him. "Are you going to get that?"

"Oh. Yeah."

He scoops it up. I hold out my hand, and when he takes it, I help him to his feet.

He dusts the dirt off his knees—a strange thing to do, considering his uniform is already covered in grass stains. "For a second there," he says, "I thought you were going to kill me."

I take him by the chin and tilt his head toward mine. Those brown eyes are electric when they meet mine. A hint of fear and...*something else.*

Not unlike being in the path of a copperhead.

You better be right about this one, dragonfly.

"Now," I say, my voice low, chastising, "where would Butch Cassidy be without his Sundance Kid?"

There it is. That crooked grin. "Are you calling me your Kid?"

"I'm calling you my *Butch.*"

I watch as, in real time, Ransom settles back into his skin.

My hands have a strange itch to roam. To blindly explore the hard edges and warm skin of the man my Claire adores. I push my thumb roughly over the scruff of his jaw, petting him roughly. He doesn't pull away, just looks at me with that blank, docile stare.

"Come on," I tell him. "Let's go find Claire."

42

CLAIRE

I'm still fiddling with the Belleflower Queen invitation when, suddenly, Everett is behind me. I don't have to look up to know it's him. I can just *feel him*. That tall, shadowy presence at my back.

He dips to reach my ear. "What's that?"

I should tell him. I should tell him about the invite, and about Arris, and the way everything feels all twisted up inside my body.

Instead, I tuck the card back into the envelope and slip it into my pocket.

"Nothing. I saw you two had an eventful game."

"Sure was eventful, alright," Ransom says, slipping into the seat across from me. They're out of the borrowed uniforms and back in their regular clothes, but Ransom's hair is askew, and just from looking at him, I can tell he smells like earth and sweat.

I want to inhale him.

"Let's get out of here," I say.

Those brown eyes meet mine. "Where?"

"Anywhere but here."

We make our rounds. I say my goodbyes to the girls, and we leave the Equestrian Club. The three of us get into Ransom's truck, and he takes me to what is quickly becoming my favorite spot.

"Look what the cat dragged in." Maeby greets us with one of her legendary, crooked smiles and hooks her arm around Ransom.

"Nothing but three blind mice," Ransom retorts.

"Twice in one week. I must be goddamn blessed."

"*Goddamn blessed*," Everett muses. "That's an oxymoron."

"We're starving to death, Miss Maeby," I say, changing the topic. "Please tell me the kitchen's open?"

"Sure, sugar. I'll bring out some menus."

"And a pitcher of your finest, please." Ransom gives her a wolf's smile, and she cackles out a laugh.

Maeby's has a small crowd, even at 3:00 p.m. The three of us hunker down in a booth with ripped seats. Maeby brings out a pitcher and three glasses. The beer is cheap, but it's crisp, and there's something about an easy-drinking beer in the middle of the day that settles me.

We order lunch.

I don't realize how hungry I am until I'm gifted a plastic basket with a burger dripping with American cheese.

Ransom—normally the one at the table to eat his weight and then some—seems distracted when the food shows up.

Everett stands. "I have to make a call. You two stay here."

With that, he slips out of the booth, passing me. The bells above the door chime as he exits.

Ransom rubs his hand up his arm. His flannel bunches up, and he grips his bicep. Everett might be able to keep secrets from me, but Ransom can't.

I nibble a fry. "Want to tell me what's on your mind?"

He folds his arms over his chest. He looks out the window, and he's got this faraway look. "You ever get this feeling...like maybe you're about to make a bad decision, but you know you're gonna do it anyway?"

The invitation burns like hot coal in my pocket.

Tell him. It's Ransom. He'll understand.

But my throat closes around my good intentions. Instead, I say, "What bad decision are you brewing up this time?"

He sets his hat down on the seat beside him and rakes his fingers through his hair. I can tell he's been sweating under his hat.

I like Ransom in all of his versions—dressed-up Ransom. Dressed-down Ransom. Working Ransom.

But *dirty Ransom* makes me feral.

"It's more like a feeling," he explains. "Like the way everything gets muggy and hot right before a big storm. This whole town feels upside down."

I have to remember: I escaped Belleflower.

Ransom didn't.

This place is as much a part of him as his beating heart. He devoted his entire life to this town and the people in it.

It has to be strange to look at the people you once trusted and know that, somewhere, there's a killer lurking in the midst.

His eyes connect with mine again. "How'd the conversation with Arris go?"

My stomach goes tight. This is it. My in. My opportunity to tell him about the invite.

But I can't stop the lies coming from my lips. "Fine."

He squints at me. *You idiot, Claire.*

I can lie to anyone, but I can't lie to Ransom.

He knows something is wrong.

Before he can ask, however, Everett returns to the table. He slides his trim body into my side of the booth. He leans over the table, picks up a knife, and cuts Ransom's untouched burger in half. His shirt rides up, just enough to give me a glimpse of the bare skin at his waist.

Eyes to yourself, hungry girl.

He takes half of Ransom's burger and takes a bite. Ransom, as if by some monkey-see, monkey-do instinct, starts eating his half.

They're in sync. In a way they weren't before today.

How bizarrely delightful.

"I put in a call to my team," Everett says between bites.

"Wolfpack?" Ransom asks.

Everett frowns at him. "Say it louder, please."

"Secret agent!" Ransom hollers. He waves dramatically toward Everett. "Hey! We got a bona fide double-oh-seven over here!" Not a single person looks up from their conversation. He settles back into his seat. "See? You may as well say you're a purple people eater from planet Zoron. No one cares."

Everett glares. I get us back on track. "What did they say?"

"I sent them images of the crowd from the Equestrian Club. They did facial scans and ran them through the database." He pulls his satchel into his lap, unlatches it, and takes out his iPad. His fingers fly over the screen. "They sent me back this."

On the iPad is a picture of Arris. Young. He could be in his twenties. His hair is jet-black, his jaw squared and strong. Those same, deep-set eyes, though.

"What is this?" I ask.

"*Who* is this, you mean?" Everett says. "Sergey Guskov. Born in Russian. Lost his parents at a young age. Was inducted to the criminal organization, Oculus, where he quickly learned how to buy and sell women. By twenty, he had a lucrative trafficking operation. He was shut down by Wolfpack Operatives, his organization dismantled. However, when they were transporting him to the United States, he managed to escape. No one has been able to locate him ever since."

"Until now," Ransom says.

My heart is pounding in my chest. I stare at the image of the hard, calculating man on the screen.

"He gave me my first horse," I hear myself say. "He treated my father like a brother. I just...I know it's silly, but I can't imagine him going into my father's room and pulling the trigger."

"It's because he didn't," Ransom says. "It was his son. Loren."

We both stare at him. "What?"

Ransom rubs his thumb up the side of his water glass. He stares at the condensation. "The night Mr. Preacher died...I heard someone run through the house. Couldn't catch them. But they got whacked in the back of the head with one of Mr. Preacher's traps." His eyes lift, meeting mine. "I saw a mark on the back of his head today."

"Then that proves it," Everett says. "Arris. Loren. The Benefactors' Society. They're all involved. Whatever they have planned, I believe they'll execute it during the festival tomorrow."

"So we should be there," I say. "So we can stop it."

"No. Not *we*. *You* should be nowhere near the festival," Everett counters. "You're the one they want, remember?"

"Right."

No Belleflower Festival. No Belleflower Queen.

I take a lengthy swallow from my beer.

The boys mirror me.

"So what happens now?" I ask.

"I've informed my team," Everett says. "They're going to come in and infiltrate the festival. They'll break it up. Arrest Arris and anyone involved. He'll be in jail. Where he belongs."

"Where he belongs is six feet under. He killed my father."

"A man you hated," Everett reminds me.

"It's complicated."

Those blue eyes hang on mine. No judgment in this. Just open acceptance. "What would you have me do? Tell me, and it's done."

My heart pinches. I think—

The invitation. Loren. Daddy. Arris—no. *Sergey.*

"Nothing," I say. "You're right. It's out of our hands now."

We don't talk much after that. We finish our lunches. Everett makes me recount the conversation with Arris, and I give him snippets of details, without revealing the invitation. He tilts his head now and then as though processing each new piece of information. Everett's tall body is splayed out, his arm resting across the table. His hand bumps Ransom's occasionally as they share fries. There's a small, subtle shift between the two men. I can't put my finger on it.

I finish my meal, swallow back the rest of my beer, and stand. The pool table is empty, so I start racking the balls.

I need to shake this terrible, dark feeling rolling around in my chest.

Time to get your mojo back, Claire.

"You two! Get over here. Grab your sticks."

Everett and Ransom join me. Everett chalks his cue. "You're not playing?"

"Oh, I am." I lift a cue from the bunch. "I'm playing against both of you. Two against one. Should even the playing field."

Before today, I didn't want them in the same *room* together, let alone on the same team.

They were oil and water. More likely to kill each other than look each other in the eye.

Now...

They're practically *breathing* in sync.

They both light up at my challenge. It's that look. The competitive glint in their eyes that makes my heart flutter and my blood race.

I've locked horns with a double-headed bull, and I wouldn't have it any other way.

Ransom snorts out a laugh. "Your funeral, princess."

Pointedly, I ask Everett, "You're not going to let me win again, are you?"

He rolls up his sleeves, revealing the ropey veins up his forearms. He's getting serious now. He instructs, "Break, Claire."

The front of my body kisses the felt green as I line up my shot and hit the mark.

It's only a little after nine when we get home, but it feels well past midnight.

I should be exhausted, but I'm not.

My blood is buzzing. We feel close—really close—to something big.

How did Ransom describe it?

The heat before a storm.

The three of us get ready for bed. This is a new routine that feels, somehow, familiar. As though we've been doing this the whole time. Dressing down. Taking turns in the shower. Brushing our teeth side by side in the sink. There's a strange, natural cadence to having both of these men in my home, in my bed, and in my life.

Now that I have it, I don't know how I ever existed without it.

I'm the longest in the shower, so I'm the last. I exit, feeling clean and steamed-fresh.

When I come out, Everett is sitting in his robe on the edge of the bed. Ransom is splayed in the tall chair in the corner, wearing nothing but gray cotton pajama pants and his Stetson tilted over his face, bandana loose around his throat. He has Everett's AirPods in his ears, which Everett is manipulating with his phone.

"This is white noise," Everett says. He presses a button. I watch him watch Ransom's expression. "This one is green noise. And brown noise. My personal favorite, but everyone has their own preference."

Ransom tilts his head. "Do it again?"

"White noise. Green noise. Brown noise."

I sit on my side of the bed. I pull out my tub of moisturizer and slide it over my legs. "Aw. Are you two swapping ear wax now?"

"There's a rigorous cleaning process." Ransom tries (and fails) to keep a straight face.

Everett, not comprehending, adds, "Clorox bleach wipes disinfect the ear pods without damaging the material."

"White noise," Ransom says, plucking them out. "Final answer."

As I rub moisturize up my calf, suddenly, Everett's hand launches out and catches my wrist, halting me. I blink at him.

"Don't do that." His eyes are dark. "Let me."

He shifts his long limbs to reach over and snatch the tub of moisturizer from the bedside table. He sets it down beside him instead. He grips the backs of my legs and pulls me across the bed effortlessly, guiding my legs into his lap.

He doesn't give me a choice, not really. He's going to take care of me, whether I want him to or not.

And *this* is Everett in his element.

Making sure everyone gets enough to eat.

Making sure everyone gets a good night's sleep.

Making sure everyone is cared for.

His dominant, disciplined affection is what drew me to him in the first place. I've been too angry to see straight these past few days. But I remember it now—why I fell in love with him in the first place, no, why I love him *now*— and my heart goes warm and soft in my chest.

Everett scoops two fingers in the moisturizer. He rubs it over his palms and slides the creamy lotion over my legs. The sensation of his strong, smooth hands gliding up and down my legs makes me shiver. As if by their own accord, I feel my legs parting. Inviting.

Everett gets close, but he doesn't take the invitation. Not yet. His hands map my inner thighs. When I look at Ransom, his gaze is lidded. He's watching us from underneath the heavy brim of his hat with a dark look that makes my core tight with want.

I'm not the only one that notices. Everett says, "Do you like watching me take care of our girl?"

"Huh?" Ransom says, blinking as though pulling himself out of a stupor.

Everett repeats himself slowly. "Do you..." His hand moves all the way up my thigh. "...like..." His fingers press underneath the brim of my panties. "...watching me..." He finds my core and pushes my wetness around. "...take care of..." My breath catches in a moan. "...our girl?"

My heart is racing.

My cheeks feel hot, and my throat is tight. Everett is touching me. Brazenly. Right in front of Ransom.

And I'm getting off on it.

"Do you want me to stop?" Everett asks, his eyes still on the other man. Watching for his reaction. His fingers curl, nuzzling and petting me idly.

Ransom shakes his head. The way he's looking at me... my nipples go hard and tight. "No. I want you to make her come."

Oh fuck.

Those thick fingers push inside my tight core. A whimper escapes me before I can stop it.

"With my fingers?"

Everett is letting Ransom lead.

Key word: *letting.*

Both of these men are so incredibly dominant, the power play between all three of us makes me dizzy with want.

Ransom leans forward, getting a better view. His elbows rest on his knees.

I want to rake my fingers through the curly hair that races like wildfire across his broad chest. I want to lick his throat.

Instead, I twist my wanting fingers into the comforter underneath, forcing myself to stay still.

Ransom answers, "With your tongue."

Everett's bright eyes light up. Then they meet mine.

He pulls his hand away. I ache, missing the touch, but...I want what's coming next even more.

"You heard him," Everett says to me. "Take it off, darling."

I pull the knot free from my robe. My hands are trembling. From want—or the nerves of being the center of attention—I'm not sure. I let my robe fall off my shoulders and puddle onto the bed behind me. I take my time rolling my underwear down my hips. Off my thighs.

They wait. Eyes trained on my every move. Looking like they might devour me.

And I so badly want them, too.

I hold up my panties and drop them off the side of the bed.

There.

I'm all theirs now.

Everett's head dips toward my thighs, but Ransom interrupts.

"Wait," he says suddenly. "Suck her tits first. Look at them. They need it."

Ransom is on the edge of his seat as he watches us. He's antsy now as he rubs a palm over his knee to distract himself. His pants do very little to hide the shadow of arousal thickening in his lap.

"As you wish," Everett says. He cups my small breast, which fits perfectly in the shell of his palm. His thumb glides over the hardened nipple, making me shiver. He kisses the tender skin softly and then pinches it between his teeth. I whine when he tugs, gently, just enough to send a lick of pain through me, one that translates to pleasure as it pools low between my thighs. Finally, he pulls my tit into his mouth, sucks, swirling his tongue in ways that make my legs clench together. I squeeze, desperate for some pressure. But his hands drop to my thighs, and he forces them apart, pinning them there. *No*, his grip says. I won't feel good until he *wants* me to feel good. Until then...

I ache as he moves on to the next breast with painful, slow, deliberate licks and sucks. I'm panting, and when I allow myself to sneak a look at Ransom...

I see my own desperate, aching need reflected in his gaze.

He's watching me. Wanting me. With our eyes locked, he moves a hand into his lap. He palms his erection, and my throat goes tight for it.

With one final, teasing nibble, Everett detracts himself from my nipples, now glistening and swollen pink. He uses his grip on my thighs to spread my legs wider, and then he gives a small, satisfied hum.

"You were right," he says. "She did need that. She's wet the bed like an untrained puppy."

If anyone else called me a dog, I'd break their nose.

When Everett does it? My insides clench.

Everett's hand clamps around the base of my throat suddenly. I gasp with surprise as my head is forced back, and my chin juts up with the strength of his grip.

This is all Everett.

My Everett, who demands affection. Who clings to the things he loves so tightly he can't help but leave marks.

His breath beats hotly on my ear. "Do you like being on display for us?"

"Yes," I admit. My voice is hoarse. I can feel it vibrating in his palm.

"Do you want me to lick your cunt while Ransom watches you come apart?"

God, I'm going to hell for this. "Yes."

He kisses the skin under my ear. "Good girl." I shiver. His

lips meet my shoulder. Between my breasts. My belly. Every small kiss plants another seed of ache inside of me. My fingers find his hair, gripping the neat, dark strands. I want to push him lower, but he's taking his time with me. Making me wait.

Making Ransom wait, too.

Everett adjusts. He's too tall, and he moves off of the bed, kneeling as though in prayer on the floor. He pulls me forward, throwing my legs over his shoulders, and only then does he dive between them.

I let out a moan of relief.

Everett knows me too well. He knows just how I like to be licked. He slides his tongue along my slit, lapping at me, and then swirls it around that bud of pleasure. He gives small, little sucks that make me rock forward against his mouth.

His hand joins in. A finger fills me, and then a second.

My toes curl, and I know I'm done for.

"Oh God," I whisper. "Oh, *fuck.*"

Nothing can stop the wave of pleasure that crashes over me. My legs lock around Everett's head. My entire body trembles, going stiff and tense. He curls his finger inside of me, coaxing me closer and closer until I'm *right there.*

I cry out. I come so hard it's almost painful. My body throbs and pulses, pulling at his fingers, dancing on his tongue.

As the waves ebb, Everett steals his tongue back. "She's flooding my face," Everett narrates for Ransom. His breath is hot on my dripping sex. "I believe our girl enjoyed that."

Our girl. I like the sound of that. So does my cunt. It throbs tightly around Everett's fingers, and I whimper, helpless with pleasure.

But then Everett's gaze shifts to Ransom.

"Come here, dragonfly."

Ransom blinks. "Me?"

"Yes. You."

But my breath catches in my throat because...

Dragonfly.

I remember the story Everett told me. How at the orphanage, the dragonfly was his only friend. His companion. His brother.

That's it, isn't it? The shift in the energy between them.

I'm his good girl, and Ransom...

Ransom is Everett's dragonfly.

Ransom gets up. He comes over to us. Everett untangles me from his shoulders, settling my legs down. He rises to his feet.

"Have a taste of her," Everett says.

When Ransom starts to lower himself to a kneel, however, Everett catches his bandana, the way someone might grab a kitten by the scruff of its neck. He pulls the other man close.

"Not there," he corrects. His tone is dark. Pointed.

Everett's face is glistening with me.

I watch as understanding blooms over Ransom's expression. His eyebrows scrunch together in brief concentration as he studies the other man. Then his hand slips over the side of Everett's neck. Ransom fits his thumb underneath Everett's chin, tilting his head up. There's a hesitation, but then—he goes in. He slides his tongue over the sharp line of Everett's jaw. Over his cheek. At the edge of his mouth. Cleaning him. Carefully licking every taste of me.

Their mouths connect for one, brutish moment.

Oh, fuck. Why is this turning me on?

Meanwhile, Everett's sharp blue eyes catch mine.

My heart tightens. I can't read the darkness in his gaze. What is it?

Possessiveness? Adoration? Absolution?

It's more like...

Your cowboy is now my *cowboy, too.*

"How does she taste?" Everett asks.

"Sweet as honey," Ransom mumbles. The stretch in his pants is working double time.

"Feel her," Everett instructs. "Feel how wet she is."

Ransom pivots. His brown eyes meet my own. He climbs onto the bed and cups my cheek. His breath tickles my face. He catches my lips in his and I can taste it. I can taste *me* in his kiss. I relish in his familiarity. The way he claims me is rough and urgent. I push my mouth against his, their eager plaything.

Ransom's hand slips between my legs. I gasp as he fondles my sex and, boldly, slips a finger inside of me. "He was right," Ransom says. "You're soaking, princess."

I whimper. My thighs close around Ransom's arm.

He tilts his gaze upward. "Y'like watching me finger her, you filthy bastard?"

Oh shit.

I've never heard anyone talk to Everett like that and get away with it.

But Everett grins. He slips his hand over my hair. He grabs a handful of it and grips. It tugs tightly at my scalp and pulls a gasp from me. "Not as much as I'm going to enjoy watching you fuck her."

His voice is a dark, syrupy thing, and it goes right between my legs.

"I need something first." Ransom removes his hand from my cunt. He points to the closet. "Toss me my jacket."

Everett does. Ransom nods to me. "Flip, princess," he says.

I twist over onto my belly. His knee wedges between my thigh. I gasp at the pressure. I find myself grinding against it.

The low, throaty chuckle from Ransom makes me ache. He smacks my ass—a quick, chastising swat. "Settle down now."

Like I'm some animal to be tamed. I bite the mattress to keep myself from growling.

These men have made me feral.

Ransom's jacket hits the bed. I hear him riffle through the pockets, and then I feel his fingers in my hair. They pull back my hair from my scalp. They make quick work, criss-crossing the strands into a neat braid.

Licking my pussy. Using me. The way they look at me, talk about me, and touch me makes me burn and writhe.

But *this*...

When Ransom gets his fingers in my hair and braids it back, it puts me into a trance.

When he finishes, it's as though I've been wrapped up in a blanket of peace. Normally, my body is buzzing, primed to fight. When Ransom cinches off the braid with a band, something in me releases. My body relaxes. I want to be touched. I want to be used. I want them to mold me like clay with their strong, capable hands. I'm ready for anything.

Anything.

"Up," Ransom says, so I sit up.

He's holding a yard of rope looped in his hands.

"Show me how good girls pray," he tells me.

I can't help the smile that crosses my lips. *We're anything but good right now.* I fold my hands in prayer position at my chest. He gets to work, looping the rope around my wrists, locking me into place. My blood goes hot at the wonderfully familiar sensation of itchy rope around my bare skin.

He finishes the knot and uses the rope to tug me forward. I love being led by him. His forehead touches mine, and I close my eyes. His breath is soft on my lips.

"Tell me what you want, princess." His voice is a low, dusty murmur. "I need to hear it."

"You," I reply. Everett's finger drags up my spine. My skin prickles, and I shiver. "*Both* of you."

Ransom captures my mouth in a kiss. I open to him, sliding my tongue along his. His breath shudders against my cheek as he shifts in place, pulling out of his clothes until he's as naked as I am. He winds his arms around me and tugs me into his lap.

I'm off-balance without my arms, but his grip holds me upright. I lock my knees around his hips, settling into the crook of his body. His skin burns like a furnace, his heat pressed against mine. He's stiff and swollen, and I wiggle in his lap, desperately wanting it inside of me. The friction draws a rough grunt from him. He reaches between us, guiding himself into me.

He's thick and strong and fills me so sweetly. I gasp, tossing my head back. I fall against Everett, who presses himself up behind me, catching me with his form.

His mouth claims the side of my throat. "Arms up, Claire."

I lift my arms above my head, my wrists still linked together. Everett guides my arms back, bending them, and loops my arms around his neck.

I'm stretched out now, my arms trapped behind me, my legs hooked around Ransom. Everett tickles his fingers down the front of my body. He draws a torturously slow line down my chest, grazing my nipple, and down my stomach.

Ransom's hands grip my hips roughly, moving me so I'm riding his cock. The dual sensations of both their hands make my head spin.

I'm not used to being helpless. But here, with both of them...

I trust them. And that trust makes me loopy with desire.

"Oh, God," I hear myself say—or someone who sounds a lot like me, except her voice is more desperate and thick than I've ever heard it. "That feels...that feels *so good...*"

I'm grinding myself closer to the edge. Everett's hand slides over my rear. His touch vanishes, and this time, when it returns, it feels wet. He presses his fingers between my cheeks, nudging against my tight hole, and I shiver.

"You're doing so well, Claire," Everett murmurs, his voice lighting up every nerve in my brain in the most delicious way. "Now, open for us. Both of us."

His finger slides inside of me, and I gasp. He invades me, reaching places that haven't been touched. I choke at the newness of it.

"Oh, *fuck.*"

"Good?" Everett asks.

He crooks his finger, stroking me from the inside out, and my toes curl. Between the two of them, I'm riding a seesaw of unrelenting pleasure, and it's all I can do to gasp out, "*More.*"

He gives me what I want. Another finger. Stretching me. Manipulating me. And then, finally, I feel *him.* Everett has worked me so well that when he presses his lubed cock into my tight hole, my body accepts him. Wants him. *Needs* him.

I'm stuffed full with both men now. I whimper, unable to control myself anymore. My eyes close, and I lose myself. I feel full—*so full.* Worshipped. Their hands are all over me.

Their lips. Their love. I'm smothered in it, drowning, and when I finally open my mouth again—

I shout. My body clenches, pulling around Ransom's cock. I fall back against Everett's form, whimpering. His hand reaches around, teasing between my legs, drawing out the waves of my orgasm.

Through my blinding pleasure, I see Ransom's eyebrows tighten together. The muscle in his jaw flexes. He lets out a small, frustrated growl and then finally says, "Grab my throat."

In my ear, Everett asks, "What?"

"*Just do it.*"

Everett's hand snakes out. He wraps his hand around Ransom's throat. I hear Ransom let out a small, surprised sound as his breath catches, and then his eyes roll back. He groans, and I feel him swell and spill over inside of me.

Everett exhales a quiet, shuddering sigh in my ear.

The energy between all three of us is intense. The connection. The heat.

Our bodies grind together, utterly entwined. One panting, sweating, heart-pounding being.

It's only once we've quieted that Everett asks, "Are you ready for me to let you down?"

I nod. He unhooks my arms from around him, letting them fall back to my chest.

Ransom makes quick work of untying the rope. My wrists tingle delightfully.

With my hands free now, I slide them over Ransom's strong chest. Then I reach back and slip my fingers up Everett's neck and dive them into his hair.

"I love you," I tell them. I don't mean to say it. It just falls out.

I've been broken open, and things I've kept stuffed inside are spilling freely out of me now.

Ransom's eyes go soft and wide. He cups the side of my face and murmurs, "I love the hell out of you."

He kisses me, and I melt into it. Everett's hand slides up the front of my body. His hand encircles my throat softly, holding me in place.

I break my kiss and twist. Our lips brush. "I love you, too," Everett says.

My heart flutters. For the first time in—maybe—forever, I'm at peace.

We unwind from each other. They wrap their arms around me, and I nestle into the warmth of their naked bodies. I'm crashing down from the intense high, and my eyelids can barely stay open. I feel their lips on my skin. I hear their lips on each other. I'm lulled by the soft touches and the beat of breath on bare skin.

The devil himself couldn't wake me from this deep blanket of sleep.

But he tries.

I jerk awake in the middle of the night. Sweat clings to my body. It's dampened my hair, and it collects underneath my breasts.

I'm short of breath, my heart pounding in my chest.

"Claire..."

That voice. My father's voice.

It's coming from the other room.

It's dark outside. The moon is just a sliver in the sky. Ransom and Everett are side by side with me. Ransom has Everett's headphones in, the white noise helping him sleep.

Everett is fast asleep and, for once, not grinding his teeth. The moonlight kisses their skin, casts dark blue shadows on their bodies.

Claire...

I want to shake them awake. I want them to tell me that the voice in my head is just that—a phantom voice. I want them to tell me there's nothing to be afraid of.

But I don't.

I have to face this monster alone.

Quietly, I move from the blankets and climb down to the end of the bed. I slip out gently so as not to disturb them.

I open the bedroom door and glance down the hall. It looks incredibly long at night, a throat of deep shadow.

Claire.

It's coming from his study. I cross the hall and twist the crystal doorknob.

It's silent in here, now that I've busted the clock. His books are still scattered around the floor. It's dark, and it takes my eyes a minute to adjust. I fumble, hunting for the lamp on his desk, and when I find it, I flip it on.

I jump when I see a woman in the room with me.

No—not a woman. My reflection.

Afraid of ghosts, are we?

I can see my naked body reflected in the glass of the old Belleflower Queen poster. My form lines up almost perfectly with hers. In the reflection, I can almost see myself wearing the Belleflower Queen crown, and my heart gets tight.

Who are you, Claire?

The daughter of a criminal?

The fiancée of an assassin?

Or are you something else?

The most vicious monster of them all, perhaps.

In that moment, I make a decision. I spent the past five years running from Belleflower, but now...

I have to get to the bottom of this. Once and for all.

This ends with me.

I sit in the big leather chair and stare at my own image. I stay there until dawn creeps up, her golden fingers touching the bookshelves. I go back to the bedroom and quietly get dressed. Everett's watch sits on the bedside table. I wrap it around my wrist. I write a note on the Belleflower Queen invitation and leave it folded on the bedside table. With Ransom and Everett asleep in bed, I slip out of the house and taste the cool, early morning frosted air.

43

CLAIRE

I saddle up Chaucer. Together, we ride to the Dagney estate.

There are dark cars parked outside. Big flower decorations drape from the balcony. The old, Grecian-style columns remind me of a time long ago.

It's a beautiful, cloudless day.

I tie Chaucer up and hop off. My boots hit the freshly manicured lawn. I can smell the earth.

I turn the dial on Everett's watch. I press it inward, and a small, blue light clicks on.

"Testing, testing," I say. "I hope there's someone on the other end of this. I'm Claire Preacher. It's six forty-five on September fourteenth. I'm entering the Dagney estate, 24 Calhoun Road, with the intent of finding the man who murdered my father." I pause. I think about Ransom and Everett...who I left in bed. *I'm sorry.* "If I don't make it out," I add. "Well. Assume I found him."

Arris stands on the porch, as though he's been waiting for me. He's wearing a light blue suit with a straw hat, satin blue ribbon around the middle.

When he smiles, the edges of his eyes crinkle. He spreads his arms.

"There she is," he announces. "Our Belleflower Queen."

"Arris."

Jade has melted into one of the seats on the porch that's woven into a teardrop shape. In her bright yellow dress, she looks like a canary in a cage.

"The prodigal daughter arrives," she drawls. She lifts her mint julep in toast. She's already slurring her words.

"Come." Arris moves his hand to the small of my back. "The girls are waiting."

As soon as we enter, we're greeted by a flurry of young women. They wear light, bright dresses and tiny rings on their wedding fingers.

This year's Belleflower Princesses.

I was one of them, once.

"You're here! Come on! You have to see your dress!"

I can't help but laugh. Was I that enthusiastic when I was their age?

Yes. Of course I was.

The floors are polished. Red and purple ribbons twist along the staircases. Even the chandelier that hangs from the second-floor gallery seems to shine brighter.

There are workers in uniforms shuffling around, moving furniture and setting up tables for the after-party tonight. Security men in dark suits linger in the shadows.

We never used to have security before.

The girls pull me upstairs, past the gallery, and into an open room. Light shines in from the wide windows, illuminating the rows of dresses, the dressing tables, and piles of decorations, including the traditional horse head masks, which look bizarre in a pile on their own.

Immediately, I'm attacked with nimble fingers and bobby pins.

This must be how a bride feels on her wedding day.

A team of professionals goes to work.

As the Belleflower Queen, it's my job to sit there and look pretty. The Belleflower Princesses keep fetching me little treats—iced scones and small nibbles to keep me going.

For hours, they work on my hair, and face, and my dress. The whole room has that thick, pungent smell of hair spray, and someone mercifully opens the window. The curtains billow like ghosts in the light breeze.

I'm in a slip with Arris comes and checks in on me. "Well, well." He puts his hand on my shoulder. "I think we have the prettiest Queen this year."

I roll my eyes. "You say that every year."

"I mean it this year." He winds his arm around me. He holds a goblet rimmed with jewels.

I remember this from my time as a Belleflower Princess. The special "Belleflower Queen" cup. Remembering Jade slurring her words downstairs, I shake my head. "Oh, no, thank you."

"It's tradition," he says. He nudges the makeup aside to set the goblet down on the table in front of me. Then he waits, expectantly.

Right. Can't break with tradition.

I lift it in both hands and swallow from the goblet. The drink inside is cold and refreshing. There's a gritty taste to it, like earth and sweet honey. I take another sip, trying to parse the flavors. "This is delicious," I admit. "What is it?"

"Just something to keep you in good spirits." He winks at me in the mirror.

Another pin in my head. My scalp feels so tight my eyes water.

"Come," my torturer/hairdresser says, "let's get you in your dress."

They fit me into the dress. One of the Belleflower Princesses—the youngest, maybe thirteen—comes over to me with a big smile on her face. In her hands, she carries the Belleflower Queen crown.

It's a beautiful vintage piece. A thin headband threaded with tiny fabric flowers, darkened with age. I crouch so the girls can fit it on my head, and then the stylist tucks it in, making small adjustments.

The crown is heavier than I thought it would be. Its teeth bite.

But then I catch sight of the youngest Promise Sister. Her eyes are bright and big.

"You're beautiful," she says. Her voice is soft with awe.

I straighten up and turn to look at myself in the full mirror.

And for a minute—

I forget why I'm here.

I forget about Daddy's murder. I forget about Oculus. I forget about every bad thing that's ever happened in this town.

I look like a queen.

Lace drips down me, tiny floral patterns beading against my skin like rain down a pane of glass. The neckline plunges down my throat and back, revealing clavicle and the squareness of my shoulders. The sleeves billow out but hug snugly at my wrists. White, flat shoes peek out from underneath the lace.

The crown makes me look like the flowers are rising

from my dress, growing out the top of my head. A royal of the wild. Delicate and feral all at once.

This is it. The moment I've been waiting for my entire life.

Now that it's happened, I can hardly feel my bones. My body is so light it's as though I'm floating a centimeter above it.

I turn to take a step, but I stumble. One of the Belleflower Princesses catches me.

"Are you alright?" she asks. Her little voice pitches with concern.

"I'm fine," I say. "Just...I think I need some air."

The room tilts, shudders, and slowly settles. When my vision readjusts, I find myself staring at the goblet on my desk.

What *was* in that drink, exactly?

My center of gravity has rolled away from me, like a spool unraveling on a string. I reach out to catch it, but a hand captures my wrist and tugs me forward.

"We don't have time," my stylist informs me. "We have to get you on the float."

I trip over my feet, and time suddenly speeds up very fast.

44

RANSOM

"Ransom."

Warm breath on my skin. The weight of his body on mine. The press of Everett's lips on my throat. One kiss. Then another. Each kiss firm. Demanding. A mark on my throat that doesn't leave even when his lips pull back.

He whispers against my skin, "*Dragonfly*."

Claiming me with his words. His mouth. Lips turn into teeth. The sharp scrape of teeth grazes the hollow of my throat. I hear myself moan and arch back, tilting my chin upward, inviting him closer.

Hell. Not inviting. Begging. Begging with my body. Begging for more.

"*Riley Ransom.*"

His voice is loud now. It punctures through my thoughts and jolts my eyes open.

A dream.

I'm dreaming.

Was dreaming.

Now, I'm wide-awake, sweat cold on my back, morning wood tenting the sheets.

Everett doesn't flinch. He's dressed, sitting on the edge of the bed. He has an earbud pinched in his fingers, the one he must've plucked out of my ear to wake me up. "Good. You're up."

"Yep. Huh. What. I'm up."

Sure am.

Everett is back to black. Black pants. A black button-up shirt. Freshly shaved. Clothes without a single crease. He laces his shoes up tightly into neat, little bows.

I sit up, pull up my knees, and rub my hand roughly over my face. I clear a tumbleweed out of my throat. "Where's Claire?"

"That's the question of the hour. She was gone when I woke up. But she left this."

He lifts a letter off the bedside table and drops it in my lap. When I read it, my blood goes from hot to cold real quick.

The note just says: *I'm sorry. I have to finish this.*

On the front is an invite, pronouncing Claire this year's Belleflower Queen.

"The Belleflower Festival. Shit. You don't think she—?"

"Yes." Everett's voice is coiled tight, like a spring ready to unload.

"But she knows they're dangerous."

"Yes. And when has that ever stopped someone as stubborn as Claire from getting what she wants?"

"Good point."

Alright. I'm up.

I leap out of bed, grab my jeans off the floor, and tug them on.

There's a lot buzzing around my brain. The way the

three of us tangled last night. The Belleflower Festival today. The dream this morning.

But I've gotta flick it away. Because there's only one thing that matters.

Find Claire. Keep that woman safe. Even if I've gotta hog-tie her and drag her home to do it.

A shadow falls over me. I glance up midway through pulling on my boots. Everett is standing over me. He's got a man-purse over his shoulder and an open palm in front of me.

"You have something that belongs to me," he says.

Huh? Oh, right—

I pluck out the right ear pod and hand it over. "Thanks."

He takes it from me, rubs it clean with a small square cloth, and then pops it back into his ear.

One of his many weird habits that I would've found annoying twenty-four hours ago. Now? It's kinda charming.

Anyway.

I pull on a shirt and tuck a handkerchief around my throat. As we walk downstairs, Everett asks, "What does yellow mean?"

I touch the handkerchief on my neck. "For good luck."

"Good. We'll need it."

My body craves coffee, pancakes, and aftercare. Instead, I get—

Everett's hand on my chest. Stopping me before we exit. His firm touch stops me in my tracks.

"One last thing," Everett says. He reaches into his man-purse and takes out a gun. He hands it over. "Take this."

"No, thank you."

Those eyebrows scrunch together. "What do you mean?"

How do I explain this to a killing robot? I try: "You ever watch *The Lone Ranger*?"

"What?"

"Every Sunday at 2:00 p.m. They play it on the Turner Classics."

"Alright."

"He never kills people. The good guys don't kill. They always just knock them out."

His lips thin. "Do you know jiujitsu?"

"No, but—"

"Krav Maga?"

"Well, no—"

"Kung fu?"

"C'mon…"

"Take the gun. If it's Claire's life or theirs, you'll wish you had it."

He tries to force it at me again, but I lift my palms. "There's always another choice."

"Maybe in the movies."

I clasp my hand on my shoulder and guide him around so we're both facing the mirror. "I want you to look at yourself," I tell him, "and then look at me." The contrast is stark. Everett in his dark clothes and tall hunch. Me in soft leather with a bright spot of color where my yellow handkerchief collars my throat. I touch his shoulder. "*Outlaw*," I say, naming him. Then I pat my own chest. "*Hero*."

Everett scowls at our reflections, which really just proves my point.

Only outlaws scowl.

"You carry the gun." I give him a pat on the back. "And I'll just—"

"Stand there and look pretty?"

"Find another way."

He slips his gun back into his holster. I can feel him stewing. I push out the door and step outside. We're met with a crowd, and I've got to blink against the burst of sun to readjust.

Three cars outside. All police. Sheriff Holden stands out front, a grim look on his face.

Relief spreads through my veins. I lift my hands. "That's what I'm talking about!" I say. "We've got backup!" I smack Everett on the chest. "See? Told you it would work out."

But he's stiff. "Riley," he says, "I don't think—"

"Sheriff Holden!" I clip down the steps, arms outstretched. "You've got no idea how good it is to see you."

"Wish I could say the same," Sheriff Holden grunts. Then he takes his gun out of his side holster and points it at me. "Hands up. You're under arrest for the murder of Randall Preacher."

"Holden, what—?"

I don't get it out before Officer West comes up behind me. He slams me up against the hood of the car. The hood is hot against my cheek, and I feel my arms yanked behind me before a pair of cuffs gets snapped on my wrists.

"Son of a...bitch..."

I watch as Everett puts his hands behind his back and they snap cuffs on him, too.

His eyes meet mine. Those blues are looking at me like this is all my fault.

Now, how the heck is this *my*—?

45

CLAIRE

I'm floating.

I'm on a float, and I'm floating.

It's shaped like the front half of a boat, with a front that narrows and a back that blooms into towering reliefs of flowers, their petals like bubbles ready to burst. Along the sides of the float stand my "studs." Men in dark suits who wear large, horse-style masks to disguise their faces. The Belleflower King rides the float, too. He's perched at the bow of the float, opposite me. I want to figure out who it is, but I can't. He's wearing a lean, white suit. Instead of a horse-head mask, he wears a mask with two faces—one on the front and one on the back, so no matter which way he turns, I can't find his face. A painted crown sits on top of each face. All I know about him, so far, is that he's only a little taller than me. He wears white gloves as he hands out plastic flowers to the crowd below, along with the studs. The crowd on the sidewalk shrieks with joy and raises their arms up to catch them.

Although horses are sculpted along the sides of the float,

they no longer actually pull the float. A bored driver sits in the tractor with a set of headphones, slumped forward, moving at a snail's pace.

And me...

Oh my God, I'm so high.

The sky is bright. I can't stop staring upward at the bursts of light. Yellows and bright greens. And the crowd—there's a warmth from them. A heat. I feel their adoration all the way to my toes. It makes me tingle.

They love me. They shout at me. They smile and reach out their hands, begging for my touch.

They. Love. *Me.*

Music pounds behind me—some pop song played too loud, fuzzy on the speakers. I had a purpose. I had a reason for being here. Something important I had to do, but...

Right now, I just want to *dance.*

I lift my hands toward the sky and feel the sun kiss my palms. I swivel my hips to the music. I pluck roses from the studs and chuck them into the waiting crowd. Every time I throw a rose, they roar with cheers.

I toss a rose with so much force it throws me off-balance. I nearly topple over, but a stud catches me.

His muscles are strong. I melt, kitten-like, into them.

"You having fun, Queen?" his voice comes from under that hideous mask.

That voice. I recognize that voice. "Rafe?"

The horse face grins at me—this big, ghoulish smile.

"Just keep dancing. Enjoy it. It's your moment!"

His hands feel so big on my waist. Strong. Like Ransom's hands. Working hands. I imagine Ransom's big, rough hands sliding up my dress, between my thighs, parting my lips, slipping deep, deep inside of me...

The thought sends a low heat burning through me. I wish he was here. Ransom. Everett. I'd like them to take me. Both of them. Right here. Right on the float. Right in front of all of Belleflower, and...oh, God...

I've never been this horny in my entire life.

Rafe gets on one knee. He procures a flower and bows his head as he gives me a single rose.

I take it. The stem is hard. A thorn pricks my thumb, making it bleed.

This one is real.

I touch the petals to my lips. The soft flesh of the flower is borderline erotic. I close my eyes and give it a gentle kiss.

When I open my eyes again, the entire town is watching me.

Go. Give them a show.

My legs are unsteady as I walk toward the edge of the float, and Rafe has to catch me a couple of times to keep me from falling off the edge. The other studs part to let me through. I lean over and extend the rose out to the greedy hands of the crowd.

A pair of small hands reach out and take hold of the rose.

It's a little girl on her father's shoulders. She has on a fancy, small dress, and her hair is tied back in a braid. Her big, sweet eyes meet mine, and there's nothing but awe in them.

"I want to be you!" she says.

When I meet her gaze, my heart jerks as though it's been yanked by a lasso.

She's me. Me as a little girl. That little prim and proper, gray-eyed girl who wanted so badly to be a Belleflower Queen she'd do anything to get it. The little girl who didn't think she was good enough unless she won. The little girl who thought love was earned and never freely given.

You're enough! I want to scream to her. *You're enough!*

But the float rolls forward through the seat of people, and the crowd swallows her and her little rose whole.

46

EVERETT

The police car hits a bump in the road. Ransom and I knock together in the back seat like bowling pins. With our hands cuffed behind our backs, balance is tricky, and our knees and shoulders keep bumping together.

"This is all one heck of a misunderstanding," Ransom says.

"Tell it to your lawyer," the sheriff says. The second officer sits shotgun beside him and snaps gum between his teeth.

Quietly, I lace my hands together behind my back.

The cuffs are on tight. I have big hands. I could temporarily dislocate my thumb and try to slide out, but even then, it seems unlikely I'd be able to fit the cuff over my hand.

Ransom, meanwhile, can't stop talking.

"Holden," he says. "Jerry. This is crazy. You know me. Heck, Jerry, we grew up down the road from each other."

The younger officer looks out the window. He snaps his

gum again, but his discomfort is written in the thin line of his mouth.

Ransom wiggles forward in his seat. "You know I ain't capable of killing no one. Especially not Mr. Preacher. The man gave me shit every day of my life, but I could take it. You want to be hunting the *real* bad guys—Arris Dagney."

"Dagney?" The younger officer—Jerry, apparently— laughs. "C'mon, man."

"I'm serious!" Ransom protests. "We solved it. All of it. This whole Belleflower Festival? It's all a front. They're selling women. Trafficking them. Real, dark, gangster stuff."

"Ransom, shut up," the sheriff barks.

Sheriff Holden's jaw is locked tight. I notice his knuckles go white on the steering wheel.

Not a good sign. I tense.

"They're the ones behind this," Ransom continues, his voice charged. "The Benefactors' Society. It's all bullshit. They killed Mr. Preacher. They've got Claire. And if we don't act quick, they'll hurt her, too. Look it up. They call them- selves Oculus—"

But Jerry doesn't get to hear the rest of Ransom's tale.

Sheriff Holden takes out his sidearm, points it directly at Jerry, and fires.

Blood doesn't bother me. Cruelty does. I look away as Jerry's head turns into a cloud of red, splattering the side of the car.

Ransom shouts and jumps back.

"I told you," Sheriff Holden says, his voice shaking, "to keep your goddamn mouth shut. That boy had nothing to do with this, and now you had to go and get him involved like that."

Calmly, he puts his firearm away. Then he turns the car

around, taking it off the main road. We roll down dirt paths, away from the center of town.

Back toward where we came from.

There's a click-click-click beside me. Ransom is shaking in his cuffs.

"Swallow it," I tell him. I don't want to be in a closed car with his sick.

Ransom hangs his head between his legs and takes deep, stomach-settling breaths.

"We aren't going to the jail anymore, are we?" he asks.

"No," I tell him. "Not anymore."

47

RANSOM

S hit.

Shitty, shitty, *fuck, fuck*.

Every time I think I know what's going on, something spins me around.

Belleflower is rotting from the inside out, and everyone
is in on it.

Dagney. Loren. Sheriff Holden, apparently.

Heck, at this point, I wouldn't be surprised if Grandmimi
was working for Oculus.

So I do the only thing I can: keep my head down. Try not
to hurl. Ignore the warm, wet feeling of stuff-that-used-to-
be-Jerry on my face.

I can't stop shaking. Everett is quiet as a tombstone
beside me.

Good. Maybe he's cooking up a plan to get us out of
here.

Because right now, I'm batting zero.

The police car drives us around back roads until we end
up at the Dagney estate. Sheriff Holden pulls the car around
back, where Dagney keeps his stables.

There's a bunch of cars in front of the main house, and I'm guessing he doesn't want to draw attention to the massacre on the passenger-side window.

"Don't do anything stupid," Sheriff Holden says. He gets out of the car and leaves us trapped in the back.

I try not to breathe too deeply. The thing-I'm-trying-not-to-think-about is starting to give off a stink.

"How're you so calm right now?" I ask Everett.

"I'm not," he says plainly.

Don't know if that's comforting or not.

We breathe in silence for a second.

"Whatever happens," Everett says suddenly, "I've got your back."

"Yeah," I tell him. "I've got yours."

Okay. *That* helped.

When Holden returns, he's got backup. Two mean-looking security guys. One of them opens Jerry's door, and the body falls out.

"Hell," the man cusses. "You have to make such a mess?"

"Dumbass was spilling everything!" Holden snaps. "Couldn't have him talking about Oculus all around the station, could I?"

The back doors open. One security guy grabs Everett; the other grabs me. I'm yanked out of the car, and I'm barely able to stumble forward before he's dragging me away.

They pull us toward the stables. It's a smaller stable than the one at the Preacher Ranch but a louder one. A couple of horses huff when we enter. I can hear pigs squealing down the way.

The guide kicks my legs out from under me, and I fall on my ass. He uses the rope to tie me down to the bars in the fence. Everett gets tossed down beside me, and they do the same to him.

Now, we're both tied up. Unarmed. Trapped with two grumpy-looking security guards.

"If you've got a rabbit up your ass," I tell Everett, "now'd be the time to pull it."

"Why would I have a rabbit—?"

We don't get to chase that hypothetical train of thought. The barn doors open, and a pair of clean, black dress shoes walks in.

Arris Dagney crouches down in front of us. Jade lingers in the shadows behind him. Her eyes widen when she sees me, but then she looks away. At the floor. At the horses. At anything but the evil her husband has created.

He checks his watch and sighs. He motions to our bound bodies, as though this is all our fault. "We have to make this quick," he says. "In ten minutes, the parade will be over, and Claire's float will pull up to the estate. I've been waiting a long time for tonight. I'm not going to have you two ruin it."

"Chaining us up isn't going to stop it," Everett says. He's got this calm, hard edge to his voice. "It's over, Sergey."

Arris's eyes flash. Then he smiles. It's a slow, creepy smile. "It takes a liar to know one, doesn't it, *Everett Hollow*?" He stretches out Everett's name like a curse. Then, he rattles off his facts: "Lived at an orphanage from ages three to eighteen, at which point you were recruited to the military. Navy SEAL for two tours. And then...redacted. Which means you either got very smart or very gutsy. Valuable traits in my profession."

Then Arris does something strange. He takes Everett's chin in his hand. He pushes his thumb into Everett's mouth and lifts his upper lip, inspecting his teeth. The same way we do when we're finding a horse to breed. "Good genes," Arris comments. He releases Everett from his grasp. "Good stock. Would be a shame to let it go to waste. Tag him and send him in with the ladies."

"Why are you doing this?" I snap. "Money?"

Arris's mouth turns downward, disappointed. "Money. The only motivation your small mind can think of. I seek *perfection*. Breeding horses is nothing to breeding heiresses. Some men will give anything for that level of perfection. The perfect legacy. Leaving nothing up to chance."

"Is that what Randall Preacher wanted?" Everett asks.

Arris lets out a short sigh. "He was a special case. He used my services. Purchased a Belleflower Queen of his very own. And when he got his legacy...I never asked for money. I only asked for one thing. That when she came of age...she'd return to the flock. You can't imagine what purebreds go for in my line of work."

Coldness seeps into my veins.

Claire. They're talking about Claire.

Mr. Preacher purchased her mother. Paid to impregnate her. And when Claire came...it was only under the stipulation that they'd sell her, too.

Rage climbs through my veins. It makes my voice shake. "You fucking psycho...you ain't gonna get away with this."

"But I have," Arris cuts in. "For thirty years. Do you think you're the first that discovered what was going on here?" He stands up then. He flicks his wrists toward us. "Send Everett in with the women. Kill the cowboy."

The security guards lift their guns toward me. I feel my body tense up. I test the limits of the rope. "Hold on a minute—"

"Wait."

Help comes in a surprising shape.

Jade steps forward. She slips her arms around Arris and looks at me over his shoulder. "Don't. I need him."

Arris narrows his eyes. "For what? His children will have bad teeth and a poor man's accent."

"I resent that," I say. "I've got all my teeth."

Beside me, Everett chuckles.

I cut him a glare. "Keep laughing, sperm silo."

He chokes on his good humor.

Jade hugs her arms around her husband's waist. "He's my...*teaser*." A strange look of surprise crosses Arris's face. His wife nestles the side of his neck. She kisses him there. "Keep him around...just a little longer. Show him what a real man looks like. Aren't I allowed a little fun?"

Arris's mouth draws into a tight line.

"He can live," Arris says roughly. "For now."

Arris links his hand in Jade's. With that, he takes her and walks her out of the stables.

My heart is pounding like a jackhammer in my chest.

The security guard comes up to Everett. He takes a small box out of his bag. It's got a syringe in it.

"Hold up," I say. "What the hell is that?"

"Something to help him *enjoy* tonight."

That's all the security man says before he fills the syringe and sticks Everett with it.

Slowly, he pushes his thumb on the stopper, injecting Everett with clear liquid.

Each push sends a new wave of panic through me.

What the hell are they putting in him?

"Quit it!" I snap. "Get away from him!"

I'm a dog straining against its collar. I'll rip their throats out. Both of them. Just for putting their hands on him. I test the limits of my bonds, but the ropes are tight. I'm helpless, and there's nothing I can do as they untie Everett and drag him away.

48

CLAIRE

The sun drags low in the sky by the time we pack into the bus to leave the parade.

How long have we been out? I'm not sure.

Time has run away from me. This morning seems ages ago. I've been in my dress all day, and it's chaffing under my breasts, damp under my arms. My hair has frizzled up around the flower crown. I'm escorted back in a tinted bus with the stallions. Horse head masks litter the floor, but the men are vibrant—sweating, talking loudly, laughing. I can't make out their words; it sounds like they're talking through tin cans attached to a string.

I sit in the back. My Belleflower King sits all the way in the front of the bus. They've worked hard to keep us apart and save the reveal for tonight. Even though it's hot in the bus, he keeps his mask on and dips his water bottle underneath the mask to take sips from it. He won't turn his double head to face me, and the secret is killing me.

I want to ask Rafe. He's the only one who might spill the details. But he's sitting too far away from me, talking animatedly with his fellow studs. His thick hair sits flat against his forehead, a sweat-band from the mask.

The bus bounces over the bumpy roads. Every time I ask for water, someone gives me a bottle of honey-sweet liquid. I let myself be parched.

The driver lets us out in front of the Dagney estate. There is no little Belleflower Princess to greet us at the door this time. This after-party is adults-only, after all.

I'm the last off the bus. I step off, and Arris catches my hand.

"Look at you," he says. "Shining like a diamond."

Jade stands next to him. She's still wearing her smile, but it looks as fake as the masks.

"It's the sweat," I say with a small laugh. "I think I need to freshen up."

"Of course. Come in first."

The two of them guide me inside. As soon as I pass the entrance, I'm greeted with a round of applause.

Lining the hallways are men I recognize. Daddy's old friends. The men of the Benefactors' Society, all dressed to the nines, wearing expensive suits and bright, white smiles. Their wives aren't here—instead, I recognize former Belleflower Queens mixed among them.

My heart does a flip in my chest.

You're here, the little twelve-year-old version of me whispers in my ear. *You made it. You're a Queen now.*

I go down the line, shaking hands. Mustaches tickle my skin when they kiss my cheek.

"Follow me," Jade says, circling her hand on my middle. "Let's get you upstairs."

I'm so light on my feet I feel like a balloon being tugged by a string when Jade guides me up the winding staircase, across the balcony, and into the same room I got ready in earlier. It's been cleared out, mostly, but there's an evening dress hanging on the dresser. It's a soft, off-white color with sequins that flow down and sparkle like diamonds.

Jade lingers in the doorway. "Do you think I could have some privacy?" I ask.

She hesitates but then widens her smile. "Of course."

With that, she exits, leaving me alone.

Alone.

It's the first time I've been on my own all day, and the silence is almost deafening.

I pluck the pins out of my hair and gently remove the crown, setting it on the dresser. I shake my braids free, and my scalp tingles with gratitude. I catch a glimpse of myself in the mirror. My makeup has, somehow, held up. But my cheeks are flushed. My irises are pinholes.

There's an adjoining half-bath. I turn on the sink and drink from it, greedy, slurping swallows, like a horse. The cool, fresh water tastes as good as running silver. Already, I feel myself coming back to life.

I wipe the back of my arm over my mouth. I don't have much time. I click the button on Everett's watch and hold it to my face.

"Claire Preacher," I say. "I'm back at the Dagney Estate for the after-party. The entire Benefactors' Society is here, along with former Belleflower Queens. They've been giving me something to drink—I'm not sure what. I think it's laced. There's security all around the building. I'm not sure if they're here to keep people out or keep people *in*."

I take off my dress. I let it fall in a heap on the floor as I step into the evening gown. There's a zipper on the side, and I pull it up.

"No sign of Loren yet," I continue to report. "Arris and Jade are here, though, so he must be here. When I find him—"

In the window to my right, I see a light suddenly flicker on in the stables.

The sun is cooling on the horizon, leaving a low, blue-purple bruise in its shadow.

A golden light spills out of the mouth of the stable flanking the back of the house. I watch from my place as two figures exit the stable.

It's hard to make it out. It looks like one man pulling another along. The taller man moves jerkily, as though his movement is limited, somehow.

I squint. Is that...?

Everett?

The knock on the door sends my nerves scattering like pins through my blood. I pull away from the window just in time to see Jade in the doorway, an impatient look on her face.

"They're waiting for you downstairs," she informs me.

I take one final glance out the window.

The figures are gone. The light still burns in the stables.

The unease in my body feels like raven claws digging into my chest.

I hear Daddy's voice. *Chin up. Back straight.*

I adjust my posture, fix the crown back on my head, and turn my insides to ice. I move to the door, but Jade blocks my exit. She holds up the goblet from earlier.

"Drink first," she says. "All of it."

I blink. They can't be this brazen. Can they?

"Why?"

Her green eyes don't flinch. "Makes the medicine go down smoother."

I hesitate. I want to toss the goblet in her face and run.

A radio chirps. There's a security guard by the door. He turns to glance at us.

"Trouble, ladies?" he asks.

"No trouble." Jade looks at me. Her eyebrows lift. "Right?"

I take the goblet. It feels cold and heavy in my hand.

Despite myself, despite knowing better, I recite the Belleflower Queen mantra in my head.

A Belleflower Queen must be perfect. She must understand that disobedience is unacceptable and a reflection of ugliness upon her character.

Well. Down the rabbit hole we go.

I tilt the goblet to the lips. It takes everything in me not to gag as the sweet-tasting liquid slides down my throat.

When I return the empty goblet to Jade, she checks the inside, seemingly to make sure I've swallowed every drop. Only then does she step back to let me pass.

"Escort her downstairs," she tells the guard.

He takes my arm. I feel myself glancing back. "Aren't you coming?"

Jade remains in her spot. Her mouth twists. "No wives allowed in this wing of the house. This is your night. Enjoy it."

She takes my arm and pulls me into a small hug.

"They're here," she says suddenly. A low whisper in my ear.

My spine tenses. "What?"

"James and Ransom. *Play the game.*"

The guard pulls me back, separating us. Jade composes herself in a tight smile, and I have to wonder if I imagined the whole thing. Jade gets smaller and smaller as I'm whisked downstairs.

The party has kicked into full gear. The guard escorts me around the corner to the ballroom, where a folksy bluegrass band is playing. A wave of heat comes over me—the bodies on the dance floor, maybe, or the drink already catching up with me.

There's a table on the other end of the room, stacked with food. My stomach pinches. I haven't eaten all day.

But before I can try to make my way there, a hand grabs my wrist.

"Come, beautiful." He smiles—Hank? Hughes?—his name has left me. He has to be twenty years my senior, but his cheeks are bright red, like a little boy's, when he says, "Dance with me."

I feel my body get pulled out onto the dancefloor.

I get tossed from person to person. Men whose faces have blurred with time. But it's the women—the former Queens—who make my heart stop when they take my hands in theirs and spin me around. I hung their pictures on my wall. I worshipped them. And here they are. Smiling at me. Welcoming me. Loving me.

I'm getting swept up in again. The wave of it all. The *want*.

"You're beautiful," they say.

"You're so strong."

"You'll be okay."

Tight, strained smiles.

"Thank you," I hear myself say. "Yes. I know."

My body bumps into another in my wild dancing.

I spin right into the arms of Maeby. Queen of '94. She doesn't look at all like the Maeby from behind the bar—her eyes are deep-set in dark eyeshadow, her hair done back in beautiful braids.

She sees me, and her mouth falls open. She holds my elbows, and I hold hers. Together, we spin.

"Claire," she says. Her voice is breathless.

"Maeby."

She pulls me in close. So close I get an airless breath of her flowery perfume.

Her voice shakes in my ear. "You shouldn't be here," she says. "*Get out.*"

I feel myself stumble backward. Her words pierce through my daze like an arrow.

She doesn't wear their fake smiles. She just stares at me, standing in the middle of the dance floor, as though she's seen a ghost.

For the first time in the whole night, real fear grips through me.

What if I've overplayed my hand?

Outnumbered. Trapped. At their mercy.

A hand slides over my shoulder, and I nearly jump out of my skin. When I whip around, I come face to...

Faces.

It's him. My Belleflower King. And the double-faced mask, grinning wickedly down at me.

My heart hammers in my chest. He lowers himself down to a single knee.

Slowly, he reaches up and takes hold of his mask. He pulls it from his head, removing it, and sets it down on the floor.

"My Queen." Loren Dagney smiles up at me. That self-satisfied smirk curls the mustache over his lip.

My throat goes tight. I can feel my heart in my neck pounding.

"My King," I whisper.

His blue eyes gleam up at me. He offers a hand.

I stare at his palm, feeling the rage rising in me like a storm.

The same hand that murdered my father.

I take it, and he pulls me in for a final dance.

49

RANSOM

Well, this is a crock of shit.

I'm trapped in the barn. Stuck with nothing but the smell of horse and barn animal.

Everett's gone. I'm left with one security guard.

"Stay put," he says.

"Or what?"

"Or I'll break your fucking legs."

"Yep. That'd do it."

I pull my legs in, sitting cross-legged.

He scowls at me. Big, bulldog face. Then he leaves me tied up and goes around to the front of the barn. He steps outside, and I hear him talking to someone on the phone.

I look around the stables. Nothing but animals on either side of me. Down on the end of the stable, there's a second doorway, wide open. I can see the mountains and the setting sun in the distance. I shift, twisting my wrists. I reach as far as I can and brush my fingers over the rope. I feel her curves, mapping out the knot in my mind's eye. It's a tight one. I'm not getting out of here anytime soon.

The sound of a horse huffing draws my attention.

Hold on…

I know that grumpy huff.

"Tssst!" I hiss, half whispering. "Chaucer! That you?"

Down the back of the stables, I watch as Chaucer slowly steps into view, craning his neck. His head swivels left to right as he chews the dandelions.

"What the hell're you doing here?"

He startles at my voice, taking a couple of steps backward. Like a kid with his hand in the cookie jar.

"Hey—no. C'mere. Quick about it."

He hesitates, suspicious. Then, slowly, he clips through the stable and walks over to me. He seems confused by me being on the ground. He pushes his nose around my hair, and I feel his hot breath as he huffs, nibbling affectionately.

"Hey, buddy. Boy, am I glad to see you."

I tilt my head against his snout. *God bless.*

I chance a quick glance toward the front. The guard hasn't noticed us.

"Listen. Chaucer. I need your help."

He looks down at me and flicks his ear. He's listening.

"Beer me."

His ears perk up. He knows that command. Loves that command. Usually means there's a carrot in it for him. He jerks his head, grabs the nearest object—a hat sitting on the railing—and tosses it at me.

Nope. That's not going to help. "*Beer me.*"

An exasperated huff. He goes, picks up a rake, and throws it at me.

Still not helpful. Actively trying to kill me now. "Beer me. Something useful."

Finally, he gets something I can use. A shovel. He drops it beside me.

"That's more like it," I sigh. "You beautiful fucking beast."

I hook the shovel under my boot. I nudge it back, rolling it toward me. It takes a hell of a lot of maneuvering, but I manage to kick it toward my hands. I use the sharp end and start sawing at the rope. It nicks me more than once. I get a jolt of pain and the wet heat of my own blood, but I don't stop. I can't stop. Claire needs me. Everett needs me.

Heroes gotta hero.

I tilt my chin down. I grab the handkerchief in my mouth. I bite down on it to muffle my groans as I power through.

After what seems like ten lifetimes, I finally hear a snap. The rope slackens, losing its grip on my wrist. I pull back, free from the fence.

Eureka! The rope is gone, but I've still got a pair of hand-cuffs to contend with. I glance back at the door.

I can see just the outline of the security guard. Still facing away from me. Still talking to someone on his walkie-talkie.

Alright then. Let's figure this out quick.

I tighten my core and push up to my feet. I nearly stumble into Chaucer getting up, and he clicks back a couple of paces to get out of my way. Hands still stuck behind my back, I find equipment hanging in the back of the stable. Brushes. Saddles. And—

Farrier nippers. Good enough for horse hooves, then there's good enough for these cuffs. Getting the thing to snap around the metal is a challenge, and when my frustration mounts, I close my eyes.

Okay. You don't need to see to do this. You know these tools. Just...*feel it.*

I go slow. I feel the mouth of the nippers catch on the

chain linking the cuffs together. I squeeze the handles hard until I hear it snap.

The nippers clatter to the floor. My hands fall to my sides, cuffs still wrapped around them, but the chain is broken, anyway. *I'm free.*

And in trouble. The sound caught the attention of the guard. He turns and heads back inside the stable.

Time to act.

I grab the rope hanging against the wall. He's so startled to see Chaucer just chilling in the stable that it takes him too long to see *me.*

I knock him down with a swift punch. I get him on the ground and leave him hog-tied.

"Real sorry about this," I tell him. "It's not personal."

He wiggles in place, his curses muffled by the rag in his mouth. I grab another coil of rope and wrap it up, looping it to my belt.

Before I leave, I ask him, "Hey, you don't got headphones on you, do you?"

50

CLAIRE

When Loren and I make our way through the ballroom, everyone clears the dance floor to let us in.

We're the center of attention.

The chandelier hanging above casts a sharply white glow. The faces of the crowd around us blur. As Loren and I move, I find myself unable to look away from his face. Every time I look beyond him, the room spins.

So I hold eye contact with Daddy's killer as we sway to the music.

He might've been handsome if another soul wore his skin. A chestnut-brown mustache curls down his mouth. His hair has deep, thick waves. He's svelte but soft.

We're close enough that when he speaks, I can feel the heat of his breath on my cheek. He smells like he swallowed an entire pack of mints in a poor attempt to cover the nicotine stain on his tongue.

It takes everything in me not to turn away.

"It feels like fate, doesn't it?" he says.

Hmm, not really. It feels like you killed my father just to bring me back home.

I play along. "How so?"

Those blue eyes glitter with a strange intensity. "We grew up together. You were best friends with my sister. Seemed like we were always...slipping in and out of each other's lives."

I was slipping out. You were slipping in.

He nearly steps on my feet. I have to dance two steps back to avoid him.

He grabs me suddenly, yanking me forward. We're just a hairsbreadth away from each other now.

"You were always too busy playing with those rough Sooter boys," he says. "Down by the lake."

I try to pull away, but his grip is too tight. "Loren—"

"It's okay." He grins. It's a terrible sight. "I knew. I saw. But I kept your secret. Because I knew eventually, you'd come crawling back. You'd find your own again."

He pushes my hair back under his thumb. He tilts in, and I can feel him inhaling me. There's a shudder in my breath, and my stomach curls. "I've been waiting all night for this."

My jaw clenches. "So have I."

You have no idea.

He twirls me, but instead of twirling back to him, I keep spinning. I pretend to trip on my own feet and stumble backward. I aim my body off the dance floor and bang right into the buffet table.

There's a couple of quick gasps. My elbow is sticky with cream puff. I feel someone grab my arm, trying to help me up.

"Sorry," I say. "I'm so clumsy..."

I'm only half-faking. The room is, in fact, tilting. Spinning. I find myself tightening my grip on the other person to keep myself from falling backward again.

Come on, Claire. Get it together.

I focus my vision long enough to grab a serrated knife off the table. As they help me up, I manage to slip the knife under my dress, fitting the blade under the elastic of my stockings.

51

EVERETT

The guard leads me through the back entrance. We enter through a narrow reading room. He stops, stands in front of me, and demands, "Look at me." I do. He lifts a finger. "Follow this with your eyes only."

He moves his finger slowly to the side. I follow the motion with my eyes, then with my head, and then my whole body follows. I find myself tilting and stumble to keep myself upright.

Shit. Whatever drugs they put in me are working fast. I don't like not being in control of my body.

He seems satisfied with my reaction and drops his hand. He reaches for a device on his belt—a small, blocky thing with a handle. "This'll pinch," he warns me. I feel him line the device up with my earlobe. There's an intense pressure and then a brief, throbbing pain, and then it's done. When he pulls back, my ear feels heavy.

He moves behind me and starts to undo the rope around my arms. "So here's the deal," he says. "While the men have their fun with the Belleflower Queens, Mr. Dagney hires local boys to come entertain the wives and ladies in the library. Rules go like this. Don't try to escape. Don't hurt anyone. Obey the ladies and give them what they want. Follow those rules, and you might actually enjoy yourself."

"And if I don't?" I hear myself say, though my voice feels foggy and distant.

"Then we kill you and your friend."

Ransom. The rope falls away from me, and I flex my hands. It's just me and this guard. Even in my intoxicated state, I imagine I could take him. Easily.

But could I take them all before they take Ransom out?

That fear is enough to keep me in check. For now.

The guard comes back around. I ask him, "What am I walking into, exactly?"

His gaze levels with mine. "A feeding frenzy. Good luck."

He reaches for a glass doorknob, twists it, and opens, gesturing me inside. I enter the room and immediately understand the warning.

What was, I assume, a once-elegant library has been transformed into a den of sin. The room is dark, lit only by flashes of blue and purple strobe lights. Grecian statues have sex toys hanging off them. The music is loud—this dull, roaring heartbeat. A sick, slow thumping. Women and men hang off each other. Clutching each other. Dancing. Moaning. Fucking.

I'm spinning. Every step I take feels like I'm pushing through wet sand. I stumble over a bottle of champagne left on the floor, kicking it, and fall forward, barely catching myself on the table.

A hand slides over my back. Female. I feel the nails. The sharpness tingles all through my body as she purrs in my ear, "Having trouble, honey?"

"Poor baby," another voice chimes in beside me. Lips find my throat. "Let mama kiss it better."

Get off of me, I want to say, but my throat is tight. Dry.

And my body...it's responding. Warming to their touches.

I hate myself for it.

The mix of uncontrollable arousal and intense revulsion makes me shake. The lionesses, encouraged, continue their onslaught of bold touches.

I need an out.

There's a sudden flash of light. I glance up and see a door open and close, a man exiting it.

Bathroom.

I extract myself from the women. Untangling them is like stepping out of an octopus embrace, but I manage it. My body is so heavy it feels as though there is someone grabbing my ankles, dragging behind me as I force myself forward toward the bathroom.

I push inside. I'm met with bright, clean light, and when the door closes behind me, it muffles that horrible noise. There are other men in here—shirtless, their bodies glistening, chatting loudly together—but I ignore them and grab hold of a sink.

I turn on the water and splash myself. My face is numb. I barely feel it.

I don't recognize the man in the mirror. Hair askance. Clothes stained with sweat. Color drained from my face.

There's a tag on my ear. I touch it. Pierced through my earlobe is a plastic, yellow tag. On the tag, a QR code.

I've been tagged. Like cattle. *Like fucking cattle.*

"Amigo!" An arm is flung around me. I'm accosted by a spicy cologne and a crooked grin. "Look who joined the party!"

It's Rafe. Ransom's friend. From Maeby's. He's wearing

no shirt, tight pants, too much glitter, too much cologne, and the same yellow tag in his ear with his own unique code.

"First time, eh?" he continues. His eyes are wide, but his irises are small, tiny dots. "First time's always a shocker. Go with the flow, yes? Look at you. The ladies love you." He catches my chin and gives me an affectionate shake. Like a dog. If my limbs weren't rubber, I'd murder him.

He reaches into his pocket and pulls out a small vial. "If you want," he offers. "Keeps you...*up 'n at 'em*, as they say."

Cocaine. Party drugs. This is not my scene.

But...

I feel like I'm underwater. I need to get my heart rate up.

I need to find Claire. I need to find Ransom.

I need to wake up from this terrible fucking nightmare.

"Fuck it," I hear myself say. I take his vial, pop off the top, and fit it under my nose. Uppers to counteract the downers.

The men give a whoop and cheer. My blood rushes. Pounding. My heart takes off, leaping against my rib cage. The roaring, underwater ocean noises in my ear...finally dissipate, like the tide pulled out to sea, never to return.

I take in a deep, gulping breath and look at myself in the mirror. I'm a wreck. But I can see. I can hear. Everything that was foggy and hazy is now painfully crystal clear.

Alive. *I'm alive.*

The wolf tattoo on my forearm snarls and growls at me. It's ravenous and ready to sink its teeth into the throats of everyone in this building.

"Okay. Let's do this."

"That's the spirit!" Rafe smacks me on the back, and like a pack, the men exit, barking and howling.

When I re-enter the library, the assault on my senses almost knocks the breath out of me.

Before, it was a low, sinking sensation. Now, I see every-thing clearly. Too clearly.

I can walk, but now I need to run. The music is too loud, like toothpicks pricking my eardrums over and over. I need my headphones. The sound makes me want to rip my ears off, and I cover them with my hands, grinding my teeth against the noise.

Dragonfly doesn't like this.

Rafe fits into the scene seamlessly. He climbs the table and starts dancing to the music. Immediately, he's flocked with hands. Lips.

Take a breath. You can survive this.

Slowly, I lower my hands from my ears. I breathe into the pain.

I notice things I didn't before. In the shadows, security men remain quiet and cold. They'd take me down before I managed to get out the door.

So I'm going to have to find another way out.

My answer comes in the form of a pair of eyes. They meet my gaze from across the room. I watch as the woman slides out of another man's lap and walks through the sea of people to get to me.

Mary-Kate. Claire's friend. She wears a thin, dark dress, the strap hanging off her shoulder.

"James," she says. "Haven't you strayed far from home. Does Claire know you're here?"

Her hands slip over my shirt. Slowly, she begins undoing the buttons.

(Don't touch me. Get your hands off me.)

I counter, "Mary-Kate. Does your husband know you're here?"

That draws a smile from her. "What they don't know won't kill them."

She has her phone tucked into her bra. She pulls it out now, and her fingers fumble over the screen. She holds the phone up to my ear and scans the QR code. I watch as she punches in a couple more buttons, then tucks her phone away, satisfied.

Her body leans against mine. Into my ear, she says, "You're mine for the next two hours."

Then she links her fingers in mine and tugs me to the door. She flashes her phone to the guard—showing her receipt for me, I assume—and he nods before opening the door and leading us out.

My feet push me forward, my heart thrumming, and all I can think is:

She's here. In this house.

Somewhere.

I'm one step closer to Claire.

52

CLAIRE

The blade of the knife is cold against my thigh.

The music winds down. Loren slips his hand to my arm. "Don't you want to see your throne?" he asks.

This is it. I keep my expression neutral.

What did Jade say? *Play the game.*

"Yes," I say. "More than anything."

He takes my hand. He guides me away from the dance floor. All around us, I can feel people staring, watching us as Loren takes me up the winding staircase.

He leads me down the hall to a door with a horseshoe nailed to the front. Without releasing my hand, Loren reaches into his pocket. He takes out a key, unlocks the door, and guides me inside.

It takes me a second to figure out what I'm seeing.

The walls are padded. Thick, green padding. The same padding we use for the horse breeding sheds. There are open shelves and hooks on the walls, which have a variety of objects. Some for pleasure—vibrators, dildos, lube. And some for pain—whips, chains, gags.

There's only one piece of furniture in the center of the room. It looks almost like a hospital bed, tilted slightly up. It has stirrups to hold a person's arms and legs in place.

A sick, dark chill slithers up the back of my neck.

"What is this?" I ask. I try to keep my voice light.

Don't let them see you scared.

Loren smiles. He gestures to it. "Your throne."

I can't help but think—what was it like with the other Belleflower Queens?

Is this the point where the fantasy died? Or were they too drugged to even notice the whip curled up and hanging on the wall?

Loren's hands move to my waist. He pulls me forward.

I put my hands to his shoulders. "Loren—wait. Let's go back outside."

"Just try it." He grins. That wicked, leering grin.

Forcibly, he pulls me over and sits me on the table. He climbs up with me. His mouth finds the side of my face. His breath hits my throat. He grips my ankle, and before I can fight it, he's already locking my legs into the stirrups, forcing me into place.

Panic surges through my chest. "Wait, *wait.* Let me look at you." I clasp my hand over the side of his face. His cheeks are spotted with pink. Exhilaration. Tenderly, I rub my thumb over the side of my face. "My King," I tell him. I hope he takes the trembling in my voice for admiration and not for fear. With my hand on his face, the watch is close to him. I want his confession, loud and clear, before I kill him. "You did it, didn't you?"

He cocks his head like a dog. "I did what?"

"My father. You killed him." His expression crumples, but I quickly add, "You *saved* me from him. He was...a terrible man. Always had me under his thumb. But you...

you killed him, didn't you? Tell me the truth, and I'll give you...anything you want."

A slow, terrible smile curls over his mouth.

"You're damn right I did. I'd do it again. You should've seen him. Lying in bed. Mean old son of a bitch. I held up the gun and blew his head clear off. He tried to keep you away. I couldn't have that. You're mine."

Now it's my turn to smile. "Loren."

"Yes?"

"I need you to hear me when I say...I will *never* be yours."

I reach between us, take the knife out from under my dress, and twist it upward, gorging him right near the groin.

He chokes in surprise. He doesn't scream. He doesn't whimper. I just watch the pure and utter shock cover his face as he looks between us.

When he gets his tongue back, it's to laugh.

"Dumb bitch," he says. "You missed my dick."

"I know," I tell him. "I hit your femoral artery."

I yank the knife out. Blood showers down on me.

53

EVERETT

Mary-Kate leads us upstairs. I hear music in the other room—not the thumping club music from the library.

This is a live band. Folksy.

Mary-Kate notices my attention shifting. "That's the Queen's coronation." She winks. "Not for us."

Belleflower Queen. Claire.

She's near.

She tugs my hand. The guard body-checks me, his shoulder nudging against mine. When he does, his jacket falls open, and I spot the firearm holstered to his belt.

Gun. I need that gun.

I let Mary-Kate lead me up the stairs. She leads us into a bedroom with white, fluffy sheets and landscapes on the walls.

The door clicks closed behind us. The guard stays inside, watching.

Mary-Kate's fingers make quick work of my shirt. She runs her palms over my chest and stomach, appreciating the muscles there.

She lets out a low hum, a near purr. "Claire always got all the best things," she muses. "My turn."

She comes in for a kiss, but I close my hand on her throat, holding her at bay. Her eyes go wide with surprise, and she gasps. In the edge of my vision, I see the bodyguard tense, his hand going to his sidearm.

My wolf is howling. I hold her here but don't squeeze. Instead, I stroke my thumb over the pounding pulse of her throat.

"You smell like other men," I tell her. "Go. Clean yourself first."

The surprise in her eyes morphs into a burning heat. She licks her lips. "Yes, sir."

With that, I release her. She gives me one last hungry look before she vanishes into the adjoining bathroom. She leaves it cracked open. An invitation I won't take her up on. The shower hisses as it starts up.

I can feel the guard's eyes on me. I lean against the wall beside him.

"So," I start. "Are you going to stay here the whole time?"

He won't look me in the eye. "It's my job."

Oh. I can read the familiar lines of repressed homosexuality like a book.

All my worst, most vile instincts are rising to the surface, but I don't care.

I'll do whatever it takes to get me closer to Claire.

And to get to Claire, I need that gun.

"I'm afraid you won't get much of a show," I tell him. "She's not my type."

He shifts his weight from one foot to the other. "Huh."

I turn to him. I pick my words carefully. "I need some-thing...*harder*."

Finally, he meets my gaze. His lips part. A hopeful, wanting itch.

It's the distraction I need.

I tilt in, as though for a kiss, and he lets me. But instead of meeting his mouth, I grab his gun. My hand wraps around the cold steel, my finger around the trigger.

Ah. We're home.

In an instant, I have the gun underneath his chin. He chokes, his eyes wide with fear now.

Past-Everett wouldn't have hesitated to blow his head clean off.

But now, Dragonfly's voice is in my ear.

There's always another way.

Fuck him for making me a better man.

I remove the gun and deal him a swift punch instead. His body slumps to the floor. He's out cold.

Just as I'm about to make my escape, I hear it.

A scream. Two screams.

The first, a man's.

The second makes my blood cold.

It's Claire's.

Claire is in trouble. And she's right next door.

I can hear her. I rush up against the wall and slam my palm on it. "Claire!" I shout.

I will break down this wall.

I will break it apart.

I will tear this house down brick by brick to get to her.

She calls back, "Everett!"

My heart is going a thousand miles an hour in my chest.

"What the fuck is going on—?" Mary-Kate leaves the shower, towel around her body. Her mouth falls open when she sees the guard slumped to the floor.

I raise my gun and aim it at her. She freezes.

"Back inside," I tell her.

She stares at me like a deer in headlights. Slowly, she walks backward into the bathroom. "Please," she whimpers. "Don't—"

I shut the bathroom door in her face. I lock her in.

Good. That's done.

I rush to the door, fling it open, and—

There she is.

Claire. My Claire.

Her hair is tangled around a flower crown. Her skin is flushed, and those gray eyes are wild. She looks like a ghost in her soft, white dress. The hem of it is splattered red.

Her knuckles are white as she grips the hilt of a bloody knife.

Immediately, I take her face in my hand. I savor the warmth of her cheek. She melts into my touch, her eyelids lowering.

"Are you okay?"

Those soft eyes look up at me. "It's not my blood." She reaches up. Her fingertips press against the bare skin of my chest. Even the smallest touch from her sends a fire lashing through me.

"I came to save you," she says.

My breath is light. Tight. My voice is a hard rumble when I tell her, "You already have."

Our eyes meet. There's a small, tense second of electricity.

And then her mouth crashes against mine, and I lose all control.

She drops the knife. I drop the gun. I need both hands to grab her. I cup her rear and the back of her head, holding her against me. She climbs me like she can't get close enough, wrapping both her legs around me. I yank her into the room and shove her against the wall.

I need to be inside of her. Nothing else matters. I've never needed anything more.

"I need you," Claire moans in my ear, her voice hoarse and desperate.

I rip her panties from her legs and bunch her dress up. Her nails dig sharply into my back as I undo my zipper and shove my aching cock inside of her. She's dripping wet. My hard length slides in easily as she soaks me.

She cries out. She shouts my name—*yes*—and *more*. I grind her against the wall. Our hips smack together. Her skin burns feverishly hot against mine.

I ravish her mouth, and she attacks me back, matching my ferocity. She launches forward, knocking me off-balance, and I stumble backward, hitting the bed. Claire straddles me here, riding me hard and fast.

My wild woman. She bucks over my body, her dress fighting to stay on. Her pink nipple slips out of the v-cut, and I attach myself, sucking and nibbling. She grips her hair and shouts as her body clenches me. I growl, her nipple trapped between my teeth, as she milks my release from me.

Her hair is a mess, trapped in the crown. She runs her hand over my chest. Her nails leave hard, red marks. I hiss. My queen isn't done.

With one swift move, I flip us over so Claire is on her back, her body dripping half off the side of the bed. I hoist her strong leg over my shoulder and drive my cock deep inside my greedy, desperate girl. Even after my release, my erection is still raging strong, and if she keeps looking at me with those lust-filled gray eyes and those slightly parted, rosebud lips, I'm afraid it's never going to slacken.

I prop myself up with a hand over her head. "Look at me," I tell her. "Eyes on mine."

She keeps those perfect, beautiful eyes trained on mine.

"Good girl." I reward her by cupping her neck, my thumb pressing in. She's sweating. There's a light puddle of sweat in the hollow here, and I lick it, drinking her like heaven's elixir. "I'm yours. Completely."

She grabs my ass. My stomach clenches as she grips tightly, holding me as deep as possible inside of her. "I'm yours," she whimpers. "Give it to me, Everett."

I choke on a moan as a second orgasm erupts from me. She mewls with pleasure, rocking her hips on my cock, her own body throbbing with me.

Her nails leave a bright trail of pain up my back, and I shiver. When I kiss her, her tongue is a balm against mine.

My heart is pounding. But—finally—we're slowing.

Those gray eyes look clearer. She blinks, as though seeing me for the first time, and slips her hand through my hair.

"You have a tag on your ear," she says curiously.

I pet her messy hair. "You have a crown on your head."

Her eyes fall to something over my shoulder. "Is he dead?"

Oh. The security guard. Forgot about him.

I shake my head. "No. I don't think so."

There's a shouting coming from the bathroom. Has she been throwing a fit this whole time? The locked door rattles.

Claire lifts her eyebrows. "Is that Mary-Kate?"

"Unfortunately."

I lift the bottom of her dress. I rub my thumb over the red stain. "Is this Loren?"

She looks at me. Her eyes look far away. "I had to," she

says. Her voice shakes. "He killed Daddy. I wanted to kill him. But I...I couldn't..."

I take her perfect, precious face. I kiss her, and I kiss her, and when I taste the salt of her tears on our lips, I use my thumb to push them from her eyes.

"It's okay," I tell her. "You're okay. That's all that matters."

She sniffs and then rubs her hand over her face. She pulls herself together, a sudden urgency in her voice. "Ransom. Is he—?"

"They had him in the stables, last I saw him."

"We need to get him and get the fuck out of here."

"I couldn't agree more."

I start to pull back, but Claire grabs my face. "Wait..."

She pulls me in and kisses me. Her kiss ripples through me. I feel it down to my toes.

"Okay," she says, her breath hitting my lips. "Now I'm ready."

54

CLAIRE

Everett and I pull ourselves together and get out of there.

My heart is thundering in my chest. I don't know what's gotten into me.

Is it the drugs? The violence? The high of the crown?

Something has been unleashed within me—something with teeth, and claws, and, apparently, an insatiable sex drive.

But also something that loves. Very hard. And now that I have Everett beside me, I'm not letting him out of my sight.

Everett takes his gun, and I clutch my knife. Together, we sneak through the halls, down the staircase, and run—

Right into Ransom.

"Ransom!" I shout. Even though I'm supposed to be quiet.

God, he's a sight for sore eyes.

I can't help it. I wind my arms around him.

"Claire," he murmurs. "Thank God."

He smells like smoke and earth. I want to bury myself in his smell.

He pries me back. It's only then that I notice he's wearing metal cuffs around his wrists, each with half a chain dangling from them. He's also got a coil of rope strapped to his belt. He glances between the two of us. "I've been looking all over for you two. Where the heck've you been?"

A heat rises in my cheeks. *Um. Having sex upstairs?*

Everett sidesteps his question and puts his hand on Ransom's shoulder. "Where's the quickest way out?"

He jabs his thumb over his shoulder. "Round the back way. Chaucer is outside. We can hightail it out of here fast."

"Then let's go."

But when Everett grabs my wrist, I feel my feet come to a halt. I can hear it. The low, twang of the band not far from here.

"Wait," I say. "The Belleflower Queens. They're all in there. Just as trapped as I was. We can't leave them."

Everett's mouth twists in a frown, but then I see a realization darken his gaze.

"They're not the only ones we can't leave behind," Everett murmurs. "Arris. If he escapes...he's just going to keep finding ways to reinvent himself all over again."

"So we've gotta end this," Ransom says.

Everett nods. "You take Claire out the back. I'll make sure we clear out."

I prickle. "I'm not going anywhere."

We lock eyes. I wait for Everett to break.

He glances away. He exhales a quick sigh. "Let's go, then."

"Wait," Ransom says. He digs into his pocket. "I got you something."

He tosses over a pair of headphones wrapped around his phone. "Thought you might need it."

Everett stares at the prize in his hands. Quietly, he says, "Dragonfly—"

"You love me," Ransom interrupts. "Yeah, I know. Focus."

55

EVERETT

Okay. It's time to crash the Belleflower party.

I step forward into the fray. The music rumbles at the stage. Men dance, swaying together with women who stumble on their feet. I wind around tables stacked with champagne glasses.

Arris stands alone, watching his flock. He's so pleased with himself he doesn't notice I'm on him until it's too late.

When his eyes connect with mine, his entire body goes tense.

"Arris Dagney," I say. "You're..." *Hmm. This isn't quite right.* "...under arrest."

Arris looks at me. He blinks. Then he laughs. "No. I don't think so. You see..." He motions to the sheriff, who has his face deep in the breasts of a Belleflower Queen. "I have all the law I need right here."

"I'll rephrase. You can come with me now and do this the easy way...or I'll kill you, your entire security team, and anyone who gets in my way. Your choice."

Now, all the humor has left Arris's expression. "I do hate

it when the livestock talks back," he says. Then he snaps his fingers.

Two members of his security team close in, blocking me from Arris. Their hands go to their guns.

"Fine. Option two."

I fit the headphones into my ears and hit Play.

Blondie's "Heart of Glass" fills my ears.

Things that are important to me about music: it should have a steady rhythm, a good beat, and should be clean enough to drown out the external sounds outside.

All the spikes and jolts of prickly, uncomfortable noise smooth out with Debbie Harry's lovely, melodic voice.

My body knows exactly what to do.

They attempt to grab me. We dance. Elbow in the stomach, hit to the throat, knee to the face. One man down. The other draws his gun, so I grab his arm, aiming it away. He sinks two bullets into the ground. I kick his legs out from underneath him, take his gun from him, and turn it on him.

I squeeze the trigger.

And then the chaos really begins.

The panic. The shouts. The rush of bodies all streaming toward the door.

I turn up the music. My focus is sharp. Clear. Singular.

There are four guards. Two down. And one target.

Arris-Sergey-Dagney.

He stares at me, eyes wide. Finally, he understands. No matter what he throws at me, I'm not going to stop until I have his throat in my teeth. Finally, he's afraid.

He tries to swim through the crowd to get to the door.

A guard grabs me from behind. I smash my elbow back, but I'm met with a horse head mask. Irritating. I just damage the thing's snout. He jabs a stick at me, and suddenly, my entire body lights up. My muscles tense, my teeth clench, and pain vibrates through me.

What is that—a cattle prod?

Fucking cowboys.

I kick him in the stomach, and it knocks the ghastly thing out of his arm. Gives me enough time to kneel on his chest and nestle my gun underneath his chin.

Blood and brain matter exit the mask's hollow eyes.

An arm locks around my throat, dragging me to my feet. It steals the breath from me, and my gun goes clattering out of my hands. My headphones pop out, the strings tangled in his forearm. Now I can hear it all. The stomping of panicked feet. The squealing of my boots against the polished floors. The ugly gasping of my own breath.

The sound of Sheriff Holden growling, "*Stay down,*" as he tries to choke the life out of me.

The cacophony of terrible noise, getting under my skin like a million fire ants.

I try to buck him, but he's strong. I smash the back of my head into his face. That works enough to get him to loosen his grip. I twist to finish it, but...

Maeby comes at him with a bottle of wine. She breaks it over his head. Holden staggers, then falls to the floor.

"Thank you," I tell her.

She squints at me. "Didn't you used to be British?"

Victory is brief.

I hear a *click* behind me, and I know immediately I have a gun pointed at my skull.

I turn. Arris is holding the pistol that slipped from my fingers. And he's aiming it directly between my eyes.

"See you in hell, Everett Hollow," he tells me.

Two things happen at the same time:

One, the gun goes off.

Two, the ground is pulled out from underneath me.

My arms snap to my sides, and my middle feels constricted, as though I've been hugged by a boa constrictor.

I blink. I'm on my back, staring at the ceiling.

But I'm *alive*. Somehow.

Suddenly, Ransom is hovering over me, rust-colored hair framing his face. "You okay?" he asks, his voice full of concern.

I glance down. His lasso is around my middle.

He yanked me out of the path of the bullet.

"Good cowboy," I tell him.

I wiggle out of the rope, grab the back of his head, and yank his mouth down on mine.

He lets out a muffled sound. His lips are warm, and the scruff of his jaw rubs pleasantly against my thumb. A low groan rumbles from me.

I want to rub myself against this man like a cat.

When Ransom pulls back, he's short of breath.

"Fight now," he says, "kiss later."

He takes my hand and helps me up to my feet. I scan the room.

But Arris is gone.

"He's getting away," I say. "If he's in the wind again, we'll never get him back."

I step forward, but—

My balance slips. *Fuck.* Stimulants are wearing off. The sedatives are seeping in again. The room is sliding out from under me, and I have to grip Ransom's shoulder to keep from sliding.

"Hey." Ransom claps my arm. I feel sturdy in his embrace. "You stay. Leave Arris to me."

I lift my gaze to meet his soft, brown eyes. "Dragonfly.

Your whole life, people have told you that you're stupid and worthless and ugly."

He blinks. "Ain't nobody ever called me ugly, but okay."

"Now is your time to prove them wrong."

He sucks in a breath. I can feel him steeling himself off. "Take care of Claire," he says. Before I can say anything else, he grabs the rope and rushes through the sea of people and out the front door.

56

RANSOM

It's chaos out here.

Women in beautiful dresses and men in pristine suits tripping over each other to get to their cars. Honking, scattering as they flee the estate.

I spot Arris's car immediately. But there's no one inside of it.

If he isn't in his car...

There's a loud roar coming from the side of the house. A man stumbles and trips, barely making it out of the way as a dirt bike zips around the corner.

Not just any dirt bike.

Loren's dumbass dirt bike. With Arris gunning the gas.

I leap into action. Even with everything going on, Chaucer just hangs out by the side of the house, comfortably chewing his dandelions and watching everything rush around him.

I grab the saddle and hoist myself into it. Immediately, he goes alert.

"C'mon!" I tell him. "Time to cowboy up."

Chaucer gets it. He lifts his head, gives a sharp snort, and takes off.

He's been pampered over the years. But that doesn't change the fact that, once upon a time, this was Kentucky's fastest racehorse on the track.

I've got a thousand pounds of muscle and strength between my thighs. I lock into the saddle and encourage him. His hooves thud on the dirt road, and I follow the high-pitch whine of Arris's bike.

He sees us coming. He zips off the road, trying to tangle us in the woods.

Big mistake.

Chaucer knows these woods. Even in the dark, it's all I can do to hold tight as Chaucer winds expertly through the trees.

We're gaining on the headlights, bouncing up ahead.

"Ha!"

The motorbike rips through the terrain. Kicks up dirt and sprays it out. Destroys everything it runs over.

Chaucer and I weave together, a wild shadow whipping through the trees. My heart pounds in time with his hooves, a low, steady *clu-clump*.

We're close now. I grip the saddle in one hand and, with the other, unspool the rope on my side.

One clear shot. That's all I need.

There's a clap, like thunder. The air sings, and a bullet cracks into the tree beside me.

Fuck.

I'm not the only one with a plan. Arris fumbles his gun, shooting at us as he rides.

He misses, but barely. I can't risk him hitting Chaucer.

Now or never.

I can barely see in the dark. Adrenaline rushes through me, making my heart beat out of my chest. Chaucer huffs and pants, his body straining to keep up with the roaring bike.

But that's the good thing about roping. I don't need my sight.

Feel it. Be the horse. Be the rope.

I spin the lasso. Once. Twice. *Now.* I toss it out, and it sings through the air...

And loops around Arris.

Bingo.

I wrap the end around my knuckles and yank. Arris goes flying back, right off the back of his bike. The force of it vibrates through my arm, nearly whipping me off Chaucer. I tighten my thighs and my grip. Pain lights up my arm, but I don't release.

Unmanned, the dirt bike spins out. It whines and screeches as it nails a tree, rolling downhill.

Chaucer whinnies and jerks against the new weight.

"We got him," I tell him. "Slow now."

Chaucer trusts me. He lessens his pace, moving away from the screaming bike.

Arris drags behind us. He's still alive. Shouting. Cursing me out. Mad as an alley cat. Wiggling like a fish on a hook. The rope is around my arm and cinched off at my middle, and I feel it constrict. I let him drag a little further until we find a clearing with a stretch of moonlight.

Chaucer's panting when we stop. I pat his side. I feel the heat of him. The sweat dampening his shoulder blades. "You still got it, old man."

He huffs, which I translate to *I know.*

I hop off. The leaves rustle below as I hit the ground. I unwind from the rope and reel the body of Arris Dagney in.

Arris has piped down finally. He's breathing heavily on

the ground. There's dirt across his face, scratches, but all in all, he doesn't look too banged up.

"Go ahead," he says. His voice is hard, though some of the fire has left it. "Kill me. I'm not afraid of death."

"Good for you," I tell him. "But that ain't my style."

I flip him onto his stomach. He tries to wiggle, but my knees trap the backs of his legs. I rope up his arms and legs, hog-tying him firmly in place.

There. He ain't going anywhere now.

"Must suck," I tell him, "getting one-upped by a Sooter and a retired racehorse."

Arris groans, which is good enough for me.

A loud whistle makes the hairs on the back of my neck stand up.

That ain't no bird—

I hear the crunch of boots on autumn leaves. When I turn, I see two men step into a clearing. I don't recognize either of them. The whistler is tall, with a leather jacket and black hair. The other has the shoulders of a linebacker and dark, intense eyes.

The tall one motions to the hog-tied form of Arris. "Aw. You shouldn't have. You wrap him all up in a pretty bow for us and everything."

I bristle. "Who the hell're you?"

The tall one lifts his shirt. It takes my eyes a second to see it in the moonlight. At his hip, I recognize that same wolf tattoo that Everett has on his arm. "Friend of your friend," he says with a wink. "We got your lady's bat signal. Smart girl."

Friends. Good guys. Relief rushes through me like a waterfall.

"You've got no idea," I tell him.

They crouch down next to Arris. The tall one clicks his tongue. "Sergey. Tsk, tsk. Couldn't stay quiet, could you?"

Arris snaps something in Russian. I make out the word *Wolfpack* and a string of something that doesn't sound all that pretty.

The tall one traces his finger along the rope. "Nice knots," he says. He cocks his head to his quiet partner. "He could give you some lessons."

The other man frowns. "We'll take it from here."

Which is a relief to hear. I'm tapped out.

I start to get up, but my legs buckle. The quiet man catches me. "You okay?"

"Yep." My side is burning up. I clutch it. It's wet. I peel my palm back and spot marks of red, spilling out through a hole in my shirt.

"Ah. Crap."

I guess Arris didn't miss all of his shots.

My knees give. I'm glad I'm in strong arms. Gently, the guy lowers me to the ground. "Slowly, cowboy."

I hear myself murmur, "Damn...lucky...bandana..."

I see the moon, staring down at me. All pearly white and full. I hope Claire and Everett are seeing this moon. *What a beautiful night to kick the bucket*, I think.

Then my lights go out.

57

CLAIRE

*T*wo weeks later.

Iᴛ's dark when Ransom comes home from the hospital.

We're lit by the hanging lamps around the Preacher estate, but the light is still dim, and we're delicate guiding Ransom inside.

I hold his crutches at the bottom of the steps. Everett has his arm around the other man, helping him up to the front door.

"Would you quit babying me?" Ransom complains. "I'm a grown-ass man."

"A grown-ass man with a bullet wound in his abdomen," Everett corrects. "One more step."

We make it inside. Even with Everett's support, Ransom is limping. His face has lost some color, and he grunts, "Okay...set me down..."

Everett carefully helps him into one of the lounge chairs left in the living room. I set his crutches up beside him.

The light walk from the truck to the house has Ransom breathless. He rests for a second, his eyes scanning the room. "I like what you two've done with the place."

It's all in a bit of...disarray. Drop cloth over furniture. Chairs stacked on chairs.

A lot has happened since the Belleflower Festival.

After Arris Dagney "mysteriously vanished" into the custody of the Wolfpack Operatives, the FBI swooped in and picked apart the scraps of what was left of the Benefactors' Society. Men and women in expensive suits walked out with their heads down and their hands cuffed behind their backs. Loren Dagney was rolled out on a gurney, screaming the whole way. He'll live to see his day in court.

Something I won't be witness to. The Preacher Ranch was purchased in full by one Everett Hollow and then promptly sold again for the high price of a nickel to Maeve Belladonna Katherine with the stipulation that she do *whatever the hell she wants* with it.

I'm washing my hands clean of Belleflower, Daddy's demons, and the haunted walls of this house. And I have three one-way plane tickets to France to prove it.

I crouch down in front of Ransom. I slip my hands over his thighs and look up at him.

"We can wait," I tell him. "Give you some time to heal. There's no rush..."

"No. We can't." Ransom's jaw tightens. "Get me out of here. If I have to spend another day in this town, it's gonna kill me."

I can't tell him this, but the relief I feel at his words surges through me like a warm elixir, all the way down to my toes.

I take his big hand in mine. I run my thumb over those strong knuckles and press a kiss to them. "Come on, hero. Let's get you to bed."

58

RANSOM

The shower is something like heaven.

It takes a long time for me to leave it. I rest my palm on the wall, drop my head, and let the hot, steamy water pound down on my neck and shoulders.

I wash away the hospital. The grit and grime. The sour memories of that night.

The doctors called me lucky. Said it was a clean shot, whatever that means. I'm grateful for it, I suppose. It'll be a cool scar, once it stops burning like hellfire every time I take a step.

I towel myself off, manage to get on a clean pair of briefs, and climb into bed. Everett and Claire are already settled in, but they part ways, making a spot for me in the middle.

I flop onto my back. I close my eyes and let out a deep sigh. "Alright. This is nice."

Claire's sweet body cuddles up against mine. The tassel around her robe tickles my hip, and she threads her leg around mine, her ankle hooking.

She kisses my shoulder. My throat. The tiny press of her lips sends a warm tingle all through me.

"God, it's good to have you back," she says.

I open my eyes to glance at the man to my right. "What about you, Everett? You miss me?"

He's propped up on an elbow. He frowns. "Not at all. It was gloriously peaceful without you around."

I snort on a laugh. "Jackass."

Everett lifts the covers. He touches my hip, his thumb carefully sliding on the edge of the scar. "Are you in pain?"

"Nothing I can't handle."

His small, tender touches and Claire's sweet little kisses are wreaking havoc on me. I've been poked and prodded for the past couple of weeks by clinical, distant hands. I'm affection-starved, and my heartbeat kicks in my chest.

I tilt my head to catch Claire's lips in my mouth, but she starts suddenly. It's tiny, just a little jump, like a spooked horse.

I stop in my tracks immediately.

Okay. Let's slow this down.

Way down.

I nuzzle against her, our noses touching. "Y'want me to braid your hair?" I ask.

Her eyes light up at that. "Yes, please."

She gets up, patters into the bathroom, and comes back with a hair tie around her wrist and a brush in her hand. I sit up, and she climbs half in my lap, giving me her back.

I run the brush through her soft, blonde hair. It glides through nearly effortlessly. When it catches, I take my time on the knots, carefully working them out. When she's smooth as satin, I put the brush down and part her hair into three sections. I start winding them together, crisscrossing them in a tight braid.

This feels soul-healing. Claire falls into a near trance in

my lap, quiet as a kitten. I love the way her hair slips between my fingers.

"Get ready, Everett," I say as I take the hair band, tying off Claire's braid. "You're up next."

He touches the back of his head. "There's not a lot to work with."

"Don't threaten me with a good time."

I pick up the brush again. I run it over his scalp.

Everett tilts his head to give me better access. He lets out a low, throaty sound.

Is he...purring?

"Oh," he says, a note of surprise in his tone. "That is good."

His small curls are tight. Not a lot of tangles here, but even after everything is nice and soft, I keep going, passing the teeth over his scalp. He sinks his body against mine.

Finally, I put the brush away. I move my hand to the side of his face, but I pause before making contact.

"Can I touch you here?" I ask.

Those blue eyes meet my gaze. "Yes."

I take his face in my hand. Strong jaw in my palm. Short hair under my fingertips. The thing that I want to say stuck behind my teeth. Finally, I come out with it: "I wanna kiss you. Is that okay by you?"

He tilts upward. An invitation. "Yes," he says.

I'm man enough to say this now: I've been fantasizing about kissing Everett for some time now.

Throwing him against a wall. Bruising his lips. An electric, vicious continuation of the power play we've had since we both set eyes on each other.

Never in a million years did I imagine kissing Everett would be a sweet, healing thing.

Warmth and affection and a deep, strong trust.

When our lips part, my breath is light. I can feel our hearts beating in sync.

We've all got scars from that night. Mine's a big, ugly, purpling thing, but theirs is like this hot, storm cloud energy, vibrating right under the surface of things.

We've all got a lot of healing to do.

"We've got nothing but time," I tell them. "Maybe we just take this part slow."

"I'd like that," Claire says. She hooks her hand on the back of my neck, and this time, she's the one to guide my lips against hers. I sink against her, tasting her. Savoring her.

The three of us spend the night wrapped up in each other, exchanging kisses until the stars fall out of the sky.

59

CLAIRE

The house is a flurry of activity.

We're moving out. Maeby is moving in. Men in blue uniforms and work gloves pace around the house, taking it apart piece by piece.

"What d'you want us to do with this?" one of the men asks me.

He motions to the painting that hangs above the mantlepiece. It's an old oil painting of me and my father. The stern, scowling man and the starry-eyed teenagers with dreams of Belleflower Queens dancing in her head.

"Burn it," I tell him.

I leave the bewildered worker and step outside. I need air.

Autumn has brought in its gusty chill. The cool air tingles on my bare arms. I should get a sweater, but I like the way Kentucky bites this time of year.

I let my feet guide me. I find myself walking around the hedges, making my way to the stables. The tall grass tickles my ankles. When I approach, I hear Ransom's voice from inside: "—gotta give him his alone time with Miss Penny, otherwise, he gets ornery. I usually give him a couple hours in the evening while I'm winding down."

I peek in through the open double doors. Ransom and Maeby are sitting in the stables by Chaucer's pen. His gate is open, and he's sniffing at Miss Penny affectionately.

"And check this one out," Ransom says. "Chaucer! Beer me!"

Chaucer steps over to the gate, takes Ransom's hat off the post, and flings it at Ransom.

"Alright, well, we're working on it."

Maeby gives a whistle. "Chaucer, beer me."

Chaucer flicks his tail. He goes over to the open cooler, picks out a beer, and takes it between his teeth. Then he saunters over to Maeby, holding it out for her.

I put my hand over my mouth to stifle my laughter. The look on Ransom's face is priceless. "How in the hell—?"

"Don't you worry about your Chaucer. He's gonna be just fine in my hands, aren't you, boy?"

Maeby tickles him under the chin and takes her prize beer. He lets out a pleased huff.

I step inside, lifting a hand in a short wave to get their attention. "Hey."

Ransom leans back to look at me. "Need something, Bear?"

"Actually...I was wondering if Maeby and I could talk."

"Of course." She gets up, dusting straw off her backside. She hands the beer over to Ransom and follows me. "Should we take a walk?"

We walk around the property line.

60

CLAIRE

Now...it's just me and Maeby.

Nerves climb my skin like tiny ants.

"What'd you want to talk about, darling?" she asks.

I bit my lip. "Actually...I wanted to talk about the Belleflower rituals. Your coronation."

She meets my gaze. Stormy, rain cloud-colored eyes. Just like my own. "Sure."

Her voice sounds casual, but I can see the muscles of her back coil up. An animal about to flee at the first sign of danger.

I hug my elbows. My jaw locks up.

Alright, Claire. Spit it out.

"I did the math," I finally say. "You were Belleflower Queen in September of '94. Then...I was born. Nine months later."

I watch her. She says nothing. We just trend forward, our shoes cracking dried leaves, kicking up the decaying last gasps of summer.

My palms are sweating. "I know it has to be hard to talk

about. I want to be clear that I don't expect anything. I understand if you want nothing to do with me, that it might be a...terrible reminder..."

"Don't you dare put that on yourself," she says suddenly. Her voice is low but intense. "You were a spark of light in a very dark nightmare."

My breath catches in my throat. I don't dare look at her. My heart beats fast, rapid hummingbird wings in my chest.

There it is. The truth.

She pulls out a pack of cigarettes from her pocket. "Do you mind?" she asks.

When I shake my head, she lights it. She inhales and breathes out a thin, smoky stream before starting. "I was twenty-four," she says. "Belleflower Festival was my entire life. Every day, I woke up and trained to be perfect. Hoped I'd be that pretty miss Belleflower Queen. When that day finally came and I got the invite under my pillow..." She smiles crookedly at the memory. "You've never seen a happier girl. We had the parade. The after-party. Randall Preacher—he was a catch back then. When I found out he was my King, I just about laid an egg. We danced. He told me all sorts of things a girl like me wanted to hear. And then he took me into that room."

My stomach turns. Knowing. Maeby looks off in the distance for a moment, toward the deep blue mountains. She absently rubs a hand over her shoulder, where those long scars climb her back. "Didn't seem to matter that I said no. Or that I fought like an alley cat. Wasn't long after that I found out I was pregnant. Course, I didn't tell anyone about what had happened that night. Not my friends. Not my parents. Not after all those years of being taught how impor-tant my purity was. Randall was the only one who knew, so even though it made me sick to do it, I told him. He said he'd help me. Make sure no one would ever have to know. I was so ashamed, but...not of you. Never of you."

Her eyes meet mine. They shimmer.

I nod, encouraging. "I know."

"It wasn't until after...when you were born...they took you away from me, just like that, and put you in his arms. That's when I realized then what a terrible mistake I'd made. But by then, it was too late. Now, they had you to hold over me."

She takes another sharp hit from the cigarette. She lets it out with a hiss.

"I wanted to run out of town, but I couldn't leave you behind. They tried to give me money. Said I could have anything I want. Except the one thing I wanted, of course. You." The edge of her cigarette has burned to a long cylinder of ash. It falls down the backs of her knuckles. She doesn't even flinch. "I gave up. Became depressed. They didn't want me around. No one wants a sad Belleflower Queen. I got them to leave me alone, mostly. Except once a year, the night of the festival. All former queens are required to show up for the coronation. Entertain the Benefactors and usher in a new Belleflower Queen. It made me sick to my stomach, leading these poor women like cattle to the slaughter. But anytime I told them to shove it, they'd find a new way to hold you over my head. Said as long as I kept coming back, you'd never have to wear the crown. Crock of bullshit that turned out to be."

She chokes suddenly. Her voice cracks, and her hand trembles.

"All those years of silence," she murmurs. "All those years I can't take back—"

I stop walking. I take her hand in my own. When she

doesn't pull away, I lace my fingers in hers. She squeezes me tightly.

"We can take it back," I tell her. "Everything they took from us. We'll take it all back. I promise."

Suddenly, she puts her arms around my shoulders. All my bones go stiff when she pulls me into a hug.

There it is. Mother and daughter.

I'm hugging my mother.

I wind my arms around her and slowly embrace her back.

"Promise me you'll start over," she says. Her voice is tight and urgent in my ear.

"I promise."

We stand there for a long time, just holding each other, as the wind picks up and tousles around the dead leaves, coaxing out the old.

61

EVERETT

Outside the wide, glass windows, workers flutter around our plane. A monster in its class. And in approximately thirty-nine minutes, it will take us across the Atlantic Ocean.

Goodbye, Belleflower, Kentucky.

Good. Bye.

Claire is at the desk when they announce they're starting to board. Despite the many times I've told him not to get up without me, Ransom puts his weight on his suitcase and rises from the plastic seat.

He stops here. I watch his gaze travel out the wide glass windows.

I slip in beside him. "Are you alright?"

"Yep. Just...need to catch my breath a second."

I repeat his words last night back at him. "Take all the time you need."

He doesn't seem to be listening, though. His gaze is distant, the clench of his jaw tight.

He doesn't need to tell me for me to know what he's thinking.

This is the first time he's ever left Belleflower. And now, he's leaving for good.

Today's bandana is *yellow*, and he's being very brave.

He grips the suitcase handle. "Okay. I'm ready."

I extend my arm. "Cowboy up."

He chuckles. It's a pleasant, rumbling sound. "Cowboy up."

He grips my arm, and slowly, we make our way to the gate. Claire's eyes flash over to us, and she quickly slips over beside us. "They said we can board early," she says.

"Yee-haw," Ransom says, but his voice is strained.

He's too stubborn for a wheelchair, but I don't mind being his human walker. The three of us settle into our seats —Claire in the middle.

Ransom flips the window open, shuts it, and then opens it again.

"Hey." There's a small smile dancing on Claire's lips. "You got on the plane."

"I got on the plane," he agrees. His color has come back now that he's settled in. "Better late than never, right?"

She grips his hand and squeezes. "Just on time."

"Is a cowboy still a cowboy even if he leaves the ranch?" I ask.

"A cowboy's home is wherever his cowgirl takes him," Ransom replies. He side-eyes me. "And his cow...partner..."

"I'd rather not be a cow *anything*, thank you."

"You got it, slick." Ransom tilts his head back. "How long's the flight?"

"Nine hours to Paris," Claire says. "And then..."

I slip my hand into hers. "And then."

And then. The rest will come. Whatever it is. We'll heal. We'll fight. We'll fuck. We'll love. We'll talk. We'll listen.

We'll learn how to live with each other; more importantly, we'll learn how to live with *ourselves*.

Whatever comes next, for the first time in my life, I don't have to face it alone.

The three of us will find it. Together.

THE END

THANK YOU FOR READING!

Thank you for reading **Double Bucked**!

I hope you enjoyed Claire, Everett, and Ransom's story.

If you enjoyed this book, **please consider leaving a review**. Authors are like fairies, and applause keeps us going!

Can't get enough? Find an **extended bonus novella** featuring Claire, Everett, and Ransom in France (and yes, it is spicy!) on my website:

www.adoracrooksbooks.com/double-bucked-bonus

ACKNOWLEDGMENTS

The first person I want to thank is...you! Your support keeps my fingers on the keyboard.

I also want to thank my editors for catching all my pesky mistakes. Plus, a big thanks to my ARC team who came through and helped spread the word!

Finally, the biggest thanks to Lizzy, who stayed up until 3 am to read the untamed first draft of this book. Your live reaction to chapter 26 was priceless.

Mission accomplished, team! Onwards to the next one...

XOXO,
Adora

THE WOLFPACK SPECIAL OPS SERIES

Book #1: Double Crossed (MMF Military)

I'm on the run with two Navy SEALs. Their only weakness? Me.

*Also in special edition paperback

Book#1.5: Double Crossed - Bonus Mission (MMF Military)

I tried to put down the gun. But trouble won't leave me alone.

Book #2: Double Bucked (MMF Cowboy)

My father is dead. The only two men who can solve the mystery?
My straight-laced fiancé and my devil-may-care cowboy ex.

Find the full series details and bonus content at
adoracrooksbooks.com.

ABOUT THE AUTHOR

USA Today bestselling author Adora Crooks writes romance with heart, action, humor, and steam.

She currently resides in the magical city of New Orleans with her beloved and their two nutty mutts. Adora lives off of coffee, cookies, and book reviews and daydreams about dirty romances with happy-ever-afters.

Sign up to Adora's newsletter to get exclusive deals on Adora Crooks stories, including ARCS and upcoming releases.

Find a full list of Adora Crooks books with tropes and content warnings on her website.

www.adoracrooksbooks.com

www.ingramcontent.com/pod-product-compliance
Lightning Source LLC
Chambersburg PA
CBHW020347220726
48290CB00014B/1300